A
STOLEN
MEMORY

ALSO BY DAVID BECKLER

Antonia Conti Thriller series
A Long Shadow

Mason & Sterling series
Brotherhood
The Profit Motive
Forged in Flames
The Money Trap

Anthology
The Road More Travelled: Tales of those seeking refuge

A STOLEN MEMORY

DAVID BECKLER

THOMAS & MERCER

Text copyright © 2023, David Beckler

Published by Thomas & Mercer, Seattle

www.apub.com

Amazon, the Amazon logo, and Thomas & Mercer are trademarks of Amazon.com, Inc., or its affiliates.

ISBN-13: 9781542034708
ISBN-10: 1542034701

Cover design by Dominic Forbes

Printed in the United States of America

This book is dedicated to Mark Astles. I worked with Mark many years ago and since he discovered my books, he's been my number one fan and cheerleader, recommending them to everyone he speaks to. Most recently, the staff treating him at The Christie. I don't know if I'd be thinking of a mate's writing at a time like that.
What a great person to have in your corner.
Thanks, Mark, you're a star.

CHAPTER 1

The phone rang and Antonia snatched it off her desk. She didn't need to check the caller, only two people knew this number and one was sitting in the next office. 'John, what's happened? I've been trying to get hold of you for a week.'

He took so long replying she feared they'd been cut off. 'A few things came up. But I've got something for you.'

'Have you got those names you promised me?'

'Do you remember the third place we met?'

'Charlton—'

'Don't tell everyone. Bloody hell.'

'I'm the only one here,' she said. 'It's an encrypted line.'

'Just meet me there in two hours.'

'Can we make it—' But he'd gone.

Blast! She'd never known John so wound up, but at least he'd agreed to meet her. She'd believed he'd changed his mind, scuppering her chances of the most explosive story she'd had in months. One that might not bring down Reed-Mayhew and GRM, his company, but would do them serious damage.

She'd need to get a move on. Should she wear a cloaking mask, or would she get away with the ghost make-up? It was cold enough to need a scarf, but she wanted freedom to move fast. She decided on the make-up and picked up her kit, heading to the bathroom. As she entered the main office Eleanor spun her chair round.

'Do you want to finalise the interview shortlist for your new PA?'

'Sorry, Eleanor, I'm seeing—' She checked who else was in earshot. Everyone looked busy and the two people nearest had their headsets on, seemingly engaged in lively discussions. 'I'm going out. We'll do it when I get back.'

She rushed into the bathroom before Eleanor could protest. There wasn't a lot of the ghost powder left. She'd need to order some more before the government made selling it illegal. She applied it with broad brushstrokes, covering her cheekbones and jaw, breaking up her profile. A line across her brow and she was ready. The fine powder made her dark skin look a dull grey.

When she left the bathroom, Eleanor studied her. 'You're supposed to emphasise your best features when you're putting on make-up, not cover them up. People would kill for cheekbones like yours.'

'It's not supposed to— Ha, ha.'

'Don't you think you should wear a mask? They're more reliable.'

'I'm going on the tube, and apart from attention from the security patrols, you always get the "If you've done nothing wrong, why do you need to hide?" mob giving you a hard time. The make-up and afro should do the job.'

'I did wonder why you'd grown it. You normally have it so short.'

She must look so tense. Eleanor was *really* trying to put her at her ease. 'Right, I'd better go.' John wouldn't wait if she arrived late. She rushed through to her office and picked up the mobile, removing the SIM card and putting it in a side pocket. It wasn't registered, but no point in taking risks. She slipped it into her backpack and strode out of her office.

Eleanor was waiting and peered again at the powder coating Antonia's skin. 'Have you overdone it? The cameras might pick you out.'

That was a risk with using ghost powder. If your changed profile looked unnatural, the face-recognition cameras would flag it and track you across the system.

'I should be okay, and anyway, I haven't time to change it.' She put her coat on. 'I'll be back by three.'

She went into the tiny anteroom they jokingly referred to as the reception area. Even before she opened the outer door, the temperature dropped. This, and a sense of unease, made her shiver. After checking the screen of the security camera, she let herself out.

A quick scan of the street revealing no unfamiliar vehicles, she strode out to the Angel tube station, relieved to see there weren't any queues at the security checkpoints. A new travel card bought with cash got her past the barriers and she made her way to the northbound platform of the Northern Line. She wandered to the far end of the platform and watched the people waiting. Seven arrived at the platform after she did, but none paid her undue attention.

With a rush of air and the smell of burning brakes, a train arrived. She jumped on, then, before the doors closed, got off. She scanned the length of the train, but nobody else got off. Satisfied nobody had followed her, she rushed to the southbound platform and caught the next train, getting off at Bank, where she charged up the escalators to exit at Lombard Street. After crossing the street, she watched the entrance for two minutes, but nobody followed her.

She set off towards King William Street, heading for London Bridge, hoping they hadn't tightened up security on it today. Working on the stable-door principle, they'd focused security on sites that had already suffered terror attacks. Four uniformed staff wearing the insignia of SecurCo hung around by the security post on the north bank. The three men and woman didn't appear to be stopping pedestrians, but they eyeballed her as she strode past. Their 'tool-belts' bulged with equipment, including batons, assorted chemical restraints and Tasers, but so far, not firearms. The recent proposal to arm all police was bad enough without giving these unregulated goons guns. Antonia crossed the bridge, checking behind her.

On the south bank, two of the guards stopped her while two more watched. 'Have you got your ID, miss?'

Stifling her irritation, Antonia retrieved her identity card and showed it. Beside her, others walked past the security post unmolested. 'Any reason you stopped me and not anyone else?'

'You seem nervous. We watched you crossing.'

'A pervert harassed me on the tube, and I thought he'd followed me.'

'He must be brave. I've seen you fight.'

Antonia studied the guard and realised she looked familiar. Apart from her near-fatal first contest in front of an invited audience of the great and the good, Antonia had only had three amateur bouts, and none attracted more than a few hundred spectators.

'I was on the undercard of your last fight.' The woman handed Antonia's ID card back. She sported a black eye.

'I hope you won.'

'Not as quickly as you did. If you tell us what the creep looks like, we'll have a word.'

A hand came towards Antonia's head. Without thinking she blocked it and threw a punch. One of the watching security guards sprawled on the pavement, a cut on his cheek.

His companion stepped toward her, a cannister in his hand. 'Get back!'

Blast! That's all I need. She held up her hands. 'He tried to hit me.'

'You've got that anti-camera muck on your face; I was wiping it off.' The man she'd hit knelt in a puddle, dabbing at the cut with a tissue. 'You shouldn't wear it.'

'I'm perfectly entitled—'

'Turn round and get on your knees,' the one with the cannister shouted. A crowd had gathered.

Antonia appealed to the woman. 'I've done nothing wrong. I just want to go to work.'

The woman paused a few seconds, then sighed. 'Go on.'

'Thanks.' Antonia strode away, pulse racing and hands trembling.

When she felt she'd gone far enough, she slowed and put her ID card away. Her relief turned to anger. Who the hell did they think they were? She arrived at London Bridge station still buzzing and made her way to the platform for the Thameslink railway. She loosened her coat as she waited. She needed to forget those arseholes and focus. The train arrived, and she got on. No time to take evasive measures.

As the carriage rattled over the rails, she rehearsed what she'd tell John. Why was he so jittery? The threat posed by Reed-Mayhew and GRM's thuggish security force hadn't changed from when he first approached her with his story. Had they found him out? If so, she doubted he'd ever meet her again. She had to say something to reassure him. But what? She couldn't protect him from Reed-Mayhew.

Without the evidence he'd promised her, *The Electric Investigator* couldn't verify his more explosive claims about GRM. She still found it hard to believe that even Reed-Mayhew would conduct brain experiments on prisoners.

The train went underground. Woolwich Arsenal station, her destination, wasn't far. They stopped and she rose, reaching the doors as they slid open. A woman waiting on the platform with a toddler and baby in a pushchair jumped as Antonia, all one point eight metres of her, materialised in the opening.

'Do you want a hand?' Antonia lifted the pushchair and swung it on to the train, using the opportunity to scan the carriage. Nobody else moved, but as she swung back, she saw movement from the next compartment. Two figures got out, one wearing a red scarf. She dropped the buggy wheels and stood in the carriage until the doors closed. The two figures got back on, and she punched the door switch. After an interminable wait, the doors slid open and she slipped out. She couldn't see the two men, but a shout told her they'd followed her. She ran in the opposite direction, dodging between the other passengers. An exit sign pointed ahead. She followed it, jogging through the tunnel to the crowded escalator.

Too many people blocked her way, so she took the emergency exit. She climbed the stairs two at a time. Warm and breathing hard, she arrived at the top and charged out, closing the door behind her. She stood for a moment, getting her bearings, then crossed the road and doubled back on herself. Five minutes later, she'd lost them.

She had half an hour to cover two miles, further if she wanted to avoid the face-recognition cameras on the main roads. The rain poured down, denser than it had appeared from the warmth of the carriage. She hurried through streets free of pedestrians and reached Charlton House, almost certain nobody had followed her. John's car wasn't there, but she'd arrived early.

A gust of wind blew water down the back of Antonia's neck. She shivered and pulled her coat tighter. Where the hell was he? If he'd changed his mind after she'd traipsed across London, she'd kill him.

She scanned her surroundings. Charlton House resembled a mini Tower of London in the gloom. Three cars sat in the small car park at the side. The lights of the one furthest from her flicked on and the engine roared into life. The car surged forward and slewed to a stop alongside her. The passenger door flew open.

'Get in.' John sat in the driver's seat, jumpy and scared.

This wasn't the car he'd driven the last time they met. Whose car was it? Antonia pressed her face against the back windows and peered in.

'Hurry!'

Satisfied nobody lurked in the back seat, she jumped in. The car pulled away before she'd closed the door. 'What's the rush?'

John checked the mirror and pulled out of the car park. 'Were you followed?'

'No. Where are we going?'

'Have you got a phone?'

'No SIM card. I've done this before, you know.'

John, focused on driving, didn't reply. His hands gripped the steering wheel as if wanting to wrench it off the column.

The stench of exhaust fumes and numerous changes of direction made Antonia carsick. 'Where are you taking me, John?'

He checked the mirror for the umpteenth time and glanced at her. 'Somewhere safe.'

She hoped it wasn't much further.

Twenty minutes later, they joined the queue for the Blackwall Tunnel. Antonia resisted the urge to ask again where they were going. Once on the north side of the river, they followed signs to the City Airport before turning off and driving along a deserted road flanked by a low concrete wall on one side and factory units on the other. Above the concrete wall, a high wire-mesh fence on steel posts barred access to the railway line, which ran parallel to the road. Without indicating, he pulled into a layby. The road ahead continued straight. Even in the gloom, they'd see a car coming from a distance, whether in front or behind them. The engine died, and the silence echoed in Antonia's ears.

'Okay, John, what's happened?'

'Nothing.' John chewed his upper lip.

Antonia glanced at the glistening tracks through the mesh and waited for him to continue.

'Someone might have overheard me and Fi—you don't need her name. Someone might've heard us talking at work.'

Antonia had once spoken to a woman on the phone. She'd appeared even more wary than John and they'd never met. 'What about?' How could he be so careless?

John swallowed and stared out of the windscreen. 'She wanted to take it to one of the bigger outlets. They've got more clout.'

'The bigger outlets won't run it because Reed-Mayhew spends so much advertising with them and he's friends with the owners and editors. We don't have adverts, so nobody tells us what to publish.'

After a few moments, he cleared his throat. 'She said they'd give her money, enough to go away and start again.'

She clenched her fists. 'You've offered the story to someone else?'

He nodded. 'One of the tabloids.' He mentioned a national paper with a readership ten times theirs.

'Blast! Is that why you've been avoiding me?'

'Sorry.' He looked sheepish.

'So, you've dragged me all the way here to tell me you're going with them?'

'No, no, I wouldn't.'

'What are you talking about? You just told me you've offered it to them. What did you tell them?'

'Nothing!'

'What, you said I've got a story for you, but I'm not telling you what it is?'

'Of course not.' He rubbed his hands on his jeans. 'We told them about the story, but no details.'

'And they said?'

'They weren't interested. They said they'd already investigated the rumours and it wasn't worth covering.'

Damn! They'd be working on it now. Most big news outfits had contacts inside GRM. She stared out of the side window. A train rattled past, its windows flashes of light, and the car rocked. She pictured her weeks of work disappearing behind it down the tracks.

'You still want it, don't you?' John didn't hide his eagerness.

'How many people know the details you and your friend have given me?'

'Not many, why?'

'Most news channels have paid informants inside big organisations, and they've probably got someone feeding them similar information. That's why they want you to think it's worthless. They don't want to share it with anyone else.' Antonia wanted to punch the dashboard.

'You think they'll publish it? That's what we want, the story out there.'

She hated the thought of someone else taking the credit for all her work. She remembered something about the editor of the paper he'd approached. He'd either gone to the same school as Reed-Mayhew or attended the same Oxford college. 'It depends on what spin they put on it. They'll probably release enough to undermine my piece, but without damaging GRM.'

'They can't do that.'

'They certainly can.' Disappointment exhausted her and she wanted to go back to the office.

'Don't tell me you'll walk away.'

'You've not left me much choice. Why the hell did you go to *them*, of all people?'

He sat hunched over for a few moments, then reached inside his jacket and produced a memory stick. 'They've not got this. The names of the prisoners they experimented on, plus their case notes.' He grinned and passed it to her.

She stared at it. If it contained what he said, it would be dynamite, but she'd lost a lot of confidence in him in the last few minutes. 'We'll see if it's any use.'

'No, you've got to promise you'll publish it. We've taken huge risks to get it.'

'I can't promise anything, John.'

He gave her a pained look, then stared out of the windscreen. A pair of headlights appeared in the gloom. As they got closer, she could make out the cab of a large lorry. The faint sound of its engine grew louder as it thundered towards them. Neither could tear their gaze away.

'He's going too fast,' John said.

The lorry grew bigger, then crossed the white line marking the centre of the road. The headlights brightened, dazzling Antonia. *It's coming straight for us.* She grabbed the door handle, threw it open and attempted to roll out, but the seatbelt jerked her back. Light flooded the cab, the headlamps creating a halo round John's head. She fumbled with the belt, finally freeing it just as the lorry smashed into the front wing of their car. Her open door slammed into the concrete wall. Would they go over it on to the railway line? Before she could ready herself for the impact, her head slammed into the doorpost, bringing blackness.

CHAPTER 2

Chapman read the report of the failed attempt to arrest a career petty criminal with a growing sense of incredulity. To his knowledge, Neil Griffin had never been violent. He'd first arrested a teenaged Griffin over ten years ago, when he'd started dealing the skunk he grew in his grandmother's loft. The account of him threatening a supermarket worker with a knife, and then attacking the two officers sent to arrest him, didn't remotely fit Chapman's experience of the man.

He retrieved the letter Griffin's mother had sent him a week earlier, soon after her son's release from his latest spell in prison. Addressed to Chief Inspector Chapman, a rank he still hadn't fully regained four years after being busted down to sergeant, the envelope bore the words 'PRIVATE AND CONFIDENTIAL' in large red letters. He pulled out the single sheet of lined paper.

Dear Mr Chapman,

I hope you remember me. I want to talk to you about my son Neil. I know hes' been in trouble so often but he isn't a bad lad, just easily led. I'm very worried about him since he cam out of prison last time. He was behaving strange the last few times I saw him, but they still let him out anyway. Now he's outand been very aggressiv and threatened me a couple of times. I don't want to get him in trouble but I know I can trust you. He told me they gave him a new treetment in prison but wouldn't tell me what. I think what they give him has messed with his brain. Can you please speak to him, I know he'll listen to you. If he goes on like this, I don't know what will happen.

Thank you.

Yours faithfully Moira Griffin (Mrs)

He finished and reached for his phone. 'Alice, can you pop in?'

A minute later Sergeant Alice Sanchez knocked on his door-frame. 'Reading your fan mail, boss?'

'Come in, Alice, shut the door.' He waited until she'd taken the seat opposite and slid the letter across the desk.

She read it, then put it back on the desk. 'Blimey, that's the second one I've heard about.'

'What do you mean?'

'I was at a Federation meeting, and someone mentioned they'd heard that prisoners were being experimented on. We all dismissed it as one of those rumours.'

Chapman, who'd been ready to dismiss Moira Griffin's letter as a mother making excuses, had a rethink. 'Have you seen the report about the attempt to arrest him?' He swung the screen round so she could read it.

Her brow furrowed as she read. 'Sounds like he went right off on one. What are you thinking, Russell?'

'Find out what the situation is with the search for him. I want us to make the arrest.'

'They'll have handed it over to Special Ops. He assaulted two officers.'

'I know, and I also know those thugs will probably shoot him and ask questions afterwards.'

Sanchez frowned. 'What do you want me to put on the paperwork?'

'Mention we've received information from a confidential informer—'

'This letter? The boss won't buy that.'

'Let me worry about her.'

Fifteen minutes later, he stood alongside Sanchez in the office of DCI Gunnerson as she read Sanchez's report.

'Okay, Russell.' Gunnerson took off her glasses and rubbed her eyes. 'I know I'll probably regret it, but I'll authorise this. Do you need an armed response team on standby?'

Chapman shook his head. 'I'm confident we won't need them.'

Gunnerson looked to Sanchez.

Sanchez looked uneasy at being asked to corroborate Chapman's opinion. 'He's never mixed with the more dangerous gangs who resorted to gunplay, boss.'

'Okay, it saves me a headache. But you'll have to take a backup team—'

'Seriously, Yasmin, my team can handle it.' The last thing Chapman wanted was a team of the wannabe coppers they were forced to work with.

'Yeah, I recall you two "handling" the arrest of a young woman not too many months ago.'

Chapman's face grew warm. His decision not to take backup when sent to arrest Antonia Conti had backfired after she'd over-powered him and escaped from Sanchez. The fact she'd been inno-cent hadn't reduced his embarrassment.

'Right, boss.' At least he'd be in charge to make sure no harm came to Griffin.

◆ ◆ ◆

The sound of motors and voices cut through the darkness. The stench of oil and hot metal filled Antonia's nostrils. She opened her eyes, unsure of where she was. Her head hurt and she felt like someone had stuck her in a tumble drier with a pile of rocks. Slowly, the memory of the impact returned. Had it been an accident or deliberate? *What's happened to John?* She hadn't heard anything from him.

'John!' Her shout came out a feeble croak. 'John!' This time louder.

Was the engine noise from the lorry? Who did the voices belong to? Lights flickered at the edge of her vision. When she turned towards them, sharp pain tore through her right shoulder, and she stopped. Why was she sitting at an angle? She moved her left arm and reached up to check her head. Her hand hit the underside of the roof. *Blast!* She must have dropped the memory stick.

'Hello, can anyone hear me?'

She jerked her head in surprise at the sound of the man's voice, and a pain like a spike through the side of her skull made her gasp.

The man repeated the question.

This time, she stayed still. 'Yes, who's that?'

Diffuse fragments of a light beam swept the inside of the car. 'My name's Adam. I'm a firefighter and we're here to get you out. What's your name?'

Relief surged through her. 'Antonia.'

'Is anyone else with you, Antonia?'

'Yes, John. He's the driver.'

'John, can you hear me?' Adam asked. 'Guys, can you keep the noise down?'

The sounds from outside diminished.

'John?' Adam called.

No answer.

'Antonia, can you see John?'

She turned slowly until she made out a slumped figure in the driver's seat. 'I think he's unconscious.'

'Okay, no worries, we'll get you both out. Without moving too much, can you tell me what your injuries are? Flex your fingers, wiggle your toes.'

Antonia did. All her limbs worked, although her right shoulder and upper arm hurt. She moved her head and pain knifed through her skull. She hissed in pain.

'Are you okay?'

'My head hurts.'

'Anywhere else?'

'My shoulder, but it's not too bad.'

'Can you tell if you're bleeding anywhere?' She heard him speak to someone else, giving instructions.

Antonia didn't want to move too much, but checked her shoulder and her head. 'I don't think so.'

'A container slid on to your car. We're getting a crane to lift it off, but in the meantime, we're going to make it safe.' His voice faded as he gave more instructions.

'Are you leaving?' The neediness in her voice embarrassed her.

'No chance. I'll stay until you're out. Relax as much as you can and call out if you need me.'

Relax? *You're joking, aren't you?* She tried not to think of what lay on top of the car. From outside, calm voices and the sound of equipment moving reassured her. They must be used to this sort of incident. Bright floodlights seeped into the cab. What time was it? She still had to do a final read of tomorrow's edition and prepare the shortlist. Eleanor would worry, but Antonia could do nothing about that. She inhaled and willed her muscles to relax, but the crash replayed. Had the lorry been driven at them deliberately? She was pretty sure it had.

'Adam?'

After a brief pause, he replied. 'Everything okay?'

'Have you seen the lorry driver?'

'Don't worry about him, just focus on yourself—'

'Is he there?'

'Hang on.' He moved away and spoke to someone else, his words too broken up for her to catch, then he returned. 'Nobody in the cab, and no signs of someone injured. We've searched the area, but I've just widened the search.'

That confirmed it. He had driven *at* them. Did the men she thought she'd shaken off at Woolwich Arsenal follow her without her noticing? A wave of guilt hit her. She'd not noticed John move. *God, I hope he's just unconscious.*

A new, sharper odour came into focus, increasing her anxiety. 'Adam, I can smell petrol!'

'Okay.' He raised his voice. 'Guys, bring the reel closer! Antonia, we're blocking the container, so it doesn't move. You'll hear banging, but don't worry.'

The hammering started straight away, reverberating through the metal of the container and making the car vibrate. It shook her shoulder and head, but she pushed the pain away. A motor strained nearby. Metal creaked and she imagined the container crashing down on to her and John.

'John?' she called again.

She listened, but no answer. A whoosh sounded behind her. Heat made her ears crinkle. Orange flames flickered in front of her, reflected in the windscreen.

'Adam!'

'Got it, Antonia. Now close your eyes, you might get wet.'

In the glow from the fire, smoke swirled around her. Outside, an engine whined. Water sprayed on to hot metal. Smoke stung her eyes, and she closed them.

'You're not hitting it!' Adam shouted.

The heat infused her flesh.

Someone outside swore. 'The container's in the way.'

Would she die in here, so close to rescue? She needed air, but smoke attacked the back of her throat. She coughed and tears streamed down her cheeks.

'Get the reel under here!' Adam sounded stressed.

The water stopped. Had they given up? She coughed again, bringing more tears. The heat was becoming unbearable. Could she smell her hair burning? Then, icy water sprayed the back of her head and shoulders, leaving her gasping. The smoke attacked again. She spluttered, snot flowing out of her nostrils. But the heat died.

'It's out now. You okay, Antonia?'

She cleared her throat, gasping for breath. 'Yes, I'm okay.'

'Great, we're still waiting for the crane, but in the meantime, we've secured the container so it can't come down on you. I'm going to come in and join you, make sure you're okay.'

The sounds of movement came closer, someone struggling to get through a tight space. After a couple of minutes, a beam of light swept the inside of the car. Antonia squinted.

'Antonia.' The now familiar voice came from just behind her. 'I don't want you to worry, but you might have damaged your neck.'

'I'm okay.' Her breath caught.

'Best to make sure. I'm going to put a support in place. I'm going to have to touch your head. Don't turn round and keep still.' Strong hands held her by her temples. 'This collar will support you.'

His hands moved away, then reappeared at her throat. She stopped herself reacting. Soft foam pressed into her neck, then, with a firm but gentle grip, he secured a collar. The beam of light bounced off the inside of the windscreen, showing the reflection of a dark-haired man.

'I'm going to give you some oxygen, it's still thickers— Sorry, smoky in here. Then I'll check on John.'

Gas hissed, then a mask covered her nose and mouth. She resisted the impulse to struggle. Clean, cool oxygen flooded her airways, making her light-headed.

'Can you hold the mask?'

The light beam moved, illuminating John. Antonia turned her head so she could see him. The top of his skull had been sheared off, leaving his brain exposed. She gagged and pressed the mask to her face.

Adam swung the lamp away from the gory sight. 'Are you okay?'

Antonia inhaled the contents of the cylinder until her nausea passed and she lifted the mask. 'I'm fine, just—'

A loud bang from above cut her off. Adam directed the lamp at the ceiling. His radio crackled and a woman's voice said, 'Are you okay in there, boss?'

'Fine. What's going on?'

Smaller explosions followed, then another big one, even larger than the first. Antonia fought against the collar, trying to see where they came from. She removed the mask and detected a familiar acrid stench from bonfire night. *What the hell?*

'Come in, Juliet.' Adam sounded less calm.

After a short pause, a breathless voice came back on. 'The container's full of fireworks.'

Choking smoke filled the car, and it grew hotter as explosions continued. The memory of being trapped in a burning house filled Antonia with panic.

'Keep the mask over your nose and mouth.' Adam's reassuring voice came from behind her right ear. 'I'll fetch a hose-reel to keep us cool. I'm not leaving you, so don't worry.'

He didn't wait for a reply, and she heard him struggling out of the space. Then she no longer heard him above the other sounds.

A sense of abandonment overwhelmed her. The fumes entered through the gap between the mask and her skin, and she pressed it tight. Her eyes streamed, so she closed them. From outside, the sounds of firefighting continued. Metal clashed against metal and engines screamed. The explosions from above continued. Unsure what would happen, her imagination filled in the blanks.

Adam's voice carried as he spoke to someone. Why wasn't he back in here to help her? To stop her panicking, she counted. She'd reached two hundred when the sound of cylinders clanking against metal came closer.

'Adam?'

The hiss of air told her he wore breathing apparatus. She resisted the urge to call him again. More metal clanked, and the hiss came closer.

'Antonia, I've brought you a BA set.' Although muffled, his voice carried over the background noise. 'I'm going to place another mask over your face, so you'll need to remove the one you're wearing when I tell you. Do you understand?'

She lifted the mask. 'Yes.' Smoke attacked her throat, and she fought not to cough. The heat made her skin prickle.

A continuous hiss overlaid the sound of Adam's breathing. 'Fill your lungs, then remove the oxygen mask.'

Antonia did so. The hiss came closer until cool air flowed over her cheeks. Then soft rubber pressed to her face, creating a seal, and Adam placed a harness over her head. The sense of claustrophobia lasted a few seconds, but faded as she became accustomed to the soft glow from a torch.

'Breathe,' Adam instructed.

She gulped air into aching lungs. The stench of the smoke remained, but her airway cleared.

'I'm going to spray water, so brace yourself. It will get hotter, then cold.'

She waited, then with a whoosh, water sprayed against the metal side of the container. The surge of heat enveloping her as it turned to steam lasted a few seconds before turning to cool spray, becoming colder. The water stopped.

'We're having to break into the container through the side to get to the fire. It's right at the back—'

Loud banging drowned Adam out and made her seat vibrate.

'The crane's been delayed,' Adam continued when it stopped, 'but don't worry. We'll get you out before it gets here, but I'll have to make some space to work and I'll need your help. Here, hold this.'

He pushed a cold piece of metal into her hand. She examined it by the torchlight.

'That's a branch,' he said. 'Point it there, over your left shoulder, if it gets too hot. This opens the nozzle.' He tapped a lever on top of a gun-like device attached to the end of a length of yellow hose which passed behind him. After confirming she had control of it, he left the light and disappeared again. Seeing her surroundings eased her panic, but she mustn't look at John. The explosions from above continued, as did the banging.

In a lull, Adam returned, bringing more light. 'Antonia, can you cool the steelwork behind you? It's getting warm in here.'

Smoke now filled the car, and she could no longer see the windscreen. The heat made the back of her neck burn, and, gripping the branch tightly, she sprayed behind her. Again, a blast of steam preceded the cooling effect. Water spray speckled the mask and the icy liquid soaked into her shoulder.

Adam's radio crackled. 'Boss, how you doing in there?' came a voice. 'The supports on the far side are getting hot.'

'Right, I'll crack on.' The reassuringly calm aura he gave off faded once again, and she sensed his unease.

'Adam, what does that mean?'

His refusal to answer confirmed it wasn't good. Then, with a loud groan, the car lurched to her left and her head jerked. Air escaped from her dislodged face mask and, dropping the branch, she tried to straighten it.

In the background, Adam's radio squawked, and he replied. Short, staccato sentences. She didn't hear the words but didn't need to. Her breathing grew ragged, and her pulse raced.

'Antonia, can you hear me?'

Stop panicking, Antonia. 'What's happening?'

'I'm going to move your seat to give me enough room to get you out.'

Behind her, Adam manoeuvred machinery and thumped pieces of metal, making her seat vibrate. Accompanied by a screech of tearing metal, her chair jerked to the side but stopped. From outside, a motor strained. Then, with a crack, the seat back gave way. She fell backwards until a firm hand stopped her.

'Okay, I've done it.' Relief emanated from the firefighter. 'Let's get you out of here. Give me the branch.' He took it off her. 'Pull the reel out!' he shouted. The yellow hose uncoiled like a snake and slithered across the back seat of the car. 'Antonia, I'm going to cut the seatbelt.' A blade slid between her hip and the seatbelt, and the fabric parted.

'We're going out the back window. I'm going to grab your jacket and slide you backwards. If you can, help me. Okay?'

'Yes, quickly, please.'

'Take a deep breath, as I'm going to have to take your mask off. Get prepared, it's thickers.'

The face mask gave her a sense of security and she didn't want to remove it, but did as she was told. Acrid fumes attacked her throat. She closed her eyes and coughed. The explosions from above their heads became more frequent.

'Right, let's get out of here.' Before she could react, Adam grabbed the shoulders of her jacket and pulled. As she moved back, she pushed, first with her knees and then her feet.

A fresh series of explosions detonated above their heads. A wave of heat and cloud of pungent smoke accompanied the deafening cacophony. She gasped, taking a deep breath of toxic fumes. As her head swam, the heat disappeared, and hands dragged her upright. She opened her eyes, blinking to clear them.

A combination of streetlighting and floodlights illuminated a hellish scene. John's car was now less than a metre high. On top of it a huge container. Flames flickered through a hole in its side and two firefighters sprayed water into the opening. More flames flickered from the car and thick smoke poured out.

'Can you take care of Antonia?' Adam addressed his crew. He'd removed his mask and tears formed tracks in the soot on his face.

Someone draped a blanket over her shoulders and led her towards an ambulance. A water bottle appeared in her hand. She held it to her mouth.

'Rinse your eyes first,' one of the other firefighters instructed.

She did, rejoicing as the cool water eased the burning. Then she drank. After a couple of gulps, she felt a lot better.

At the ambulance, they placed her in a wheelchair.

'Sit there until they check you over.' The firefighter took her details and returned to help Adam, who strode around the scene giving instructions.

Antonia accepted the oxygen the paramedic offered as he examined her. Her thoughts turned to John. Did he have a family? Would someone get the worst possible news tonight?

The flames from the car had died down. The fire would have burnt John's body. But what about the memory stick? She needed to get hold of it. She struggled to her feet, but a coughing fit disabled her.

'Hey, hey, take it easy.'

'I need to get something out of the car.'

The paramedic studied the smouldering ruins. 'You'll be lucky.'

'Please, it's very important.'

'I'll see what the fire bobby says. You sit here and drink some more oxygen.'

He returned with Adam a few minutes later. 'How you doing?'

'Okay and thank you for getting me out.'

'Yeah, well, it's our job.' He wiped at his cheek with a sleeve, spreading the soot.

She couldn't recall seeing a Chinese firefighter, especially not one with green eyes. She guessed he must be in his forties. 'Can you get something from the car?'

He frowned. 'It's now a crime scene. Those lads are here to take charge of it, but they're not saying why.' He frowned and pointed at an unmarked car she'd not noticed. Three figures watched the scene. One of them turned to them. Unease made her hackles rise.

'Please, Adam, it's really important. It's probably why—' She checked on the paramedic, but he'd gone inside his vehicle. 'It's why they took us out.' She hoped she didn't sound too ridiculous.

'Took you out?' Instead of doubting her, Adam considered her words. 'You reckon the lorry deliberately hit you?'

'Did you find the driver?'

'No, and someone stole the lorry this afternoon. What did you want from the car?'

'A memory stick. I had it in my hand.'

'What's on it?'

'I . . . I don't know. Evidence to help me show corruption in high places.'

'Hmmm. Those guys in the car aren't regular police.'

The sense of unease she'd experienced earlier intensified. 'Will you do it?'

He studied the scene for a long moment. 'Yeah, if I can. I'll drop it off. Take care, Antonia.'

As he returned to the incident, the man who'd studied them intercepted him. The two men entered the pool of light illuminating the incident, and she recognised one of the men from the train.

CHAPTER 3

The phone on Russell Chapman's desk vibrated, and he scooped it up before the first note of 'Needy' rang out. He'd kill his daughter for replacing his ringtone with it, once he'd had her change it for something more grown-up.

'DI Chapman.'

'Boss, Griffin's arrived back and has just taken the lift to the fifth.'

'Great, Alice, we'll get over there pronto. Don't let him leave.'

'Do you want us to—'

Chapman cut the call. Now she'd made sergeant, Sanchez needed to learn to use her initiative. He grabbed his stab vest and jacket and ran out into the detectives' office. 'Okay, guys, he's back. Let's go.'

The three members of the burglary team dropped what they were doing and followed him into the lift. Chapman punched the button for the basement garage. He slipped the stab vest over his head, studying his team as they descended. All three looked ready for action – even Greville Sanderson, a veteran of twenty-eight years who made no secret of his desire to draw his pension as soon as possible.

'Who's coming with us, Grev?' Chapman said.

'Err, well.'

Sanderson's reaction told Chapman all he needed to know. 'Who have we got?' He tried not to let the disappointment show in his voice.

'They've sent a team from SecurCo.'

'Oh, for fuck's sake.' Louisa Walker punched the metal wall, her savage scowl a world away from her normal cherubic expression. 'I thought they'd sacked those tossers.'

'I wish! They just haven't extended their contract. They're giving it to GRM.' Darren Baxter, the third member of the team, didn't look happy about this.

'Bloody hell.' Walker punched the wall again. 'More of the same. What's the betting they hire the same set of Neanderthal goons with just a new badge on their uniforms?'

Chapman sympathised, but couldn't let this continue. 'All right, nobody's happy about it, but we have to work with them, so let's have a bit of professionalism.'

Walker opened her mouth to speak but turned away, muttering.

Chapman continued dressing, thoughts racing, remembering his experience of GRM six months earlier. No doubt their CEO, Gustav Reed-Mayhew, would extract the maximum 'value' from the contract. Chapman had thought that once plans to privatise the Met foundered, the mania for privatising the security services would end, but it had recently resumed. At least since he'd regained some of his lost rank he had tenure again, and didn't have to worry about losing his job.

With a ping, the lift stopped at basement level and, slipping his jacket over the bulky vest, Chapman led his team out.

'I'll get the car.' Walker held up a set of car keys and strode away.

The stench of stale exhaust fumes and burnt rubber filled his nostrils. As his vision grew accustomed to the harsh strip lighting, he searched for the backup team. Several bulky uniformed figures waited near a dark minibus with the SecurCo logo on the front doors and a row of blue lights on the roof. He approached them, searching for their leader. The men stopped talking and stared at him.

Chapman halted two paces away. The armoured figures towered over him. 'Right, guys, you know where we're going?'

A bearded figure with sergeant's markings detached from the others. 'Yeah, the boss briefed us.'

'Good, so you know who we're searching for. Don't forget, silent approach, so no lights or sirens.'

'As I said, we've been briefed.'

Chapman swallowed his irritation. 'No harm in checking we're on the same page.'

An unmarked people-carrier pulled up alongside them with a squeal of tyres, Walker in the driver's seat and the other two in the back.

'Follow us,' Chapman told the SecurCo crew, 'but if we get split up and you arrive first, wait for me.' He opened the passenger door and got in.

Before he could close it, Walker leant across him and gave the finger to the crew gathered around the minibus. 'Eat my wake, arseholes.'

The car surged forward, slamming the door and leaving Chapman steadying himself with a hand on the dashboard as he fumbled with the seatbelt. The two in the back joined in with Walker's laughter. Chapman couldn't suppress a grin and decided not to reprimand her. They reached the exit barriers and the huge steel gate slid aside. By the time it opened enough to let them through, the minibus had caught up and stopped a few inches behind them, engine revving.

Chapman glanced back to see the bearded sergeant and a scowling driver glaring at them. Then the people-carrier raced out into the daylight, tyres squeaking on the concrete ramp, and on to the slip road. A steady drizzle had replaced the earlier sunlight. With barely a pause, Walker joined the traffic on Harrow Road. The lights on the junction with Edgware Road showed red, but Walker surged forward, past the waiting traffic. Arriving at the front as the lights changed, she swerved across the stationary vehicles, eliciting a volley of angry toots, until she flicked the blue lights on for a moment.

A siren sounded behind. The minibus followed them through the junction, its light bar flashing. Chapman snatched up the handset on the dashboard and pressed the speak button. 'What part of no lights or sirens didn't you understand?'

After a silence, an aggrieved voice replied, 'Your driver started it.'

'What are you, a kindergarten kid? Do it again and you'll find yourself looking for another job.' Chapman slammed the handset back in its bracket and glanced at Walker, who mouthed, 'Sorry, boss.'

Despite not using the blue lights, she made good progress through the early evening traffic. Walker took risks Chapman wouldn't have, but he'd learned to trust her and focused on what he'd likely find when they arrived. They left the main road and drove down a side road. A row of shops on their left faced a block of flats six storeys high on the opposite side.

'Alice is in an office above the newsagent. There's an opening between the florist and bookmakers.' Chapman pointed with his left hand. 'Go down there and pull up behind the bookies. Give the woodentops room to pull in.' He checked behind, but they'd left the minibus a long time ago.

Sanchez's car sat at the bottom of a concrete staircase leading to an open deck that ran above the shops, and Walker parked in front of it.

'Wait for me.' Chapman left the vehicle and climbed up the stairs to the deck.

Open to the elements, with a stained concrete floor and a weathered wooden handrail, it ran the length of the shops, and a row of doors led to the individual offices.

Sergeant Alice Sanchez appeared in a doorway with a 'To Let' sign alongside it. 'You made good time, boss. Let me guess: Walker drove.'

'Right in one.' He gestured at the doorway. 'Do you want to update me?'

Sanchez led him back into the office. Instead of the smart business suits she'd started wearing since her promotion, she'd changed into jeans and trainers and tied her brown hair into a short ponytail. She led him through a dingy corridor with peeling wallpaper and worn carpet into a darkened room at the front. The lingering odour of ancient cooking permeated the walls. Two chairs sat against the window and a seated figure peered through binoculars pointing at the apartment block opposite.

Chapman acknowledged the constable, who wore a headset. 'Are we monitoring their phones?'

'Just a landline in the flat. I couldn't get a blanket warrant for the mobiles, sorry, boss.' Sanchez looked crestfallen.

'Never mind. What's our target doing?'

'Neil Griffin is holed up in a flat on the fifth floor with a married couple.' Sanchez reeled off two names.

'Are they involved in his operation?'

'Not according to our records. He went to school with the husband, but we think they're legit.'

If Sanchez had investigated them, he trusted her findings. He gave her a signal to continue.

'He returned forty minutes ago and he's still up there.' Sanchez then gave him a rundown of the access points to the building. The prospect of using the stairs didn't faze him, as it would have done six months ago. The fitness regime Antonia started him on had made a big difference, and although nowhere near her level, he now felt he could hold his own.

'You two stay up here and keep a lookout,' he told them. 'Tell me if anything changes, or anyone we recognise shows up. I don't want us caught by surprise by Griffin's oppos.'

He left them, his thoughts on the forthcoming operation. Out back, the team from SecurCo had arrived and Walker appeared to be taunting them. She stood alongside Sanderson, facing a group of bulky security operatives. One of them stepped towards her, mouthing something and finger-pointing.

The side door of the people-carrier opened, and Darren Baxter got out. With what sounded like a sigh of relief, the springs of the car rose. The pointer shut up and stepped back. Chapman didn't blame him. At nearly two metres and over one thirty kilos, Baxter wasn't someone to take lightly. Despite his bulk, he kept himself fit. Chapman once saw him deal with a gang of football hooligans on his own, sending four of them to the local hospital. At Chapman's arrival, the rest of the SecurCo team got off their bus and joined their colleagues.

'Right, everyone,' Chapman said into the silence, 'listen up. Team leader—'

'It's sergeant.' The bearded man scowled at Chapman.

'Team leader, our target is on the fifth floor of the block across the road. Take five of your men and secure the exits. There's the main entrance in the centre at the front and two fire exits at each end that come out round the back. I want two of you on each—'

'I decide how I deploy my force.'

Chapman descended the final three steps and walked up to the man. 'You clearly don't understand how this works. I'm running this operation and you're here to assist me. Do you want me to quote the relevant sections of your contract?' Chapman tried to recall which they were. Sanchez would know.

The team leader clearly didn't know them, as he scowled and gave Chapman a glare that would strip paint before assenting.

Chapman continued. 'Two of you at each entrance. Don't let anyone in or out.'

Once they left, Chapman briefed his officers and the rest of the security guards. The advance party confirmed they were ready, and Chapman led his force to the main entrance of the block of flats. Two SecurCo men waited inside the foyer. At least they'd done what he'd told them. Chapman sent pairs of the remaining security guards to each end of the building to secure the fire escape stairs, telling them to proceed to the fifth floor.

Sanderson made for the lifts, but Chapman stopped him. 'We're using the stairs.'

'Fifth floor, boss?'

'Yeah, fifth, not fifteenth.' Chapman started up the stairs and the three constables followed, Sanderson muttering under his breath and making his feelings clear.

By the second floor, Walker had heard enough. 'Shut it, lard-arse. Why don't you wait for us downstairs if it's too much trouble?'

Baxter's laugh drowned Sanderson's wheezy retort.

By the fourth floor, Chapman's calf muscles ached. He paused on the landing and tightened his stab vest. Walker looked like she could do fifty floors and Baxter, even carrying the sixteen-kilo battering ram, wasn't blowing. A red-faced Sanderson stumbled up the last step and joined them.

'When we get to the next floor, Darren, you go first and take the door while we—'

'Boss!' Sanchez's urgent call sounded in his earpiece.

'Go ahead.'

'He knows we're here. Someone rang him.'

'Shit! Okay, I'm on my way.' Chapman addressed his team. 'Someone's tipped him off.' He set off up the last flight, sensing an impatient Walker behind him.

As he burst out on to the top landing, the door to their target flat flew open and Griffin charged out. On seeing Chapman, he ran in the opposite direction. Ignoring his tight muscles, the inspector followed, but within three steps, Walker overtook him. A loud clang behind him told Chapman Baxter had discarded his battering ram.

Griffin charged through a pair of doors dividing the corridor and Walker followed. Chapman reached it and pushed the left leaf aside as Griffin disappeared through a door at the far end of the corridor. *Where the hell are the pair I sent to secure the stairs?* Walker arrived at the door and as she reached for the handle, it slammed back into her, catching her in the face. With a cry, she fell back and hit the floor.

A surge of anger energised Chapman. He got to Walker as she sat up, blood streaming down her face.

He slowed, but she waved him on with a bloody hand. 'I'm fide, get the bastard.' Blood bubbled out of her nostril.

Baxter had reached them and even Sanderson put on a spurt as he saw his colleague felled.

'Daz, come with me, and, Grev, take care of her and call an ambulance.'

Ready for the same to happen again, Chapman reached for the handle and dragged the door open. It led to the landing on to the fire exit stairs. Voices came from the floor below.

Chapman ran to the banister. 'Have you got him?'

'Nobody's come down here.'

Chapman led the way up to the top floor, where the stairs ended. Two doors led off the landing at ninety degrees to each other. He burst through the first, which led to an empty corridor.

'This way, boss?' Baxter stepped back on to the landing and opened the other door.

'Yep.' Chapman brushed past him and stepped into the darkness, hand sweeping the wall for a switch. He found one and flicked it, but nothing happened. Shapes resolved once he grew accustomed to the dim light. He found himself in a dusty room with no windows. A narrow metal staircase led upwards. As he climbed the first flight and turned one-eighty degrees, the light increased. A narrow doorway at the top of the stairs hung half-open. Chapman climbed towards it, comforted by Baxter's heavy tread a few steps behind him.

He threw the door open and blinked. Dregs of daylight illuminated the rain-slicked roof, and he stepped out on to it. Ahead of him a zinc-coated walkway in a valley between two pitched roofs led to a small brick structure with a door in it at the far end. A sign on the door identified the other fire escape stairs. The apex of the roofs extended above head height. Behind him, a similar brick structure housed the door he'd just come out of. Chapman checked round it, but Griffin wasn't there.

He returned to the doorway where Baxter waited. 'Boss, do '

Chapman gestured Baxter to shut up and signalled his instructions. Baxter nodded and led the way to the far staircase. They'd almost reached it when they heard a scraping sound behind them.

Chapman spun round to see a figure on the ridge of the roof behind them. Griffin had almost hauled himself over the top. The three men froze for a few moments. Then, with a cry of panic, Griffin disappeared over the other side of the ridge.

This turned into a shrill scream of terror which made Chapman's pulse spike. He rushed to the place where the fugitive had disappeared and, throwing himself on to the roof, scrambled up to the ridge. Icy water leached through his trousers as his thighs scraped along the wet tiles. His head cleared the ridge and below him, in the gutter at the edge of the roof, crouched Griffin, his terror obvious.

Thank God! 'All right, Neil,' Chapman said between breaths. 'How's your mum?'

'Oh, it's you.'

'Yeah, it's me. Why don't you stop playing silly buggers and get back up here?'

Griffin hesitated.

'Where you going to go, Neil?'

Griffin didn't move.

'It's a long way down, mate.'

'I fucking know it is,' Griffin said between clenched teeth and closed his eyes.

Shit, he's paralysed with fear. 'Neil, you just need to stand up and I'll grab you.' Chapman looked down the slope behind him and addressed Baxter. 'I'm going to reach over the other side. Grab my belt and stop me sliding off.'

Baxter scrambled up the roof behind Chapman, pushed a huge hand under Chapman's stab vest and grabbed the top of his trousers. Chapman edged forward, raising his torso above the ridge and peered down at Griffin, whose body trembled.

'Neil. Come on, mate.'

With an obvious effort, the young man rose to his feet. Chapman held his breath and stretched out towards him. Baxter's grip made him feel he was in a harness. Griffin stood, but he faced away from the ridge.

'Come on, Neil, this way. Turn to your left.'

Griffin didn't react straight away. Had he heard him? Then, slowly, he followed Chapman's instructions and stood facing him on trembling legs.

Chapman exhaled in relief. 'You can open your eyes now.'

Griffin squinted at him.

'Great, but you're going to have to help me here, mate. Lean forward and lie on the tiles.'

Griffin lowered himself to the roof.

'That's great. Now you need to push yourself up the slope so I can reach you.' Chapman reached forward and draped himself over the roof, his arms reaching down to the fugitive.

Griffin reached upwards, but still came up short. Chapman stretched, willing his arms to extend to the young man. He glimpsed the pavement far below. Several figures gawped, pointing upwards. A bus swung round the corner and into the street. Chapman's eyes lost focus, and he closed them until the dizzy spell passed. Less than six inches now separated their hands.

'Can you get higher, Neil? I've nearly got you.'

With a low groan, Griffin edged further towards him. Then, with a screech of metal, the guttering under Griffin's feet broke away. He screamed and his hooked fingers scrabbled for grip as he slid away from Chapman. Below them, a bystander echoed his scream.

CHAPTER 4

Sabirah's optimism faded as she entered the reception. When the summons had arrived from the Internal Security Agency to attend an interview, she'd panicked. But Eleanor convinced her they probably wanted to discuss her Leave to Remain. She could barely entertain the idea of being safe for five years. Nadimah would be eighteen. Already, she was becoming a woman and Sabirah noticed the attention from boys.

Now she'd arrived, she didn't think people came here to get good news. A large room with a low ceiling and a stained carpet, it needed a thorough clean. The odour of unwashed bodies combined with the stink of damp fabric. As she queued at the crowded reception desk, she studied those waiting. They sat on cheap plastic chairs, either alone or in small groups, heads bowed and silent or talking in whispers. 'A room of sorrow', Mama would have called it.

Sabirah reached the front of the queue, and a harassed woman took her details. She entered them on her tablet and, giving Sabirah a case number, told her to wait. She found an empty seat and checked the clock above the reception desk.

The time on her letter passed. Next to the clock, a display clicked on to the number twenty. Her card read forty-seven.

How long before they reached her? She'd told the children she'd be less than two hours. She hated leaving them alone, but wouldn't bring them somewhere like this.

The couple next to her argued.

'They told us one, it's now after two,' said the man, a bundle of nervous energy. 'I've got to go back to work.'

His heavily pregnant wife took his hand. 'Please don't make a fuss. It won't do any good and we don't want to draw attention to ourselves. This is their country, they do what they want.'

Sabirah gave the woman a sympathetic smile. If she had to wait as long, the children would worry.

An hour later, the speaker near the ceiling called her name and told her to go to room seven. A sign directed her down a gloomy corridor lined with doors. As she passed one, a man's raised voice carried. A woman sobbed and, after hesitating a moment, Sabirah hurried past. She reached the right door and knocked, worried about the woman.

'Come in.' The man who spoke sounded annoyed.

Sabirah entered a small, stuffy office with a narrow window near the low ceiling. A harsh strip light illuminated a table with two people behind it. The man peered at her over rimless glasses. The woman wore a friendlier expression.

'Sit, Mrs Fadil.' The man indicated a lone chair in front of the table and consulted his tablet as Sabirah sat down. After making her wait two minutes, the man began.

'Can you confirm your address?'

Sabirah clutched the letter they'd sent her. 'Vincent Terrace. You have the address.'

'I asked you to confirm it.'

She recited the address.

'That's an expensive place to live. I couldn't afford it, could you?' He spoke to his companion, who agreed with him. 'How can you afford to live there? It says here you work as a shop assistant and a cleaner.'

'Mrs Curtis is very generous. She doesn't charge me rent. She says I should spend my money on the children.'

He jabbed a finger at her. 'We expect people like you to pay your way, not sponge off gullible pensioners.'

'She said she'll let me pay when I can do my profession. Once my English is better, I will work as architect.' She could hear her English getting worse. *Don't let him upset you.*

The man snorted. 'How long have you been here?'

He must know. 'One and a half years, but I only have English lessons for six months.'

The woman leant forward. 'Your children changed schools. Why?'

'The first one made them unhappy, so Mrs Curtis arranged.' Would they make her send them back to the other school? Was this why she was here?

'So, you completely rely on a disabled pensioner in a wheelchair.' The man didn't hide his sneer.

'Mrs Curtis is happy to help us.' Sabirah's voice faded.

'Her daughter isn't happy, though.'

'Antonia?' He must be lying. Antonia gave them her apartment, and she would never talk to these people.

'She's complained that you've used her mother's confusion since her stay in hospital to inveigle your way into her affections.'

Sabirah couldn't stifle a laugh. 'Mrs Curtis isn't confused. She has a very clear mind.' *She would eat a stupid man like you for breakfast.*

The woman leant into the man and whispered something. His annoyed expression intensified. 'Her daughter's called Kate. Who's this Antonia?'

'She is Mrs Curtis daughter. A refugee like me, who she adopted, so she *is* her daughter.'

'I am speaking of her *biological* daughter.' He glanced at his tablet. 'Kate Curtis is very concerned. As her mother's so frail, she's worried you're taking advantage of her. How would you support yourself if anything happened to this old woman?'

The question often kept Sabirah awake. She'd have to move out of the beautiful apartment and find somewhere like the cold and damp place they'd lived in before. She'd survive, but she hated the thought of her children having to endure it again.

'As I said before, you must show you can support yourself, and you're not. Therefore, we have no choice but to cancel your Permit to Reside—'

'You can't.' Were they sending them back? She hadn't imagined they would do this.

'Can't we?' He held out a hand.

'Why do you do this to me?'

'Your papers.' He clicked his fingers. 'Unless you haven't got them.'

Everyone knew the punishment for forgetting your papers. Sabirah reached in her bag for her permit. The green card sat in a zipped pocket, ready to show at a moment's notice. She remembered how relieved she'd been to get it in exchange for the yellow Asylum Seeker's Pass. She stared at it, reluctant to give it up.

The man snatched the card and stared at her with a nasty grin, then cut it into four with a pair of scissors, the blade slicing through the likeness of her face.

Sabirah could have killed him. She swayed in her seat, unable to think. Without a card, they would arrest her and take her to a detention centre.

The woman said, 'You've got two weeks to appeal.'

'You'll be wasting your time,' the man said. 'Eighty per cent are refused.'

Sabirah didn't need him to tell her. Like every refugee she'd met, she'd memorised the success rates of every part of the process.

The woman produced an envelope which she pushed across the table. 'The letter will tell you how, and there's a temporary pass to make sure you don't get arrested.'

Sabirah opened the envelope and the bright yellow card she'd so hated fell out. She never thought she'd be glad to see one. At least she could go home with the children, but for how long?

Sabirah stood in a daze, a hollowness inside her. She hadn't felt this helpless since she'd gone to prison on trumped-up changes. What could she tell the children?

Chapman ran down the stairs to the ground floor and rushed out of the fire exit at the rear of the block of flats. Instead of finding Griffin's broken body on the tarmac, a huge red fire engine sat in the car park. Of Griffin there was no sign. The engine of the hydraulic platform strained as the white booms lowered. A small crowd, including the SecurCo men he'd deployed, watched.

Chapman approached the nearest. 'What happened?'

'Someone called the fire brigade when they saw the bloke on the roof. The guys set this thing up, and they were getting it up there when matey flew over the edge.' He pointed at the descending cage. 'He landed on top of the fireman in there.'

With a huge sense of relief, Chapman studied the figures returning to ground level. Neither looked injured. If Griffin had suffered the fate Chapman imagined, not only would Chapman have faced the wrath of his commanding officer, but he'd have had to explain himself to the young man's mother. He searched for his team and found Sanchez.

'I've sent Louisa back in our car, boss. There's nothing broken and she didn't want to go to casualty, but I told her to book off duty and not return until she looks a lot less like the runner-up in a boxing match.'

'Thanks, Alice.' He gestured at Baxter and Sanderson. 'Lads, can you take charge of our prisoner?'

The cage came to a stop half a metre from ground level and the firefighter in it lifted a rail and invited Griffin to get out.

Baxter helped him down and held him. 'Cuffs, boss?'

'Are you injured?'

A very chastened Griffin shook his head. A small bruise on his forehead could have been there earlier.

'Yes please, Darren. We don't want any mishaps.' Chapman led his team and Griffin back to the people-carrier and, after removing all evidence of their surveillance from the office, they set off for the station.

Despite the fact Griffin hadn't come to harm, Chapman suspected he'd have plenty of paperwork to complete. He examined their prisoner, cuffed and looking forlorn between the two bulky constables. He intended to speak to him about the contents of his mother's letter and he'd have to do it tonight.

Back at the station, Chapman accompanied the two constables and Griffin to the custody suite.

The sergeant, an old friend, studied the prisoner. 'Ah, Mr Griffin – or Superman, as he thinks he is. Don't make yourself comfortable, your chariot awaits—'

'Could I have a quick word with him?' Chapman said.

The sergeant frowned. 'I received explicit instructions to make sure the team collecting the prisoner were informed immediately he arrived. They've been up in the canteen for the last hour.'

'They're keen.'

'You're telling me.' The sergeant checked the time. 'I'll be contacting them in half an hour, as soon as you arrive.'

'Cheers. Is interview room one free?'

'Booked by Inspector Chapman, I'm afraid.' The sergeant winked.

Thanking him again, Chapman led Griffin to the interview room. 'Take the cuffs off, Darren.'

'Do you want us to stay, boss?' Baxter unfastened the handcuffs.

'No need, you two get off, I'll sort the paperwork out.' Not that I've got a life to be getting home for.

The two constables escaped before he could change his mind. Chapman sat across from Griffin. The young man's hands hadn't stopped trembling since they'd collected him from the fire service.

Chapman sought a way to put him at his ease.

'Do you want me to get you a drink, tea, coffee, Neil?'

He shook his head.

'I got a letter from your mum, Neil. She's worried about you.'

'Keep her out of this,' Griffin snarled.

Chapman had to stop himself flinching at the unexpected response. 'I meant no disrespect. But she is worried about you.'

'Oh yeah, what she say about me?' Griffin seemed to notice his tremor and entwined his fingers.

'She's worried about what's been done to you in prison.'

Griffin focused on his hands, squeezing them together until they turned white.

'Do you want to tell me what they've done?'

'Why aren't you recording this?'

'This isn't an official interview, Neil. I'm just trying to help.'

He snorted. 'Yeah, like you let me fall off the roof.'

I didn't make you climb up there. 'You're not injured, are you?'

'Take more than that to injure me.' A flash of the cocky youth Chapman knew.

'Glad to hear it. So, what's been happening? She mentioned a treatment.'

Fear crossed Griffin's features and he hunched further over. 'I haven't had any treatment.'

'Not even any counselling—'

'No! Nothing.' Griffin glared at him. 'I was just winding her up. Anyway, have you seen her recently?'

Chapman tried to recall the last time he'd seen her. 'Not for a while.'

'Well, she's lost it. I wouldn't listen to anything she says.'

'She seemed quite lucid in the letter—'

'Well, she fucking isn't, okay?' Spittle sprayed across the table and Griffin clenched his fists.

'Okay, Neil, I'll take your word for it.' Chapman held his hands up in a placatory gesture. 'Do you want to tell me what happened yesterday? You can take care of yourself, but I've never known you attack anyone.'

Griffin hunched over again, biting his lips. He almost spoke, then changed his mind. Chapman waited. In the quiet, he could make out distant voices. As the silence stretched, Griffin made a decision.

'They told me—'

The door burst open, and the custody sergeant appeared. 'Sorry, Inspector—'

'What's going on?' Chapman rose.

Behind the sergeant stood three men in the uniform of one of the private prison providers, one evidently senior, judging from the shit on his shoulders. He addressed the sergeant. 'We told you to let us know when the prisoner arrived.'

On hearing the man's voice, Griffin seemed to shrink and began to rock.

'He doesn't take orders from you, and neither do I.' Chapman stepped towards the door.

'But you do from me, Russell.' DCI Gunnerson emerged from behind the prison officers. She turned to them. 'Sorry for the misunderstanding. There's your prisoner.'

The two junior prison guards brushed past Chapman and grabbed Griffin, dragging him to his feet. He let them, his beaten demeanour making Chapman fear for the young man.

◆ ◆ ◆

Still in a daze, Sabirah went looking for her children. What could she tell them when she found them? She'd given them instructions to wait opposite the central fountain in the Italian Garden at Hyde Park. On a day like today, few people visited the park. She was late – it was almost four – but they had warm clothes, courtesy of Mrs Curtis after they outgrew their last set. The thought made her feel guilty. Did she rely on the old woman too much? Was she a parasite, like those two officials suggested? She'd never met the daughter, but Antonia's reaction whenever her name came up told her all she needed to know.

She reached the Italian Garden. A few tourists wandered the grounds, studying the browning reeds in the ponds. Then she saw two figures sitting on the bench inside the stone shelter at one end, and the anxiety she always experienced when she wasn't sure where to find her children faded. She opened her mouth to call them, but realised her mistake. They sat with their heads together, oblivious to their surroundings. Clearly a courting couple.

Her unease crept back. Had they wandered off, bored of waiting? But they knew not to. Her anxiety growing, she completed a circuit of the gardens and approached the couple.

'Excuse me, I'm sorry to bother, but have you seen my children? A pretty girl this high' – she held her hand at head height – 'with long black hair, and a boy?' She held her hand above her shoulder.

They blushed and shook their heads. Were they foreign, and didn't understand her? The urge to repeat herself, but louder, almost qualified her as a native. She resumed her search. The café wasn't far. The children could have gone there. Her optimism faded as she got closer. An elderly couple wrapped up against the cold sat on a bench in front of the darkened building. Sabirah's unease changed to a sense of panic. Something *must* have happened to them.

The fear of the authorities, something she'd only experienced since the secret police back in Syria took her beloved Rashid, made her reluctant to go to them. She'd ring Antonia and ask her what to do, but Antonia had her own worries. The idea of asking Mrs Curtis made her uncomfortable. She would happily help, but the words of the bully still stung.

'Mamma, where have you been?'

The shout from Nadimah startled her. Sabirah spun to see her daughter, smiling, holding a takeaway hot drink in both hands. Next to her Hakim and behind them a woman she didn't recognise.

'Nadimah, where did you go? I told you to wait for me.'

'Sorry, Mamma, but you were so late.'

'It's my fault.' The woman approached, wearing an apologetic smile. 'They seemed so cold, I took them for hot chocolates.'

The children's cold and pinched faces made her ashamed of her anger. But why were they with this woman? Sabirah had warned them about trusting anyone.

45

'We got one for you, Mamma. No sugar, how you like it.' Hakim offered her a cup.

'Thank you.' She lifted the lid and inhaled the chocolate aroma. Then sipped the thick, warm drink and nodded her thanks to the woman. 'Children, thank this lady for your drinks and we'll go.'

'Rosemary Juma.' The woman held out her free hand. Fortyish, about the same age as Sabirah, she wore an elegant grey wool overcoat which must have cost more than Sabirah's wardrobe. 'It's my fault. I took your charming children away and worried you. Can I buy you supper, by way of an apology?'

'No! Thank you, you have done enough.'

'Please, it's not far.' She gestured at a hotel across the Bayswater Road.

Sabirah had planned to treat her children to a meal, but not somewhere so expensive.

Before she could refuse, Nadimah piped up.

'Please, Mamma, she's from Idlib.'

The mention of her home city made Sabirah pause, and she studied the woman. Although she'd taken her for English, her Syrian surname sank in.

'My husband worked at Al Rayyan Hospital,' Mrs Juma said.

That's where she'd given birth to Nadimah. A mix of emotions filled her – joy, nostalgia and sorrow for what she'd lost.

'Please,' the woman pressed. 'It would give me great pleasure to spend a short while with someone from home.'

Her children's pleading expressions swung her decision. 'Okay, but you must let me pay.'

'No, I wouldn't dream of it.' Mrs Juma took her hand and, linking arms, led her towards the hotel.

They walked, chatting of home and familiar places they'd both frequented. Sabirah tried not to dwell on the ordeal of this afternoon and the inevitable fallout as she relived happy memories.

Conscious of the shabbiness of her clothes, the grandness of the hotel intimidated her. It was the type of interior she hated and would be embarrassed to design. One that shouted about itself, 'Look how impressive I am,' rather than lifted your spirits when you walked in. She'd not visited anywhere this imposing, apart from to clean it, since they'd escaped from Idlib. Mrs Juma didn't suffer from any such inhibitions, and, untangling her arm from Sabirah's, swept up to the reception desk.

Within five minutes, the four of them were sitting in a smart dining room overlooking the park. Under her coat, Mrs Juma wore a peach designer suit with matching shoes, making Sabirah feel even more like the poor relative. They ordered, Mrs Juma insisting that the children, who'd become used to checking the prices before choosing anything, order whatever they wanted.

Watching them enjoy their surroundings and listening to Mrs Juma's conversation of places in their past filled Sabirah with longing. She missed Rashid more than ever, but the knowledge of what they'd done to him contaminated the memory. The thought that this might be the last time she'd see the children happy almost overwhelmed her.

'Nadimah tells me you visited the Internal Security Agency,' Mrs Juma said. 'Trouble?'

The fear and uncertainty she'd experienced at the end of her interview rushed back. Sabirah studied her host. Could she trust this woman? They shared a background, but plenty of people from Idlib supported the devil who masqueraded as their president.

'They tried to remove me because I got involved in political activity.' Mrs Juma scanned the nearest tables, but nobody sat near them. She still lowered her voice. 'A group of us called for the removal of the evil son-of-a-bitch. You know who.'

'What happened?'

'My brilliant lawyer squashed it and got me Indefinite Leave.' She speared a piece of asparagus with her fork. 'I can give you his number.'

That would be a prize Sabirah couldn't even imagine. Just the return of her green card seemed too much to hope for. 'I can't afford—'

'Nonsense, he's Syrian, and will do it pro bono.'

'I already have a lawyer.' It wasn't strictly true. Mrs Curtis had a lawyer and she let Sabirah use him. She should learn to stand on her two feet. If she had her own lawyer, they couldn't claim she depended on someone else. 'But it might be useful to talk to your man.'

Mrs Juma pulled her Hermes handbag to her and produced a business card from inside it. She wrote on the back using a gold pen. 'Tell him I recommended you. You won't regret it.'

Sabirah took the card and read the name. If this man got rid of the threat of deportation hanging over them, even for a few months, she would give thanks.

Mrs Juma closed her handbag with an air of satisfaction that puzzled Sabirah. A tremble travelled down her spine. Was she making a big mistake? Mrs Juma smiled at Hakim, who grinned back, teeth covered in pink ice cream. *You're being paranoid, Sabirah, this woman just wants to help.*

CHAPTER 5

By the time Antonia walked to her office in Vincent Terrace, the leg she'd injured in the crash moved much more freely. Perhaps the damage wasn't as bad as she'd feared. The day she'd spent getting intensive treatment seemed to have paid off. However, negotiating the steps down to the offices of *The Electric Investigator* made her reconsider. She unlocked the entrance, hobbled to the alarm and reset it.

She struggled out of her jacket, wincing as she moved her damaged shoulder. This definitely wasn't a great idea. She should have taken another day off, but they'd scheduled interviews to select her new PA, and she wanted to see every candidate. She also wanted to work on her story. Not that she had much to add from her meeting with John since she lost the memory stick, but she had another potential source from a prison visitor who'd left a message on their confidential whistle-blower's line over the weekend.

She made a coffee and sat at her desk, massaging her ankle. The joint felt hot to the touch, but a few moments of kneading eased the pain. She opened the folder relating to her article. A flashing icon told her someone had added notes on the shared system. She never used it while working on a story, preferring to share completed articles. She opened the link and read the notes with growing irritation.

'What are you doing here?' Eleanor demanded from the doorway.

'You made me jump.' Antonia should have heard Eleanor's arrival – if not the lift bringing her down, at least her wheelchair motor. 'We've got the interviews this afternoon and I've got a news—'

'We won't fall apart if you take a few days off. Don't forget, I ran it for donkey's years and I'm sure Miles and I can manage it for a few days.'

'Yes, I'm sure you can. Why did Miles contact the woman who left us the message?'

'You weren't here—'

'It's *my* story.' Antonia realised how childish she sounded, but she had a huge investment in this story. She had to be careful. Being in charge, she didn't need to remind everyone how young she was.

'I wasn't sure how long before you returned. Anyway, now you're here, was the meeting worthwhile? Did you get anything we can use?'

'The poor guy's dead, but your priority is the story.' For all her compassion, Eleanor could still shock her with her insensitivity.

'Balderdash. I'm sorry the poor man's dead, but being mealy-mouthed won't bring him back. And I'm certain he'd want us to publish his story. That's why he came to us.'

'And I'm sure his family and friends wish he hadn't.' Antonia sipped her coffee, wishing she could unsee the scenes that kept returning.

Eleanor broke the silence. 'I'll get a drink, let you cool down.'

'I'll get it.' She stood, regretting it as she put weight on her ankle.

'I can manage, thank you.' Eleanor spun away in her chair.

Antonia didn't have the energy for this. She finished reading Miles's notes. He hadn't completed his account, but he'd planned to speak to the woman again. Now she'd returned, she could do it.

Eleanor returned, accompanied by a sweet fruity aroma that momentarily overpowered the coffee. She placed a steaming mug on the desk and manoeuvred her chair into place. 'We need some new mugs.' She gestured at the chipped crockery. 'You can ask your new PA to get some.'

Antonia smiled, recognising the peace offering. 'Good idea.'

'How are you, Antonia? I imagine it was traumatic. The reports said your source died at the scene.'

An innocuous-sounding phrase for what she'd witnessed. 'It wasn't pleasant, but I'm okay, thanks.'

'Something's bothering you. What is it?' Eleanor's shrewd eyes appraised her.

'I think I was followed to my meeting with John.' The confession made her cringe.

'How? You're usually so careful.'

'I . . . I don't know.' She'd gone over the journey so many times she felt dizzy. 'I'm pretty sure two men followed me on the train at Woolwich. I saw one of them at the scene of the crash. The lorry that hit us did so deliberately.'

Eleanor took a sip of her drink. 'I thought the lorry hit you north of the river. How did you get there?'

'I walked to Charlton House and got in John's car.'

'If they'd followed you to Charlton House, they must have followed John's car. He must have taken precautions to avoid being followed.'

Antonia replayed the torturous journey in his car. He appeared to have been careful, but as she didn't drive, she wasn't sure how difficult it was to spot a tail. 'If I hadn't led them to his car . . .'

'I doubt you did.' Eleanor's look of sympathy only made her feel worse.

'How else did the same man appear at Woolwich and the crash?' She hadn't wanted to sound so aggressive and mouthed, 'Sorry.'

'What happened to your hair?'

The change of subject threw Antonia. She didn't want Eleanor to know what she'd been through. 'I wanted a change.' She'd got the mobile hairdresser to come round and chop off the singed ends.

A knock at the door made her look up.

'I asked Miles to join us.' Eleanor moved her chair to give him more room.

The thought of finding out what he'd discovered lifted Antonia's mood. Would it make up for losing the memory stick?

Miles stepped through her doorway. 'Good morning.' His good-natured smile faded when he saw Antonia. 'Should you be at work?'

'Not you as well.'

He held up his left hand in surrender. 'Just concerned about you.' He placed his Pavarotti mug on the desk, the string from his tea bag draped over the handle, and dragged the visitor's chair into position.

Eleanor addressed Miles. 'Antonia was telling me about her meeting with the unfortunate John.'

Antonia said, 'I'd rather hear about what you discovered yesterday, Miles.'

'I think it would be useful if *you* brought us up to date first,' Eleanor said, 'seeing as you've, yet again, not used our file sharing software.'

Antonia counted to five and drank some coffee. 'Okay. Unfortunately, John didn't tell me much before he died, but he brought information on a memory stick. I had it in my hand when

52

the lorry hit us. I asked the firefighter in charge to get it for me. I'm assuming he hasn't contacted the office.' She doubted he'd have got it. That spook from the train would have definitely warned him off.

'Not yet,' Eleanor said. 'What had John told you so far? All you've told me is GRM are conducting memory experiments on prisoners. Has he told you the nature of these? Had the accident been more serious, and you'd been' – she searched for a word – 'injured, we'd have nothing.'

Antonia ignored the implied rebuke. 'John worked for GRM Corrections, which is the arm that manages their prisons. He took care of the prisoners who were being experimented on. He observed the changes in their behaviour, loss of memory and personality changes, acute paranoia and violent outbursts. Those who were already violent or paranoid got worse.'

'Why didn't they stop treating the prisoners? Surely they didn't want them to get worse.'

'It didn't affect all the prisoners, and it often happened days or weeks after the treatment.'

'But we don't know exactly what this "treatment" is, do we?'

Antonia realised Eleanor wanted to play devil's advocate, but a bit of support would be nice. 'John tried finding out, but the medics gave them some sort of sedative before they subjected them to the treatment, so most recall nothing about it.'

'What have we got, then?'

'We've got case studies, with dates and exactly how their personalities changed, but no names.'

'Do we know how they selected the prisoners?'

'They completed a questionnaire, then they interviewed those who "passed". He had nothing to do with that side, or in administering the treatment.'

'So, he didn't know how they did it?' Eleanor took another drink from her cup.

'Not in any detail.' Antonia couldn't ignore this weakness in their information.

'Can I butt in?' Miles said. 'Anne, the lady from the prison visitors, spoke to several families whose relatives were experimented on. It sounds like the sort of thing the Nazis did. Why haven't more people come forward to expose it?'

'Incremental dehumanisation,' Eleanor said. 'They degrade people in small imperceptible steps, until suddenly, they're not even human.'

'Did she tell you any more than you've put on the system?' Antonia said.

'She's given me details of incidents which occurred once they released the prisoners. Although their treatment caused them serious problems, they got no follow-up or help to adjust.'

'What sort of problems?'

'One prisoner refused to acknowledge his children. He behaved as if he and his wife had just left school. They're in their late thirties. He remembers nothing from after the first time he went to prison. Another assaulted his best friend, nearly killed him, accusing him of breaking into his house.'

'John mentioned several assaults and an attempted murder in the prison.'

'According to Anne, she can link two deaths to people they experimented on and released—'

Eleanor slammed her mug down, splashing rose-coloured jewels on the desk. 'I can't believe they released people with such serious issues.'

Antonia agreed. 'They offered them shorter sentences if they signed up. They also got better food and single cells. What were these deaths?'

'One killed himself, a habitual burglar. In fact, they were all recidivist non-violent prisoners. He'd been easy-going, never letting anything get him down, but he changed, becoming introspective and melancholy. After months of trying to get therapy, he took an overdose.'

'And the other one?'

'He killed someone who he claimed abused his sister. He'd never been violent, either. And, more worrying, he didn't have a sister.'

'What the hell happened to these people?' Eleanor rarely used expletives.

'I don't know, Eleanor,' Antonia said. 'I'll see if I can get any more out of Anne.'

Miles examined his treacle-like brew. 'I spoke to her last night. She made it clear she wasn't keen to speak to us again. She mentioned John's accident. Sorry.'

This landed like a punch in Antonia's gut. 'Will she give us names, so we can contact the families?'

'Sorry, she made that very clear.'

Antonia drained her mug. 'The fact they killed John shows they're rattled.'

'Can we prove it wasn't an accident?' Eleanor said. 'I believe what you told me, but we need to be careful what we publish.'

'If I can show the lorry hit us on purpose, we might not have enough for a court of law, but it's plenty to run the story. And once we publish it, the families of the affected prisoners should come forward.'

Miles became more miserable. 'Again, I'm sorry to deliver more bad news, but they gave the families large payments to keep quiet.'

Blast. 'I'm still going to run it, I'm not wasting weeks of work. Someone *must* come forward.'

Eleanor drank more of her fruit tea. 'Okay. You're the editor.'

She was, but at times like this, she wished she wasn't.

'Boss!' Sanchez stood in the doorway to Chapman's office.

Chapman, lost in recollections of yesterday's near miss, started. 'Sorry, Alice, miles away.'

'I noticed. The boss wants to see you, now. She's not happy.'

He could guess why. He'd just sent his report on Griffin's arrest. He roused himself, made his way to DCI Yasmin Gunnerson's office and, after knocking on the door, walked in. She sat at her desk studying her tablet and, without looking up, waved him to a chair.

He sat and waited. She looked exhausted and more harassed than she usually did. She'd aged years in the last six months, but it wasn't surprising. The diagnosis of her husband's motor neurone disease must have devastated the devoted couple. Chapman wondered if she'd hand in her ticket soon. He'd only been a DI for a few months this time, but he'd been DCI for long enough before his fall. Apart from everything else, he could do with the money. This office wasn't great, thirty square metres of worn carpet, filled with cheap steel and MDF furniture, but it beat the tiny cubicle he had.

Gunnerson finished reading and studied him. 'What am I supposed to do with this, Russell?'

'File it?'

'You're joking?'

'Why not?'

'You take your officers clambering on a slate roof fifty feet off the ground in a rainstorm—'

'A light drizzle.'

Gunnerson continued. 'You didn't do a risk assessment. You didn't wait for backup.'

'We had a team from SecurCo.'

She snorted. 'And you pissed *them* off. I've got a complaint from their district manager about you, and your, I quote, "lack of respect, failure to adequately brief and plain rudeness".'

He waved this away. 'They're lucky I didn't send them back. Useless liabilities, every one of them.'

'That's as may be, but we have protocols.' She pinched the bridge of her nose. 'We don't have to put up with them for much longer.'

'You, or us?'

The right side of her mouth lifted. 'I'm going nowhere, Russell. But we'll soon have brand-new auxiliaries from our new "partners".'

'What's the betting it's the same monkeys in new—'

'We're not here to discuss the politics of policing. We have clear protocols. If a fugitive is in a precarious position above ground level, you're supposed to wait for our High-Level Recovery Team.'

'Last time, they took fifty minutes.'

'If there's an issue on attendance times, you can call the fire brigade.'

He snorted. 'And disturb their snooker game?'

She fixed him with a glare. 'You're behind the times.'

Bugger! He'd forgotten her nephew had just joined and would fill her head with bullshit. 'Anyway, they got him.'

'Yes, thanks to your sergeant. You got away with it. You should have waited.' She sipped water from the fancy flask on her desk. 'Luckily, Mr Griffin survived, although his solicitor has intimated they may apply for compensation for his "near-death" experience.'

'Okay. If he wins, I'll put in a counterclaim for recklessly putting me at risk. I still get nightmares, it's probably PTSD—'

'Oh, shut up, Russell. Rewrite this, but this time I want you to address the reasons you failed to wait for the HLRT and the complaints from SecurCo.'

'Are you serious?'

'Deadly.'

'No problem.' He rose. 'How's Rex?'

Her brow clouded. 'He's got the new wheelchair, and he's practising with the synthetic speech software.'

'Already?' *He must be going downhill fast, poor guy.*

'He can still speak, but it's becoming slurred, and no harm in being prepared.'

'Tell him I said hi.' He walked to the door.

'Russell, we're having a few friends round at the weekend, if you fancy joining us.'

His mind went blank for a moment. 'Erm . . . I've got Abby for the weekend.'

'Oh, right. Let me have the report today.'

He clicked his heels and stepped into the corridor. Rex wasn't a bad guy, but they had little in common and the thought of making polite conversation while pretending to ignore his deteriorating health wasn't Chapman's scene.

His phone vibrated. 'DI Chapman.'

'Russell, Antonia.'

'Antonia, long time no hear.' He'd been thinking they'd not seen each other for too long. 'How can I help you?'

'A lorry hit a parked car a couple of days ago, next to the City Airport, and I wanted to find out if it was deliberate.'

'Someone you know involved?'

'The driver. He died.'

'Sorry to hear that. How can I help?'

'I've spoken to the investigating officer, but she won't tell me much. Can you find out anything?'

'It depends who it is.'

Antonia told him the details and, luckily, the investigating officer owed him a few favours. He arranged to find out all he could and meet her for a drink after work. What had Antonia got herself involved with now? Six months earlier, her boss had been murdered and they'd both come close to joining him when he got involved with a story she was investigating.

◆ ◆ ◆

Chapman arrived first and secured a table in a quiet corner of a wine bar off Russell Square. The owners had created a horrific mash-up of retro fifties kitsch and nineties animal prints. Why the hell did Antonia choose this place? The eagerness with which he anticipated their meeting surprised him.

He'd told the waitress who greeted him he'd arranged to meet someone and, hanging his coat on a chrome coat stand, sat in the furthest booth, facing the entrance. The list of cocktails on the menu read like the author had swallowed the script of a Carry On film. Out of habit, he studied the other patrons as he pretended to peruse it. They seemed to be groups of colleagues out for an after-work drink. Probably 'team-building'. What a load of bullshit.

A lone figure entered the wine bar and came towards him. Antonia's purposeful stride seemed a bit off, not quite a limp, but she wasn't moving with her usual grace. Several men at other tables fell silent as they followed her progress. *In your dreams.* Chapman stood, proud to be seen with such a striking woman.

'Antonia, good to see you.'

He'd pondered how to greet her, but she took his shoulders and kissed his cheek, enveloping him in a subtle scent. 'Russell, thanks for coming. You're looking good. Still following the exercise regime I gave you?'

'More or less,' he said, pleased she'd noticed.

He studied her as she removed an elegant overcoat, grimacing as she did so. Although she'd never been skinny, her shoulders were bigger than last time he saw her. Then he stared at her face. 'What the hell happened to you?' He pointed out the graze on her cheek. It wasn't the only mark on her and, combined with her uneven gait, it suggested she'd been in the wars. 'Short hair suits you, by the way.'

Antonia ignored the compliment and his question. The waitress scurried over and took their order, disappointed they chose a beer and sparkling water.

Antonia waited until she'd left. 'Did you see the report of the RTC?'

'Not the final report, but I spoke to the investigating officer and scribbled a few notes.' He produced a sheet of paper and passed it to her.

Antonia read his notes. A group who'd arrived earlier sang a ragged rendition of 'Happy Birthday' at one of their number. Chapman gave thanks he wasn't the poor sod in the middle.

Antonia slapped his notes. 'How can they treat it as an accident?'

'I'm not sure what you're getting at.'

'How well do you know the investigating officer?'

'She knows her job.'

'I could tell when she questioned me, but I meant, could she be compromised?'

Chapman would once have reacted angrily to the suggestion one of his colleagues could be bent. 'We worked together as constables, and she was always dead straight. I've not heard anything different. Why are you so sure it wasn't an accident?'

'The guy drove at us. I told the officer who interviewed me.'

'Bloody hell, you're the passenger?' Chapman studied her injuries anew. He'd seen images of the remains of the car after they'd removed the container. 'When I heard the account, I imagined the passenger would be in intensive care.'

'I was lucky.' She touched her cropped head. 'I had to get the singed hair cut off.'

'Right, a stolen forty-foot trailer full of fireworks landed on your car, then burst into flames. I don't call that lucky.'

'They tried to kill us. Succeeded with John.'

The waitress arrived with their drinks and Chapman took the opportunity to compose his thoughts. He'd assumed Antonia was investigating the crash.

The waitress left, and he took a sip of his beer. 'You'd better rewind and fill me in. Why were you there?'

'I'd arranged to meet John, the driver. He's an informant who works— worked for GRM. We were working on a story, and he had some information to give me.'

'You still pursuing GRM's big boss, Reed-Mayhew?'

'Of course, wouldn't you?' She shuddered and stared into her drink.

'What's the story about?'

Antonia looked thoughtful then checked the nearest tables before leaning towards him. 'They're experimenting on prisoners.'

'Seriously?' He placed his bottle on the table. 'I might have something on that.'

'Yeah?'

He told her about the letter from Griffin's mother and the rooftop arrest.

'What did he say when you questioned him about it?'

'He clammed up. Claims he'd been winding his mum up.'

'Did you believe him?'

Chapman thought for a moment. 'I've got to know him over the years, and he was definitely different, which backs up what she said. But I've not seen him for at least three years, and I've seen prisoners change a hell of a lot in that time.' But that much? He wasn't sure.

'Do you think he'd talk to me?'

Griffin had been adamant nothing had happened, becoming quite aggressive when Chapman pushed it. 'I'd say no, and under the new rules he wouldn't be allowed to talk to you while he's on remand.'

'I'd forgotten prisoners can't speak to the press before their trial.' Antonia's look of disappointment made Chapman want to do something to help her.

'I could ask his mum if she'll talk to you.'

'Okay, that could be useful for background information.' She gave him a tight smile.

'No problem. Did you get the information from your informer before he . . .'

'He gave me a memory stick, but I dropped it when the lorry hit us. Someone promised to get it for me, but I've not heard from him.'

'Do you want me to see if it's amongst the guy's personal effects? As we're treating it as an accident, I should be able to get hold of it.'

She smiled. 'Thanks, Russell, but I doubt it's still there. I told you someone targeted us, and some dodgy security types arrived later. I'm sure they'll have searched the car and I don't want you to get involved.'

He tried to hide his relief. The last time he and Antonia got involved with 'security types' he'd shot two men dead, and he still suffered nightmares about it.

◆ ◆ ◆

Antonia took a cab back to the office. Her first interview for her new PA started soon and she didn't want to be late. She sat in the back, lost in thought. She planned to publish the story she'd worked on with John. They'd deliberately killed John to shut him up. She knew that was what happened, but if the police were treating it as an accident, it weakened her accusation. She needed the information on the memory stick, but didn't expect they'd ever find it, and she'd given up on the firefighter. He'd either not found it or he'd decided she was a neurotic conspiracy theorist and not bothered looking. She couldn't blame him.

They arrived in Vincent Terrace, and, giving the driver a tip, she got out. The row of terraced Georgian buildings shone in the autumn sunlight. Last night's wind had got rid of the last few leaves on the trees screening the house from the Regent's Canal. Antonia strode across the pavement, conscious of her need to focus on the forthcoming interviews. The person they took on would be her first hire.

Eleanor and Alan Turner always did the interviews. Antonia never went a day without thinking of Alan, and the memory of his courageous final act returned as she reached the top of the stairs. After receiving death threats, he'd hired a team of security guards and they'd turned on him. Antonia still blamed herself for failing to warn him about them. She and Chapman had attempted a rescue but had gone into a trap. Turner had saved them by taking on a gunman, armed with just a chair.

She blinked to clear her vision and descended to the main entrance. Someone had polished the plaque beside the main door. A small blob of Brasso had collected in the corner of the bottom rail of the 'E' of 'The Electric Investigator', etched across the top of the plate. She looked at the Louis Brandeis quote below – *Sunlight is said to be the best of disinfectants; electric light the most efficient policeman* – as she wiped the Brasso away with a tissue and let herself into the office.

Eleanor and Miles looked up when Antonia entered the main office, an air of concern enveloping both.

'Where have you been?' Eleanor demanded.

'Sorry, took ages to get to the meeting. I got a cab back. Anyone here yet?'

'First candidate rang saying he's going to be ten minutes late. Lucky for you.'

Antonia resisted the urge to apologise again and rushed through to her office. Someone had tidied the profusion of documents and reference books, which she never got round to sorting, and cleaned her office. It looked almost presentable. She slumped into her chair and checked her emails, but saw nothing urgent, and she retrieved Chapman's notes from inside her coat.

'Got your questions ready?' Eleanor asked, wheeling herself into the room.

Antonia slid her chair across, giving the owner of *The Electric Investigator* room to get her powered chair in. 'Here somewhere, I prepared them last night.' Antonia slid open the top drawer and took out three pages of questions she'd printed out, replacing them with Chapman's notes.

'How did it go with Chapman?'

'They're saying it's an accident.'

'How ludicrous. Do you think they've been got at? Did Chapman think the investigating officer could be corrupt?'

'He didn't think so, but it's not the sort of thing you discuss with colleagues.'

'You shouldn't dwell on—'

The buzzer carried from the front door. They waited in silence as Miles's baritone welcomed their visitor and led them across the office. He knocked on the door, pushed it open and ushered a tall, gangly young man with round silver-framed glasses into the room. For a moment Antonia imagined she saw her dead predecessor, Alan Turner.

'Tomasz Zabo,' Miles announced.

The silence dragged until Eleanor said, 'Welcome, Tomasz.'

Antonia roused herself and scrambled to her feet. 'Hello, this is Eleanor, our founder, and I'm Antonia, the editor.' She still wasn't used to the title.

Once his nervousness wore off, he radiated an air of friendly openness, reminding her even more of Alan. By the end of the allocated time, she thought she'd found the perfect candidate.

As they discussed him, Eleanor issued a warning. 'Make sure you keep an open mind about the other candidates. He came across very well, but . . .'

'Of course.'

The rest of the afternoon passed in a blur of candidates and repeated questions. The last applicant left, and the two women sat in silence for a few moments. Antonia felt like she'd gone ten rounds and the low-level headache, a legacy of the smash, let her know it had gone nowhere. Eleanor looked exhausted. Miles came in with a tray, a teapot for Eleanor and a coffee for Antonia, plus a plate piled high with assorted chocolate biscuits. Antonia hadn't realised how hungry she was and grabbed a couple, wolfing them down then picking up another.

Miles returned with his drink and a pad covered in his spidery shorthand. Revived by their refreshments, they discussed the candidates for half an hour. Antonia wanted her favoured candidate, but Eleanor championed a woman Antonia had struggled to connect with.

Miles tried to mediate. 'Shall we sleep on it and decide in the morning?'

Eleanor jumped at the suggestion. 'Good idea, Miles. We—' The doorbell interrupted her. 'Oh God, did we miss one?'

Miles laughed. 'Not from my list. I'll see who it is.'

Antonia checked the time. Six thirty already. She'd planned to go to the gym for a massage and sauna to help her recovery.

'Someone to see you, Antonia.' He ushered a figure into the room.

Adam. She'd assumed he'd decided not to get involved after he'd cut her out of the car. He smiled, stretching his tanned skin across his cheekbones and showing even teeth. Her insides fluttered as his green, almond eyes studied her.

After the introductions, Eleanor and Miles left and Antonia sat in awkward silence. 'Sure you don't want a drink?'

'I just wanted to drop this.' He placed a memory stick on her desk.

She picked it up. 'Wow, you got it. Thank you, I assumed . . .'

'When we lifted the container, we had to cut the driver out. I took over at the sharp end and found this in the footwell.' He gave her a sympathetic look. 'Sorry for your loss.'

'We weren't close. I didn't even know his name.'

He raised his eyebrows. 'Really?'

'He was a whistle-blower. He gave me a false name.'

'Who was he blowing the whistle on?'

'Do you mind if I don't say? I'm still working on the story.'

He frowned. 'I'd like to know who followed me.'

'Someone followed you? When?'

'To the gym the next morning. And someone else searched my flat before I got back. They must have known the driver had the memory stick, and when they didn't find it in the car, decided one of us took it.'

'How come they didn't find this?' She held it up.

'I took it with me, planning to bring it to you, but I spotted the tail and I changed my plans. That's why I didn't come until today. If I'd evaded them, they'd have guessed I'd spotted them, so I just let them follow me until they got bored.'

'You don't seem too concerned that someone followed you.'

'It's not the first time, but it's been a while.'

Why would a firefighter be used to being tailed? 'Are you sure nobody traced you here?' She'd convinced herself nobody had followed her from Woolwich station, but they'd still tracked her to John's car and killed him.

'You can never say a hundred per cent. It depends who's following you.' He waited for her to tell him.

Antonia had too many questions about him to tell him more.

He gave a wry grimace. 'I'm pretty sure those spooks who turned up at the crash were involved. They usually change teams so they don't get spotted.'

Antonia's heart skipped a beat. 'So, they could have followed you.'

He didn't hide his irritation. 'I parked in a multistorey in a shopping precinct three miles away. I left via the fire exit of a pizza restaurant and walked here. Not a very direct route. It took me two hours, and I sat in the window of your friendly local for half an hour before coming here.'

'I'm sorry. I appreciate your efforts. It's just, I . . .' She hesitated. 'They followed me to my meeting with John, that's why he . . . I thought I'd shaken them off.'

'Maybe you had. I checked the underside of the car when they came to take it. I told the spooks I needed to check for residual heat so I could get close. Someone had stuck a tracking device on it.'

Does that mean it was John they'd followed? 'Why did you check?'

'You seemed pretty sure someone had targeted you. A tracking device is the surest way to make sure you don't lose someone.'

Again, how come he knew so much about these things? The relief she hadn't caused John's death surged through her, but also a wariness. Who was Adam, and could she trust him?

CHAPTER 6

'What's wrong, Mama?' Hakim's question as they arrived at his school cut Sabirah.

'Nothing. Come on, you'll be late.' She should have known it would be her son who saw through her attempt to hide her fears.

Hakim would have pursued it, but the sight of two of his friends in the playground distracted him and with a perfunctory goodbye, he ran off. Sabirah's insides constricted as she watched them. How many more days would he be able to enjoy the carefree company of his friends? The memory of the traumatised little boy who'd cried in his sleep every night broke her heart.

She roused herself and hurried away. She'd not taken the morning off work to mope outside her son's school.

The fearful thoughts that had filled her mind since the devastating visit to the Internal Security Agency two days earlier accompanied her on her journey to the address Rosemary Juma gave her for the solicitor she'd recommended. The imposing exterior of the building made her pause, and she admired the classical proportions. Sweeping marble steps led to double doors flanked by gleaming white pillars. Self-conscious, she climbed the stairs, glad she'd brought the beautiful handbag Antonia had given her, the only stylish thing she owned. The idea of Antonia, who never wore dresses and rarely carried anything more stylish than a backpack, choosing such an item still amazed Sabirah.

She pushed the doors open and stepped into a grand entrance hallway with wood panelling and gleaming parquet floors. A strong smell of polish overlaid with the scent of flowers enveloped her. The blooms sat in a huge vase on a table in the middle of the reception area, underneath a crystal chandelier hanging from the ceiling several metres above.

A uniformed man stood behind a lectern desk. 'Good morning, Madam. Can I help you?' His expression suggested she'd come to the wrong place.

Fighting the impulse to slink away, she held his gaze and told him who she'd come to see. After checking, he directed her to the two lifts on the wall beside his desk. She rode up to the third floor convinced she was wasting her time. She couldn't afford to hire anyone who would occupy offices in this building – although Mrs Juma had assured her he wouldn't charge.

The reception area for the solicitor had a more modern style, but you couldn't mistake the smell of money.

The young receptionist rose from her chair to greet Sabirah, and, after offering her refreshments, asked her to wait. Although she looked Syrian, she spoke perfect English, sounding like Mrs Curtis. Sabirah perched on the edge of the luxurious leather sofa facing the young woman. Her thoughts returned to her and her children's fates. Visions of the horrors of the refugee camp they'd escaped less than two years ago filled her head.

After five minutes, a door opened and a short plump man in a beautiful silk suit appeared. He wore his thinning black hair short and his moustache and beard neat, as if trimmed that morning. His teeth gleamed against his pale brown skin.

'Mrs Fadil, welcome.' He gestured towards the open door.

Sabirah stood. 'Mr Al Rahman, thank you.' She snatched up her handbag and scurried through the opening.

The room beyond contained an enormous mahogany desk in front of a tall window flanked by towering bookcases. Al Rahman gestured to a chair in front of his desk and sat in his throne-like armchair behind it.

'We can speak Arabic or English, whichever you prefer.'

He sat half a head higher, so she had to look up at him. 'English. I'm trying to learn.'

He gave a sympathetic smile. 'I understand they've revoked your Permit to Reside.'

'Yes.' Her voice came out a whisper.

'Do you have the paperwork?'

She reached into her handbag and retrieved all the documents relating to her dealings with the Internal Security Agency. She stood to reach the desk and slid the papers across its leather-covered expanse. Al Rahman opened a gold glasses case, and, retrieving horn-rimmed half-moon spectacles, read them. His lips moved as he read. He put the papers down before studying her over the tops of the glasses.

'This is very unusual.'

'Is it bad?' she blurted out, her stomach clenching.

'If you have a Permit to Reside, it's either renewed after twelve months, or you get Leave to Remain. On the rare occasions they revoke it, it's usually for breaking the law. But you haven't.'

'What does it mean?'

'I don't know, Mrs Fadil. I've never come across it.'

'Can you help?'

'Of course.' One of his canines had a gold cap. 'This letter mentions your failure to support yourself and your children. It's frowned upon, but not usually a problem if you have private means or a sponsor.'

'I support us. I work very hard, but Mrs Curtis, my landlady, tells me to have English lessons so I can work as architect like back in Idlib. The lessons are expensive, so she lets me live for free.'

'And what's your relationship with this Mrs Curtis?'

'She is the mother of my friend Antonia.'

'So, a family friend?'

'Yes.' But the term didn't do her justice. Mrs Curtis had been more than a friend to her family and treated the children as a loving grandmother would.

He picked up the papers again and sat staring at them for some minutes. Then he laid them aside and removed his glasses, leaving a red mark on the bridge of his nose. 'I'm going to appeal the decision as an abuse of process.'

The woman had mentioned an appeal. 'They say I only have two weeks.'

'Don't worry, once we lodge an appeal, the clock stops. It will go to a tribunal. This Mrs Curtis will probably have to appear. Will she do that?'

'Yes.' Mrs Curtis would surely help.

'Good, good. I'll apply for the appeal and once we have a date, I'll arrange for you to come in and rehearse your testimony. Is there anything I need to know about your time here?'

Should she tell him about her time in prison? But they'd dropped all charges and apologised. 'Do you know when you'll be given a date?' She couldn't relax until they'd won.

'We'll request a fast-track. The fees are the same whether—'

'Fees? Mrs Juma said you don't charge. I don't have money.'

'No, no. I won't charge for my time. We have to help each other, don't we?' He showed his teeth. 'Maybe sometime you can help me. Say, when you're practising as an architect?'

'Of course.' His manner made her uneasy.

'No, they're court fees which we have to pay. You can cover those?'

'How much?'

'A few hundred.'

A few hundred! But she had no choice. 'Okay.' If the appeal failed, she would need all the money she had to make their lives easier in the camps. 'What if the appeal fail?'

'That's a possibility, but I'm confident we can overturn this. I've never failed yet.' He stacked the papers together. 'I'll keep these, and my assistant will give you the bank details for the fees. She'll email the amount as soon as we have it. And my driver will give you a lift to wherever you're going.'

'Thank you, but no need.' She'd planned to go straight to the rundown warehouse where she cleaned the offices. The thought of Al Rahman's driver knowing she worked as a cleaner at such a scruffy place embarrassed her.

'Nonsense. He'll take you wherever you want.'

She'd have time to go home and change instead of going to work in her best clothes. 'Thank you.'

Pleased but apprehensive, despite Al Rahman's assurances, Sabirah made for the door. She suspected Al Rahman wasn't some-one to forget a favour, but she'd happily design him an entire house if he could remove this threat blighting her life. The thought light-ened her step. She'd get a treat for the children tonight.

'Mrs Fadil?'

She paused at the door.

A troubled frown had creased his forehead. 'Even if the appeal succeeds, there's no guarantee they won't try something else.'

'What do you mean?'

'I said it was unusual . . . If someone is determined to . . . We'll see, shall we?' He seemed embarrassed, like he'd said something he shouldn't. 'I'm sure it will be fine.'

Was someone doing this to get at her? But who, and why? Sabirah left, numb and with her newfound optimism crushed.

◆ ◆ ◆

The sound of operatives at a dozen or more keyboards carried through the open doorway of the scruffy office as Antonia waited for the ageing computer whiz on the other side of the desk to finish his work. The memory stick Adam recovered hadn't worked on any of their devices. Even Miles, the most tech-savvy of them, couldn't access its contents.

Unwilling to concede defeat, she'd brought it to the offices of a team of cyber security experts she'd used before. The last time, they'd accessed the network of traffic cameras around London and identified two men who'd dumped a body in the canal near her office. Antonia had used the information to track down a team of killers. The team had moved since then, but their new offices, although bigger, had the same temporary vibe. The walls and faded carpet tiles showed the outlines of the previous occupier's furniture and fittings and a musty, dusty smell suggested it needed a good clean. She flexed her ankle and massaged her shoulder. Neither was back to normal.

'Okay.' The chief hacker pushed his chair away from the screen, then rose to close his office door. His thick hair seemed greyer since last time and more lines creased his tanned face.

'What have you found?'

'Mixed news.' He leant down and unplugged a memory stick from his computer. 'I've copied the few uncorrupted documents I retrieved on to this. The majority, forty-three of fifty-one, I can't recover.' He retrieved another stick and placed both on the desk in front of Antonia. 'What did you do? Place it in the oven?'

'Something like that.' She reached for the memory sticks.

'A word of warning. If you want to hide your IP address, don't rely on any old commercially available VPN.'

'What do you mean?'

'The documents were part of email exchanges where the participants had hidden their origins, but I tracked the address of one email.'

'Can I have a copy of that address?' Could it be John's colleague, the woman he didn't mention?

'You've got it.' He waved a hand at the memory sticks. 'I've pasted it on to a document.'

Antonia thanked him and made her way back to the office. The fact they'd got something from the memory stick, plus a possible contact, lifted her spirits. Although eager to examine the contents, she made sure she took her usual precautions on the way back, avoiding the face-recognition cameras on the main thoroughfares. The extra walking took its toll on her ankle, and she arrived at Vincent Terrace limping. A vintage Rolls Royce with personalised number plates drew away from outside the house as she approached it. Who owned a car like that? Someone Eleanor knew? The car seemed familiar.

'Antonia.' Sabirah stood before the front door.

'Weren't you seeing your new solicitor?'

'Yes, that's his car.' She indicated the disappearing Rolls.

'Very nice, but what did he say? Can't he help you?'

'No, is good, he can help. How are you, your injury?' She waved at Antonia's leg.

'Too much walking.' Despite Sabirah's assurance, her anxiety seemed as bad as it had been this morning. 'Is there anything I can do to help?'

'Maybe, can I speak tonight? I have to go. Work.'

Antonia watched her enter the house. If this guy could do anything for her, why wasn't Sabirah more upbeat? Anger at the way they treated her friend made her want to hit back. Deciding to speak to Eleanor about what they could do, she made her way inside.

'How did it go?' Miles asked.

'They recovered something but not sure if it's enough.' She made herself a coffee and took the memory stick into her office. Although she never left her computer connected, she still checked it wasn't connected to the internet, and inserted the stick into a port. She'd opened all the documents when Eleanor tapped on her door and manoeuvred her chair in.

'Miles told me. Let's see what we've got.' Her eyes shone with enthusiasm.

'I've just opened them.' She powered up her second screen. 'Did you see Sabirah?'

'She rushed off to work.'

'I don't think it went well.'

'What did she say?' Concern etched Eleanor's face.

'It was more her manner. She's very stressed, almost as anxious as before she went.'

'Oh dear, was her English deteriorating?'

Antonia nodded. 'She'd been doing so well with her extra lessons.'

'I offered to find an architect's practice to give her work experience when I saw her yesterday, but she insisted she'd find her own. And I'm not sure why she's gone with this new solicitor when Geoff Stokes has done such a good job of representing her.'

'She probably wants to stand on her own feet. You can be a bit overpowering sometimes.' Antonia smiled to rob her words of offence. 'She came home in a fancy vintage Roller which I assume is his. It looked familiar.'

'Someone you know?'

'I'm not sure. It could be someone we investigated for a story.' Antonia knew to leave it alone and let her memory work in the background and it would identify where she'd seen the car before. 'Here they are.' She angled the second screen towards Eleanor so she could read the contents of the memory stick.

They read the documents in silence. Antonia suppressed a twinge of disappointment. She'd hoped for more, but they already had enough to run a story. And if the email address they'd recovered led to John's colleague she'd once spoken to on the phone . . .

Eleanor finished reading. 'How much couldn't they recover?'

'Forty-three unreadable documents.'

'That's a shame, but this gives us enough to run a story, yes?'

'I think so, Eleanor. We know they've experimented on prisoners without their consent, messing with their memories. This gives us the location and names of a few of them, so we can verify what's happened to them.'

'Do you think you can speak to any of them this week? They're all at the same prison.'

'I don't know. I'll focus on their families first. And try this email address we recovered.'

'Good idea, but don't you think you should speak to some of the prisoners?'

It made sense to have first-hand accounts, but she wasn't keen. Her last prison visit, when she'd gone to see Sabirah, ended with her nearly getting shot on the way home when a team from the same rogue security company that killed Alan followed her home. 'Do we need them?'

'You're the editor, so it's your decision. But I think it would be a mistake not to.'

Eleanor rarely made a direct intervention, and Antonia wasn't comfortable going against her wishes. 'I don't want to draw attention to what we're up to.'

Eleanor gave an exasperated sigh. 'Let's be frank, Antonia. What happened Monday makes it clear they're already aware of what we're doing. We either back off and give up or show the bastards. You owe it to John, or whatever his real name was.'

They did. But the old woman was right about GRM knowing of their investigation. Gustav Reed-Mayhew also knew that neither of the women would give up. What would he do next, and how far would he go to stop them?

◆ ◆ ◆

Losing herself in an afternoon of mindless cleaning had helped to calm Sabirah. Although having her Permit to Reside taken away was a setback, she'd been in worse places and survived. And she had good friends who would help her. She let herself back into the house in Vincent Terrace. Having to work later than usual to make up for her morning at Al Rahman's office meant she hadn't been able to collect her children from school.

As she made her way to the stairs, the sound of her children's laughter came from behind the door to Mrs Curtis's living room. With a smile she reached for the door handle, but hesitated. Mrs Curtis was sure to ask how it went this morning and Sabirah didn't feel up to explaining why she'd changed solicitors, abandoning the one the old lady had provided her with.

She made her way down into the offices below. Most of the staff had left, but a light showed through Antonia's open door.

'Come in, Sabirah.' Antonia's frown turned into a strained smile.

'I can come back if you're busy.'

'Nothing that can't wait. Grab a seat while I finish this.'

Sabirah studied her friend. Bruises didn't show up as much against her dark skin, but there was no mistaking the grazes on her face. Sabirah had noticed her limp earlier and could tell from the way she held herself she wasn't comfortable. Mrs Curtis had told her about the accident, but she hadn't known much about it.

Antonia finished typing with a flourish and shut off the screen.

'How is your shoulder, Antonia? What happened?'

Antonia looked into the distance. 'A lorry hit the car I was in, and I got bashed about a bit.'

'Mrs Curtis said your friend died. I'm sorry.'

'I didn't really know him. What about you? I heard you've lost your Permit. Did your new solicitor tell you why?'

Al Rahman's warning had preyed on her mind. 'You must not tell Mrs Curtis. I don't want her to worry.' Sabirah leant forward and lowered her voice. 'He didn't tell me why, but he said maybe someone wanted to harm me.'

'Was it—' Antonia suddenly stopped. 'Did he say who?'

'I think maybe he' – Sabirah hesitated, wishing her English was better – 'regret? Yes, he regret telling me, and he said he thinks everything will be okay.'

Antonia looked thoughtful. 'How well do you know this Al Rahman? Can you trust him?'

'Yes, he's from back home. I think he's an honest man.'

'Is that why you changed solicitor, because you wanted someone from back home?'

How could she tell her without sounding ungrateful? 'I . . . I worry that I rely too much on Mrs Curtis. She gives me the beautiful apartment, find wonderful schools for the children. She pay for her solicitor to act for me, so I think I need to do things on my own.'

Antonia studied her. She had this way of looking into you that sometimes made Sabirah uncomfortable, like she could tell what you were thinking.

Antonia laughed and the tension flowed out of Sabirah. 'Eleanor can be a bit intense sometimes. I miss living here, but I'm glad to have my own place. What about money? How much is this guy charging you?'

'No, it's free. Pro bono, but I have to pay a fee for the appeal.'

'I'll pay it, let me know how much.'

'I'll pay you back.'

'Of course. And I'll look into Al Rahman.'

'Thank you.' Sabirah felt disloyal. After all, the man was helping her for free. But what harm, if he was honest? She gestured at the ceiling. 'I'll go and feed the children.'

The two women stood and hugged. Antonia had the screen back on before Sabirah left the room. Who had she thought would be trying to harm Sabirah? She should have asked, but Antonia obviously didn't want to tell her. Was it someone she'd crossed? Sabirah shivered. Antonia had some terrible enemies. Had another one of them noticed her?

CHAPTER 7

The two uniformed security guards led Antonia and her solicitor Geoff Stokes through grand corridors and into a meeting room on the first floor of the headquarters of the newly formed Ministry of Patriotism. The Ministry had taken a ninety-nine-year lease on their new headquarters for an astronomical sum. Antonia had discovered the owners' links to a party donor, but her exposé had caused barely a ripple. She stepped into the room and studied her surroundings. Ornate cream plasterwork lined the walls below a dado rail. Above it, wallpaper featuring golden herons stretched up to the elaborate plaster of the cornice five metres above the parquet floor. Apart from the huge table in the centre of the room, and the eighteen chairs surrounding it, the only other furniture comprised a matching sideboard with an array of bottles on a tray at one end. Antonia suspected she wouldn't be offered their contents anytime soon.

Five of the chairs had name plates in front of them. Two, alongside each other on one side of the table, read 'Conti' and 'Stokes'. She checked the other three. The middle one had the name of the woman who'd summoned them, but the others were blank. Puzzled, she took her seat and massaged her ankle.

'Sure you're okay?' Stokes said. 'It's only a week since you endured a very upsetting ordeal. We can still ask for a postponement.'

'I'm fine, thanks, Geoff. Anyway, we're here now and I want to get this over.'

'It would have been helpful if they'd given us a bit more detail as to why they've summoned us.'

Antonia was sure the summons had everything to do with John taking her story to the tabloids. Her request to speak to three of the prisoners mentioned on the memory stick would also have sounded an alarm. Why had she gone along with Eleanor's idea of speaking to the prisoners? She'd known it would backfire. Without a doubt, Reed-Mayhew had the clout to get the story spiked. She'd hoped to have more time to get it out and wrote most of it before she'd put in the request. She ran her hand over her cropped head. The stench of burnt hair filled her nostrils, a vivid memory more real than her surroundings. A cloud moved, flooding the room with sunlight, straight into her eyes.

Before she could suggest moving to the opposite side of the table, the door opened and Millie Forman, the civil servant who'd summoned them, marched into the room. In her wake, two figures towered over her. The first of the men, a bulky giant with no neck, stood several centimetres taller than Antonia's one-eighty. His companion, slim and not as tall, wore black-rimmed glasses and brought up the rear.

Forman took the middle of the three chairs opposite, her cerise outfit contrasting with the monochrome suits of the two men, who resembled nothing so much as minders. The sun haloed the three figures, making it impossible to see their features. Antonia struggled to read their moods, making her imagine she faced three automatons.

Forman introduced the men. 'Mr Grist' – she indicated the giant – 'and Mr Palmer are here to observe and, going forward, will be monitoring your publication.'

The two men remained impassive, but Antonia got the impression of facing two predators, ready to do her harm.

Forman continued. 'Ms Conti, Mr Stokes, I'm disappointed to have to ask you to come in again.'

'Why have you summoned my client, at such brief notice?'

'It's been brought to our attention that you're working on a particular story involving GRM and government contracts.'

'Who brought it to your attention?' Antonia didn't need to ask.

Forman made a gesture of dismissal. 'That's irrelevant. The fact is, we've put restrictions on publishing stories about confidential government contracts. Something you're clearly aware of from previous conversations.'

'Our article isn't about government contracts, confidential or otherwise.'

'I'll decide when you submit your copy. And if I decide it compromises the government, you can't publish.'

'You can't do that!' With an effort, Antonia restrained herself from smashing her fist on to the gleaming conference table.

'Oh, can't we?' Millie Forman raised her plucked eyebrows. 'You'll find that's exactly what we can do.'

'You're censoring the press—'

'What we're doing, Ms Conti, is preventing the proliferation of fake news: something which has caused untold harm to this country, and undermines trust in our institutions, especially the government.'

'We're exposing abuses of the human rights of prisoners—'

'They've been convicted in a court of law.'

'They still have rights.'

Forman snorted.

'You can't experiment on people without their consent.'

'You have absolutely no evidence that's what's happened.'

'Only because you won't let us talk to them.' Antonia glared at the civil servant.

'You're also making accusations of wrongdoing against a government contractor, and by implication, HMG.'

'They're free to take us to court.' She would love to see Reed-Mayhew trying to defend this in front of a jury, but he'd send a suit, protected by a phalanx of expensive lawyers.

'That's not going to happen, Ms Conti. You've a history of a vendetta against this company, and if I recall, you had to withdraw the last story about them because of lack of evidence.'

Anger surged through Antonia. The memory of the government spiking her story still hurt after all those months. 'That's not what happened, and you know it.'

A shake of the head from Geoff Stokes stalled her, and using his most conciliatory tone, Antonia's solicitor intervened. 'Of course, Ms Forman, we have no desire to add to the misinformation being promulgated to the British public. I don't believe *The Electric Investigator* has ever been guilty of publishing untrue stories.' The lawyer adjusted his tie. 'Despite what some ministers may desire, we still operate on the principle of innocent until proven guilty '

'Don't lecture me on the principles of our legal system, Mr Stokes.' Spots of colour appeared on Forman's cheeks.

'I wouldn't dream of it. I'm merely pointing out that you're convicting us, not only without a trial, but in the absence of any evidence of wrongdoing.'

'Sorry if you don't like it.' Forman fixed first Stokes, then Antonia, with her stare. 'But those subjects are out of bounds until we specifically tell you otherwise. In the meantime, you're free to publish your exposé of the local vicar's affairs, or whatever it is you write stories about.'

Antonia took a deep breath to calm herself. Eleanor was right. She got too involved and needed to step back. The odour of furniture polish mingled with the powerful scent emanating from Forman. The sun's rays illuminated motes of dust in the air. It had moved, enabling her to see the two men flanking Forman. Neither made any contributions to the discussion, but studied her with cold, blank expressions. Antonia still struggled to read them. With a jolt, she realised she'd seen the smaller one before, but couldn't place him.

A response to Forman's barb came to her. 'Okay, we'll lead with Reed-Mayhew's affair with—'

'Any stories about *him* need to go through *me*. Provided your article is truthful and doesn't mention Mr Reed-Mayhew's dealings with HMG, I'll give you permission to publish it.'

'How's that not censorship?'

'I have no intention of revisiting this argument, Ms Conti. We have no interest in muzzling the press, we're just protecting the country from malign influences and making it a safe place to live. Isn't that one reason people like you come here to claim asylum?' Forman gave a smug smirk.

Antonia pictured the self-righteous official with a bloody nose.

'Now, thank you for coming in, Ms Conti, Mr Stokes. My colleagues will escort you.' Forman indicated the men flanking her.

Stokes pushed his chair back and rose. 'Thank you, Ms Forman, gentlemen.'

Antonia, unwilling to give in, reluctantly got to her feet. Her ankle had stiffened but, determined not to show weakness, she forced herself not to limp and followed Stokes into the corridor. The three civil servants followed. Grist indicated they should accompany him, and Palmer brought up the rear. The notion she knew him became stronger. Forman's heels beat a fading tattoo on the tiled floor as she went in the opposite direction. Antonia and Stokes walked to the security post at the entrance of the building in silence. Even the familiar security checks, which had become a daily part of life, annoyed her. Anger and humiliation made her hot. The low sun shone through the glass doors, making her squint. She snatched her jacket off the security guard and, holding it in her hand, strode towards the exit. A cold gust as she opened the door reminded her winter was on the way. Autumn leaves swirled around her denim-clad legs as she hurried towards their car at the far end of the very full car park. Stokes struggled to keep up.

Once out of earshot of the security guards, she let her frustration boil over. 'Bastards! How can they protect a criminal?'

'Gustav Reed-Mayhew has never been convicted of a crime,' he said in his conciliatory tone, 'so technically, he's not a criminal.'

'Not you as well, Geoff.'

'I'm merely pointing out the legal position, Antonia. You know I'm fully behind you in your efforts to expose his crimes.'

Antonia slowed to let him keep up. 'I can't believe we've passed a law permitting a jumped-up civil servant like her to ban us from investigating government contracts.'

'You ran a very creditable campaign to highlight the inequities of the Security and Borders Bill, highlighting its potential to cover up the actions of the government on the pretext of protecting "national security".' Stokes made quotation marks with his fingers. 'I don't think you can castigate yourself on that front.'

'Fat lot of use it did. It passed, first time.'

'Hmm, yes, the downside of a big government majority—'

'And a mostly supine press.'

'With a few honourable exceptions.' He nodded at her. 'The fact you can't publish the story shouldn't prevent you investigating Reed-Mayhew.'

'What's the point if we can't use the material?'

'In my experience, people prepared to bend the law in one area aren't usually scrupulous about following it in other situations. I'm sure Reed-Mayhew engages in a variety of shady practices. You of all people should know that.'

The fact she'd been unable to prove he'd been behind the deaths of several women, including one of her friends, despite knowing it to be true, still hurt. And worst of all was his part in Alan Turner's murder. 'But nothing sticks to him. He's too clever to get personally involved and always works through third parties.'

'The ones we're aware of. There's always something they overlook. We just need to find it.'

'Easier said than done.'

'Most things are.'

Antonia reviewed the resources they'd spent on the story Forman had just scuppered. Could they afford to risk the same happening again and, more importantly, could she persuade Eleanor to spend more time and money on another investigation? Eleanor's determination to nail Reed-Mayhew burned less brightly since she'd come out of hospital after surviving a near-fatal attack by men sent to harm Antonia. He'd not been the one who sent them, otherwise Eleanor would have doubled her efforts. They reached Stokes's car.

'I don't know if we can risk it, Geoff.'

'It's not like you to give up, Antonia.'

'I'm not giving up.'

Stokes held up a hand. 'Okay, okay.'

The recollection of Reed-Mayhew taunting her in his office, just before his henchmen drugged her, filled her with determination. 'You're right, I'll get the bastard. An arrogant shit like him will have slipped up somewhere. We'll continue our investigation. The woman working with John will have the information we need and hopefully she'll come forward.' Although so far, nobody had responded to the message she'd sent to the email address they'd recovered. What if it was one John used and nobody responded?

Stokes smiled and Antonia realised he'd played her. A shrill ringtone broke the silence in the seemingly deserted carpark. They followed the sound.

The one called Palmer lurked behind an adjacent car. He must have followed them using the cars as cover. He made no move to answer his phone, but leered at Antonia. How much had he heard? The dead-eyed man stared, making her shudder, then he saluted them before heading back to the entrance. As she watched him, she remembered where she'd seen him. He hadn't worn glasses, and he'd had a haircut and shave since, but she recognised the man who'd spoken to Adam at the crash.

◆ ◆ ◆

Gustav Reed-Mayhew studied the report his head of security had prepared. Like all his reports, it was thorough, but expressed in the stilted language that betrayed his previous career in military intelligence. Still, Reed-Mayhew didn't employ him for the quality of his prose.

He turned the page to reveal a photo of his brother with his eldest daughter at her graduation. She was a good-looking girl, and bright, with a first from Cambridge. She'd never suffered a setback in her life, being too young at seven to remember her mother's death, so this would probably do her good. Toughen her up. Anyway, with help from her ex-international rugby player father, she'd doubtless pick herself up following a period of reflection.

Underneath were the photos of the incident that would bring her down. Silly girl, but she'd brought it on herself. The memory of overhearing her at the graduation party he'd paid for at London's glitziest venue returned, vivid as a nightmare.

'Fab party. It's so nice of your uncle to pay for this.'

'Nice? He did it to embarrass Dad. To show him he might be a popular celebrity, but he can't compete when it comes to money.'

'He seems very charming.'

'Don't be taken in. The guy's a snake. A real grade A creep. And never accept an invitation to go to one of his parties.'

Just the memory made him clammy and part of him wished he hadn't listened in, but he couldn't ignore it. Time she paid. He buzzed his PA and moments later, a knock came at the door.

'Come.'

Reed-Morgan studied his head of security. The man still looked like a soldier, despite wearing a decent suit. He stopped in front of the desk, and if he hadn't held a tablet, would have probably thrown up a salute. 'Afternoon, sir. Have—'

'What have I told you?'

Red-faced, the man glanced behind him and, realising his mistake, moved from between his boss and his mirror. 'Sorry.'

Reed-Mayhew checked his reflection, then studied the grainy stills taken from a surveillance video.

'Have you decided yet, sir?'

'Let me see the original again.' Reed-Mayhew held out a hand.

His head of security offered him the tablet. Reed-Mayhew's phone buzzed. The red light told him it was an encrypted line. He waved the tablet away and checked the number before taking the call.

'Mr Reed-Mayhew, it's Millie Forman—'

'Have you done it?'

'Yes, I left her in no doubt that you were off-limits.'

'Good. You'll get your usual—'

'There could be a problem.'

He took a few deep breaths to calm himself. 'Go on, now you've interrupted me.'

'Sorry. She was overheard promising to continue investigating you. Do you want me to—'

'I'll deal with it.'

'I can make sure—'

'I'll deal with it!' He could almost sense Forman's fear. If he'd been alone, he'd have prolonged the call to savour it. He slammed the phone down and took the tablet. He hated using such a small screen, but wanted nothing incriminating on his computer. The security footage showed six young people in evening dress walking along a darkened riverbank. They passed under a streetlight, each identifiable, including his errant niece.

One of the young men vanished into the shadows, followed by a second. They returned, holding a struggling, ragged individual between them. After tormenting him for a while, they pushed him into the river, where he struggled for a few moments before disappearing under the water.

Reed-Mayhew returned the tablet. 'She didn't have much to do with it, did she?'

'Because the young man died, they'd class her as an accessory to murder.'

'Manslaughter, surely.'

'They had the opportunity to save him. If you play it further, the young man surfaced and you can see them messing with a life belt, pretending to throw it to him.'

'So, life?' His niece didn't deserve that.

'Very unlikely. The individual was an undocumented immigrant. A failed refugee.'

He'd make sure she didn't get more than a few years, if any at all. He didn't want to ruin her life, just teach her manners, and, of course, get justice for the poor victim. 'And how come it's taken four months for this to come out?'

'The boy who instigated it has contacts, father's an MP.'

'Not as good as my contacts. See if you can make it clear the father instigated the cover-up, get him deselected or even charged. That should keep the others on their toes.'

'Yes, sir.'

'And talking of refugees, the other . . . problem you were dealing with. It appears she may need more persuading.'

'Shall I use the subcontractor again, or some of our—'

'I've told you. I don't want to know, but make sure none of it ever comes back to me.'

The door closed and, alone again, Reed-Mayhew studied his reflection in the mirror on the wall in front of his desk. The memory of the indignity he'd suffered when his last head of security failed to deal with the meddlesome immigrant Conti still hurt. He'd lost several government contracts he'd been promised and, even worse, he'd had to put up with sniggers and innuendo from the same type of bastards who'd made his schooldays such a misery. He'd make sure she didn't do the same to him again.

◆ ◆ ◆

Stokes pulled up at the kerb outside *The Electric Investigator*'s offices. 'I won't come in, but give my love to Eleanor.'

'Of course, and thanks again, Geoff.'

'By the way, how is your friend Sabirah doing with her job-hunting?'

'Have you spoken to her recently?' Had Sabirah told him she was going with another solicitor?

'She wanted advice on whether her architecture qualifications would be accepted over here. I told her there shouldn't be a problem. Her English is coming on well.'

'A more stimulating job will do her good.' Antonia remembered her own short stint working as a cleaner. She'd not minded some aspects of the job, but couldn't imagine doing it long-term. 'Did she mention her problems with the immigration people?'

'Only in passing. She did tell me she had a new solicitor. It was quite touching. She explained it was nothing to do with my competence, but she wanted to stand on her own feet. Do you know how she got on with him?'

'She says it went okay, but I suspect she's not happy.'

'Hmmm.' Stokes pursed his lips.

'What?'

'It surprised me when I saw who she's gone with. Al Rahman usually deals with commercial law and has some very high-profile clients. He's not cheap.'

'He's doing it pro bono.'

'He doesn't usually.' He hesitated. 'I don't want to disparage a fellow solicitor, especially one who's taken a client off me, but I would be careful.'

'What do you mean?' The thought of Sabirah falling for a scam infuriated her. Was the money she'd asked to borrow for the court fee, or to pay this solicitor? 'Is he crooked?' Antonia's enquiries into him had turned up nothing concerning.

'No, no. Not at all. When I said his clients are high profile, I meant notorious. He'll represent anyone if the money's right.'

Was that when Antonia had seen his car, while he was representing one of the dodgy businessmen they investigated? 'He'll be disappointed if he's expecting to fleece Sabirah, but I'll tell her to be careful.'

'No need. I'm speaking out of turn. He has a reputation for getting the right verdict, and I'm sure he'll do an excellent job for Sabirah. Forget I spoke.'

Should she say anything to Sabirah? Or would it just worry her friend further? She decided to stay quiet, but would keep tabs on Sabirah's appeal. 'Okay, if you think so.'

Antonia exited the small electric hatchback and stood on the pavement stretching her long legs. She watched Stokes pull out into the traffic and considered her next move. If she intended to continue investigating Reed-Mayhew, she needed to hurry. If the creepy guy who'd followed them had overheard her, Reed-Mayhew would soon know.

Without the enhancing effect of sunlight, Eleanor's house appeared neglected. She'd suggest a coat of paint and maybe a refurbishment of Eleanor's flat on the ground floor. She missed living there, but loved the mews house she'd inherited from Alan. Her friend's fate reminded her how dangerous taking Reed-Mayhew on could be. The police still hadn't linked the men behind his death to the businessman, but Antonia knew one existed and she was still searching for it. She shivered and descended the stairs to the basement entrance of *The Investigator*'s offices.

The reinforced security door closed behind her with a solid clunk, and she manoeuvred through the cramped reception room into the main office. A figure sat behind her old desk in the corner. 'Nadimah, what are you doing here?'

The young girl looked up from her tablet with a guilty start. 'I'm doing my homework. Hakim is playing *Call of Duty* and I wanted some quiet. Aunty Eleanor said it would be okay.'

Antonia checked the time. Nearly five. They couldn't agree on which of the two candidates to take on and had decided on a final interview. The first would arrive in half an hour. The successful candidate would be using that desk. She didn't want them thinking they acted as a crèche for the children who lived upstairs.

'Is it okay if I stay?' Nadimah wore a worried expression.

'For a bit, yeah. Do you know where Eleanor is?'

'I'm here.' Eleanor Curtis reversed out of the staff room, which doubled as their stationery store. 'How did it go?' She studied Antonia, concern on her lined features. 'Not well, I'm guessing.'

'Can we discuss it?' Antonia gestured to her office.

'As soon as I've finished this for Nadimah.' Eleanor smiled at the girl.

'We haven't long before our interview.'

'I won't be long.' She turned her attention to the girl.

Antonia couldn't hide her irritation. Eleanor's lack of commitment to *The Investigator* had coincided with Nadimah and her family moving into Antonia's old flat on the upper floors of the house. Well, she was in charge now and needed to focus. She pushed open the door to her office. For a moment she imagined Alan behind the solitary desk in the room, but that would never happen again. She shook herself, and, taking her seat, powered up her computer. She'd grown into the role of managing editor of *The Investigator* since taking over after his murder six months earlier, but she still missed his wise counsel, especially at times like this.

A knock at her door, and it opened. The whirr of the electric motor told her Eleanor had finished with Nadimah. Antonia leapt up and pushed aside her visitor's chair so her adoptive mother could manoeuvre into the space.

'Did you have to do that?' Eleanor asked when Antonia closed the door.

'Do what?'

'Make it so clear to Nadimah she wasn't welcome.'

'This is a working office. We've got serious problems to discuss and I'm interviewing in less than half—'

'No need to be so ungracious. The girl admires you, but when you're like this, I don't know why.'

Antonia's face grew hot. 'That's not fair. I've got a lot on my shoulders.'

Eleanor's expression softened. 'I know, but she's still very fragile. Not everyone can deal with what she's had to. I know *you* did, but you're . . . unusual.'

Antonia wasn't sure how to take that. 'Sorry.'

'You need to apologise to Nadimah. She's cooking supper, and it would be nice if you came.'

Antonia had planned to go to the gym for some more rehab, followed by a quiet night in with a takeaway. 'Okay. Yeah, I look forward to it.'

'I'll tell her. Now, what happened with the fragrant Ms Forman to put you in such a bad mood?'

'Do you know her?'

'Oh yes, she and Kate shared a flat at uni.'

Eleanor rarely mentioned her daughter. The last time Antonia had seen Kate, they'd nearly come to blows when Kate called her 'Mummy's little orphan'. 'I can imagine they'd be friends.'

'What did she have to say?'

Antonia told Eleanor the outcome of the meeting.

'That is a blow. All your work down the drain.'

'I'm not giving up.'

'What do you mean?'

'I'm still going after Reed-Mayhew—'

'What's the point if we can't use the material? We don't have unlimited funds.'

Before her hospitalisation and weeks in a coma, Eleanor would never have suggested backing off from investigating Reed-Mayhew. Whatever the obstacles. 'I appreciate that, but we've made good progress with contacts inside his organisation. He's bound to have made a mistake and if we find evidence of illegality, they can't stop us publishing it.'

'Don't be naive, Antonia. They're protecting him, and they'll stop us publishing whatever we find.'

Antonia had the horrible notion Eleanor was right. 'If we knew who in the government is protecting him, we could find a link between them.'

'There is no link, not like you're suggesting. They're not doing it because he's one of them. He's always been an outsider, so he must have something on them.'

Antonia thought back to the underground fight club she'd uncovered, almost losing her life in the process. She believed Reed-Mayhew blackmailed the people who attended the fights where women fought to the death. He'd escaped unscathed by blaming it on Mishkin, his head of security. Antonia knew Reed-Mayhew ultimately ran them and collected the secretly filmed footage. She just couldn't prove it. Someone like him would also have set other traps for the rich and powerful. She just needed to find his source of blackmail material.

'I intend to find out what, Eleanor. And when I do, I'll bring the bastard down.'

Eleanor's concern increased. 'Be careful he doesn't bring us down and destroy you, Antonia.'

CHAPTER 8

The forensic garage echoed as Chapman walked across the polished concrete floor. Oil and fuel odours mixed with the rubbery smell of the non-slip coating on the floor. He checked the numbers above the bays lining the main workshop. The remains of the car Antonia had been in when the container smashed it sat in bay six. You needed a good imagination to recognise it as a car. The container had crushed it to half its original height and the posts supporting the roof had sheared. Most of the paint had blistered and a mixture of soot and rust coated much of the metal. The roof lay on the floor behind the car.

As he got closer, the stench of burnt rubber increased until it dominated. How the hell had Antonia survived? Dark stains on the driver's seat reminded him her companion hadn't. The car sat on a hydraulic lift to facilitate examination and Chapman flicked the switch, turning the power on. Then he pressed the up button. With a creak and a hum, the rig rose.

Chapman stopped it, crouched, and peered up into the underside of the car. Years of road muck coated the metal except in one small patch, where someone had scraped the dirt away. He examined it. Perfect for a tracking device.

'What the hell you doing?'

Chapman jumped and turned to face his inquisitor. 'DI Chapman,' he said. 'I've signed in.' He produced his ID.

The man confronting him had a lined face, prominent yellow-brown upper incisors and a receding chin. He wore spotless grey overalls with the company logo on one breast and the title Garage Manager on the other.

The manager examined his ID. 'You shouldn't wander around here on your own.' He noticed the raised car. 'Did you do that?'

'Yes.'

'You're not supposed to use the equipment. In fact, you shouldn't touch anything. Who signed you in?'

The young woman who had signed him in appeared just then, red-faced and breathless.

'There you are. I told you to wait.' The manager turned his ire on her. 'You shouldn't let visitors wander about on their own.'

'Sorry, boss. I told him to wait while I dealt with a call.'

'She did.' Chapman addressed her. 'Sorry, I wasn't sure how long you'd be.'

The manager returned his attention to Chapman. 'What were you doing under the car?'

Chapman resisted the temptation to tell him to bugger off. Then his phone rang and, glad for the distraction, he took the call. 'Chapman.'

'Boss,' Sanchez said, 'we've got a possible aggravated burglary and kidnapping in Eaton Square.'

'Text me the address.' He slid the phone into his pocket. 'Sorry, I've got to go. Thanks for your help.' He waved at the young woman, hoping he'd not got her into trouble, and strode back to the exit.

Half an hour later, he arrived in Eaton Square, parking behind the patrol car opposite the address Sanchez had texted him. She met him at the front door.

'Which floor, Alice?'

'It's one house.'

Chapman paused. Whoever lived here must be worth a mint. He stepped past Sanchez and into an entrance hall with a white marble floor. A huge gold chandelier glowed like a small sun and the light reflecting off the white walls made him squint. 'What have we got?'

'I'll show you.' She led him through a door higher than his ceiling at home into a gloomy corridor. He saw nothing for the first three steps and followed the sound of Sanchez's shoes clacking on the black parquet. Dark red walls absorbed the light from faint downlighters scattered along the corridor. She halted outside a dark wood door and threw it open.

Light flooded in through three floor-to-ceiling windows, illuminating a room the size of his apartment. He squinted and scanned the space. Pale furniture lay scattered about on what looked like a field of snow.

'What's the bloody idea of the contrasting décor? It's like someone's let an idiot with no taste and too much money loose.'

'That's a pretty accurate description of my husband,' a woman drawled.

Chapman's face grew warm. The woman stood to the left of the door in front of a wooden shelf unit. Around it lay the remains of smashed trinkets and photo frames. The woman was tall and pale, with a long face and dark hair arranged over her left shoulder.

'Mrs Snowden, I asked you to stay in the kitchen.' Sanchez tried to hide her irritation.

The woman rolled her eyes. 'I've touched nothing.'

'Mrs Snowden, this is my boss, Inspector Chapman.'

'Gwendolyn, please.'

'She returned home to find this' – Sanchez swept a hand round the room – 'and called us.'

Now he'd grown accustomed to the light, Chapman noticed the disarray. Someone had smashed every ornament in the room and put a vase through the screen of a huge TV fixed to the wall above the marble fireplace.

'Who else lives here?' Chapman said.

'Just my husband, Ellaby. He runs a hedge fund.'

He'd need to, to afford this. 'Do you know where he is?'

Sanchez replied. 'He works from home, but we've searched the house and he's not here.'

Mrs Snowden gave her a condescending look. 'He's not the most observant individual, but even he wouldn't have missed this.'

'How come the alarm didn't sound?' Chapman asked. 'The box outside belongs to a monitoring company.'

'Ellaby often forgets to set it.'

Sanchez had obviously not discussed her suspicion that the man had been kidnapped.

'Do you know where he might be?' Chapman asked her.

'I've given your assistant a list of places I could think of.'

'We're checking them now, boss,' Sanchez said.

Chapman needed to speak to Sanchez. 'We need to examine the scene, Mrs Snowden. It's easier if you're not here.'

'Of course, Inspector. I'll return to the kitchen like a good little woman.' She gave a regal wave and sashayed out of the room, accompanied by a cloud of perfume and whisky fumes.

Once he and Sanchez were alone, he said, 'What makes you think it's a kidnapping? He could have just gone out.'

'Look at this.' She led him to an area behind one of the huge cream sofas dotting the room. Someone had slashed the covers, and foam stuffing protruded. Spots of blood sprayed the luxurious carpet. 'There's more here.' She pointed him to one of the book-lined alcoves flanking the fireplace. More blood stained the carpet in front of it.

His mind racing, he scanned the room. 'How many rooms like this?'

'The main bedroom and his study.'

'What's missing?'

'Nothing obvious from this room or bedroom, but she never goes into his study, so couldn't say.'

'So, kidnapping could be the motive, but why wreck the place?'

Sanchez indicated the sofas. 'It looks like they were searching for something.'

'This *looks* like they've vandalised it, not searched.' Something about the alcove struck him as wrong. He checked the one on the other side. 'This is the only part of the room left undamaged. But over there, every book is on its side or on the floor. And how come there's one light above it, but two switches?'

He turned them both. The light dimmed, and the bookshelf slid open to reveal a lift door. He pressed the button alongside it and motors whirred. Then the doors opened on to a car big enough for two people.

'I'll get Mrs Snowden.' Sanchez left.

Chapman stepped into the lift car, closed the doors and pressed the solitary control button. Nothing happened. He opened the doors to find Sanchez and Mrs Snowden.

He stepped out. 'Where does this go?'

Gwendolyn Snowden looked like she'd topped up her whisky intake. 'Oh, God, this leads to Ellaby's panic room downstairs. We never use it. Waste of money.'

He could think of a few people who wished they'd never had to use their panic room. 'How do you get it to work? Do you need a key?'

She regarded him like she thought him stupid. 'You just press the button.'

'I just did.'

She shrugged. 'I've never used it.'

'Does it come out anywhere else?' Sanchez asked.

Snowden pointed at the ceiling. 'Up in his study and in our room above.'

'I didn't see any doors.'

'Behind the shoe cabinet in our room and a bookcase in his study.'

The lift doors closed, and Chapman pointed at them. 'Who maintains this?'

'A specialist company. Our housekeeper deals with them.'

Sanchez opened the lift doors and stepped in. 'Their number's here on a metal plate, boss.' She hesitated, then addressed Snowden. 'Who monitors this alarm?'

'No idea.' Snowden sounded bored.

Sanchez pressed the alarm button, but nothing happened. 'I'll give them a bell.' She punched the numbers into her phone and stepped out of the lift, then a speaker in the lift crackled.

'Piper Security, did you have a problem?' a metallic voice asked.

Chapman stepped past Sanchez. 'Inspector Chapman here. I'm in one of your lifts but it doesn't work.' He gave the address.

'How do I know you're who you say you are?'

'I'm here with one of the owners. Is there a password?' If there were, he doubted Snowden knew it.

'And how do I know you haven't threatened them?'

Give me strength. 'I'm assuming you have a direct line to our control room.'

'Yes.'

'Why don't you ring them?'

The speaker went dead for several minutes, and then the voice returned. 'Okay, Inspector Chapman, we've received confirmation of who you are. If the lift doesn't work, it means someone's using the panic room.'

'How do you communicate with people in there?'

'We do it from here. A colleague is trying to contact them, but so far, no response.'

He exchanged a look with Sanchez. This felt wrong. 'How can we get in there?'

'Our team will override the controls when they get there. ETA seventeen minutes.'

'Thanks.' Snowden had wandered off and sat in a relatively undamaged armchair. 'You can go back to the kitchen, Mrs Snowden.'

With a loud sigh, she left.

'Do you think the intruders went down there with Mr Snowden instead of taking him with them?' Sanchez asked.

'Why would they do that? It makes no sense.'

'Could his wife have surprised them when she came home, and they've gone down there to hide until we've gone?'

Chapman doubted it, but his sense of unease didn't diminish. 'Shall we call for backup?'

'The two uniforms haven't left yet, and I'd imagine the security company will send at least two. Six of us should manage.' He didn't want to call out an armed response team for nothing.

He toured the other two ransacked rooms upstairs, becoming even more certain someone had trashed, not searched them. But why? Voices at the front door brought him downstairs again. Three figures in green uniforms stood at the door talking to Sanchez. Two generic heavies and a third, a studious-looking young woman with an aluminium briefcase, who had to be the technician.

Chapman introduced himself and, with instructions to the heavies to wait at the entrance to the room, led the technician to the lift. She entered, and removed a small cover from below the control panel. Producing two cables from her case, she plugged them in, then punched a code into a keypad inside the case.

'All yours, Inspector. It should work now.' She disconnected everything and, replacing the cover, exited the lift.

'Shall I get the two uniforms?' Sanchez asked.

'Just one. There isn't room for more.'

Sanchez returned with the bulkier of the two officers, a young constable wearing a determined expression. Chapman got in the lift and beckoned the constable to join him. The door slid shut, and he pressed the down button. After a brief pause, the motor whirred and descended. Relief and apprehension competed in Chapman's gut.

The lift stopped and the two police officers waited in silence. Then the door slid open.

Chapman stepped out into a well-lit room three metres by five. At one end was a sofa with a figure sat on it.

'Oh fuck!' the constable said.

The figure sat splay-legged with his head, or what remained of it, thrown back on the back of the sofa. Blood and bits of brain covered the wall behind and an automatic lay on the floor.

Chapman silently echoed the constable's exclamation. They'd found Ellaby Snowden.

Antonia had prevailed in her preference for the new PA. It wasn't just because Tomasz Zabo reminded her of her predecessor, Alan, but he'd been the best candidate. Eleanor's favourite, while better qualified and more experienced, had unsettled Antonia, and she'd learnt to trust her instincts. Tomasz had arrived early and was waiting outside in the rain when Antonia arrived. She let him in and, making them both coffees, took him through to her office.

'Eleanor's usually here to welcome new colleagues, but she's got a hospital appointment. She sends her apologies.'

Zabo's brow furrowed. 'She's not ill, is she?'

'Just a check-up.'

'How long she been in the chair?'

'Since I've known her, but . . .' Antonia was uncomfortable discussing Eleanor. 'She used a manual chair until a few months ago.'

'Is she getting worse? I mean, is it degenerative?'

'Oh no. She lost the use of her legs due to an accident.'

'Good.' He turned bright red. 'That sounded awful. I meant good, she's not getting worse. I lost my mum to motor neurone disease last year.'

'Oh, I'm sorry.'

'Thanks. So, why's Mrs Curtis now in an electric chair—' He looked even more embarrassed. 'Sorry, that's what Mum called hers. I meant powered.'

'A gang of thugs broke into the house and attacked her. She clocked one with a lamp, but they knocked her about. She's still determined to get back to propelling herself around, but it's a slow process.' The fact the thugs had been searching for Antonia still filled her with guilt. 'Shall we start with a summary of what we do here?'

'As I said in my interview, I've read *The Investigator* since my eleventh birthday.'

'You're aware then, we're often contacted by vulnerable people taking risks to expose wrongdoing. Often, you're their first point of contact, and how you deal with them can determine if they trust us enough to continue.'

'I hadn't realised.' His Adam's apple bobbed. 'Will you give me training?'

'Miles did your job for a few years, and he'll go through it with you. Don't worry, I'm sure you'll be fine.'

She'd finished giving him the welcome talk and tour when Eleanor arrived back from the hospital.

'Tomasz, I'm so sorry I wasn't here to meet you.'

'No problem, Mrs Curtis. They've taken good care of me.'

'The least I can do is give you a history lesson about *The Investigator*, if Antonia hasn't already done so.'

Antonia held her hands up. 'I wouldn't dare. I'll leave you to it.'

Antonia returned to her desk and focused on working on the lead story for the next day's edition. With the proliferation of private contractors willing to offer civil servants inducements, they had plenty of material, but they needed to break another big story soon. Zabo settled into his role and by mid-afternoon, he was confidently putting calls through to Antonia. She'd finished tweaking her copy when Miles tapped on her door and came in.

'We're going for a drink with Tomasz after work if you want to join us.'

Antonia checked the time. Five already. 'Sure, I'll see you there.'

Warm, damp air infused with a mixture of cooking odours and alcohol fumes hit her as she entered the pub. The after-work crowd made it pleasantly full. The small team from *The Investigator* had commandeered a table in the far corner of the main bar. Miles's cheerful baritone carried as he regaled them with one of his shaggy-dog stories. As she went to join them, two men at the bar observed her progress. They weren't the usual types you saw in here and the attention made her uncomfortable. As she passed them to join her colleagues, the odour of a distinctive aftershave mingled with fruity vape fumes.

Miles stood. 'My round, Antonia. What will you have?'

'Usual sparkling water please.'

He lowered his voice as he passed her. 'Tomasz is fitting in well. Good choice, boss.'

Zabo held a bottle of beer and chatted easily with his new colleagues. Antonia congratulated herself on having made the right decision. As she sat talking to her colleagues, however, a prickling sensation traversed her scalp. The two men she'd noticed now occupied the table behind her and one turned away too quickly. Like most young women in London, she'd got used to being ogled, but this was different.

Half an hour later, her colleagues drifted off and soon, she and the 'new boy' remained.

'Do you want another, Tomasz?'

'I'd better not, I've got a long journey.'

'South Norwood, isn't it?'

'A bit further, but it's an hour if I'm lucky.'

They put their coats on, and Antonia checked on the two men. They appeared deep in conversation, but one held a phone. She checked them again as she left the room. They hadn't moved, but she was certain they were watching her. She shouldered her backpack and fell into step beside Zabo as they approached the door.

'I'll walk you to the bus,' she said. 'It's on my way.'

Cold air enveloped them as they left the warm glow of the pub, and she shivered. Antonia's thoughts drifted to tomorrow's edition. Zabo said something she didn't catch. A dark shape came out of the shadows, moving at speed. Her mind emptied and adrenaline flooded her system. Hands grabbed at her backpack and pulled her sideways. She spun round, elbow leading. She hit a torso and her assailant grunted.

Zabo let out a cry. Another figure grappled with him. Her assailant still held on, and she stamped on his shin. With a cry, he let go. She leapt forward and punched Zabo's attacker in the neck. He released Zabo, who fell to the ground.

Antonia kicked out at his attacker, catching his thigh. A second kick smashed into the side of his knee, and with a cry of pain, he fell. She moved in to finish him but jerked backwards as the first man grabbed her backpack again. She resisted, but he outweighed her and swung her round. The distinctive aftershave identified her attacker as she fought to keep her balance. She stayed upright and slid one arm out of the straps, then abruptly the second.

Her attacker jerked backwards, and she spun to face him. He swore and threw her bag at her head. She ducked.

Zabo cried out.

Another figure detached from the shadows, suddenly illuminated by headlights at some distance. His ski mask told her it wasn't a good Samaritan. An engine growled, the vehicle coming too fast for the road. The driver must have seen what was happening. Aftershave Man barrelled into her. She rode the impact, keeping her feet, but staggered towards the edge of the kerb. Hands grabbed at her. A punch to his face made Aftershave Man release her. For a moment, she couldn't see the newcomer. Then he grabbed Zabo, who'd struggled to his feet.

The headlights raced closer, the engine noise now a roar. She glanced at the blinding light. Aftershave Man charged at her. His shoulder hit her in the ribs, shoving her towards the road. Pain and panic energised her and, smashing a forearm into his face, she spun away from him. Air rushed past her. Then a sickening thud, brakes screeched, and the vehicle halted twenty metres past her.

It must have hit Aftershave Man. She checked around her, but he crouched on the pavement, clutching his nose. A shout from his injured companion roused him and he ran to help him. A bundle lay on the pavement just ahead of the stationary van. Had it hit the newcomer? Then she saw him rush to help Aftershave Man.

'Tomasz!' she shouted and, checking the three men posed no immediate threat, ran to Zabo. He lay crumpled in a foetal position, blood leaking from his ear.

CHAPTER 9

The faint sound of sobbing tore at Sabirah's heart. She waited on the darkened landing, not wanting to intrude on her daughter. After a few minutes, unable to stand any more, she rapped on the door and opened it.

'Nadimah?'

The sobbing paused.

'Nadimah, can I put the light on?' She waited a few seconds, then hit the switch. Warm light flooded her daughter's bedroom.

The fact her children no longer shared a room was one of many joys of living here. They'd each had their own room in Idlib, a lifetime ago. The idea they might have to leave here made Sabirah sick.

Nadimah had pulled the bedclothes over her head and Sabirah carried the chair from in front of her dressing table to her bedside and stroked the bump of the duvet covering her.

'Come on, dear, let me see you.'

Slowly, Nadimah emerged, blinking. She'd wiped her face, but the tracks of her tears shone.

'What's wrong?' Sabirah stroked her daughter's cheek with the back of her finger.

'Nothing.'

'Why are you crying?'

Nadimah looked away. 'I was thinking about Daddy.'

Tears stung Sabirah's eyes. She thought of her beloved Rashid every day. The memory of the secret police taking him away still raw. 'He would never want you to cry, my child.'

Nadimah took a shuddering breath. 'I know, but I can't help it.'

Sabirah reached for her daughter's hand. The top of her pyjamas fell open, revealing the edge of a bruise. 'What happened?'

Nadimah snatched her hand away and pulled the edges of her top together. 'Nothing.'

Sabirah held her gaze.

'I fell over.'

'Let me see?'

'No, it's okay.'

'Nadimah!'

Her daughter held out for a few seconds before exposing the edge of the bruise. Sabirah pushed the opening wider and more discoloured flesh appeared. Despite her daughter's pleas, she undid the next button and pushed the fabric as far back as it would go. The extent of the injury made her gasp.

'Who did this?'

'I told you, I fell.' Nadimah's voice almost disappeared.

'Come on, sit up and take your top off.'

'No, Mama.'

'Yes.'

The bruising continued round the girl's torso. Sabirah recognised the pattern. She'd suffered something similar when a group of women attacked her in the shower during her nightmare ordeal in prison.

'Please don't lie to me and tell me you fell. Who did this?'

Nadimah's eyes brimmed with more tears. Sabirah resisted the temptation to take her in her arms and draped the girl's top over her shoulders. She waited until she'd pushed her arms through the sleeves and fastened the buttons.

'Some girls outside school. They called me a dirty Arab terrorist and one hit me. I hit her back like you said, but she just laughed and then they pushed me down and kicked me.'

'From your school?'

'No, they're from another school nearby.'

'Right, tomorrow we'll see their head teacher and you can identify them—'

'Please, Mama, no.'

'Do you want them to get away with it?'

The tears overflowed and ran down her cheeks.

Sabirah hesitated as she remembered how reviled 'snitches' were in prison. Even the guards treated them with contempt. She didn't want her daughter to be stigmatised. At least it wasn't happening at her school.

'Okay, I will not speak to the head unless they attack you again. But you must come home a different way, and I want you to go with Antonia to the gym. So next time you hit someone back, they won't mock you.'

'I don't want to fight, Mama.' Snot coursed out of her nostrils and Sabirah gave her a tissue.

'I know, my darling. But sometimes we have to.'

She held her daughter, whose sobbing intensified until she exhausted herself. Nobody messed with Antonia, and she wanted her daughter to have the same confidence. They were strangers here and some people would always dislike them for it.

◆　◆　◆

The team from CrimTech, led by Senior Crime Scene Technician Jolanta Dobrowski, had finished processing the panic room and, having completed their work in the other rooms, packed their equipment away. Chapman once considered Jo a friend, but since she'd betrayed him and Antonia to the security services six months earlier, their relationship had understandably cooled. She stepped out of the living room into the gloomy hallway, where Chapman and his team waited.

'What can you tell me?' he asked.

She addressed Sanchez. 'What we found is consistent with suicide. The blood spatter pattern, gunshot residue on his hands and no signs of restraints. The only inconsistencies were the cuts to his hands and damage to his knuckles.'

'Like he'd punched someone?' Chapman said.

'Or something.'

This added weight to Chapman's theory. 'What about the cuts?'

'Broken glass or pottery, but you'll have a better idea after the post-mortem.' Dobrowski still addressed Sanchez.

Chapman wouldn't let her off the hook. 'Do we need to preserve the trashed rooms?'

'We don't anticipate coming back, but it's up to you.'

'Okay, thanks. I'll look forward to getting your report.'

'You'll have it by the close of business tomorrow.' She didn't meet Chapman's gaze as she left.

'Awkward,' Sanchez said.

'The fuck she think she is?' Louisa Walker asked. 'Just because she's married to the creep in Financial Crimes.'

'That's no way to refer to a senior officer, Constable Walker.' Though yet again, Chapman agreed with Louisa. His old boss had the knack of pissing off the people he worked with while seeming to keep *his* bosses happy.

'Do you want me to tell the Murder Squad not to bother?' Walker said.

'Not on your life. I know what Dobrowski said, but until we've received the PM results it's a suspicious death, and we treat it as a potential murder.'

'Right, boss. What do you want us to do?'

'You and Darren question the neighbours, see if they heard anything or saw anyone arrive or leave.'

'I'll make sure he doesn't go to the door first, otherwise no bugger will answer.' Walker hurried away.

Sanchez waited until she'd left. 'Nobody could have heard the shot.'

'But whoever smashed this place up would have made a racket.'

'I don't think we're after anyone else.'

'You're no dummy, Alice, and I'd put money on that, too, but . . .'

'Yup. Shall we speak to Mrs Snowden?'

They found her in the kitchen sat at the long refectory table. A distinctive Port Charlotte whisky bottle sat in front of her. He hoped she hadn't drunk too much. The stuff was lethal.

'Do you want some?' She lifted the bottle.

'No thanks, Mrs Snowden. Are you up to answering some questions?'

She gestured at the chairs on the opposite side of the table, and he and Sanchez sat. He signalled to Sanchez to take the lead.

'Do you mind if we record you?' Sanchez placed the voice recorder next to the bottle.

'Whatever.' She took a sip of her drink.

'Can you tell us about your husband's state of mind?'

'You mean, did I think he would kill himself?' Whisky splashed from her glass as she made an angry gesture. 'And I just let him?'

'Sergeant Sanchez wasn't suggesting you did. I'm sure your husband would have given you no sign of what he intended, but did you observe any changes in him?'

The anger drained from her, and her head slumped.

Please don't cry. But she held herself together.

Sanchez resumed her questions. 'Was there anything worrying him? Business problems, money?'

She snorted. 'Does it look like it?' She gestured round the huge kitchen.

He wouldn't be the first bankrupt living like a millionaire, but Chapman let it go. They would find out soon enough.

Sanchez ploughed on. 'Anything else which might have been on his mind? Did he display any changes in behaviour you might have wondered at?'

Snowden plucked at a thread on her sleeve. 'He appeared more introspective recently. He's never been one to think much. I don't mean he was stupid, but he didn't ponder life's mysteries. He lived life at full pelt, without worrying about the consequences.'

Sanchez leant forward. 'What changed?'

'He started getting therapy at a clinic in Kensington.'

'Do you have the name?'

'Their brochure's somewhere on his desk. Do you want me to get it?'

'No, we'll find it. Please continue.'

'The first time he went, he was buzzing, on top of the world. He suggested I go, but I can't stand that bullshit. Anyway, after a few weeks he became more subdued, introspective.' She stared into the distance, then picked up the glass. A thin layer of whisky coated its bottom, and she drained it before topping it up.

The aroma of malt filled Chapman's nostrils and he signalled to Sanchez he'd take over. 'Why did he continue to attend?'

She shrugged. 'I asked him. He said he needed to.'

'Needed to?'

'Yep, like some sort of penance.'

'And how was he when he came back?'

'Like someone had caught him.'

Chapman waited for her to continue, but she didn't. 'What do you mean?'

'A few years ago, he had an affair, and I found out. A young girl who worked in his office, gold-digger trying to get her claws into him. That's how he behaved, like he had when I'd caught him.'

'You think he was having an affair?' Sanchez said.

'He gave me no clue last time. It wasn't until I found out and confronted him his behaviour changed. He didn't like being caught.' Mrs Snowden gave Sanchez a sad smile. 'You'll find out how devious they can be.'

Chapman doubted Sanchez would ever have her heart broken by a man. 'And you think he exhibited the same behaviour? He felt guilty about something.'

Mrs Snowden sipped her whisky and nodded.

'When did he last go?'

'A couple of weeks ago? He's got an online concierge service. They can tell you.' She drained her glass and stared at the bottle. 'If you don't mind, Inspector, it's been a very long day.'

'Sure, we'll leave it for—'

'Could I just ask one question?' Sanchez cut in. 'Why did he choose that clinic?'

'An old school friend recommended it. Don't ask me which one. There's a group of them who still get together. Ellaby hinted they were working on a big project that would make our fortunes, but I suspect they just wanted an excuse to meet up. Overgrown schoolboys reliving their childhoods.'

Chapman stood. 'Thank you, Mrs Snowden. We'll just need to check his office, find the brochure. We've already taken his electronic devices to check for any communications which might cast a light on his— on what happened.'

She waved her free hand. 'Whatever you need to take. But there's no sense in asking me for any passwords.'

Glass clinked before they'd left the kitchen and Chapman waited until Sanchez closed the door. 'She's got you pegged as the little sister who needs a bit of advice. It could be useful next time.'

'Yeah, like I need advice not to get into bed with a man.' She gave a theatrical shudder and led the way upstairs.

On the second floor she stopped outside a door with a 'CRIME SCENE DO NOT ENTER' sign taped to it. They put on disposable gloves and overshoes. She opened the door and put the light on. 'The intruder must have started in here.'

Chapman checked over her shoulder. What must have once been a beautifully decorated study looked like a herd of buffalo had trampled through it. Books lay askew in front of dark wood bookshelves, wadding hung out of the wounds in the green leather covering two Chesterfields and a captain's chair. Papers covered the floor, desk and tops of the filing cabinets, except where the crime scene technicians had removed a laptop and desktop case. A large monitor on the desk lay on its side with a hole in the screen.

'And we're supposed to find a leaflet?' Sanchez said.

'We'll give it ten minutes. Then contact the concierge service if we don't find it.'

He approached the desk and stared at the carnage. The handle of an ornamental paperknife, in the shape of a mini Samurai sword, stuck out of a pile of papers in the middle of the desk. Chapman moved them aside. The knife fastened a small piece of glossy paper to the wooden surface of the desk. A fission of excitement dispelled his apathy. A dusting of fingerprint powder told him it had been checked, so Chapman grabbed the handle and pulled, but it didn't come out. By levering the blade sideways, he loosened it and it came out with a creak.

'What have you got?' Sanchez paused her search of a pile of papers in front of a filing cabinet.

Chapman freed the paper from the blade. One side showed part of a grand stately home, and the other a swimming pool and a few words beneath it. 'Part of a leaflet for a health club. Someone had ripped it into pieces first.'

'Let's see.'

He handed it to her, and she examined both sides.

'It's Parview Hall, near Bedford. I recognise the tower. You can just see the clock.' She placed a thumbnail on the image.

'What is it, a spa?'

'It's owned by Parview Complete Health. They claim to treat the whole person, including your mind.'

Chapman had forgotten Sanchez's partner was into all that alternative therapy crap. 'You reckon this is the place he went for his therapy? He wouldn't have gone to Bedford.'

'They've got a place in Kensington, different name. I can't remember what it's called.'

He checked the time. Gone ten. No wonder he was starving. He'd get a takeaway, again. 'We'll go in the morning.'

'Shall I meet you there? I'll research it and text you.'

'Thanks.' His phone buzzed, and he checked the caller display. Control. He hoped it wasn't another callout. 'Chapman.'

'Inspector. A flag's come up on this incident. Someone's on the way to take over from you. Wait until they get there to hand over to them.'

'Why? It's almost certainly suicide.'

'Mr Snowden is a prominent citizen. This will need handling.'

'I can manage the investigation—'

'They'll arrive within the hour.'

'Who's coming?' They didn't answer. 'I'm going to find out when they get here.'

'Superintendent Harding.'

'But he's in Financial Crimes—'

'Don't touch anything.' The line died.

Sanchez studied him. 'Trouble?'

'*Don't touch anything*! Cheeky sod.' Chapman kicked the overturned bin. 'They're taking it off us. They don't trust me to handle it. And they're sending "the creep in Financial Crimes".'

'Harding? Why? He couldn't find his arse if you gave him a map.'

'Probably some dodgy deals to cover up.' Chapman suspected Harding's loyalties weren't to the police.

'Arsehole.'

'Snowden probably went to school with someone in the cabinet. Cue a whitewash, "shot himself while cleaning his gun".'

'It stinks. Do you want me to wait?'

'No point in both of us hanging about. You get on home.'

'What about Mrs Snowden?'

'Probably in a coma by now. The stuff she was drinking is sixty per cent. I'll stay up here.'

'I'll check on her before I go. See you in the morning, boss.' She paused as she reached the door. 'Don't touch anything.'

The desk diary he threw hit the wall as the door closed. Chapman scanned the room. While he waited, he'd have a rummage, see if he could find anything of interest. He wasn't convinced Snowden's death had anything to do with a clinic, and Harding's involvement made him more certain something dubious had happened.

◆ ◆ ◆

The smell of disinfectant and sickness she always associated with hospitals filled Antonia's nostrils, mingled with the sickly-sweet odour of the hot chocolate her neighbour was drinking. Around her, in the waiting room of University College Hospital, a mixture of the walking wounded and friends and relatives sat. The murmur of low voices and electronic pings provided a background accompaniment to her thoughts. The laptop resting across her knees had gone to sleep long ago.

She kept replaying the moments leading up to the van hitting Tomasz. She was sure her attackers were the two men she'd noticed at the pub. They'd targeted her, and Tomasz had paid because he'd been with her. If she'd let him walk to the bus alone, he wouldn't be here, but maybe she'd be in the theatre getting repaired. The medics had taken Tomasz Zabo's broken body away over an hour ago. She'd washed off the blood she'd got on her skin from giving him CPR, but the stain on the sleeve of her jacket remained.

The room fell silent. Two uniformed officers stood in the doorway, figures made bulky by stab-vests and equipment belts. They saw her, and the taller of the two, a young South Asian sergeant with a pockmarked face, came towards her.

'Ms Conti?'

Her heart flipped. Had Tomasz died? 'Is he okay?' His surprise told her she'd made a mistake. Of course, a medic would give the news here.

'I'm not sure. Could we have a word in private?'

She put the laptop in her backpack and followed him out, the attention on her making her skin prickle. They led her out into the now-silent corridor and to a small office with three desks in it.

The sergeant arranged chairs round one of them and invited her to sit. 'I'm sure you know why we're here. What can you tell me about what happened?'

She recounted the events leading up to the attack.

'So, you reckon the two men followed you from the pub?'

'There was also another one waiting.'

'Can you identify them?'

She'd only seen them when the van's headlamps swept over them. 'They wore ski masks.'

'How did you recognise them as the men from the pub?' The constable spoke for the first time. He'd taken notes in silence, his watery blue eyes under almost invisible brows appraising her.

Antonia hesitated, remembering a much earlier attack, one she wished she could forget again. 'One of them wore a distinctive aftershave.'

He snorted. 'Is that it?'

The sergeant gave his colleague a disapproving look. 'Okay, Ms Conti, what happened next?'

'I thought they wanted my backpack. It had my laptop and phone in it, so I let them have it, but they threw it back at me. They could have taken it when I tended Tomasz, but they left it.' She picked it off the floor at her feet. 'You can get his fingerprints off it.'

'No chance,' the constable said. 'Waste of time and money.'

Antonia waited for the sergeant to contradict him, but he just said, 'Why do you think they attacked you?'

Which one of you is in charge? 'They were there for me. The van should have hit me. One of them definitely pushed me towards the road but I spun away.'

'So, the van driver was working with them?'

'Why would they attack you?' The constable folded his arms. A fine down covered the freckled skin on his ham-like forearms.

'I edit *The Electric Investigator*. People don't always like what we write.' Should she mention what happened to John? But they'd already dismissed it as an accident, and she didn't want to muddy the waters.

'So, this was a hit on a fearless reporter to shut you up.'

The mocking tone irritated her.

'We think it was something else,' the sergeant said before she could respond. 'Gangs target attractive young women to kidnap and exploit – I'm sure you can use your imagination.'

'Why target me when they saw I wasn't alone?'

The sergeant ignored her. 'What happened after the van hit your friend?'

She replayed the scene where she'd knelt alongside Tomasz. 'Two of the men helped the one I'd kicked. I smashed his knee—'

'I hope you didn't use excessive force,' the constable said.

'What? The men attacked us, we defended ourselves.'

'You're allowed to use *reasonable* force. It's not a licence to cause mayhem.'

She glared at him. 'One of my friends is in there fighting for his life.'

The silence stretched until the sergeant broke it. 'Which knee?'

She replayed the attack. He'd led with his right. 'Right knee. He'll have ligament damage and a severe bruise on his thigh.'

'We'll check the hospitals. What happened next?'

'I focused on Tomasz. He wasn't breathing and I couldn't detect a pulse, so I gave him CPR.' The matter-of-fact statement didn't reflect the distressing minutes while she tried to keep the young man alive. 'I heard the men get into the van and it drove off.'

'Did you see them?' the constable said, a challenge in his tone.

She wanted to say yes, wipe the smirk off his face. 'There weren't any other vehicles there.'

The sergeant stepped in. 'We've visited the site. It happened near the junction with Quick Street. Could their car have picked them up there? You said one of them waited in the shadows.'

'The door I heard was much closer. Definitely the van.'

'Could it have been the driver, getting back in?'

She tried to recall the sounds. The sense of panic she'd experienced as she worked on Tomasz returned, making her pulse race. 'It was one of the sliding doors in the back.'

'Okay, Ms Conti, if you remember anything else, give me a bell.' The sergeant slid a card across the desk.

'What happens now?'

'We'll try to find the van and check the hospitals for the guy you injured.' He stood and, after hesitating a long beat, the constable did the same and they left.

Antonia's chest seemed to vibrate. The stress of relating the incident, reliving working on Tomasz, and her anger at the constable sent adrenaline spiking through her system. She should have taken his name, but she could recall his number and scribbled it on to the card the sergeant had given her. She picked up her backpack by the straps and stepped into the corridor. Despite what the constable said, she'd get it checked.

A medic in scrubs almost ran into her, swerved, then stopped. 'You the woman who came in with the RTC victim?'

'Yes.'

'Can you get hold of his next of kin?'

Antonia's stomach dropped.

CHAPTER 10

Wearing the same clothes as on her last visit made Sabirah even more self-conscious as she sat in Al Rahman's waiting room. The fee for the appeal had been far more than she'd expected, although Antonia had been happy to let her have the money she needed. The phone on the receptionist's desk buzzed.

'Mr Al Rahman will see you now.' She rose and opened the door to his office without catching Sabirah's gaze.

Sabirah entered Al Rahman's office and he watched her, expressionless.

'Sit.' He waved at the chair in front of his desk and dismissed his assistant with a nod of his head.

Sabirah sat, the feeling of something badly wrong growing by the second. Al Rahman placed his glasses on and studied a sheaf of papers. Unlike the correspondence she'd given him, these were stapled together. Tension built up in her chest until she thought she'd burst.

Eventually, he spoke. 'Why didn't you say you'd been incarcerated?'

'Sorry?'

'You went to prison for theft.'

The memory of the pain, humiliation, and above all, fear she'd endured came flooding back. 'It was a mistake. They acquit me.'

'Your employer dropped the charges as an act of compassion. They didn't acquit you.'

Sabirah couldn't speak.

'Can you imagine my embarrassment when I discovered my client had a criminal record I wasn't aware of?' His lips curled back in anger.

'Sorry.' She should have told him at their first meeting.

Then his anger dissipated. 'You must trust me, Mrs Fadil. We must have no secrets. I can't represent you if you don't tell me the truth.'

'Sorry.'

'Now tell me what happened. I'll record you, so we don't have any inconsistencies.' He pressed a button on his telephone.

Sabirah took a deep breath. She hated thinking about her time in prison, but she needed this man's help. 'I worked at GRM office, cleaning Mr Reed-Mayhew's office. He lost papers, and they said I took.'

'Did you take them?'

Would Antonia get into trouble if she told him she'd stolen them for her? Could she explain all this to the well-fed man in the expensive suit? Would he understand? It was six months ago, but she couldn't betray her friend. She shook her head.

'So, what happened?' His piercing stare over the tops of his glasses seemed to search her soul.

'The head of security, Mr Mish—' She couldn't say his name. Even though she knew Antonia had killed him, he still appeared in her nightmares. 'He accuse me of stealing. He made me touch Mr Reed-Mayhew glasses case, so they find my fingerprints. Then police arrest me and send me to prison.' The beatings she'd received from the other inmates still gave her trouble, especially her knee, but for the first time since she'd fled her home, she'd fought back.

'What happened then? They just let you go?'

'Yes, the prison people said I could go free.'

Al Rahman studied her for a few moments, then read the document in his hand. 'It says they also investigated you for links with terrorist groups.'

'No! I'm not terrorist. To some people, we are all terrorist.' She included him in her gesture.

He nodded. 'There's a xenophobic minority which lumps us all together.' He gave a sympathetic smile. 'Did you receive any paperwork confirming they'd dropped the charges?'

'My other solicitor, Mr Stokes, asked, but they said it's on public record.'

'Okay.' He laid the papers on the desk. 'I'll put this in a report and push for another appeal hearing. They'll want another fee.'

'Why? I already pay.'

'They rejected your appeal. We have to do it again.'

'I don't have.' She couldn't ask her friend again, even though she doubted Antonia would mind.

'Well, if you'd told me everything last time, we would have got the first hearing request granted.'

Shame made her hot. 'But they dismiss charges, so I didn't think it matters.'

'I'll see if they'll make an exception in this instance. But you must tell me everything and let me decide what to disclose. Do you know what client confidentiality is?'

Did he think she was stupid because of her bad English? 'Yes, Mr Stokes explained.'

'So, whatever you tell me, I can't disclose. Do you have anything you want to tell me before I put in another appeal?'

'No.'

'Okay.' His expression softened. 'Would you like some tea, or something to eat?'

'No, thank you.' She just wanted to get out of there.

'Is everything okay with the children? Are they happy at school?'

'Yes, very happy.' But for how long?

'What about the woman whose house you live in?'

Why was he asking about her? 'Mrs Curtis is a wonderful woman. Very generous and so kind to me and the children.'

'She has a reputation as a very tough businesswoman. Someone who will pursue her objectives ruthlessly and isn't afraid to cross lines or trample on people to get what she wants.'

Sabirah stumbled to translate some of his words but understood his meaning. 'She is tough and determined, but always honourable. A woman to admire.'

'Of course, of course. Can I give you some advice? In this country, it's difficult to tell what people think. They are so polite, but you can't tell what they want. Someone who comes with an open hand of friendship could strike you down.'

'Mrs Curtis isn't like that.'

'No, of course not. I didn't mean her. But be on your guard.' He held her gaze. 'I'm telling you as one Syrian to another, some of them don't consider us their equals, so they have no qualms about using us for their own ends.'

She wasn't sure who he meant if not Mrs Curtis. Not Antonia? 'Thank you for your advice. I will remember it.'

'Good. Now, I'm afraid I've got another appointment. My girl will tell you when you need to come again.'

He swept the papers on the desk together and slid them into a drawer before focusing on his screen. Sabirah thanked him and left the room. No offer of a lift in his car this time. She'd have to manage on the tube. The whole meeting had unsettled her. What did he mean about Mrs Curtis's reputation? Sabirah trusted her completely, but she relied too much on the old lady.

◆ ◆ ◆

Chapman was already waiting when Antonia walked into the dining room. Whenever she'd met him, he occupied a table at the furthest corner of the room with a clear view of the entrance. She made her way through the crowded room. The noise of diners attacking their food, chatter and glasses clinking mingled with the indistinct music issuing from the speakers attached to the faux beams above her head. The smell of roast meats and gravy filled the air. Heavy, chunky furniture she remembered from her last visit combined with the dark walls and patterned burgundy carpet to make the room claustrophobic.

He stood when she reached him, and she greeted him with a hug. 'Remind me why you like it here?'

'This is payback for the uber-trendy place you dragged me to last time.' He winked at her. 'And they serve superb roasts.'

'I vaguely remember.' She recalled punching the mirror in the ladies and shattering it. She hoped they'd forgotten.

Despite the place being busy, Chapman had secured a table for four and she hung her jacket off the back of a spare chair. They ordered from a waitress in an imitation medieval serving wench's outfit.

'You paid last time, so it's my turn,' Chapman said. 'I don't want any arguments.'

'We just had a drink when I paid.'

'My bad luck then.'

'So, is this like a date?'

Chapman opened his mouth to say something then cleared his throat, and she laughed.

'Funny, ha, ha.' Chapman updated her on what he'd found at the forensic garage. 'Your water squirter was right. Someone placed a tracking device on the car, but they removed it.'

Chapman's obvious antipathy towards Adam amused her. 'Do you think someone at the forensic garage took it off?' Further confirmation she'd not led their enemies to John lifted another burden.

'Difficult to say. The guy in charge seemed keen I didn't get close, but it doesn't mean he's dodgy. The spooks you saw at the incident could have removed it. How is your investigation into GRM going?'

'It's not.' She told him of her meeting with Forman.

'That bloody stinks. So are you dropping the investigation?'

'No, but I need a new source of information.'

'I thought you'd got the memory stick?'

'We did, but the story we wrote using the information on it is what Ms Forman closed down.' Antonia worried she might never get to publish this story. 'How about your prisoner?'

'I've been trying to get hold of his mother. I can't justify a visit to him in prison unless I can link him to a case I'm investigating.'

'But you arrested him.'

'Yeah, that was a favour from my boss, one she regrets. But he's inside for assaulting two officers and that's not my case.'

The smell of rosemary and roast potatoes preceded the food, ending their discussion until the waitress left. Antonia examined the oval plate stacked with meat and vegetables and picked up her cutlery.

'You want to fill me in on what happened to you last night?' Chapman speared a chunk of roast lamb with a fork and cut it.

Antonia had told him some men had attacked her, but not the details. She checked the surrounding tables. Their occupants, engrossed in eating and chatting, paid her and Chapman no attention. She related the events of the previous night between mouthfuls. Even though she'd told the story a few times, having had to repeat details to the police in the hospital and again to Eleanor and Miles this morning, she still found it an ordeal.

When she'd finished, he let out a low whistle. 'Remind me not to go anywhere with you. That's two people who've come to a sticky end.'

'Not funny, Russell.'

'Sorry. How's the lad?'

A surge of guilt almost overwhelmed her. 'They called in his family last night, but he's hanging on.'

'And the investigating officers are treating it as an attempted mugging and hit-and-run?'

'They want to treat the men's attack as either a mugging or an attempted abduction. The sergeant suggested they could be sex traffickers.'

Chapman laughed.

'What's so funny?'

He held up his hands. 'I'm not suggesting they wouldn't be interested in you, but I can't imagine any who'd try to kidnap a six-foot, obviously fit woman, especially with your new muscles.'

She hunched her shoulders self-consciously. Maybe she'd overdone the weights. 'They wanted to shut me up, not kidnap me.'

'Yeah, a hit-and-run is easier to cover up as an accident than a bullet through the skull. But what if they got the right target?'

'What, you think they targeted Tomasz?'

'Why not? What do you know about him?'

'What he put on his CV, plus we did a background check.' Was the inoffensive young man the one they'd been after? 'No, I'm not having it.' She'd do a more thorough check, just in case.

'Just saying don't ignore the possibility. It sounds to me like the investigating officers don't want to escalate this. I'm willing to bet that by the time their superiors finish, they'll record it as an attempted mugging which went wrong, and an unfortunate accident where the driver failed to stop.'

'Not an abduction?'

'A lot more hassle for them if they treat it as that. Not as much as for attempted murder, but too much for some of the lazy sods in the job. Have you got the name of the sergeant?'

She retrieved the card and slid it across the table. 'Keep it. I've scanned a copy, I've written the badge number of his sidekick on the back. He's a nasty piece of work.'

Chapman studied the card. 'Islington. I know a few people there, so I'll ask around. Find out what they're up to.'

'Thanks, but' – she hesitated – 'I've got another favour to ask.'

'Sure, what do you want me to do?'

'The guy who grabbed me, he pulled my backpack off my shoulders. I wondered if you could get prints off it.'

He studied the material. 'They shouldn't have any problems.'

'I mean, can *you* get it checked for prints? Don't you know someone?'

'Yeah, but if you recall, our last meeting ended badly. You were there.'

Antonia remembered. They'd arranged to meet his 'friend' to get her advice, but she'd informed Reed-Mayhew's forces, and Antonia and Chapman had escaped through the kitchen of a restaurant. 'Nobody else?'

'My primary contacts were with the last company which had the contract. I'm sure they'd do it, but it will cost.'

'Will their results carry the same weight as one from your forensics team?'

'They're still Home Office certified, so yes.'

'Can you give me their details?'

He tapped the card she'd given him. 'How come the two clowns who saw you last night aren't doing it?'

'The constable said it would be a waste of time.'

'What did the sergeant say?'

'Nothing. He deferred to the guy, clearly intimidated by him.'

Chapman didn't look impressed. 'Did the men who attacked you wear gloves?'

Antonia had replayed the incident so often she didn't need to think. 'He didn't when he grabbed me, straight *after* he'd thrown the backpack.'

'He wouldn't take them off, so you can guarantee he didn't have any on. Lazy sods didn't want to do the paperwork.' He turned his knife over in his hands. 'I'll make sure it's tested. Keep it safe until you hear from me. There's a difference between being idle buggers and passing up the chance to catch a thug.' He speared another piece of lamb, and the prongs squeaked against the glazing of the plate.

'Thanks, Russell, I owe you, and for investigating what happened to John.'

He yawned. 'Sorry.'

'Late night?' She wanted to ask him if he was seeing anyone. She knew he'd split with his girlfriend the last time they'd worked together, although he never mentioned it.

'Not what you think. I worked until gone midnight.' He checked around and leant towards her. 'You can do me a favour in return. I attended a burglary last night, but it turned into something a lot more interesting. A posh bloke wrecked his house then topped himself.'

'Eaton Square?' The sudden death of a prominent citizen like Ellaby Snowden hadn't gone unremarked. The fact it was Chapman's case gave her a great opportunity.

'Yeah,' he said, disappointed she already knew. 'Nobody's reported it yet.'

'Not officially, but don't forget, I'm in the business. What's the favour? I should ask you for the inside gen.'

'They've taken the case taken off me and given it to my old nemesis, Harding.'

She remembered an inspector with the same name who'd signed a warrant for her arrest. 'And you want me to . . . ?'

'I found some information indicating Snowden was getting some big backers for a project he was working on, suggesting this isn't just about sparing his family's blushes because a guy's gone off the rails. If I access anything about the case, it will raise a flag But, as you've demonstrated, you have access to information the average person doesn't. And you can also put stories out there to stir things up—'

'Hang on, I'm not getting involved in settling any internal spats with your colleagues. I'll support you however I can, but I'm not compromising my integrity, or exposing *The Investigator* to any risks. We're having a difficult enough job keeping our licence.'

Chapman held up his hands. 'There's no way I'd do that. Harding is married to Jo, who set us up last time. She's also the senior forensic investigator on this case.'

Information started falling into place. 'She works for one of Reed-Mayhew's companies, doesn't she?'

'Yep, and Harding is suspiciously close to another company the creep owns.'

Antonia didn't need to think. 'No problem. Now, since you're paying, do they have a sweet menu?' The more fronts she had against Reed-Mayhew, the more chance of finding the mistake that would bring him down. Last night's events reminded her someone was also working to bring *her* down.

Chapman drove back to work, his thoughts racing. The account of what sounded like another attempt on Antonia worried him sick. Although he'd played devil's advocate, he had no doubt she *had*

been their target. Although well able to take care of herself, fists offered no defence against a sniper's bullet.

A car in a visitors' space triggered a faint memory. Probably a senior officer coming to give someone grief. As long as it wasn't him. He returned to his office. Sanderson and Walker were the only ones in the outer room. He closed his door and rang Islington, asking to speak to the chief inspector. They'd both reached the rank together, but Chapman was ten years younger and had hoped to go much further. George would happily retire without further advancement.

'Russell, how can I help you, mate?'

'Two of your lads picked up an incident on Vincent Terrace.'

'Attempted mugging of a girl gone wrong and a young lad in hospital?'

Chapman gave a wry smile. 'I'd say either a botched abduction or an attempt to injure or kill one of the victims.'

'You know the girl?' George would have made a good detective.

'She's a reporter who's ruffled a few feathers. This is the second RTC involving her in a month. Someone died in the last one.'

The sound of George's keystrokes filled the silence. 'Shit! I should have guessed. Your friend's ethnicity should have raised a flag. My fault.'

'What's up?'

'The constable has "issues". He's got a swastika tattoo on his ankle. Claims his mates did it while he was pissed.'

'Can't you get rid?'

George sighed. 'I've tried. He's not a member of any proscribed groups and he knows exactly how far to push it. I've put him with the sergeant to tone him down, but the poor guy's struggling. I'll get him in and tell him to upgrade the incident.'

'This could be your chance. Your Nazi ignored evidence of a serious crime.'

'What evidence?'

'One attacker grabbed Antonia's, the young woman's, back-pack. No gloves. Your Nazi dismissed checking it as a waste of time.'

'Hmmm. Unfortunately, my sergeant would take the heat.'

'If he's not up to it . . .'

'You were always a hard bastard. The guy's recently promoted, he just needs a bit of encouragement to grow into the role.'

'You're too soft. Put your Nazi with someone who can manage him. Haven't you got any women?' Neither Sanchez nor Walker in his team would take any shit.

George laughed. 'You've changed your tune, but I'll consider it. Have you got the backpack, or can you get your friend to drop it off? Tell her to ask for me.'

He thanked George, and with vague promises to meet up for a drink, ended the call. He sent Antonia an encrypted text with the information, hoping she bothered switching her phone on.

A knock and Walker stuck her head in. 'Got a minute, boss?'

'Come in, Louisa.'

She came in and closed the door. 'The wanker in Financial Crimes was here earlier asking after you.'

'What did you say?' What did he want? Chapman had already briefed him about the case at the house last night.

'I wanted to tell him to eff off, but Sanderson smarmed over him like a cheap suit. He told him what you told us, you went out to see an informant.'

'Thanks, Louisa. I'll keep a lookout for him.'

He didn't have long to wait until voices in the outer office warned him of visitors. Harding didn't bother knocking.

'Come in, take a seat.' Chapman held his anger and gestured to three chairs stacked against the wall opposite his desk.

'I'm not staying.' Harding stuck his chin forward. 'Did you take anything from Mr Snowden's office?'

'Why would I? It's your case. If something's missing, ask your wife. CrimTech took a load of stuff.'

'They haven't got it. You sure you didn't take anything?'

'I know I'm older than you, but I can still recall stuff from yesterday.'

'What about your team?' Harding jerked a thumb at the outer office.

'Not to my knowledge. Why don't you ask them?' Harding had a talent for pissing him off, but he was abusing it now.

'It's just a leaflet. You might have picked it up inadvertently.'

'Do you understand what *no* means?'

'You've not actually denied taking it, just deflected with another question—'

'I'll deny it now. I removed nothing, zilch, nada, from Snowden's house.'

'Hmm.' Harding spun on his heel and stalked to the door. He paused in the opening. 'Before you get too smug, Mrs Snowden made a complaint about you. I believe Professional Standards are speaking to your DCI. Have fun.' He slammed the door behind him.

Chapman remembered where he'd last seen the car in the visitor's space. It belonged to Chief Inspector McGee from Professional Standards, and she hated him. 'Shit!'

A louder commotion preceded her entrance. She arrived at his office accompanied by his DCI, Gunnerson, and two uniformed heavies behind her.

Gunnerson spoke first. 'Russell, we've received a very serious complaint about you by Mrs Snowden. CI McGee is here to investigate.'

'DS Sanchez and I were together every time I saw Mrs Snowden.'

'The incident occurred after DS Sanchez left and before Superintendent Harding arrived—'

'I didn't see her at all then, I stayed in the study.'

'So you say,' McGee said. 'Because of the seriousness of the allegation, I'm suspending you while I investigate.' She then recited a caution.

Chapman decided not to say any more without a representative. He'd made that mistake last time. Once they spoke to Sanchez, they'd clear him. She'd checked on Snowden before she left, and the woman had passed out in the kitchen.

'Do you have anything to say?' McGee said.

'No comment.'

'Whatever. These two officers will escort you off the premises.'

He shut his computer down and stood. The two officers looked embarrassed as they flanked him and escorted him through the outer office.

'By the way,' McGee said, 'there's video evidence to support Mrs Snowden.'

He stopped. 'There can't be.'

McGee gave a smug grin.

CHAPTER 11

Antonia put the handset on speaker and glanced round her office as she waited for the connection. Although not immaculate, it was far tidier than usual, ready for her to welcome the newest member of staff. At the sound of the automated response, she ended the call and exhaled in frustration. Chapman still hadn't switched his phone on, and he hadn't responded to any of her messages. Ringing him at work led to more frustration. The response 'He's not in' greeted every enquiry. Despite two detectives interviewing her about the attack when she'd taken the backpack in for fingerprinting a week ago, they'd not been in touch with the promised update.

The faint vibrations caused by the lift coming down from Eleanor's flat made her coffee tremble. Antonia guessed Eleanor would want to be part of the welcome too. She rose and opened her door. The owner of *The Electric Investigator* manoeuvred through the outer office towards her.

'Our new girl not here yet?'

'Morning, Eleanor. It's not nine yet.'

'Hmm, I thought she might get here early on her first day.'

'I suspect Jean Sawyer is the sort of person who will arrive exactly on time every day.'

'You're probably right, dear. She does seem to be on the spectrum.' Eleanor hesitated. 'Sorry, I know I'm not supposed to use such language, but I'm a very old dog.' She studied Antonia. 'Is that why you don't like her? Does she remind you of someone in your past?'

'I don't dislike her. But she's difficult to read. I can't tell what she's thinking. It makes me think she's hiding something.'

'She's just different. I'm sure you'll get used to her. She's an excellent candidate, as good as Tomasz. We're lucky she took this job after we'd initially turned her down. Have you heard any more about how he is?'

'His sister said they're keeping him in a coma until the swelling subsides and they can assess his injuries. She thought he might lose a leg, but whatever happens, he won't be fit to work for several months.'

'Have they caught the driver yet?'

Antonia had hoped the fingerprints of his accomplice would lead to his capture, but she now doubted it. 'They found the van, burnt out.'

'No CCTV? I can't imagine much of the city remains without cover.'

'Apparently, hackers had disabled the cameras in the area where they abandoned the van. Will you do the welcome speech?'

'I thought you could do it, dear. You're in charge now.'

Eleanor had welcomed the staff who worked for *The Investigator* since she'd set it up as a magazine over thirty years earlier, missing only the unfortunate Tomasz Zabo. She'd given Antonia the same speech, even though Antonia had lived with her since Eleanor adopted her as a traumatised teenager, and they'd ridden down in the lift together. Antonia wasn't sure how she felt about this change. She'd welcomed Zabo last week, but only because Eleanor had gone to hospital. This felt like the ending of an era.

The doorbell rang. Nine exactly. Antonia went to answer it and checked the security camera. A woman of average height in her mid-thirties stared at the door. Her brown hair looked like she'd cut it herself and her multicoloured tweed coat would fit someone bigger. Antonia opened the door.

Jean Sawyer smiled, showing a smear of lipstick on her teeth. 'Good morning, Ms Conti.'

'Antonia, please. Come in, Jean.'

Sawyer wheeled a small cabin bag in behind her. 'Don't worry, I'm not moving in. I like to have my own things around me at work.'

After giving her the welcome talk, Antonia left it to Eleanor and Miles to continue her induction. She shut herself in her office and focused on getting the next day's edition ready for publication. Although being online meant they could publish stories as they occurred, they continued to break the bigger investigations on Tuesdays. Forman had blocked tomorrow's big story. The replacement story about modern slavery was too depressingly familiar.

She'd sent several messages to the email address they'd recovered from the damaged memory stick she'd got from John, but still hadn't received a reply. Antonia had convinced herself it must lead to John's colleague, a woman she'd spoken to fleetingly. She'd appealed to the woman to help them avenge John's death. The messages hadn't bounced back, so she hoped whoever monitored the address read them and would eventually get in touch. Although she couldn't blame them if they didn't.

Two hours later, she'd done her best to make her lead story compelling, and recognised she'd reached the stage of tinkering for the sake of it. She needed to escape from her stuffy office and get some fresh air. The light on her desk phone flashed.

'Ms Conti, I've got a caller who insists on talking to you. I've questioned her, but she won't give her name or where she's from. She just says she's a friend of John's—'

'Put her through.'

'Are you sure? At my last place—'

'We don't interrogate our callers. Lots of people who contact us want to remain anonymous.' Eleanor and Miles should have covered this.

'If you insist, Ms Conti . . .'

The phone beeped to tell Antonia she had the external line. 'Hello?' Instead of a reply, the line echoed. *If the caller put the phone down because of Jean . . .* 'Hello?'

'Antonia?'

Thank God. 'Yes, how may I help you?'

'I don't appreciate being grilled.'

'I apologise, we've got a new PA. She's . . . enthusiastic.'

After a long pause, the woman said, 'Sorry I seem jumpy, but you understand . . .'

'Sure. I presume you've decided to work with us. Do you want to meet?'

'This afternoon. I want to do this soon.'

Antonia checked her diary. Nothing she couldn't change. 'What about fifteen hundred – three o'clock – at the place I used to meet John before he changed it to Charlton House?'

'No!'

'So where?'

'I've got the number you emailed me. I'll send you an encrypted message.'

She ended the call, and inserting the SIM into her mobile, Antonia powered it up. It beeped straight away, and she opened the message. Kew Gardens. It would take a while to get there, and she'd need to leave soon. She replied, giving her description.

She took the SIM card out and slipped it, and the phone, into her pocket. Keys, cash, and a new travel card went in other pockets. In the outer office, Jean Sawyer sat at her desk. A variety of knick-knacks, neatly arranged in rows, surrounded her workstation.

'I'm going out, Jean. Won't be back before six, so we'll have a chat tomorrow.'

'Okay, where shall I say you've gone if anyone rings?' Her big brown eyes studied Antonia.

'Out.'

'Can I have your mobile number?' Her fingers hovered over the keyboard.

'I don't believe in them.'

'Wise decision.' Sawyer's reply surprised Antonia. 'I'll email any messages which arrive while you're out to your desk.'

The tall blonde woman in a smart suit stood at the top of the shallow steps outside the glass and steel gallery building. The description fitted the one Fiona had given Antonia, and she carried a bright red umbrella, as promised. The journey to Kew Gardens, including her precautions to make sure nobody followed her, had taken longer than she'd expected. A gust of wind blew autumn leaves around her ankles. Antonia strode towards the woman, who noticed her.

'Antonia?' she asked.

'Fiona?' Antonia studied the woman. A few years older than her, she stood the same height in her heels.

'For our purposes.' She shook hands, her pale blue eyes appraising, then checking behind Antonia.

Antonia detected wariness, but also relief. 'Shall we go somewhere warmer?'

'I could do with a bite, I missed lunch.'

Antonia nodded. So had she.

'The brasserie is usually quiet at this time.'

They walked the way in silence, Fiona's heels clicking on the path. They reached the brasserie and slipped inside. A gaggle of tourists waited by the doorway deciding what to do. As Fiona said, the place was almost deserted, and they took a table in the far corner where they could see everyone else.

Once they'd ordered, Antonia produced her phone. 'Do you mind if I use voice transcription?'

'I'd rather you didn't have a recording of my voice.' Fiona stared at the device as if studying a dangerous animal.

'It transcribes your words as text, so there's no recording of your voice.'

'You can't name or quote me in your report.'

'You have my word. Anyway, I don't know your name, so I couldn't.' Antonia recalled her last conversation with John. 'We can't pay you for this.'

'Of course, I don't want any money. I . . . I just want to tell people what's going on.'

Oh, really? 'Great. If there's anything you disclose which is only known to you, you need to tell me, and I'll make sure it doesn't come back to bite you.'

Their order arrived, and Fiona waited until they'd both started eating before getting down to business. 'Where do you want me to start?'

'Pretend John's told me nothing.'

'I'd better start at the beginning.' She looked to her right. 'When I trained as a psychologist, I became interested in cognitive neuroscience. I don't know how much you've followed the study of memory, but we've discovered it isn't fixed and we can manipulate it to reduce the emotional impact of traumatic incidents or overcome phobias. We can even make people forget specific incidents.'

'Don't those techniques rely on drugs?' Ten sessions of therapy hadn't even taken the edge off Antonia's nightmares, and she'd refused to let them drug her. After years of using her own techniques, she'd managed to bury them, but her run-in with Mishkin earlier in the year, and witnessing John's death, had reawakened them.

'A combination of drugs and therapy, but it doesn't always work, and the memory may return. Also, in many cases, trauma results from several incidents or a prolonged exposure to abuse. In those cases, the existing techniques are less effective. This is where our method is revolutionary.' A note of pride entered her voice.

'What's your organisation called?'

Fiona took a sip of her drink. 'I'd rather not say.'

'I understand.' She could easily find all the companies in the field.

'We can identify all memories associated with a particular trauma and erase them.'

'How?' Antonia leant forward. The idea of wiping out some of her memories appealed. 'John mentioned they drugged the patients.'

'I don't want to give too much away, but it doesn't need drugs. They sometimes make it easier if your subject is difficult, but the process involves using intense light, lasers, on the part of the brain affected.'

'Wouldn't you have to penetrate the skull?' Antonia shuddered. Having a hole bored in her skull sounded worse than taking drugs.

'That isn't necessary.'

'Okay, so far, so good. But John told us they experimented on uninformed subjects. I've spoken to the families of three prisoners, and they confirm their relatives are behaving strangely.'

Fiona ate a mouthful of the quiche she'd ordered as she pondered. Antonia ate another sandwich from the afternoon tea she'd treated herself to and realised she'd already finished the others.

'It wasn't our decision.'

Antonia waited for her to continue.

'Our client has—'

'GRM?'

'Of course, John's told you. Yes, GRM used it on prisoners in one of their establishments.'

'What exactly do they do?' So far, Fiona had confirmed what Antonia already knew. 'John wasn't very clear.'

'John worked for GRM. He wasn't aware of the details of what we do.' Fiona sipped her drink. 'We hoped to use our process on people who'd suffered trauma, to treat conditions like PTSD. GRM thought they'd use it to "cure" criminals.'

'How?'

'Often a traumatic event, or series of events, triggers criminal behaviour.'

'How did you use this "treatment" on the prisoners?'

'We didn't. As part of our contract, we were training their staff and provided them with three devices. They were supposed to use this to treat prison staff affected by trauma and PTSD as well as prisoners. One of the trainees took it to his boss, and unbeknownst to us, they set up a programme to "cure" prisoners. Had we known, we'd have put a stop to it. Not only were the trainees not ready to start treating people, but to do what they wanted would have required a lot of additional training and carefully formulated treatment plans.'

'John said they didn't consult the prisoners.'

'They offered them better accommodation and food if they helped with "medical research".'

'So, what happened?'

'Their staff didn't understand the importance of vetting the subjects properly. We've not done a huge amount on this, but our research suggests it will only work on people who turned to crime *because* of trauma. Not those predisposed to crime because of a combination of their personality and upbringing. They're often the worst offenders, so, of course, they focused on them.'

'With what outcome?'

'They used the devices without considering the effect. Where abuse occurred in a family setting, they removed all memories associated with the subject's family. When family members came to visit, the prisoners didn't have a clue who they were. They became untethered and often became more violent. These memories were vital to their sense of self.'

'What did GRM do?'

'Nothing. Not only hadn't they completed our training course, but they weren't psychologists, just technicians. Someone trained wouldn't have made such a catastrophic error.'

'So, the process is irreversible?' Antonia studied her last cake.

'It's not straightforward. You can reimplant the memory, but you need to have taken steps to preserve it first. They didn't.'

'And how do you preserve the memory?'

Fiona looked uncomfortable. 'It would take too long to explain in detail, but we've developed a process that converts the memories into an electronic format like a computer file, which you can store on hard drives.'

'John said they covered up crimes to hide what they'd done, but he wasn't specific.'

'They've hidden at least one murder. One guy, a very violent offender, lost memories of his father. It turned out the father had been the only person who'd treated the guy well during a shitty childhood. He'd built up a good relationship with an older prisoner who'd reminded him of his dad. Once they removed the memory, he became even more unmanageable until he turned on the old guy, killing him.'

'How awful. Do you have a name?'

'I'm sorry. But' – she fixed Antonia with an eager expression – 'I'm going to offer to treat the prisoners, undo the harm they've done. I'll get the details for you.'

If *The Investigator* published the details of these crimes without explicitly mentioning that GRM had carried out the experiments that caused them, then Forman wouldn't find out until they published the follow-up. But by then it would be too late. The recollection of her two henchmen, especially the smaller one with glasses, gave Antonia pause and reminded her of what had happened to John. 'I can't let you, it's too dangerous.'

'I'm not doing it for you. If it gets out our procedure has caused these crimes, they'll shut us down. I've not spent the last six years working my guts out to see all the work go down the pan.'

'Promise me you won't take any risks, after what happened to John.'

'What do you mean? It was an accident, wasn't it?'

Antonia hesitated. Although she'd welcome anything Fiona found out, she couldn't let her take such a risk without warning her how GRM had dealt with previous whistle-blowers. 'The police are treating it as one, but someone tracked his car.'

'How do you know?'

'Two people I trust told me.' Could she trust Adam? She didn't know him well, but sensed she could, and Chapman had proved himself many times.

'It means someone knew where to find him?'

'Yes, and when they did, they sent a lorry which drove straight at us.' Should she mention the other guy GRM had killed, disguising it as a suicide?

Fiona studied the dregs of her tea. 'I'll think about it and get in touch.'

Antonia wondered at Fiona's reaction. She'd seemed unsurprised by the revelation and unperturbed at the prospect of putting herself in the same position. Why?

CHAPTER 12

Chapman sat in his too-small living room, half-watching another daytime programme. His phone buzzed again for the umpteenth time, and he checked the caller ID. He'd decided to ignore it, but, bored out of his mind, relented. 'Yes, Alice?'

'Don't you ever answer the phone?'

'Not when I'm suspended. How can I help you?'

'Gunnerson asked me to ring you. She's given up trying. She wants you to come in.' Sanchez sounded exasperated.

'I gave her the contact details for my Police Federation rep.'

'She's not told me in so many words, but I think they're dropping the charges.'

Relief, then anger, surged through him. 'I'll wait until I get it in writing. Anything else?'

'Don't get snappy with me. I offered to stay, and I gave a statement confirming the drunken cow was unconscious when I left.'

'Yeah, sorry.' He'd grown bored of staying at home. 'Give me an hour.'

He made sure someone from the Federation could meet him at work and set off. By the time he arrived, he'd focused his anger on Gwendolyn Snowden. Why had she made the false accusation? He'd gone over every moment he'd spent in her company and couldn't imagine any reason he'd have upset her. Had someone put her up to it? But who or why? He'd find out.

McGee's car was back. Why the hell was she here if they were dropping the charges? Good thing he'd arranged for someone to accompany him.

Sanchez met him at reception.

Chapman cast about the corridor. 'You seen anyone from the Federation?'

'Yeah, me.'

'Are you qualified?'

'I've done the advocacy course.'

He remembered her taking time off over the summer. 'How many times have you done this?'

'Let me see.' She made a show of counting on her fingers. 'You'd be the first.'

Sanchez was an excellent officer, bright and tenacious. 'Okay, but if I feel you're out of your depth . . .'

'No problem. Shall we go up?'

After a brief conflab, they made their way to Gunnerson's office. CI McGee sat to the side of the desk, wearing a sour expression. Gunnerson frowned, puzzled, when Sanchez came in behind him.

'I'm here in my role as Federation rep, ma'am.'

'Russell, you didn't need to bring anyone with you.' Gunnerson looked uncomfortable.

'You have.' He indicated McGee.

'CI McGee is here to inform you they're dropping the charges—'

'That's not strictly true,' McGee said. 'Because of the stress of her husband's recent death, Mrs Snowden has decided to drop the charges. We will therefore discontinue the investigation.'

'Will you clear DI Chapman completely?' Sanchez said.

'Not until we've completed the investigation.'

'But you've paused the investigation, so will never complete it, and the charge will hang over him forever.'

'It's only fair to give Mrs Snowden time to recover from her ordeal. She may wish to resurrect—'

'Or she may decide she doesn't. You can't keep an open ticket on DI Chapman in case someone decides to resurrect an accusation they've already withdrawn.' Sanchez emphasised her words with hand gestures.

'You're a witness defending him, so you shouldn't be here.' McGee looked at Gunnerson for support.

'This isn't a court of law,' Gunnerson said, 'and we're not discussing DS Sanchez's evidence. I would suggest she has a point.'

McGee gave Gunnerson a glare that should have felled her.

Chapman tried not to smile. 'What happened to your video evidence?'

McGee studied her hands. 'Because Mrs Snowden is withdrawing her complaint, it's not relevant.'

'What you mean is, you've got none. If you had evidence, you wouldn't need her to make a complaint, you'd charge me.'

McGee reddened. 'It's not relevant.'

Sanchez leant forward, eyes blazing. 'You've got a choice. You can either exonerate the DI immediately, or he'll put forward a complaint of malicious bullying and I'll recommend the Federation backs him all the way.'

McGee recognised she'd get no support from Gunnerson and snatched up her handbag and coat. 'I'll get a letter sent.'

They sat in silence for several seconds after the door slammed. A big grin broke out across Chapman's face, reflected on Sanchez's, and even Gunnerson looked pleased.

'Was that okay, boss?' Sanchez said.

'Not bad. Worth a few drinks.'

'Well done, Alice,' Gunnerson said. 'But watch your back with McGee. Can I have a word with you, Russell?'

Sanchez left and closed the door. Gunnerson searched for how to start. 'I don't usually listen to tittle-tattle, but I heard a rumour there was never any complaint against you.'

'What? You mean Mrs Snowden was lying? I've said all along—'

'No. She never made a complaint.'

Chapman needed a minute to take this in. 'You mean they instigated a disciplinary process without receiving a complaint?'

'Exactly.'

Chapman let out a whistle. 'Bloody hell. I *have* upset someone, haven't I.'

'We both know McGee will do anything to bring you down, but she wouldn't have done this on her own. It had to be someone higher up.'

'Harding?'

'At the rate he's going, he'll soon be in a position to do you serious harm. But I'd say not yet, and not this. Too much risk for him if it went wrong.'

Chapman agreed; Harding wasn't a risk-taker, unless he'd been put up to it by someone above him. But who, then? And how high did this go?

The nightmares had kept Antonia awake most of the night. They hadn't been this bad since she'd been a helpless teenager at the mercy of monsters. She sat at her desk, her body too heavy for her. When she closed her eyes, she imagined she saw her mother – not a person she recognised, but a victim being abused by the men. And then breaking free to attack the man holding Antonia, giving her life so her daughter could escape. The fact that her mother hadn't

149

escaped still filled Antonia with guilt. Her logical brain told her a nine-year-old girl had no hope of outrunning men on horseback. But that didn't lessen her shame. The memory of what happened next was too much to bear and her eyes snapped open. She couldn't function like this.

Sawyer knocked on the door and pushed her head in. A short-sighted tortoise. 'Out partying, Ms Conti?'

Antonia yawned. 'I'm working too late.'

'Try chamomile tea or valerian, and if they don't work, ask your doctor for Zolpidem. Works every time for my mother.'

Antonia had tried the suggested remedies, plus a few more, but wouldn't take sleeping tablets. She suspected the staff at the Towers had fed them to her and some of the other girls. More of the memories that had kept her awake rumbled into view.

'Are you okay, Ms Conti?'

'Sorry, Jean, what did you want?'

'I was going to offer you a coffee, but maybe it's what's keeping you awake.'

'A coffee would be lovely. Thank you.'

She stared at the screen for three minutes after Sawyer left, her brain not taking anything in. She couldn't continue like this. If she wasn't going to take drugs, she needed to do something else. She made the decision she'd avoided and hunted for a name on a medical search engine. He was still in the same offices. After punching his number into the phone, her thumb hovered over the red button. *This isn't just you, Antonia. You need to sort yourself out. People rely on you.*

'Caldecot Clinic. Can I help you?'

Antonia's mouth had dried. 'Can I make an appointment to see Professor Haller?'

'Your GP must refer you, I'm afraid.'

At least he hasn't retired. 'I'm an existing patient. Antonia Conti.'

'Hang on.' Keys clacked, and a computer beeped. 'Here we are. You discharged yourself. The professor doesn't normally—'

'Could you just ask him if he'll see me?'

'I can ask.' The phone went dead, and after a long minute, it clicked. 'He said he'd see you. He has one free slot today at twelve?' Her voice could have made ice cubes.

'Today?' She wanted longer to get used to the idea.

'He's usually fully booked. The next free session is in seven days. Shall I put you down for then?'

Seven more days without sleep. She couldn't face it. 'No, I'll see him today. Thank—'

The phone clicked and Sawyer appeared with a coffee. Antonia checked the time. Just over an hour. It would be tight. 'Sorry, Jean, I've got to go.'

'What about this?' She put the coffee on the edge of the desk.

'I'll have it later.' She picked up her backpack. 'I'll be out of contact.' She didn't want anyone to know where she was going. After scooping everything she needed into it, she grabbed her jacket and raced out before anyone could question her.

She decided to abort her journey at least six times, changing her mind on each occasion, but eventually arrived at the nondescript terraced house where Haller based his practice. It lay within easy reach of the Maudsley Hospital and his more serious patients.

The young receptionist's manner contrasted with her iciness over the phone. Antonia sat on one of the new grey leather armchairs, idly glancing through the magazines on offer as she asked herself why she'd come. She could still leave.

A name in the subheading of an article stopped her. Under the heading, a picture featured two figures standing in front of a stately home. One resembled a caricature of a country gentleman wearing a tweed suit and brogues. His short brown hair still had the side parting and, despite the smile plastered on his face, his hazel eyes were dead. Antonia had last seen him when he told her she had to take part in a cage-fight with two women to secure Sabirah's release from prison. He'd neglected to mention Antonia wasn't meant to survive. She read the first paragraph.

> *Gustav Reed-Mayhew is known to most of our readers for his high-flying business GRM, whose employees keep us safe in our beds and the country running smoothly. What they may not know of is his extensive philanthropy, something he is very reticent about. His latest act of generosity involves the donation of this magnificent property to the nation. 'You effectively saved it from ruin, didn't you, Mr Reed-Mayhew?'*

> *'I stayed here as a schoolboy and saw the dreadful state it had fallen into. When the opportunity came to buy it, I jumped at the chance. I spent seven million restoring it and intended to live here, but have decided to share it with the nation.'*

Antonia recalled a conversation Sabirah had overheard when she worked at Reed-Mayhew's offices. He'd instructed his accountant to force the previous owners into bankruptcy over a debt their son had secured on the house. Had he then become bored with it? Antonia had investigated the story and discovered their son went to school with Reed-Mayhew.

'Antonia, what a pleasant surprise.' Professor Haller's voice took her back to the awkward and disturbed fifteen-year-old she'd been the last time she heard it.

'Hello, Prof.' She put the magazine down and stood, uncertain.

'Come in.' He gestured at the open door behind him.

His hair had gone completely grey since she'd last seen him. She went through the short corridor, which ensured the privacy of the consulting room. Unlike the waiting room, this hadn't changed. A small, unobtrusive desk sat in one corner and a seating area with four armchairs were arranged in a U in front of a fireplace.

'How's Eleanor?'

'She's well.' Eleanor had introduced her to Haller. Antonia suspected they'd been lovers. 'But she doesn't know I'm here.'

'I understand.' Haller waited at the door. 'Do you want to take a seat?'

She strode to the furthest chair and sat facing him. She used to perch on a middle chair, staring at the paintings above the fireplace while he sat nearest his desk. He took the same place now and, as then, waited for her to speak.

Her first words surprised her. 'I killed Mishkin.'

'I read something six months ago. You killed him in self-defence. Who was he?'

Of course, he'd never known him as Mishkin. 'He used to call himself Videk.'

'Ahhh.' He gripped the chair arm with his left hand and his pinkie finger lifted, a sign he was formulating a question. 'How did it make you feel?'

'Exhilarated. Free.'

'But now?'

'I'm still comfortable with what I did. Mine wasn't the only life I saved. But meeting him again revived the memories . . . The ones we worked on.'

'Not very successfully, if I recall. You resisted my attempts to get you to face your demons. What's changed now? You know I almost told my assistant to turn you down.'

A surge of panic seized Antonia. He couldn't refuse her. 'I thought I could hide what happened in a compartment in my head, so I'd never need to look at it again, but I realise it was never going to work.'

'Because they've now come back?'

She took a deep breath to still her dread. 'Yes.'

'Did they come back straight away, or have they grown more intense?'

'The latter. I've experienced a couple of . . . incidents lately, which have added to my . . .' She wouldn't think of herself as traumatised.

'Okay, we can address those. What do you want our sessions to achieve?'

'A good night's sleep?' She gave a smile.

'You know how this works. You must be prepared to face the memories that are troubling you, not run away from them. Are you prepared to commit to seeing this through?'

The thought she'd run away didn't fit with her self-image, but that's what she'd done. And it had led her to where she was. 'I don't have a choice.'

He considered her reply and Antonia waited. Part of her wanted him to say no, but she had to do it.

He nodded. 'Let's get started then.'

What, now? She took a deep breath. 'Okay, I'm ready.'

Antonia outlined the incidents she wanted to address, starting with her mother's murder and finishing with John's. The worst, she'd already gone through with Haller, so thankfully she was able to skim over them. He filled his notebook in dense, spidery writing using a cheap plastic biro. When they'd finished, Antonia felt she'd had an intense workout and sat back in the chair, exhausted.

Haller studied her. 'Do you recall the exercises I gave you to deal with the panic attacks?'

'I'm using them, but they no longer help.'

'We'll take a few minutes to recap the techniques and I'll try some new ones.'

He took her through relaxation exercises he'd taught her eight years earlier. When they'd finished, he said, 'Don't forget, these techniques help you cope with the symptoms. They will not deal with the problems plaguing you.'

'I know.'

He retreated behind his desk and opened his laptop. 'I've got another session free at the same time next week. Shall I book you in?'

A week, is that all? Would she be ready? 'Yeah, thank you.'

He confirmed the appointment on his system. 'I know you're an adult, and more able to deal with setbacks, but it will be a challenging time for you and the fact you've already tried this and failed will make it that much harder.'

Antonia hoped she'd have the strength to go through with it. If not, what was her alternative?

◆ ◆ ◆

Antonia finished reading the early feedback from today's lead story. Few people had bothered commenting, suggesting the subject hadn't gripped them. The idea that modern slavery didn't shock or move people any more depressed her. She realised they needed a big story of high-profile corruption to get their teeth into. Did she spend too much energy on Reed-Mayhew? The early information she'd got on Ellaby Snowden through her contacts in financial services looked promising – he was mixed up in something big that involved a lot of money and high-profile politicians – but she'd come up against a brick wall. Chapman still hadn't got back to her with what he'd discovered about Snowden's business, and although he'd intimated he couldn't investigate it, he could have been in touch out of courtesy. She wasn't impressed.

Jean Sawyer knocked on the door. 'Coffee, Ms Conti?'

'Yes please, Jean.' She'd given up getting her to call her Antonia.

While she waited, Antonia rang Islington police station. The detectives investigating her attack still hadn't contacted her. She wondered if they'd dropped the investigation. Tomasz Zabo had lost his left leg but would survive. Had they moved the case down the list as a result? To her surprise, one of the detectives came on the line.

'Hello, Ms Conti. We were just talking about you.'

'Have you got any news?'

'Sort of. The fingerprint analysis on the backpack's come through—'

'Have you identified someone?' They didn't sound too certain.

'That's the problem. Obviously, most are yours, but we've found some from one or more unknown persons, probably male. It will confirm we've got the right person once we get a suspect, but it doesn't take us further forward.'

Her excitement ebbed. 'Do you have any other leads?'

The detective hesitated. 'A few, but nothing solid.'

'I can still produce Replicants of the men I saw in the pub, and one of the bar staff says she recalls them clearly.' Six months earlier, she'd used the Replicant software to produce a 3D likeness of a man who'd attacked her.

'As I explained, because you didn't see him when he attacked you, we can't use it—'

'Not even to find him and check his fingerprints?'

'I'm sorry, Ms Conti. But believe me, it's great we've got a fingerprint to check.'

She ended the call as Sawyer came in with a coffee. The large sheet of paper Antonia used to plot connections when working on a story covered most of her desk. However big a screen she used, paper still gave her a better overview.

'Hang on, I'll move it.'

Sawyer placed the coffee on the cleared space. 'What's this?'

'It's a cross between a Spider Diagram and a Mind Map. I use it when I'm working on a story.'

Sawyer pointed to the name at the centre. 'Ellaby Snowden. The gentleman who shot himself in his panic room last week?'

'Yes.'

She studied it for a few moments. Antonia had become more tolerant of her once she'd got accustomed to her unconventional ways.

'It says "Allies" in this one.' Sawyer pointed to an oval above his name with a network of lines leading to more name-filled ovals.

'They're people he has, or had, good relations with. Friends, business partners and so on.'

'And this one?' Sawyer pointed to the oval with 'Enemies?' in it.

'Those are people who *might* want to harm him. I'm not certain about them, hence the question mark.'

'You've got three against this name.' Sawyer pointed to an oval connected to 'Enemies' with a trio of question marks after the name in it.

'I'm almost certain he's not relevant, but I'll keep him there until I'm sure.'

'Are we doing an article about him?' She fixed Antonia with her steady gaze.

'I'm not sure yet. He's potentially interesting, but we may find nothing worth investigating.'

'These contain what you know about him?' She pointed at rough circles full of Antonia's dense writing. 'And these empty bubbles?'

'That's what we don't know.'

'Hmm, fascinating.' Jean stared at the diagram for a minute before leaving.

Antonia folded it and put it away. She'd just finished her coffee when Sabirah arrived, a nervous Nadimah behind her.

'Are you still going to the gym?' Sabirah said.

'Of course. It will be fun, won't it, Nadimah?'

She gave an uncertain nod.

Antonia stood. 'I'm sure you'll love it. And if you don't, that's okay, you don't have to do anything you don't want. And as I promised, we'll go for a pizza afterwards.'

Nadimah brightened and Antonia collected her new backpack containing her training kit and set off for the gym with Nadimah in tow. The girl relaxed during the walk, telling Antonia about the bullying she'd experienced. Antonia had learned how to deal with bullies the hard way, after enduring a year of torment at the children's home when she'd been Nadimah's age.

'Are we going in there?' Nadimah asked, pointing to the unprepossessing industrial unit with the sign 'Boxing and martial arts' on a weathered board above the double doors.

'It doesn't look much, but it's the best gym in London and the people are great.' And one place Antonia felt completely safe, but what if Nadimah hated it? Antonia suddenly felt nervous. 'I've asked Milo to take care of you. He seems really scary, but he's a sweetie. I call him Tweedledum and his twin Tweedledee.'

Nadimah laughed.

'If you can't tell them apart, check his left ear, there's a bit missing.'

'What happened?'

'He says a lion tore it off when he was a kid, but he's from Bermondsey, so I think he made it up.'

She punched the keycode into the lock and led the way in. The changing room smelled of shampoo and mould. Few women used the gym, so Antonia rarely shared it with someone else. She waited to change her top until Nadimah went to the loo so she wouldn't see the scars on Antonia's back.

Once changed, she led her to the entrance of the main gym area. A full-size ring occupied one corner and bags of all shapes and sizes hung opposite. An aerobic zone, containing a variety of machines, and a weights section filled the other two corners of the vast space. The sounds of metal weights clanking, punches landing on leather and explosive breathing overlaid the background driving beat of the music Milo preferred. Other members paused in their training to greet Antonia, wondering who she'd brought with her. Nadimah stared, mouth open.

A gigantic figure stopped pummelling a heavy bag and made his way to them. Sweat glistened on his shaved head, which resembled a huge black cannonball. His T-shirt strained to contain his massive torso and, although taller than Antonia, he appeared short.

'Is this Nadimah?' He pulled the bag mitt off his right hand and held out an enormous paw, made bigger by layers of bandages.

Nadimah gulped.

Antonia bent down and whispered. 'Tweedledum.'

With a grin, Nadimah clasped the hand in both hers.

'Okay, young lady, I'm going to take you through the basics while my brother sees if he can get Antonia here to regain some of the speed she's lost in the last few weeks.'

'I've a session planned.'

Milo shouted, 'DARIUS!'

His twin appeared in the doorway to the smaller room, nick-named the 'torture chamber'. 'Okay, Ant, you're late. Get in here. I've got the perfect circuit set up for you.'

'I'm going to do some weights and a bit of bag work.'

'No more weights until after your fight. Now come on, the clock's ticking.' He gave a scowl, which would have terrified anyone who didn't know him.

Antonia didn't want to abandon Nadimah, but she heard giggles as the girl tried on some gloves as big as her head. An hour later, she staggered out of the torture chamber, her legs like rubber and lungs burning.

A cry of 'Antonia, over here' greeted her and Nadimah executed a perfect left-right-left combination on a floor-to-ceiling ball before looking at her with a big grin.

Despite her arms feeling like concrete lumps, the relief at seeing Nadimah so clearly enjoying herself made her punch the air. 'Brilliant.'

'She's a natural,' Milo said. 'Far better than you were during your first session.'

Antonia remembered herself as a gangly teenager, all uncoordinated arms and legs. It had taken her months to achieve the same level of proficiency. She thanked Milo.

'My pleasure, she's a great kid.'

The goodbyes of the others in the gym accompanied them as they left. Nadimah was still bubbling with enthusiasm and excitement when they arrived at the restaurant in Covent Garden for the promised pizza. As they waited for their order to arrive, Nadimah's grin faded.

'There's a man looking at us.'

Checking out the rest of the room, Antonia found Chapman standing in the doorway, a young woman at his side. Abby, his daughter, she guessed. She was almost the same height as her dad.

Antonia waved them over. 'Do you want to join us?'

Chapman checked with Abby, who nodded.

'Nadimah, this is Abby and her dad, my friend Russell. You met him a while ago.' It had been a traumatic time for Nadimah and her brother, and Antonia wasn't sure if she'd suppressed the memory.

'You bought me and Hakim a pizza,' she said. 'But you were fatter.'

Abby laughed and Chapman reddened before recovering. The two girls soon fell into deep conversation. Antonia reminded herself that despite the size disparity, they were the same age.

'How come you didn't return my calls?' she asked him.

'What's happening with Islington? I've not checked up how it's going.'

'Not great.' She updated him.

'Hmmm. I'll give their boss another bell.'

'You still haven't said why you ignored me.'

'I wasn't in a good place. They'd suspended me and I felt sorry for myself.'

Antonia felt hurt he'd not told her, but he wasn't any more of a 'sharer' than she was and had probably told nobody. 'What happened?'

She listened in silence until he'd finished. 'Any idea who's behind launching the phony disciplinary process against you?'

'Not a clue. How's your investigation into Snowden going?'

'There's not much information about him. I found out he went to school with Reed Mayhew—'

'That guy again. Don't you think you're a bit obsessed?'

'I thought you might say that.'

'They all went to the same few schools.'

He was probably right, which was why she'd not followed up the discovery. 'He was involved in raising a lot of money and I think he was planning to bid for government contracts.'

'Really? His wife said something about a big project that would make them extremely rich.'

'That sounds like a government contract, he's donated to a few politicians. But I thought your mate Harding was investigating him.'

Chapman glared, then realised she was teasing him. 'The rumour is, Financial Crimes are investigating Snowden for money laundering.'

'He wouldn't come anywhere near a government contract with that hanging over him—'

'Well, duh!' He winked at her.

'Oh, right.' She knew a few businessmen who weren't above sabotaging a potential rival. The mere fact he was being investigated would scupper his chances. 'Do you have any more on that? It could point us to who had it in for him.'

Chapman glanced at the two girls. 'I'll pop round tomorrow, if that's okay.'

'Thanks, I'll look forward to it.'

They finished eating and, with promises for the girls to meet up again soon, parted. Despite the hour, the streets still thronged.

As they walked to the tube, Nadimah said, 'Abby said she doesn't live with her dad.'

'Yes, it's all too common.' Antonia wondered where her own dad was, or even if he was still alive. She'd got as far as tracing his family to Palermo but had chickened out. Maybe she'd go back to it one of these days. They waited to cross the road.

'Antonia, there's another man looking at us.' Nadimah's voice rose.

Years of checking over her shoulder had made the girl hyper-sensitive. Antonia knew the sensation, and suspected it was just a creep ogling them. 'Where is he?'

'He's in that doorway.'

Antonia followed Nadimah's finger to a man examining the window display beside the door of an electronic cigarette shop. She recognised something familiar about him. His body language told her he knew she'd seen him. Antonia took two steps closer. He spun away, but she saw enough to recognise one of the men from the pub. He ran.

Two police Security Auxiliaries ambled towards them from the opposite direction.

'Nadimah, go to them and tell them I'm chasing a thief.'

She ran before Nadimah could object. The man's bobbing head appeared fifty metres ahead and Antonia wove through the crowds, making her way after him along the wide pavement. She'd gone three hundred paces when the thought he was a decoy to get her away from Nadimah hit her like a slap.

'Blast!' She spun on her heel and ran back the way she'd come. She reached the spot she'd left Nadimah in full panic mode. When she could see neither Nadimah nor the two officers, her adrenaline spiked even further. She did a three-sixty, hoping to see the caps of the officers. Were *they* also decoys, collaborating with the man she'd chased?

A *Big Issue* seller approached. 'You after the girl you was with?'

'Where did she go?'

'A car stopped, and she got in it.'

Antonia's heart lurched. 'You saw her get in?' Nadimah wouldn't get in a stranger's car.

'Well, not as such. But when it drove off, she'd gone. I couldn't see her behind the two uniformed fatties.'

It wouldn't take much to overpower her. 'What kind of car?'

'White. Pale. Sorry, I don't know cars.' He showed a mouthful of yellowed stumps.

Not expecting a positive result, she asked, 'Did you get the number plate?'

'With these eyes? Sorry, luv.'

'What did the two police do?'

He sucked his teeth. 'They got on a bus and went that way.'

Antonia's gaze followed his finger, a sense of dread gripping her.

CHAPTER 13

Chapman's phone rang, and taking it off speaker, he held it to his ear.

'Russell, where are you? Someone has snatched Nadimah—'

'Calm down—'

'Don't tell me to calm down. I'm going to ring—'

'She's with me.'

'What? Why?'

'Let's not do this over the phone. Cross the road. I'm just down the lane which leads to the church. I've got my hazards on.'

He got out and watched as Antonia ran across the main road, not waiting for a gap in the traffic.

She strode up to him, finger jabbing. 'What are you playing at? I've been frantic.'

'You abandoned her.'

'I did not. I left her with two police—'

'You left her with two people you didn't know. They're not even real police. They work for a private company that recruits anyone with all their limbs and who enjoys wearing a uniform.'

'I saw one of the men who attacked me and nearly killed Tomasz.'

'Maybe you were supposed to see him and go haring off. Did you think of that?'

Her anger faded and the tips of her ears grew darker. 'Yes, which is why I rushed back.'

'When you're responsible for a child, you can't just leave them.'

'I know,' she whispered.

'Come on, get in. Or do you still not want a lift?'

She shuffled towards the car. Abby had got in the back, so Antonia headed for the passenger seat.

He followed close behind, worried he'd maybe laid it on with a trowel. 'If you want to make a complaint now, you could persuade the two clowns at Islington to let you produce a Replicant.'

She stopped and turned. 'Seriously?'

'The guy is obviously stalking you. You saw him clearly, did you?'

'Yes.'

'Ring them in the morning.' He suspected they'd try to fob her off, but he'd see what he could do.

She hugged him. 'Thanks, Russell.' Then, leaving him paralysed, she got into the car.

His face hot, he composed himself and strolled to the driver's door. Antonia was apologising to Nadimah when he got in.

'Have you seen this, Dad?' Abby passed him her phone.

He put the overhead light on and examined it. This wasn't Abby's phone. He'd just forked out for the latest model for her as an early Christmas present. The screen showed a blurred image at the end of a short video. He replayed it. Antonia's shoulder blocked the left edge of the screen, but the rest showed a gloomy shop doorway. A man stood with his back to the camera. Then Antonia moved forward. The man stumbled out of the doorway and ran. As he did so, he appeared in three-quarter profile. Chapman paused the footage. 'Who's this?'

'The man Nadimah saw.'

Chapman twisted in his seat. 'Did you take this just now?'

165

Nadimah kept her gaze on the back of the seat, biting her lip, and nodded.

'Well done.' He turned the screen to Antonia. 'That him?'

'Yes.'

'Great, we'll put him through the system in the morning.'

'Why not now?'

'We've got to take these two young ladies to their mothers, and we can't just barge into work in the middle of the night. I'll deal with it in the morning. Abby, can you send the video to my phone?'

They dropped Nadimah off first. Antonia got out, reassuring him she'd make her way home alone. He was already late so didn't argue. The last thing he needed now was a row with his ex about getting their daughter home late on a school night. She wasn't above making a mess of his plans for seeing Abby over the Christmas holidays. He dropped his daughter off without incident and made his way home. He turned up the volume of his police radio.

The almost constant chatter told of a busy night. Then a series of messages for a major incident on the other side of the city filled the airways until they changed channels. Glad he wasn't on duty, he continued on his way. Straight away, a call went out for officers to respond to the sighting of a body, a potential suicide. The address sparked a memory. Chapman pulled over and retrieved his phone. There, amongst the images of the documents he'd copied from Snowden's desk, he found the address. It must be linked.

He picked up the handset. 'DI Chapman here, I'm not on duty, but I'm five minutes away.'

The operator didn't respond immediately. Chapman decided to go, even if they didn't want him, but then the relieved-sounding operator accepted his offer. He pulled out into the traffic and focused on what he might find, needing to get his incident head on, smartish. He put on the blue lights but didn't need his siren.

A patrol car with an illuminated light bar identified the site of the incident. The two officers had stopped the traffic and cordoned off a black Range Rover parked to one side, but something looked odd about it. Was the body in the car? By the time he'd manoeuvred past the stationary cars and parked, he could see the body. Whether by design or accident, the victim had landed squarely on top of the SUV. The roof of the car sat a good twenty centimetres lower than normal, the windscreen and side windows shattered. Broken glass covered the roadway and pavement.

He retrieved some disposable gloves, locked his car and studied the building. Shops at ground level and offices above. Blinds fluttered from a window about twenty floors up. *Jesus!*

He approached, taking his time to take in the incident. The cordoned area included the extent of the blood spatter. A constable intercepted him and he introduced himself. She didn't hide her relief.

'Do we have any ID for the victim?' Now he'd come closer, the stench of faeces hit him.

'There might be in his jacket, but . . .' She gestured at the broken body.

He didn't blame her; he didn't fancy rummaging around in the victim's clothing. He didn't need to get any closer to identify the expensive watch on the wrist that hung down the side of the car. An elegant shoe sat on the damaged bonnet, confirming that whoever this was, it wasn't a cleaner.

'Who have you called out?'

'Nobody yet, boss. An ambulance is coming . . .'

A siren confirmed it had almost arrived. 'We need body recovery and CrimTech. Get them out and I'll see what we've got up there. I'll want them to come up, so I'll let you know where to send them.'

A uniformed security guard loitered in a gap between two shops. Behind him, two glass doors sat in the middle of a plate glass wall ten metres wide. Beyond it, a well-lit reception area with seating and a desk on one side. Two brushed steel lift doors faced the entrance.

Chapman showed his warrant card and introduced himself. The guard studied his identification.

'I need to examine the office the man came from.' Chapman indicated the body. 'Shall we go inside?' A series of brass plates beside the right-hand lift listed the names of the occupants. 'It looks like he came from about the twentieth floor. Do you know who's in the building?'

'Only came on at nine, but I can check which floors are still occupied. We arm the alarm system when they're unoccupied.' He went behind a high reception desk and stabbed at a keyboard. 'There's nobody above the thirteenth until you get to the twenty-second, there's someone in Blackthorn Capital.'

The confirmation that he'd guessed right sent a frisson of excitement through Chapman. 'Right, we're getting somewhere. How do I get into the offices up there?'

'I'll see if the cleaners are still up there.' He picked up a phone, mumbled into it, and two minutes later, the lift pinged.

A middle-aged man with cropped grey hair, a military air and wearing smartly pressed overalls came out. After being briefed by the security guard, he escorted Chapman up to the twenty-second floor, let him into the offices using a key card on a lanyard round his neck and after giving Chapman instructions on how to contact the front desk, left him to it.

Chapman put disposable gloves on and pushed the door shut behind him. The lights had come on when they'd opened the door and he examined an opulent reception area. The name Blackthorn Capital in large chrome letters dominated the room. Cameras

168

followed him as he headed towards a pair of doors facing him. They'd have to get the footage from those. A long corridor stretched ahead, with half a dozen doors on each side. It didn't take him long to find the room he wanted. The name tag on the door read 'Aaron Futcher'.

The temperature dropped significantly as he walked in. A large window had most of the glass missing, a few jagged pieces stuck in the frame. It would have taken a lot to break the triple-glazed window. A wooden oar lay on the carpet below the window. 'What the hell?'

He glanced round the room. Above the huge desk, which faced the windows, was an empty display cabinet about four metres long. The inscription underneath read 'Oxford 2000'. Photos in dark wood frames scattered around the room showed teams of rowers in various poses.

He made his careful way towards the window. Broken glass lay on the carpet. Pieces stuck out of the frame like teeth; as he got closer, he could see blood on some of them. He took out his phone and rang down to the officers guarding the body, telling them to send the CrimTech team to the twenty-second floor.

While he waited, he checked the office. A Port Charlotte whisky bottle stood by an empty crystal glass on the desk. Chapman checked the level. Half empty. Next to it lay a leather-bound diary, and he flicked through it. He found the name he was looking for: Ellaby Snowden.

Antonia yawned as she waited for her computer to open the pages of the news agency they subscribed to. She'd slept badly again. She didn't recall most of the dreams that had disturbed her, except for the familiar one of John, accusing her of causing his death. Haller had warned her his sessions weren't a quick fix.

She tried to ignore the memory and scrolled through the news headlines, checking them for stories she needed to follow up. The main one concerned a dramatic prison break by a crime kingpin, but his helicopter had crashed into a row of houses, bursting into flames. She clicked on the story, certain it would be front page news on every outlet. The site listed the publications that reported on each story, showing the prominence and space they gave it.

The suicide of Aaron Futcher, described as a financier, piqued her interest. She'd read about him recently, but the fog inhabiting her brain stopped her remembering where. As she scrolled down, the name of the investigating officer made her pause. Chapman hadn't been on duty last night. She checked the time; still too early to ring him.

She decided to continue digging into Snowden's story. Was that where she'd read about Futcher? An internet search for both names brought up thousands of hits. She focused on the images. One drew her attention: a group of youths in a sports uniform and standing behind a long, narrow boat. The name of the school stopped her. The fact Reed-Mayhew had gone to school with both men *couldn't* be a coincidence. But she was sure there was another link between the two men.

Energised by the discovery, she got another coffee and took out her Spider Diagram for Snowden. She drew a new oval and wrote, 'Being investigated by Financial Crimes team headed by Superintendent Ian Harding.' She drew a line from it to the one headed 'Government contracts' and added a new name: Aaron Futcher. She'd just finished when she heard movement outside.

'Miles?'

'No, it's me.' Jean Sawyer appeared in her doorway.

'You're early.'

'I wanted a word in private.'

Had she found another job? 'Come in, close the door.' Part of Antonia wouldn't have minded Sawyer leaving, but she didn't want the hassle of having to recruit another PA.

Sawyer sat in the visitor's chair and rested a folder on her lap. 'I've done a bit of moonlighting.' She pulled a sheaf of papers out of the folder and handed them to Antonia.

The top sheet showed a letterhead from the Inland Revenue addressed to Ellaby Snowden. 'What's this?'

'It's a letter from the Inland—'

'I can see, but why have you got it?'

'I accessed Mr Snowden's computer and you can complete your diagram now.'

'How? You know they can trace it back to you. You didn't do it from here?' She imagined them not only losing their licence, but being arrested.

'Oh no. I used a VPN—'

'They can still find you.'

'Not with the ones I use. Anyway, I logged into the Wi-Fi at a shopping centre a few miles from home and sent the signal round at least seventeen servers all over the world.' Sawyer looked pleased with herself. 'I've done this before, you know.'

Antonia studied her assistant with renewed interest. 'You clearly have. Why?'

'An awkward dumpy girl with a fascination for mathematics didn't make many friends at my school. Online, I could be who I wanted to be, and you get to know such interesting people.'

'I'll bear that in mind.' Having an in-house cyber expert could be useful.

'Shall I leave those with you then?'

'I still can't use them.'

Sawyer pouted. 'Why not? You've used whistle-blowers before.'

'But they've given me information obtained legally, through their work. You've hacked someone's computer. It's like breaking into somebody's house and stealing.'

'It's more like walking in through an open door. He'd not even used basic—'

'The fact a house is easy to break into isn't a defence. We must be careful how we get our information. There are some grey areas, but having our employees hack people's computers, especially someone who's just died, is not one of them. The way you did it shows you knew it was wrong.'

Sawyer replaced the papers in the folder but paused at the door. 'Why can't you use this information to tell you where to investigate?'

'What do you mean?'

'You think he was breaking the law, but you're not sure how. If you read these, you will know, and decide where to focus your investigation.'

Antonia recalled using a similar argument with her predecessor. 'Leave them here and I'll destroy them.'

With a conspiratorial grin, Sawyer put the papers on the desk. 'Another coffee?'

'Thanks.'

Antonia waited until she'd closed the door before removing the documents and skimming through them. Futcher's name jumped out and she focused on that page. He and Snowden were setting up a company with a high-powered board, including a former Home Secretary and several peers. The proposed balance sheet showed they'd have a huge war chest of several billion. This must be the company bidding for the government contracts, but for what exactly? The answer lay on the next page. They intended to bid for the new generation of prisons being planned by the government and it looked like they had a good chance of success. That would be a direct challenge to GRM and Reed-Mayhew.

Conflicting emotions gripped Antonia – excitement, tinged with disappointment she couldn't use these documents. Or could she? Despite what she'd told Sawyer, Antonia considered ways they could use the information without risking *The Investigator*'s licence. She quickly realised it wasn't possible, not without compromising her integrity. Maybe Chapman could suggest something when he came in.

Sawyer returned with the drink. 'I've been thinking. What if someone sent you these papers through the post? Anonymously. Someone who worked for Mr Snowden—'

'Just don't, Jean. And don't mention this to anyone else. Ever.'

Sawyer flinched, then, with a curt nod, scurried out.

Antonia finished reading the papers. Sawyer was right. These gave Antonia all the information she needed. If Reed-Mayhew knew what was here, he'd realise what a threat to his empire Snowden and his pals presented. It gave him all the motive he needed to get rid of them. But how do you get two men to kill themselves? Although it wouldn't be the first time he'd staged fake suicides. And what about the other people involved? Would these two deaths be enough to derail the new company?

She reread the papers, consigning as much as she could to memory and making cryptic notes on a pad. If anyone found these in their offices, they'd be in serious trouble. She fed them into her shredder, checking it had destroyed them. She still had a few sheets to go when a knock at her door made her jump.

Sawyer popped her head round the door. 'Ms Conti, you've got a visitor. Adam Sterling.'

It took a few seconds to place him, but then she felt a mixture of surprise and relief. 'Show him in.' She checked she'd placed the papers face down and stood. 'Adam.'

173

He took her hand in a firm grip. 'Hope you don't mind me popping in.'

'Of course not. Coffee?'

'Thanks.' He paused while she asked Sawyer to make it. 'I wasn't sure if I should come. I've had some hassle at work. Two Special Branch bods accused me of taking items from an incident.'

'John's car?'

'Yes. They interviewed me under caution.'

'Seriously. I'm so sorry. What did you say?' Had he admitted to them that he'd given her the memory stick? She couldn't expect him to lie to the police.

'I told them I didn't make a habit of taking items from burnt-out properties.'

'When did they question you?'

'Two days ago. I've been on nights, otherwise I'd have come earlier.'

'Did they say why they spoke to you a month after the incident?'

'New information, they said. They mentioned you, asked if I knew you.'

Sawyer brought in two coffees, giving Antonia time to think. 'What did you say?'

'I told them I'd met you when we rescued you and you invited me for a drink to thank me.' He flushed. 'I thought if someone saw me coming here, I needed an explanation. Hope you don't mind.'

'I should apologise. I got you involved.' Why would they resurrect this now? They'd killed the story. 'Do you think they believed you?'

'I can be pretty convincing.' He yawned and sipped his coffee.

'Late night?'

'Some idiot crashed his helicopter into a row of houses.'

'You went to *that*?'

'They posted me to Twickenham for the night and I expected a quiet shift but ended up on first attendance.'

'Can I interview you? You've not spoken to anyone else, have you?' This could be a good angle on a big story.

'I avoid the press. Had my fingers burnt. What would you want to ask me?'

'What you found when you got there, your impressions. Nothing to get you in trouble with the higher-ups.' Someone rang the front doorbell.

'I don't see a problem. When?'

'Now?' She retrieved her voice recorder. She needed to focus on the questions.

Raised voices, then a knock and Chapman walked in. 'Sorry, I didn't know you had a visitor.'

Behind him, Sawyer's expression of outrage confirmed his lie.

Antonia glanced at the papers still next to the shredder. 'Russell, meet Adam.'

'The water squirter?'

Adam rose. He stood a few inches taller than Chapman, who pulled his stomach in and puffed his chest out. Antonia stifled a grin.

'Glad to meet you, Russell.'

Chapman took his hand. 'Can we talk, Antonia? I don't have long.'

'I'll get going,' Adam said. 'Regarding the interview, shall I jot a few impressions down and email them to you?'

She expected a terse, jargon-ridden report. 'I might have follow-up questions.'

'No problem, bell me or we can meet up. I only live in Clerkenwell.'

She rose. 'I'll show you to the door.'

When she returned, Chapman sat in the chair Adam had vacated. 'What's he doing here?'

Although she and Chapman had ended up on the wrong side of the law together, she suspected he'd be less forgiving of Adam's indiscretion. 'He attended the helicopter crash. I thought we'd do a different angle to the others.'

His expression made his disapproval clear. 'How's Nadimah?'

'Great. Thanks for bigging her up about taking the video. How come you went to the suicide after you dropped us off?'

'Short-staffed. You know about the prison break? They'd set up a fake drug deal at the same time, supposedly involving the main crime syndicates in London. They dragged all the spare officers there, then the prison break happened and all hell broke loose. Someone's going to get their arse kicked.'

'Sounds like there's a story there.'

'Yeah, but I'm too far out of the loop and if you speak to anyone else, they'll deny it.'

'I'm more interested in the suicide. He—'

'So am I. I volunteered to go because I recognised the address from Snowden's papers. I found more documents in his office. His company, Blackthorn Capital, did business with Snowden.'

'Yes, they're mentioned—' She glanced at the papers near the shredder.

Chapman waited. 'Mentioned where?'

'I found out more about those government contracts. Snowden and Futcher are setting up a company to bid for prison contracts. Or were.'

Chapman whistled. 'Stepping on Reed-Mayhew's toes.'

'Now who's obsessed.'

'Ha, ha.'

'You agree Reed-Mayhew is mixed up in the two suicides?'

Chapman frowned. 'I wouldn't put it past that bastard to sabotage their bid, but get rid of both of them? I don't buy it.'

'You sure they were both suicides?'

'Snowden was locked in a panic room, and Futcher was the only one in his office. I've checked his CCTV, both the system in his office and the one covering the common areas. Nobody went in or out after he arrived at about eight.'

Antonia couldn't hide her disappointment. 'I was hoping there was a doubt.'

'I think it's more likely Reed-Mayhew instigated the money laundering investigation. Don't forget that Harding, the guy running it, is dodgy.'

'Would you be able to check if there's any substance to it?'

Chapman shook his head. 'Even if there wasn't bad blood between me and Harding, checking up on an ongoing investigation like that is a sure way to get into trouble.'

'But surely, if it's unfounded they'll have to drop it.'

'They'll do that after any contracts are awarded. They can drag it out, especially if they're waiting for information from foreign banks.'

Antonia realised he was right.

'Cheer up, we've got some good news. We've got a hit on the image Nadimah took.'

'Great, can we track him down?' She'd almost given up on catching the men behind what happened to Zabo.

'He's from Darlington – apparently well known to the lads up there. He acted as a freelance enforcer for local drug dealers.'

Antonia had no trouble believing it. 'What's he doing in London?'

Chapman looked uncomfortable. 'He should have been on remand for attempted murder, but the prison cocked up and they let him out by mistake.'

'Let me guess, a private prison.'

'Good guess. They run almost eighty per cent of prisons now.'

Antonia hadn't realised they'd expanded so far, and that was before they built these new ones. 'How come you didn't have his prints?'

'They cleared them off the system when they released him, another cock-up.' He cleared his throat. 'We found him on CCTV getting on a train to Darlington last night, not long after you saw him.'

'Can the local force pick him up? I'm assuming he's wanted for the attempted murder.'

'No need. They found him in a derelict house. A syringe in his arm.'

'I'm sure he wasn't a junkie.' Antonia put herself back in the pub. 'He resembled a bodybuilder.'

'The local lads think the gangs topped him because he'd become a liability.'

'Because I could identify him?'

'Yep. These guys are serious.' Chapman still seemed unhappy.

'I'd worked that out, but what aren't you telling me?'

'They found a phone. They've linked one of the numbers it called to the Albanian mafia. He rang it just before he attacked you, and again just after you chased him yesterday.'

Antonia's insides fluttered. Everyone knew about the Albanian mafia. 'Why would they be after me?'

'Have you investigated them?'

'No.'

'It doesn't matter. We're going to move you and Nadimah's family to a safe house. And the old lady – remember what happened last time.'

As if she could forget. 'I'm not hiding from anyone.'

'Antonia, these guys don't mess about. If you're a target, you need protection.'

CHAPTER 14

Chapman was still worrying about Antonia as he drove to visit Neil Griffin's mother. The memory of watching him fall off the roof still gave him nightmares. As he'd expected, he couldn't talk Antonia into moving, but after what happened to her predecessor Alan Turner when he'd taken refuge in a 'safe house' – one of his guards shot him – he didn't blame her. He hoped she was right and the Albanians would need a few days to find a replacement for the man they'd disposed of, and the one she'd damaged. He'd have to see if he could arrange something.

Ahead, his destination loomed, a drab seventies council block. He parked the car somewhere he hoped it would stay safe and got out. Why had Moira Griffin rung him? He suspected she wanted to discuss her son's treatment in prison. She'd mentioned her letter when she rang, although apart from checking he'd received it, she'd refused to discuss anything about it on the phone.

He climbed the external concrete staircase to the first-floor flat. Discarded nitrous oxide cannisters lay underfoot and the stench of skunk pervaded the atmosphere. Even the late afternoon sunshine couldn't disguise the dismal state of the building or lift his sense of despondency. He identified flat seven by the number inexpertly painted on the brickwork beside the door. A faint tinkle sounded in the distance when he pressed on the bellpush. Nothing happened for so long he reached for it again, but then he heard movement.

'Who is it?' a cracked voice demanded.

'Mrs Griffin? It's DI Chapman.'

Bolts scraped, a chain rattled and the door opened, releasing the sickly-sweet smell of vaping fumes. 'Mr Chapman, thank God! Please come in.'

Chapman tried to hide his shock. The tall glamorous blonde he'd met the first time he'd arrested her teenaged son had morphed into a haggard middle-aged woman, although she wasn't much over forty. Her velour tracksuit bottoms and bulky cardigan didn't disguise her thinness. Red rimmed her once vibrant blue eyes.

'Moira, good to see you.'

'Come in.' She stepped back from the opening. 'Excuse the mess.'

The odour of stale cooking joined that of the vaping liquid. A short hallway led to a living room with an aged sofa and mismatched armchair. Instead of an oversized screen, an untidy bookcase full of paperbacks dominated the cramped room. A vape kit lay on the coffee table next to a dirty mug and bowl containing a puddle of discoloured milk.

'Sit.' She pointed at the chair before scooping up the dirty crockery. 'Tea, coffee?'

He wasn't keen but recognised she needed a few moments to compose herself. 'Tea, please. Milk, no sugar.'

He undid the zip on his jacket, but it wasn't much warmer than outside, so leaving it on, he sat down. She returned with two mugs, placing one on the table in front of him.

'Hope it's okay, I don't have much milk.' Her hand shook, spilling some of the tan-coloured liquid.

He refused the offer of biscuits and waited for her to tell him what she'd summoned him to say.

She sat at the far end of the sofa, cupped her mug between both hands and stared into her tea as if reading his future. 'Neil's dead.'

'What?' They should have told him. 'When?'

'Yesterday morning.'

'What happened?'

'They say he died trying to escape, but he couldn't have. He was promised they'd let him out early, so why would he try—' She choked on her words and tears coursed down her lined cheeks.

Chapman waited for her to gather herself. 'Do you want to start from the beginning?'

'Sorry.' She sniffed, held the mug in one hand and produced a tissue from a pocket in her cardigan. 'After you helped get him off the roof, he was really grateful. I know he didn't say it, but he was.' She sipped her tea. 'Anyway, they put him back in Bradwell.'

'The new private prison?' The one that had released Antonia's attacker early.

'Took me all day to get there, arse end of nowhere. Really grim. You been there?'

'Nah, I hate prisons.' None more than those privatised monstrosities.

'I don't blame you.' She shuddered. 'Anyway, they told Neil he'd be kept there for the duration—'

'Wasn't he on remand?'

'He was out on licence, so instead of trying him for assaulting those coppers, they made him serve the rest of his sentence.'

And save money by not having a trial, and reduce the compensation they paid to the coppers. Bastards. Chapman gestured for her to continue.

'Neil hated it there, said the guards were sadists and at night they let the inmates run free. Him and his cellmate barricaded their door, but he said the guy disgusted him. I think he must have tried it on with him, but Neil wouldn't say.'

'Is that why he attempted to escape?' He remembered the lad's fear when the guards came for him with a stab of guilt. Could he have stopped them? But on what grounds?

'No! That's what *they* said. But he wasn't trying to escape.' Her violent gesture made the tea slop over the side of her mug, and she wiped it on her tracksuit bottoms. 'Sorry, but what they said didn't make sense. He agreed to let them do those experiments again, like I said in the letter.'

'Do you know exactly what those experiments were? You weren't too clear in the letter.'

'Sorry, he didn't really tell me much about it. He said they weren't supposed to discuss it, but I don't think he really remembered what they'd done.'

'You said it messed with his brain? What do you mean?'

'I told you he became aggressive, but he also forgot things.' The tears returned, running freely down her cheeks.

Chapman had witnessed the aggression. He'd also followed up the rumours Sanchez had heard, but nobody seemed to know anything definite, and several people suggested the prisons used electric shock therapy. 'What exactly happened?'

'He didn't remember stuff we did when he was a kid. When he said about how you'd arrested him, I mentioned the first time you'd caught him, but he couldn't remember it.'

'He probably wanted to forget it.'

'Nah. He always told it at family get-togethers, how you'd dragged him out of the slurry pit. It was funny, the way he told it.' She dabbed at her tears.

Chapman imagined he detected the stench of slurry, even ten years later. 'He didn't remember it at all?'

'Nope.'

Strange, but not something worth investigating, and Chapman wondered why she'd asked him to come. 'But you say he was having the treatment again?'

'Yeah. Well, I told him not to, but he reckoned they did it better now, so he let them, and they said he could come out early again. But I only seen him once since he started it, and it was awful.' She sobbed and wiped more tears. 'Sorry, Mr Chapman.'

Again, he waited for her to gather herself.

'He said he deserved to be there. He talked about killing kiddies and said what he'd done was unforgivable.'

'But until this last time, he'd never been violent.' Chapman forgave the time the lad had almost brained him with a walking stick; he'd been high on something.

'I know, but what he said he did was so horrible. He told me he picked kids up at funfairs, took them in his caravan.' She told Chapman what her son had claimed to have done to them. 'I felt sick when he told me.' She broke down, her sobs punctuated by shuddering breaths.

Chapman resisted the urge to put an arm round her to comfort her. A chill settled on him. Had he misread Griffin, taking him as a young lad who'd gone off the rails, when in fact he was something far worse? For something to do while she recovered, he sipped his tea. Full of sugar. He gagged. A vague memory of having heard of similar crimes nagged at him. He'd check the missing persons' files.

He waited until she'd recovered once again. 'Are you sure he did those things?'

'I don't know. He hasn't even got a caravan, but then I think, why would he make stuff up like that? He must have been sick. I told him he needed to tell you, then you could have got him treatment. I still get nightmares . . .'

Chapman hoped she didn't break down again. 'What do you want me to do, Moira?'

'Find out what happened?'

'I can't open an investigation without a good reason, it's not even my area.' Chapman couldn't recall if he knew any officers who covered that part of Essex.

'Can't you do a private investigation?'

'I'm sorry.'

'I've saved up some money.' She produced a screwed-up bundle of notes from her pocket.

He held up his hands. 'I can't take your money, Moira.'

She put the notes away and buried her face in her hands. 'I've let him down. I'm supposed to protect him, but now he's dead and I can't do anything.'

He imagined something happening to Abby and being unable to find out what had gone wrong. 'What did the prison tell you?'

She shot out of the room, returning a minute later with a plastic document sleeve. The email inside, from *Bradwell Prison Ltd (Part of the GRM Corrections family)*, informed Moira they'd found her son dead in the grounds of the prison. The circumstances of his death shocked Chapman, and he read it twice. That couldn't have happened. What the hell was going on at Bradwell?

◆　◆　◆

The second session with Haller ended. Antonia had found it difficult to speak about what really bothered her, and they'd spent the first half searching for a way to get started. The memory of such tough sessions from eight years earlier depressed her.

'Prof, is there a treatment where you can erase my memories?' She wanted to test what Fiona had told her, but she also wished she could do it.

'Not a treatment.'

Had Fiona lied or just exaggerated? 'So, it's not possible.'

'This isn't my area of expertise, but there is research into the way memory works which suggests we can manipulate memories. There are a lot of studies into this area and it's possible we might have a treatment, as you call it, in the not-too-distant future.'

'But no such cures available now?'

'The authorities haven't approved any yet. But the nature of research is such that people don't share their early results. I've heard that some clinics are involved in a controlled trial of a treatment which sounds like what you're describing, but I would imagine they've already selected their subjects. And it's experimental, very much at your risk.'

'What are the risks?'

'The potential risks would take too long to elucidate. I'm sure the clinics have a much better idea of the actual risks.'

'Do you know which clinics are doing this work?'

'I would strongly counsel against it. Anyway, the clinics involved are very expensive.'

'It's not for me. I'm working on a story.'

He studied her sceptically.

'Is everything I tell you covered by patient confidentiality?'

'Of course, provided you don't intend to put yourself or anyone else at risk, in which case I'm duty-bound to report it. It's not a sacred confessional, much as some people would like it to be.'

'Even if it's nothing to do with me?'

'Everything we discuss is about you.'

She couldn't imagine him betraying her confidences. He'd even rebuffed Eleanor's probing of her progress when Antonia came here as a teenager. 'I've heard there's a company erasing prisoners' memories, to "cure" them of their criminal behaviour.'

He considered this for several seconds. 'Gaining approval to use prisoners as guinea-pigs is almost impossible.'

'It's unofficial. Even the prisoners aren't told what's happening.'

His bushy grey eyebrows rose on his wide forehead. 'That's completely unethical and illegal. How do they get access to the prisoners?'

'The people doing it run the prison.'

'Ah.' He thought for a moment, then shook his head. 'It would make their job easier, I suppose.' He clasped his hands together. 'It's possible they can manipulate the prisoners' memories. But I'm not sure how effective erasing them would be. If you're investigating the prisons, why do you need to know about the clinics? As far as I know, *they* have approval for their work.'

'I'm speaking to a whistle-blower, and they tell me their company's carrying out legitimate tests, but a rogue employee has passed their techniques on to the prisons.'

'So, you want to check on the veracity of your informant.' He sat for several moments, then rose and opened his laptop. 'There are two clinics I've heard are trialling this treatment in London. I'll get their details.'

'Are they trustworthy?'

'What do you mean?' He studied her, suspicion blooming.

You idiot, Antonia. 'I meant, are they likely to be involved with the people experimenting on the prisoners?'

'Hmmm. I very much doubt it. They would have had to jump through several hoops to be accepted for the trial.'

'Oh, good, I can trust them then?' She held her breath.

He nodded and punched keys for a minute, then produced a notepad and pen. 'Here you are.' He scribbled on the pad, ripped off the top sheet and passed it to her. 'The top one is the most likely to be fruitful. Neither are cheap, but the other's very expensive and is frequented by the wealthy and, therefore, paranoid, so are unlikely to speak to you.'

'Thank you. You wouldn't know who's behind the research?'

'I'm sorry, my dear. It could be one of several people, and I'm not prepared to set someone like you on to them without good reason.'

She studied him, gauging his intention, and detected amusement.

'I have great admiration for your abilities and tenacity, Antonia. I wouldn't want you investigating me.' He returned his attention to the screen. 'Shall we see when you can return?'

'Yeah.' Antonia studied the paper he'd given her. Could one of these clinics erase her troublesome memories? No, she couldn't risk it.

◆ ◆ ◆

Despite the sunshine, Sabirah shivered while she waited on the pavement outside the house Mrs Curtis let her live in. She'd begun to think of it as her home, but that had changed over the last few weeks. Her stomach rumbled. She'd been too nervous to eat lunch or even much breakfast. She pulled at the hem of the nice dress she'd found in a local charity shop.

'Don't fuss, you look marvellous.' Mrs Curtis reached for Sabirah's hand and gave it a squeeze.

'Not too bright?' She'd loved the vibrant fabric, but the English didn't always appreciate colourful clothes.

'I wouldn't worry. It's perfect.'

A large top-of-the-range people-carrier approached.

Mrs Curtis studied it. 'Is that our lift?'

'I think so. Mr Al Rahman usually has a limousine, but this must be for you. I said you are in a wheelchair.' Although Al Rahman already seemed to know.

'You don't afford a limousine on legal aid.' Mrs Curtis still didn't trust Mr Al Rahman.

'He's Syrian, he wants to help.'

'I know, dear. Now let's see if they can fit my chair in.'

The car pulled alongside, and the back door opened before Sabirah reached it. A vision in a pink Chanel suit came out, enveloped in a cloud of expensive perfume.

'Mrs Juma, what are you doing here?'

'Rosemary, please. I wanted to support you on your big day.' Mrs Juma hugged her, then studied Mrs Curtis. 'Mrs Curtis, wonderful to meet you. Sabirah and the children have told me many good things about you.'

'Eleanor, please.' She looked annoyed but held out a hand, which Mrs Juma clasped.

The driver got out and retrieved a metal ramp from the boot. Mrs Curtis wheeled herself in, her electric motor straining. Sabirah followed her and sank into the leather upholstered seat. How had Rosemary Juma known Sabirah was appearing before the tribunal today? Too nervous to chat, she let the other two women talk. Despite Mrs Curtis's initial reaction, she seemed to get on with Rosemary Juma.

All too soon, the car stopped. Sabirah peered out, expecting to see Mr Al Rahman's office building. 'Why have we come straight to the court? Where is Mr Al Rahman?'

'He had another case. He's been here all morning. Don't worry.' Mrs Juma took her right hand in both of hers. They felt like silk, unlike her rough and cracked skin.

Sabirah wasn't ready. She'd expected to have the journey rehearsing her testimony with Mr Al Rahman. She followed Mrs Juma out on to the pavement while the driver retrieved the ramp. Mrs Juma produced a crystal-encrusted phone in a shade of pink matching her outfit, stepped away, and made a call as they waited for Mrs Curtis to join them.

She ended the call and put the phone away. 'Shall we go in?'

Sabirah kept step with the wheelchair as it ascended the ramp alongside the marble steps. Her legs seemed impossibly heavy. After going through a series of security checks they entered an expansive entrance hall. A marble staircase rose ahead of them, winding round a lift shaft containing three lifts. Two wide corridors led off left and right, teeming with people moving purposefully.

'There he is.' Mrs Juma waved at a figure down the right corridor and set off, her heels clicking on the marble.

They set off in pursuit. Mr Al Rahman spoke to a well-dressed man who shook his hand and strode away before they reached him.

'Sabirah, good to see you again. I presume you're Mrs Curtis, a pleasure to meet you.' He took her hand. 'Shall we go through your testimony? I've booked a room. We've got forty minutes. I'll only need twenty with you, and don't worry, Sabirah. We will have time to go through yours. Rosemary will take you for a coffee. Now, try to relax.'

Despite Mrs Juma's best attempts, Sabirah felt like a trapped bird as they sat in the café. Images of the nightmare camp they'd stayed in before crossing to Lesvos kept flashing before her. And then, when they thought they'd reached safety, an even worse place, populated with feral predators who preyed on their fellows. A surge of panic paralysed her.

'Sabirah. Come on, we must go. Please don't worry. Mr Al Rahman will win.'

Sabirah stumbled to her feet. Her coffee sat on the table, untouched. She followed Mrs Juma to the room on the floor above, and they waited outside. It opened to let Mrs Curtis out, laughing as she shared a joke with Mr Al Rahman. Sabirah went in and they reviewed the key points of her testimony. She'd been taking extra English lessons, even though her two jobs left her exhausted. She hoped her newfound proficiency didn't desert her, as it often did if she was stressed.

Mr Al Rahman's phone pinged. 'Time to go. Just remember what we said. Mrs Curtis will be excellent, and she will do you proud.'

They made their way to the tribunal room, Mr Al Rahman leading the wheelchair and Sabirah next. At the door, a steward only allowed Sabirah and her solicitor through. She looked at Mr Al Rahman in panic, but he reassured her.

Three people sat facing her, two women and a man. Mr Al Rahman introduced her, then told her to sit at a table facing the triumvirate before calling Mrs Curtis.

As she'd expected, Mrs Curtis gave a confident presentation. Sabirah, wrapped up in what she intended to say, only heard snatches, but the old lady made her sound like a saint before giving Sabirah an encouraging smile and being escorted out. Then it came to her turn. She teetered on unsteady legs.

The questions ran as Mr Al Rahman had outlined and by the time they finished, Sabirah felt almost sure they'd done it. Only one member of the tribunal hadn't asked a question. She did so now.

'Mrs Fadil, we've heard how you're holding down two jobs whilst improving your English, which although far from perfect, is better than some we hear.' The other two smirked. 'You're also providing a good home, albeit through the generosity of Mrs Curtis, to your children, who both seem to be doing well at school.' The woman, small and shrewlike with half-moon glasses perched on her narrow nose, glanced at something on the table in front of her. 'My concern is your attitude to this country.'

'I'm sorry, what do you mean?'

'Mrs Curtis is a prominent person, but has a history of attacking the government and our institutions.'

Sabirah looked at Mr Al Rahman, who avoided her gaze.

'We don't want someone like her to influence you. She's already corrupted another refugee, a young woman she adopted. What's to say she won't do the same to you?'

Mr Al Rahman spoke up. 'My client just wants to bring up her children in a peaceful, tolerant country. This other person was young and impressionable—'

'Like your client's children.'

Sabirah waited for him to speak. What could she say to defend Nadimah and Hakim? The words she needed flew her mind.

The three tribunal members put their heads together, muttering, then the man addressed her. 'Your solicitor persuaded us to overlook your incarceration, however, we can't ignore the possible negative influence of your landlady and sponsor. We need further reassurance—'

'I promise I will not—'

'Tell your client not to interrupt me.'

Mr Al Rahman looked annoyed. 'Mrs Fadil, please.'

'As I said, we will need further reports. Shall we reconvene in three weeks, just before Christmas?' He glanced at his two companions.

Shrew-Face and the other woman nodded.

'Three weeks, then. Social services will contact you. Make sure your client makes herself available—'

'What happens?' Sabirah said.

'You're this close to getting a deportation order.' Red-faced, he held his thumb and forefinger together. 'Your solicitor will explain to you. I assume he speaks your language.'

Mr Al Rahman gave her a warning glare, put his papers away and stalked out of the room. She followed, panic and fear consuming her.

CHAPTER 15

The information from Chapman about the involvement of the Albanian mafia in the attack on her gave Antonia a headache. She'd checked every story they'd covered during the six months since she'd become editor, and then searched another year back to check any she'd worked on as a reporter. Nothing linked to the Albanian mafia.

She checked the name of the man her attacker had phoned. Agron Lika. An Albanian who appeared a legitimate businessman, although Chapman assured her he belonged to their mafia. Had one of his business associates asked him for a favour to scare her off?

She started a Spider Diagram and filled in the information she found on the internet. She'd had to use specialist sites to get most of the details she needed.

Her email flashed up a new message from Adam.

Hi Antonia, I've written a few words. Let me know if you want to get together and tidy this up. Ax.

She read his account, clear and informative without using too much jargon, but it needed work to appeal to the general reader. She jotted down the questions she needed to ask to make the story clearer. Before she could respond, her mobile pinged with an incoming encrypted message. She opened the phone and read a message from Fiona.

I've got an update. Usual time and place?

Antonia checked the time. Two. She'd make it if she went straight there, but after her recent run-ins with the thugs on her tail, she intended to take a circuitous route. Add an hour? She typed and received a thumb emoji.

She snatched up her backpack. Adam's email sat on the screen. She should reply, but didn't want to rush and would deal with it when she got back. She buzzed Sawyer and slid the SIM card out of her phone.

Sawyer came in, her tablet at the ready. 'Yes, Ms Conti?'

'Jean, I'm going out.' She picked up the Spider Diagram. 'Can you fill in as much of this as possible?'

Sawyer's face lit up. 'It will be my pleasure. And don't worry, I'll confine myself to legal sources.'

Antonia hesitated. Finding out Lika's movements could save her life. 'It's not for a story, so we don't have to . . . restrict ourselves.'

'Oh?'

'This Agron Lika orchestrated an attack on me and a colleague which put him in hospital.'

'I understand.' Was that a mischievous glint in her eye?

Antonia had her reversible coat, black on one side but powder blue on the other. She put it on, blue side out. Anyone watching out for it would easily miss the black version. She stuffed a baseball cap in her bag for another change of appearance, although now her hair had grown back, she'd need to adjust it.

Two hours later, she entered the restaurant where she'd met Fiona a week ago.

Fiona sat nursing a cup at a table in the far corner and when Antonia joined her, surprised her by giving her a hug.

Once they'd ordered, Antonia said, 'You're going to get me the information about what they're doing to the prisoners?'

'Nobody else will do it.' She gave a self-deprecating smile.

'Have you got anywhere?'

'I spoke to the head technician at GRM the day after we met. I saw something was eating him and he let it slip they'd lost another prisoner.'

Why hadn't she heard anything? 'Do you know what happened?'

'He clammed up as soon as he realised he'd implicated himself. I offered to help them reverse the harmful effects of their treatment. I saw how much that appealed, but I didn't push. Just hinted I needed money because of a personal indiscretion.'

'Clever. Then what happened?'

Antonia's drink and their cakes arrived.

Fiona watched the waitress leave. 'He left it three days, then asked to meet. He had a "proposition" for me, pretended to be offhand about it. Not very successfully.'

'How did the meeting go?'

'He talked round the subject, but was obviously keen to broach it. I let him blather on for half an hour, then put him out of his misery. Honestly, these guys think they're so clever but they're completely transparent.' She jabbed at her carrot cake with a fork. 'He offered me a chunk of money to help them. And I mean, a lot.' Her eyes sparkled.

Could they follow a trail? 'How are you getting paid?'

Fiona swallowed. 'Cash. Cold hard cash.'

'It's harder to trace, but not impossible. If you give us a date and tell us how much, each time they pay—'

'Why? I'm keeping it. I'm the one risking my neck and doing the work.'

'You're welcome to it. But if we can put in dates and amounts, it strengthens our story, even if we can't match them to their accounts.'

'Oh, okay. Anyway, they've paid me the first instalment for two days' work.' She leant forward and whispered, 'Twenty-five K.'

'Wow, when do you start?'

'I can only do weekends and evenings. I'm going this Saturday, three days' time.'

'Do you think you'll have anything for me next week?'

'I doubt it.' Fiona focused on spearing the last piece of cake. 'It might take a few weeks.'

And a few payments of twenty-five K. 'What exactly will you do?'

'Will you include this information in your article?'

'I won't put anything in the article that can come back to you, but I need to understand what's involved. I have done this before.'

'Of course. I don't want to disclose too much about our techniques. But I'm happy to discuss it in general terms. Take, for example, the man I told you about last week.'

'The killer?'

'Yeah. I'd have to find out about the memories they'd destroyed and try to replicate them.'

'How do you do that? You can't ask him.'

'Unfortunately not, but although they didn't do a brilliant job, the technicians produced reports. There's also information from personal records, friends and relatives and, if by any chance they've had therapy, there will be notes.'

'Aren't they confidential?' The thought of anyone accessing the records of her therapy horrified Antonia.

'Of course, but they're my patients, and I'll use the information to treat them, so there are no ethical dilemmas. I'll then use the data I've gathered to construct a duplicate set of memories, or at least near enough to undo the damage.'

'It sounds like a lot of work. How many patients did they want you to treat?'

'He said four, but those are just the ones who've presented with problems so far. There may be others.'

'How many prisoners have they experimented on?'

'He wouldn't tell me, but I'm sure I can find out for you. I get the impression, up to fifty.'

Antonia whistled. *How many names were on the damaged part of the memory stick?* 'Are they still doing it?'

'I doubt it. He seemed pretty shaken up by the latest incident.'

'If your therapy's so dangerous, how do you persuade people to undertake it?'

'It's not dangerous.' Fiona's pale blue eyes darkened. 'The people using it don't understand it well enough. We've treated well over a hundred patients, with their full consent, and have had zero serious problems. Not one.'

Antonia held out her hands, palms forward. 'I wasn't having a go.'

'Sorry.' She gave a dazzling smile. 'It's just what they've done makes me so angry.'

'I understand. How do *you* find your patients?'

'They're mostly people we're already treating. If they're suitable, we explain the treatment and ask them if they're interested. They're given the full facts and give consent at each stage. We don't remove a memory without having a record of it—'

'Like a recording of what happened?'

'Not quite. It's not a record of what actually happened, but of your recollection, which, as you know, is often vastly different.'

'You said "mostly". Do you get some subjects from elsewhere? Could someone volunteer to take part in the trial without undergoing therapy?'

'No. They need to undergo therapy so we can determine if they're a suitable subject.'

'What about people who have memories they've suppressed and want to remove them without reliving them?'

Fiona studied her. 'We run a programme where you undergo intense sessions of therapy and then get the treatment. It's controversial because it doesn't give you time to process what you're dealing with, but it's more of a data collection exercise, and it's in-house, so we monitor you twenty-four seven. It takes a few days, but once you get treated, the memories disappear, so you only endure them for a short period.'

The thought of never reliving what Mishkin had done to her, or even forgetting what had happened to John, appealed. 'Would . . . Could I volunteer?'

'I might as well give you my name and employer's address.'

'If I wanted to find out who you are, how difficult do you think it would be to do so? I know what you do. How many organisations do what yours does? Or I could just have you followed.'

Fiona glared at her. 'Have you?'

'I wouldn't want the responsibility of knowing.'

'But if I told you where I work, you'd soon discover my real name. And I don't want my colleagues to find out I've spoken to you. I'm doing it to help them, and me, of course, but it's not something I want them to know. I'm sure you understand.'

Antonia swallowed her disappointment. 'Of course.'

Fiona picked up her cup and swilled the dregs as if searching for an answer. 'There is a possibility.'

'Yes?'

'What sort of memories do you want to forget? No, don't tell me. I can probably guess.'

'If you can't help me . . .'

'We can't, but someone else may. We've enrolled a few private clinics to enable us to get a bigger sample for our trials.'

'Could I go to one of those?'

'They've already treated their patients and are now following them up, but I could ask if any of them will take on new subjects.' She lifted her eyes to Antonia's. 'It won't be cheap.'

'That's okay.' Apart from his house, Alan Turner had left Antonia money from a life insurance policy.

'Okay. I'll make discreet enquiries and contact you in the usual way.'

'Thank you.'

The waitress ambled over. 'We close in five minutes, ladies.'

Antonia checked the time. *Blast*. She should have got back to Adam. 'I've got to go. Thanks for everything.'

'A pleasure.' Fiona gave her another hug, longer than the first.

Unaccountably unsettled by this, Antonia rushed off. Although Fiona had promised nothing concrete, a sense of lightness accompanied her.

◆ ◆ ◆

The taxi stopped outside the pub in Clerkenwell where she'd agreed to meet Adam. The icy night air enveloped her as she got out and strode to the entrance.

A warm fug of beer fumes, garlic and ginger enveloped her as she left the chilly night behind and entered the pub. The murmur of voices and clink of glasses drowned the faint sound of the jukebox. She scanned the crowded room. Halfway along the long left-hand wall, Adam waved. She made her way over. Although it was busy, he'd snagged a good table. A half-empty pint glass sat in front of him. He wore a lumberjack shirt, open at the neck, with a black T-shirt underneath. A brown leather jacket hung off the back of a hook on the wall alongside the table.

'Sorry I'm late.'

He stood to greet her. 'No problem. Can I get you a drink while you settle in?'

By the time she'd removed her outer gear and sat down, he'd returned with her glass of red wine and a half of beer for himself. They studied each other.

'Cheers.' She clinked her glass against his. 'Sorry I didn't get back to you earlier, I had to . . . Something came up.'

'I'd have come to your office, or the pub near it. Saved you a trip here.'

After her last visit to their local, she didn't want to return. 'This is nice.' She studied the traditional décor, dark paint below a dado rail, pale embossed wallpaper above, with a scattering of etched mirrors and framed boxing posters around the walls. 'Is it your local?'

'It's one of a couple I visit. Food's good. It's Thai if you want to eat, and you get served fast, even if they're busy.'

'Shall we address the article before we eat?'

'Sure. Did you like the piece I sent?'

'It was great, I just wanted to clarify a couple of points which are probably obvious to you, but not so much to us laypeople.'

'Sure, whatever you need to ask.' He topped up his pint with the half.

After asking if she could record him, she retrieved her tablet and powered it up. 'You mentioned you'd experienced some unusual challenges that night. Can you give me a better picture of these?'

'We'd removed a couple of casualties from the helicopter when two large SUVs roared up and a load of heavies got out. I assumed they were the security detail for whichever celebrity was on board, but I've learned different since, and their behaviour makes more sense.'

'What did they do?'

'They tried to remove the casualties.'

'What did *you* do?'

'There were half a dozen of them, but I had some big lads and a couple of handy lasses on my crew. We told them to back off.'

'What about the police?'

'They came in just one car, and they were busy evacuating residents.'

'I heard the police had problems. They went on a wild goose chase.'

'That explains it. Anyway, the heavies got the message, especially when they saw the state of the casualties.'

'Were they bad?' John's missing skull flashed before her.

Adam checked nobody was in earshot, then leant towards her. 'You can't report this until the police have informed all the relatives, but nobody survived.'

'You're okay if I mention you had to put up with threats from the heavies?'

'More interference than threats.'

She'd think how to word it afterwards. 'The reports I saw said the helicopter had been used in a prison break. It also said they'd flown into some cables, which seems particularly unlucky. I appreciate you wouldn't carry out the investigation, but did anything suggest that's not what happened?'

'Although there weren't many police there, a team from Internal Security turned up pretty smartish and took the wreckage away almost before we'd removed the bodies.'

'Did you get an idea what the hurry was?'

He leaned closer, and she smelled his spicy aftershave. 'You definitely can't use this, but I'm pretty sure a surface-to-air missile brought the chopper down.'

'Pretty sure?' Wow. None of the reports she'd read mentioned this

'I saw a few in Iraq a while ago.'

'Were you in the Iraq war?'

'The first one.'

She realised she'd underestimated his age. 'Were you in the army?'

'Royal Marines.' He laughed. 'Don't mix them up. It would be like me calling you a gossip columnist.'

'Sorry.' Weren't they supposed to be especially tough? 'Did you tell the police?'

'The Internal Security guys, but it didn't surprise them, and they told me to keep my mouth shut.'

'Where would you get a missile in London?'

'Not too difficult, if you have the money. But you'd need time to get it, it won't be a last-minute purchase.'

'Someone who knew about the prison breakout?'

He nodded and took a sip of his beer.

'Who was in the helicopter?' The reports still hadn't said when she checked on her way here.

'I'm not sure, but the guy in the prison guard's uniform had a tattoo of a double-headed eagle on his forearm.'

'A prison guard?'

'Someone posing as one.'

Her cheeks grew warm. 'Of course. You seem to know a lot about these things.'

'Amazing what you learn in my job. You get to go places and see things most people aren't aware of.'

She tried to put this new information together. The double-headed eagle meant something. She retrieved her phone to open her browser, but she hadn't replaced the SIM card since meeting Fiona. She'd use the London Transport Wi-Fi, but she wasn't logging into the pub's.

'Albanian mafia,' Adam said in a low voice.

Her stomach did a flip, and she scanned the pub, then realised what he meant. The fake prison guard in the downed helicopter. 'You sure?' Her thoughts churned as she worked to piece the story together.

'You got any more questions for me, or shall we order? I need some scran.'

'Sorry, of course. I've got a couple more, but let's order first, my treat.' She waited for him to object.

'Okay.' He reached for the menus at the far end of the table, and they studied them in silence.

Was the prison break and the subsequent downing of the helicopter connected to what happened to her? She still hadn't found any links between *The Investigator* and the Albanian mafia that could account for Lika sending his men after her.

'You ready?'

'Oh, sorry.' She'd not taken in any of the menu. 'What do you recommend?'

'They do a nice shrimp panang, but I'm having a green curry.'

'Shall we have one of each and share?'

'Good idea. There's no table service, so I'll order because they know me. Give me your card if you're paying.'

While she waited, she focused on the additional questions she wanted to ask him.

He returned with a jug of water and two glasses. 'Ten minutes. Did you want another wine?'

'Water's fine.' She asked him her questions, then said, 'I don't want the Internal Security guys giving you any more grief, especially after the hassle you got about the memory stick. I'm going to mention someone saw a firework flying towards the aircraft before it crashed.' She waited for him to object.

'Okay. When will you get your story out there?'

'I'll go back to the office and post it tonight.' Another late night.

They made easy conversation and shared each other's food. Adam looked disappointed when she ate as much as he did, obviously hoping to get more than half, but she was starving.

As the waitress removed their empty dishes, Adam yawned. 'Sorry, I'm always like this after nights.'

He offered to walk her back to the office, insisting it wasn't much of a detour. Although she doubted Lika would have got his replacement team ready yet, she was glad of Adam's reassuring presence. The sky remained clear, and a half moon shone above the skyline. Frost coated the pavement, making it treacherous. They walked in silence, Adam tense. He kept checking behind them and his unease infected Antonia.

They crossed a narrow lane full of parked cars and he stared into it. A few paces later, they drew alongside a dark passageway between two buildings. He glanced back, then grabbed her arm and pulled her into the passage.

'What are you—'

He clamped a hand over her mouth. 'Shhh!'

Her surprise and shock wore off. She prepared to retaliate, but this didn't feel like an attack. What was he doing?

Then he whispered, 'Stay here,' and disappeared into the passageway.

She followed him, cautious until her vision grew accustomed. The passage joined another at right angles. She saw movement on her left, a figure in a brown jacket. Adam. He moved fast, back the way they'd come. Her foot slipped as she turned, but she steadied herself and ran past rows of bins and piles of plastic bags.

As she shot out of the alley into the narrow lane they'd just walked past, she saw a large SUV in a parking space. The back doors were open, and two figures grappled in the roadway. One landed a series of blows on the other, and his opponent fell.

Was it Adam who'd gone down? No, the man in the brown jacket still stood. The figure on the ground wore black. Another figure in black came round the back of the vehicle, fist raised.

She shouted a warning.

Adam blocked the blow. His assailant flew over him, legs and arms windmilling, and crashed on to the road. Adam dropped to his knee and landed a vicious punch to the man's head.

He turned to her and shouted, 'Stay where you are!'

Like hell I will. She ran towards them, her feet sliding on the icy tarmac.

The first man in black was back on his feet. As Adam focused on him, something moved in the shadows behind him. Another man. He raised his arm, and with it a weapon. She uttered a yell and launched herself at him, catching him at the top of his chest.

He staggered a couple of steps back and turned on her. The extendible cosh in his hand glinted. He swung it at her head, and she ducked. It whistled above her. She leapt in and punched him in the face before he swung it back. He swore, and she hit him again. Something cracked in her hand, and she gasped in pain.

Blood dripped down her attacker's cheek, but he raised his cosh. She retreated. He ran at her, and she sidestepped him and punched him with her left as he flew past. He lost his balance, and she attacked, catching his right shoulder with a heavy kick. The cosh clattered out of his hand.

Before she could press her attack, an engine roared. She glanced back. The SUV headed away down the narrow lane, one door still open, then it slammed shut. A body lay in the gutter behind it. She glanced at her assailant. The cosh lay where he'd dropped it, but he'd gone, limping towards a parked car. A door flew open, and he jumped in, then the car pulled out and surged past her, following the first.

With a sense of dread, she stepped towards the body in the gutter. She saw the brown jacket and ran to it.

CHAPTER 16

The ambulance wailed as it pulled out of the lane. A police car followed. More police vehicles filled the narrow lane and blue flashing lights reflected off the windows of the buildings lining it. Despite the cold and the hour, several residents had come out on to the pavement to gawp. Antonia shivered and examined her right hand in the light from a floodlight the crime scene investigators had set up. The swelling and pain told her she'd done some damage. Dried blood coated her knuckles.

'You cut yourself?' Adam said.

She hadn't broken her skin. 'It's from the man I punched.'

'They should get DNA from it. Get the crime scene guys to swab it.'

'I will. How are you feeling?' She leant in and examined the cut on his left cheek.

'A lot better than the guy who did this' – he indicated the cut – 'and his mate in the ambulance.'

When she'd reached the body in the gutter, she realised her mistake. She recognised the man whose knee she'd smashed three weeks earlier. Then, to her relief, an out-of-breath Adam had jogged back from the main road where he'd pursued the cars in a vain attempt to identify the number plates.

One of the crime scene technicians returned to their van and opened the back doors. Antonia flexed her hand, wincing as a sharp pain shot up her arm. 'I'll see if he can swab this now.'

Before she could, the senior police officer joined them and after greeting Adam by name, she became serious. 'The paramedics said he might not make it. What exactly happened?'

Antonia waited for Adam. They'd agreed he'd take the lead, but she hadn't realised the extent of the man's injuries. Would the fact the police officer knew Adam change how he responded?

Adam wasn't fazed. 'A guy I recognised stuck his head in the pub, saw us and went straight back out.'

'He recognise you?' the inspector said.

'He wasn't interested in me.'

Antonia shivered again, but not from the cold.

The policewoman focused her attention on Antonia until Adam continued.

'Someone was watching the doors and when we came out, they rushed off, coming this way.'

'They knew which way you were going?'

'Unless they made a lucky guess.'

The inspector checked if Adam was joking. 'Same guy?'

'I couldn't see. But I suspect so. We set off, and I waited for something to happen—'

'Why didn't you warn me?' Antonia said. 'I almost took you out when you dragged me into the alleyway.'

'Sorry, I wasn't sure they'd try anything, and didn't want you panicking—'

'I'm not a helpless damsel.'

'Yeah, I saw. Sorry.'

'And what *did* happen?' the inspector demanded.

'When we passed this lane, I saw him get into the driver's seat of an SUV. He wasn't alone. Then, when we walked past, one of them followed us. I knew where the passageway led, so I doubled back—'

'You told me to stay. If I'd been a helpless damsel and he'd come after us . . .'

'I gambled he wouldn't follow two of us on his own, especially when he realised I'd spotted him.'

'And what happened then?' The policewoman sounded impatient.

'He must have run back to their car. He'd reached it when I got there. We had a bit of a tussle and I put him down, then his mate joined in. Antonia shouted a warning, and I threw him. I hadn't realised they'd come in two cars so didn't see the third guy, but Antonia sorted him.' He nodded his thanks.

'What about the guy in the ambulance?'

Adam hesitated. He'd told her he pulled the door open and grabbed the guy's collar. He'd not been wearing a seatbelt and flew out, smashing his head on the kerb as he landed.

Adam held the inspector's gaze. 'The driver started forward and as the car swung out, the passenger threw open his door and leapt out at me. I got out of his way, and he hit his head. The other two jumped into the back and they drove off.'

She could sense his tension as the inspector considered his words, but the officer didn't seem to notice.

'You said you recognised the driver?'

'He used to work for a gangster in Essex—'

'Albanian?' Antonia said.

They both looked at her.

Adam said, 'No. Local guy, family from Georgia, but the driver was a South African.'

'How do you know *him*?' the officer asked.

'I interrupted his brother beating his girlfriend up in a car park.'

Not for the first time, Antonia reflected that Adam seemed to get involved with a lot of odd people.

The inspector grimaced. 'Charming, their parents must be proud. Can you remember his name?'

'Something like Meyer, ex-police or army back in SA. You've probably got him in your files.'

'Okay, we can check. You think he's still working for the guy in Essex.'

Antonia racked her memory. Who had they investigated from Essex?

Adam gave a rueful laugh. 'No chance. The guy . . . he disappeared, fifteen years ago.'

He was keeping something back. She'd ask him later.

The inspector addressed Antonia. 'Anything you'd like to add? Did you recognise the South African? You're not from South Africa, are you?'

'No, I'm not. And I didn't see him.'

'And you've no idea why he might be interested in you, apart from the obvious?'

Antonia shook her head.

The policewoman's radio crackled. 'Okay, Mr Sterling, we'll need a statement, and one from you as well, Ms Conti.'

'Sure. Can I get this swabbed? It's from the man who had the cosh.'

'That would be very useful.'

Antonia made her way to the crime scene van and after swabbing the blood, they let her wash her hands in a sink. She examined the swelling and hoped it wasn't too serious.

Adam and the policewoman remained together, their body language more intimate than before. The policewoman laughed and left to speak to a subordinate.

'You seemed to get on.'

'I went out with one of her colleagues a few years ago and met her at a do. She asked me if I remembered her.'

'Did you?'

'Of course. A gentleman always knows what to remember, *and* what to forget.'

'Do you think she believed what you told her about the guy in the ambulance?'

'Why wouldn't she? She wants to, so . . .'

'You mentioned the gangster from Essex. Is there any chance he might be back on the scene?'

His pupils darkened. 'If he is, he'll be the first since JC.'

'JC?'

'Didn't you go to Sunday school?'

For an instant Antonia could smell the incense and hear the sonorous voice of the bishop in St Therese Cathedral in Juba as they celebrated the canonisation of Josephine Bakhita. Her mother had been so proud that a woman with one Italian and one Sudanese parent, like Antonia, had achieved sainthood.

'Understood. Shall we give our statements? I'm shattered.'

She realised the affable firefighter wasn't someone to make an enemy of, and gave thanks he was on her side.

◆ ◆ ◆

Chapman walked out of Southminster station and scanned the small car park. He spotted Kirsten in a powder blue Q7, one of only three cars waiting. The engine roared into life and the car rolled towards him before stopping alongside. Chapman waved and reached for the passenger door. The odour of leather and polish pervaded the spotless interior.

'Russell, good to see you.' Chief Inspector Kirsten Ballard leant across and offered her left cheek for him to kiss.

Her blue-green eyes sparkled against her tanned skin and her black hair shone. They'd last seen each other when she'd been a young probationary constable and he, her sergeant. Their brief relationship had soon run its course, but they'd stayed friends until she transferred out of the Met to get promotion. Now in her mid-thirties, she'd reached the rank of chief inspector.

'The country air obviously agrees with you.' He fastened his seatbelt as the car surged forward.

She glanced across, smiling. 'You're looking well.'

'So are you.' He indicated the pips on her shoulder. 'How long you been a CI?'

'Three years. I'm about to get made up to super, but that's not common knowledge.'

'Congratulations.' To reach the rank so young suggested she'd get to the top, unless something derailed her progress.

'I'm amazed you haven't got there yet,' she said, 'but I hear you hit a couple of snags.'

'That's one way to describe it.' He'd been lucky to keep his job, dropping two ranks from DCI to sergeant. It had taken four years to get one of those back.

'You were unlucky. Everyone knew the bastard was on the take.'

'But only one person stupidly accused him without evidence.'

'I heard you rearranged his face.' She winked at him. 'Couldn't have happened to a nicer bloke. You know he tried it on with me? He grabbed my hand and stuck it down his trousers.'

'Did you report him?' Chapman would have landed a few more blows if he'd known.

'Yeah, right? Me, a probationer, and him a chief super. Get real.'

Some of his colleagues made Chapman ashamed.

The car left the outskirts of the small town and increased speed. Kirsten drove with an intense competence. Her unadorned left hand rested on the gear lever.

She noticed his attention. 'D. I. V. O. R. C. E,' she sang in a passable imitation of Tammy Wynette.

'Any kids?'

'You know what it's like for us girls. Kids or . . .' She tapped her rank markings with two fingers before glancing out of the side window, blinking. 'So why are you coming to visit a shithole like Bradwell on your day off?'

He'd given her an outline of the case but hadn't gone into the details over the phone. 'His mother's owed an explanation.'

'And you want to give her one?'

He laughed. 'I arrested the lad regularly since he was fourteen until five weeks ago. It's down to me and my team that he ended up here.'

'I read the report from our guys. There's a copy in there.' She tapped the glove compartment. 'You can read it, but it stays in the car. The inspector who conducted our investigation is very able. What makes you think there might be anything dodgy?'

Chapman hesitated. If Kirsten thought he intended to challenge the findings of her investigation team, she might just turn the car round and drop him at the station. He wanted to make sure his misgivings weren't unfounded. 'I don't, but I promised his mother I'd check. Thanks for taking the trouble.'

'You've changed. The Sergeant Chapman I worked with would have put her straight. You're getting soft in your old age.'

He recognised the catalyst for the change: the case he'd worked on with Antonia at the start of the year. Sent to arrest her for murder, he'd realised she wasn't the killer and joined forces with her to pursue a monster. Apart from being almost shot and beaten to death, he'd seen a different side of life, one that challenged his rigid views of right and wrong. 'It happens to all of us, Kirsten.'

He retrieved the report and read as they drove through the flat landscape, the only relief an occasional clapboard house. Up

212

ahead, a dark smudge appeared on the horizon. The ozone smell he associated with childhood holidays told him they were nearing the sea. As they got closer, the smudge separated into walls and towers. A six-metre-high concrete wall surrounded a group of nondescript buildings, the design of which hadn't troubled a talented architect. In the distance behind the building, dark clouds gathered over the sea.

'Lovely, isn't it?' Kirsten said, seeming to read his mood.

Remote cameras followed their progress and Chapman's despondency increased with every metre closer they got. She found a visitor's space in a large car park in front of the main entrance. Chapman stared at the prison through the windscreen for a few moments. A brick building, at least ten metres high but with no openings above ground floor, sat in a gap in the wall. Floodlights pointed outwards from beneath the eaves. The walls stretched away at least a hundred metres on each side. Concrete towers rose above the wall at regular intervals. As well as lights, these supported cameras.

He opened the door and inhaled the dank atmosphere. Shivering, he fastened his jacket. Kirsten got out, and he joined her at the front of the car. The engine ticked as it cooled.

'Shall we do it?' She started towards the main entrance.

Chapman joined her, manoeuvring round the steel bollards keeping cars away from the building.

Kirsten gave an encouraging smile as they waited for someone to answer the door. 'At least we get to go home once we're finished.'

The guard inspected Kirsten's ID card and led them into a well-lit reception area, more suited to an education establishment than a prison. She noticed him taking it in. 'Staff entrance, the visitors go in round the side.'

A tall balding man ambled towards them. His dark serge trousers needed an iron and he'd rolled up the sleeves of his off-white shirt, the left below the elbow and the right up round a bulging bicep. 'Kirsten, good to see you. Is this your colleague?' He held out a large hairy hand. 'Stefan Harries, deputy governor, for my sins.'

Chapman took it. 'DI Russell Chapman. Not colleagues any more. I'm here in an unofficial capacity, searching for closure for the family.' He managed not to blush as he used the well-worn phrase.

'Well, if Kirsten says you're okay, I'm sure it will be fine. Do you want to come through to my office?'

He led them to a room with a large pale-wood desk facing the door. A bookshelf full of files and a few hardback manuals stood behind it. He invited them to sit in the chairs and produced a file from a drawer.

'We're fully electronic, but for accident investigations, we like to keep paper copies.' He slid the file across the desk. 'Do you want to have a read? It will speed things up.'

Chapman offered the file to Kirsten, who waved it away, and read the account in silence. Two guards had discovered Griffin's body at dawn and raised the alarm. Much of the account confirmed what he'd read in the police report Kirsten lent him. A series of glossy photos illustrated the report, including several close-ups of the body lying on the concrete yard.

Chapman examined them. 'These bruises on Neil's forehead. What caused them?'

'The *prisoner* got into a fight with two other inmates.'

'Would it be possible to speak to them?'

'I'm afraid not. We've moved both. We have zero tolerance for acts of violence.'

How convenient. 'So that's why you put him in the infirmary.'

'Yes.'

'Why did you sedate him?'

'What?'

214

'The autopsy found traces of sedative.'

Harries gave Kirsten an exasperated look, and she said, 'If he was in pain, or possibly aggressive. I'm sure we'd have investigated it thoroughly.'

That told me. Chapman closed the folder and placed it on the desk. 'Has anyone escaped from here?'

'No, and few bother trying.' Harries gave a complacent smile.

Chapman couldn't resist a dig. 'I suppose they can rely on getting released by mistake.' If the thug they released by mistake had injured Antonia, as intended, Chapman would have done more than make a cutting remark.

Harries glared. 'A full investigation exonerated us.'

'Shame about the young lad he attacked losing his leg.' He could sense Kirsten giving him daggers, and moved on. 'What makes you certain Griffin was trying to escape?'

'It sounds like a cliché, but we found him with a rope made from knotted sheets, and he'd discussed it with his cellmate. They'd become very close.'

That contradicted what Moira had said. 'Can I see the relevant locations?'

'Of course. It's a fair walk. It's the tall building at the back of the compound. You'll see then why few try to escape.' He held his hand out for the file.

'Could I refer to this while we wander round?'

Harries exchanged another look with Kirsten. 'If you must.'

Harries had to collect the keys they'd need, and as he closed the door, Kirsten turned on Chapman and hissed, 'I thought you said you wanted a box-ticking exercise.'

'I just want to make sure we tick the right boxes.'

'Our guys did a thorough investigation, and I didn't bring you here to tear it apart. If I'd known that's what you intended . . .'

'I'm not here to tear anything apart, but if your people did a good job, it should stand up to scrutiny.'

She snorted. 'Let's get one thing straight. Stefan's doing *me* a favour. Don't make me regret bringing you here.' She turned away. 'I forgot what a right royal pain in the arse you could be.'

They sat in frosty silence until Harries returned and then followed him into the body of the prison. Once they left the offices, the place became much more like the prisons of Chapman's experience – stark corridors separated by steel doors, but with one difference: muzak played over hidden speakers.

'It keeps the inmates docile,' Harries said, sensing Chapman's question. 'I didn't believe it when they introduced it, but it has a significant impact. At least thirty per cent fewer incidents while it's playing.'

The prison officer was trying to mend bridges, but Chapman needed to probe more. 'You said two prisoners attacked Griffin. Was he being bullied?' He nearly stepped on the prison officer's heels as he halted, and Chapman took a step back.

'We're very hot on bullying. I take personal pride we have none here.'

'I'm not suggesting it's rife, but you can't monitor them twenty-four seven.'

'We. Do. Not. Tolerate. Bullying. Is that clear, Inspector?'

'Crystal.' Chapman avoided Kirsten's eye. He anticipated a frosty journey back to the railway station.

They arrived at the building at the back of the prison and made their way up to the fourth-floor infirmary in silence. Harries used a key card to open doors on to deserted corridors, an indistinct murmur in the background the only sign of life. He let them into the reception area of a medical facility. Several staff in scrubs wandered around behind half-glazed doors.

'Could I speak to the staff who treated Griffin?'

'What for?' Harries snapped.

'I wanted to determine his state of mind. Were you aware of anything bothering him?'

'You mean bullying? I've already told you—'

'He was desperate enough to attempt to escape against incred ibly long odds. Something must have been bugging him.'

Harries sighed and picked up a handset on the reception desk before mumbling into it.

Chapman peered through the vision panel into the rest of the unit, aware of the waves of disapproval wafting off Kirsten.

'He's on his way,' Harries said. 'Don't even ask to see the medical records.'

'It's a large unit for a prison clinic.'

'There isn't a hospital nearby and, as you know, prisoners no longer get NHS treatment, so we deal with most ailments on site.'

Chapman wanted to ask about the experiments Griffin's mother mentioned, but he'd wait to speak to the medic. The doors to the clinic opened and a stocky figure in scrubs stood in the opening. A bushy beard and shaved head suggested he'd put his head on upside down.

'Dr Saunders, these police officers want a quick word about Griffin.'

The doctor pushed his thick brown-framed glasses back up his nose and swallowed.

'Russell Chapman.' He held out a hand, taking the doctor's limp and damp paw.

'Err . . . how can I help you?' Saunders pushed the glasses again, although they hadn't moved.

'Inspector Chapman wanted to know the prisoner's state of mind,' Harries said.

'Well, I'm not a psychiatrist, so I'm speaking as a layman on this matter. He seemed happy, considering.' He gestured at the surrounding brickwork. 'No particular issues.'

'So why did he attempt a breakout?'

The doctor shrugged. 'I'm afraid I can't help you. Why does anyone try to escape?'

'According to your boss, nobody does.' Chapman studied the doctor, who seemed fascinated by his own footwear. 'Why did you have him in here?'

Saunders's gaze flicked towards Harries, then the floor and walls. 'We, erm, we were treating his injuries . . .' He tailed off.

'I'm speaking as a layman, but they didn't appear serious.'

'Concussion can be fatal, Inspector.'

'I'll take your word for it, Doctor. So, what about the experimental treatment he underwent?'

Saunders blinked and adjusted his glasses again.

Before he could reply, Harries intervened. 'We're trying psychotherapy on volunteers. See if it helps them come to terms with their offending behaviour.' He glanced at Saunders. 'We take our responsibility to rehabilitate them seriously.'

'Who carries out the treatment?'

'Our staff here.' Harries gestured at the medic. 'Now, if you've finished, Inspector . . .'

Saunders telegraphed his relief. 'If that's all, Inspector, I've got patients.' He gestured with a thumb and slipped back behind the door, closing it with a loud click.

'Shall we go?' Harries retrieved his electronic key.

Chapman indicated the key card. 'How did Griffin get out of here without one of those?'

Harries looked embarrassed. 'One of the medical staff left theirs unattended.' He operated the lock and swept out with Kirsten following on his heels, and they started back the way they'd come without waiting for him.

One prisoner released by mistake, and now a second allowed access to keys. This place was hardly the fortress Harries made out. 'Hang on, we haven't seen where he fell from.'

Harries stopped and turned, slowly. 'Okay then.' He rolled his eyes at Kirsten, who wore an annoyed scowl.

Chapman keeping the deputy governor between him and the CI, they ascended two more floors and arrived at a solid door with an old-fashioned key lock.

Harries retrieved a key and inserted it in the slot. 'Before you ask how Griffin got through here, this is new. We replaced the electronic lock after the . . . accident.' He pushed the door open and gestured to Chapman to enter.

Moist heat washed over him. Lights flickered on to show a large, low room full of the paraphernalia required to maintain such a building. The odour of dusty concrete pervaded. A huge boiler occupied one corner, producing the heat. A row of water cylinders lined the adjacent wall. At the opposite corner, a ladder bolted to the wall led up to a trapdoor.

Harries gestured towards it. 'That's where he tried to get out.'

Chapman approached it. 'Can I?'

'Be my guest. The light comes on automatically.'

Chapman handed the file to the deputy governor, and gripping the uprights, ascended. The trapdoor moved easily on hinges. A light flicked on, and he studied the space. Much smaller than the room below, the ceiling sloped down, following the roofline. A lift motor sat on the floor to his left and in the ceiling in front of him, at head height, an openable skylight reflected the bare bulb. Griffin must have got out through there.

Chapman tried the handle. 'The window's locked.'

The murmur of voices from the room below ended and Harries shouted, 'You're not going outside?'

'I just want to see what he saw.'

With more huffing, keys jangled and Harries' face appeared in the opening. 'Here, catch.' He swung an arm and light flashed off a key on a fob.

Chapman caught it. 'Cheers.'

He opened the skylight and chill air rushed in. He pushed his head out. Although still a couple of hours before sundown, a gloom had descended. Below him, instead of the sea view he expected, lay the prison, the concrete yard twenty metres away. Anyone wanting to escape would need to crawl through the skylight and climb back over the roof behind him. Chapman pulled himself up to the frame of the skylight and perched on the edge. A flash of vertigo made everything sway, and he gripped the frame.

It passed in a few seconds, and he twisted round towards the ridge behind him. It rose steeply, far higher than he expected. Anyone wanting to get to it would need to traverse seven metres of slippery tile. He remembered Griffin's reaction on the roof of the flats. There was no way he'd have attempted it. But if he wasn't there to escape, why did he come up here?

CHAPTER 17

The nurse finished tying the bandage round Antonia's right hand. Although she'd applied ice and compression overnight, by mid-morning the swelling hadn't subsided, and she'd reluctantly gone to casualty.

'It's not broken,' the nurse said, 'but you need to elevate it, so we'll give you a sling. Don't get the bandages wet and change them every couple of days. Get someone to tie them if you can't manage it. Swelling should go down in a day or two.'

Antonia thanked him and went to find the police officers she'd arrived with. She found them in the cafeteria. After two attacks in less than three weeks, plus the death of one of her attackers and capture of another, the police took her safety seriously. She'd refused round-the-clock protection, asking they just accompany her to and from work and on any essential journeys. The panic alarm Alan Turner had put in his house after an intruder had taken him hostage there still worked, and they'd tightened security at the offices.

She dozed on the way back to the office. They'd left the police station after three and she'd managed less than four hours of broken sleep. The vivid memory from childhood had reawakened less wholesome ones from her time imprisoned by her mother's killers. The officers dropped her at the office and, thanking them, she asked them to come back at six and take her to the gym. Although in no shape to train, she'd promised to take Nadimah.

She fumbled with the key, not used to using her left hand, but couldn't open the door. Frustration boiling over, she rang the bell and Sawyer replied.

'Sorry, I can't open the bloody door.' She held her bandaged hand up to the camera.

'Mrs Curtis told us to put the bolts on. I'll come and let you in.'

Careful not to let her frustration, tiredness and the pain affect the way she treated Sawyer, she thanked her and disappeared into her office. She tried to catch up with the work she should have done this morning instead of sitting in casualty for four hours, but her head was full of cotton wool. The pain when she caught her right hand on the edge of her desk made her think they'd examined the wrong X-ray. She wished she hadn't refused the powerful painkillers they'd offered her.

The police still hadn't released the names of the people in the helicopter crash, so the story stayed prominent in the news cycle, mainly people speculating about the identity of the victims. Her disclosing a missile had brought the aircraft down would cause a stir. Adam's account didn't take long to knock into shape. She added the information she'd got from him last night and changed a few phrases. The advice Turner had always given her when editing her work guided her revisions: 'Don't tell the reader what to think, but make sure they see the truth and come to the right conclusions.'

When satisfied, she sent it for proofing before uploading it to their site. She ordered a sandwich and a coffee and while she waited, checked on something Adam had told her. A search for the double-headed eagle brought up millions of hits. Most weren't of interest, but she checked the tattoos and found what she wanted. Albanian gangsters frequently had them. She should have believed him.

She'd met a journalist who'd spent a year undercover with them and written a book. It romanticised their history, the only reason he stayed alive, albeit in self-imposed exile in the US. Antonia had met him twice, but he'd been drunk both times, and she hoped he'd remember her. He took her call. A good start.

'Antonia? Remind me?'

She described herself.

'Yeah, yeah, of course I remember you. Legs, we called you. The rest of you wasn't bad if I remember right.' He laughed. 'I'm in London in a couple of weeks, let's get together.'

In your dreams, creep. She swallowed her distaste and with a promise to meet in London as a carrot, he offered to tell her whatever she wanted.

Fifteen minutes later, she'd discovered the name of the head of the Albanian mafia in the UK, and he had the same tattoo Adam described. He'd been out of circulation for seven months, which coincided with the date of incarceration of the man who'd died in the helicopter crash. She'd also discovered that his subordinates did nothing without his explicit say-so. He must be behind the attacks on her, but why? Did his death mean she no longer had to worry? But he'd died over a week ago. Were they still carrying out old orders, and, once the new man took over, would they leave her alone?

She finished the call, wishing she could go for a thorough wash.

A soft knock at the door announced Sabirah's arrival. 'Antonia, you're hurt. You don't have to take Nadimah.'

'I need to see the people at the gym, and I'll have a sauna. Relax my muscles.'

'If you're sure?' Dark smudges under her eyes told of her exhaustion and she looked beaten.

Guilt snapped at Antonia. She knew her friend had problems with the immigration authorities, but she'd been too focused on her own worries to talk to her about it. 'Shall we do something together this weekend?'

A smile and Sabirah resembled her old self. 'That would be good, but only if you're not too busy.'

'Great. Where's the junior champ? We'd better get going.'

Nadimah wasn't too keen to get in the police car; hearing what they'd done to her father had coloured her opinion of them. When they arrived at the gym, she disappeared into the changing room while Antonia got a drink from the small health bar at the back. She found both Dekker brothers there, and Antonia acknowledged them with a wave. Although she'd planned a sauna, she couldn't face the faff of having to seal her hand in a plastic bag. She'd brought her laptop and had plenty of work to do.

'How come you're not training?' Milo demanded as he served her.

She held up her hand. 'Not broken, but I've got to rest it for two weeks.'

'Let me see.' He probed the bandaged flesh with surprising gentleness. 'You should elevate it to help the swelling go down. Didn't they give you a sling?'

'Too much messing about.'

'That's the trouble with you kids, can't do anything which needs a bit of effort. Use it. Otherwise you'll be out twice as long. Tell her, bro.'

She laughed. 'You're only thirty, grandad.'

Darius looked up from the book in front of him. 'What happened?'

'Guy with a cosh. I punched him in the face. Twice.'

'What have I told you? The guy's armed, you run. At him if he's got a gun, and away for everything else.'

'He was about to hit a . . . friend with it.'

'And this "friend", why couldn't he defend himself?'

'Who said it's a he?'

He exchanged a glance with Milo, who said, 'Your voice goes up if you're talking about someone you like.'

Her cheeks grew hot. 'He's twice my age. He's a fireman, writing a story for me about the helicopter crash.'

'So, grandad needed you to protect him?' Darius said.

'He was dealing with two other guys.'

He raised his eyebrows. 'Not so old, then.'

Nadimah appeared in the doorway. 'I've put my gloves on how you showed me, Milo.' She held up two fists encased in bag mitts.

'Hey, princess,' Milo said. 'Let's do some training. Leave these two crocks in here. She's broken her hand because she forgot how to punch, and he just forgets everything.' Laughing, they headed to the gym, leaving the room suddenly silent.

'Who've you upset?' Darius said.

'I'm trying to find out. Probably the Albanian mafia.'

He whistled. 'Start at the top. You know if it kicks off, your police escort won't be worth a damn.'

'They're more of a deterrent.'

'Yeah? I've never heard of a couple of coppers deterring the Albanians. If you need any help, you know where we are.'

A surge of affection washed over her. 'Thanks, Darius.' They'd offered to help her before, and she knew they meant it. Having the two brothers' protection would give her peace of mind, but she didn't want them dragged into her problems.

◆ ◆ ◆

Everything about Griffin's death felt wrong to Chapman, and he wasn't prepared to let it go. The claims Griffin made about abducting kids had stayed with him since he'd spoken to the lad's mother. After his visit to Bradwell yesterday, his determination to investigate what they'd been doing to the prisoners increased. And he wouldn't ignore the failings he'd uncovered. He'd tried persuading Kirsten to do the same during the long drive back to Southminster. But she wasn't interested and left him in no doubt it wouldn't be worth the bother asking her to do him a favour again.

He rang a friend in the Prison Inspectorate, leaving her a message to get back to him. While he waited, he searched databases for unsolved crimes involving children abducted from fairgrounds. There weren't any, so he searched for missing children. Although he found a depressing number of these, the number going missing from fairgrounds wasn't recorded. He'd have to check each record. *Bugger*.

Sanchez knocked on his doorframe. 'Morning, boss. You either arrived at the crack of dawn or someone sneaked in last night and did all your paperwork.'

'Both,' he said. 'I got back from Bradwell fired up, so came in and did a few hours.'

'I've never had the urge to come in when I've taken a day's leave. Mind you, I've never taken a day off to visit a prison. How did it go?'

'Shit. I burnt another bridge with a former colleague, and I've upset the governor. I'm probably banned from all the facilities owned by the group.'

'That's a good thing, isn't it?' Sanchez shared his antipathy to prisons.

'Yeah, you're probably right.'

'Do you want a coffee?' she asked. 'I planned to tie up a few loose ends, but you've already done them.'

The mug he'd made when he'd arrived remained half full, but cold. He held it out to her. 'Thanks, Alice, and I could do with picking your brain.'

He continued searching through the cases while he waited for her to return. She came in, placed two steaming mugs on the desk and closed the door.

'Right, brain ready to be picked.'

'I'll tell you what I discovered and why I'm not happy.'

He'd already informed her about Griffin's death, but not the claims about the medical experiments the young man had made to his mother. She listened in silence as he told her about his visit and conclusions.

'I would agree, Russell, you knew him much better than I did, but there's no way the man I saw after he'd been on the roof would have tried to climb over what you described.'

'What the hell was he doing up there?'

'The thing you mentioned about the kids and a caravan is familiar.'

'I thought so, too. Maybe we both went to the same briefing about it. I'll narrow my search to areas in and around London.' He activated his screen and changed the search parameters.

'Could I see?'

He turned the screen and Sanchez wheeled her chair round so she could see it. 'How come you're only going back seven years?'

'I went back to his sixteenth birthday. I doubt anyone younger could do it. They'd need a car.'

'I'm pretty sure I heard about the case I'm thinking of on my recruit's course, eight years ago. Could I?' She reached for the keyboard, and he slid it across to her.

Her fingers flew over the keys. The scent of apple shampoo wafted off her hair. She'd let it grow longer than normal and her usual razored bob looked ragged. Was everything okay at home? They'd applied to adopt and maybe they'd had setbacks.

'There you are.' She wheeled her chair back.

Chapman read the case outlines on the screen. They described Griffin's claims perfectly.

He checked the details. 'That can't be right, he'd have been two or three at the time of the first abduction.'

'They've also got someone else for it, and look where he is.' She pointed at the bottom of the screen.

'Bradwell Prison. What the hell?'

'You said his claims surprised you. What if he hadn't done it, but he'd met the guy responsible and decided to claim his crimes?'

'If the guy was an armed robber or jewel thief, I could understand it, but nobody claims to be a nonce. Anyway, the guy would have been in solitary or at least in a special wing.'

'Is there any way to find out? How burnt is your latest bridge? Scorched or—'

'Charcoal.'

'Ah. Well, you always did these things thoroughly.' She gave him a sympathetic smile. He'd once almost driven Sanchez to demand a transfer.

Something else Griffin's mother said came to him. But that can't have happened.

'What is it, Russell?' Sanchez peered at him.

'Just . . . No, it couldn't be true.'

'What?'

'Moira, his mum, said something about him finding his cellmate disgusting. Had they put Griffin in a cell with this monster?' He tapped the screen.

'But this specimen would go into a segregation unit for sickos.'

'Griffin said they mixed the prisoners.'

'But even if by some perverse chance that had happened, as you said, why would Griffin claim those crimes?'

Louisa Walker came for Sanchez, and they left Chapman to his thoughts. Just before lunch, he got a call back from his prison inspector friend. He'd met her through his ex, but they'd always got on.

'Maeve, thanks for ringing back. I wanted to ask you about Bradwell Prison.'

'And here's me thinking you wanted to arrange a farewell party for Brigitte.'

'Why?'

'She's going back to Germany. Us Irish are the only Europeans welcome now.'

'Is it that bad?'

'Not quite. So, what do you want me to tell you about Bradwell? There's not a lot I can tell.'

'Isn't it one of yours?'

She snorted. 'It's not anybody's.'

'What do you mean?'

'It's one of a new breed they've designated as "super prisons". A special Home Office team inspects them and produces confidential reports.'

Chapman wanted to swear. 'Who investigates if things go wrong? They released the wrong prisoner. The man committed a very serious assault following his release, and is now dead.'

'Oops, not very clever. That would be the Home Office, the same people who gave them their licence and a clean bill of health during their first annual inspection three months ago.'

'Very transparent.'

'Tell me about it. It gives the rest of us a shocking reputation. Is it the assault victim or dead man you're interested in?'

'Neither. Another prisoner I arrested was there. He died in very odd circumstances.'

'The local police should still investigate. Don't you have contacts there?'

Did. 'I've seen the report, but I'm more interested in what happened before he died. He appeared to share with a very nasty child killer.'

'Sharing a cell?'

'Hmmm.' Would it shock her?

'That would be very irregular. They should make sure they segregate prisoners like that from the general population.'

'Irregular, but not impossible?'

'Nothing's impossible, Russell, I still have ambitions to play centre forward for United.' She laughed. Maeve stood just over five feet tall and Chapman had never known her to take exercise. 'But if I came across it in one of my prisons, the governor's feet wouldn't touch.'

'What about a rumour they're experimenting on the prisoners?'

Her manner changed. 'Don't be too quick to believe rumours and definitely don't start spreading them. It wouldn't be good for your career.'

'What do you mean?'

'Nice talking to you, Russell. Say hello to Abby when you see her and take care of yourself.' The line went dead.

What the hell happened there?

◆　◆　◆

'You're refusing point blank to tell me who gave you the information about the missile?' Millie Forman sounded irritated.

Antonia adjusted her grip on her handset. If she needed to answer this many calls, she'd have to think about getting a headset. 'First, we never disclose a source—'

'So, you know who it is.'

'In this case, we don't.'

'That's irresponsible. How do you check it's true if you can't identify the source?'

Antonia didn't have time for this. Despite coming in to work early, she'd not done any of the catching up she'd planned to do, and seemed to spend all her time fielding calls from various agencies.

When she didn't answer, Forman continued, 'The terms of your licence put the onus on you to check the veracity of your stories before publishing.'

'Don't threaten me, Ms Forman. And are you telling me the story's untrue?'

Forman didn't reply.

'I'll take it as a no. Have a good day.' Antonia slammed the phone down and resisted the temptation to swear.

'Do you have a few minutes, Ms Conti?' Sawyer stood in the doorway to Antonia's office.

'Will it take long?'

Sawyer raised her eyebrows. 'It's about the job you asked me to do. The *special* one.'

Antonia reminded herself never to use Sawyer for any subterfuge. 'You gave me the completed diagram yesterday.' It hadn't revealed anything exceptional. If Chapman hadn't told her of Agron Lika's links to the Albanian mafia, she'd never have guessed it from what they'd found out.

'I've got some more information.'

'Come in, then.'

Sawyer closed the door and took a seat, placing her tablet on the desk. 'You know the separate encrypted email account the subject used—'

'You said you couldn't access it.'

'Yesterday, I couldn't.' Her eyes shone behind her glasses. 'I tried something different last night and intercepted a message. He doesn't use it often, but it's clearly one he uses for nefarious purposes.'

'What did the message say?' Had he discussed the attack on her and Adam the night before?

'Here.' She slid the tablet across, and Antonia read it.

The single-line message read, I've paid K the balance. Job well done. Antonia couldn't hide her disappointment. It gave her no useful information, and anyway, it wasn't anything to do with Wednesday's attack. That 'job' had been anything but well done. 'How did you deduce this is nefarious? It might be for a perfectly legal transaction.'

Sawyer gave a smug grin. 'The message gave me an "in" to the others. I downloaded them all.'

'Really? Have you got them?'

Sawyer produced a memory stick and handed it to Antonia.

'Have you read them?'

'They made little sense to me, but you might understand them.' She stood. 'I'll let you read them.' She paused at the door. 'I identified some people he messaged, but some used very sophisticated software I couldn't penetrate.'

'Thanks, Jean. Great work.' Antonia's hand shook as she inserted the stick into a port. Sawyer had copied the messages on to a series of spreadsheets, one per thread. She clicked on the first one. The first column gave the date of the message. The earliest in this thread started seven months earlier and the last one dated from July. She'd check it later.

The next one started five months ago. Lika sent a message, Received details of Subject 2, awaiting instructions.

The reply arrived three days later. Monitor Subject 2. 24/7

The next message made her stomach flip. Monitoring Subject 2 causing problems. Can we use a tracker?

The next reply, OK, but remove afterwards, arrived a week before they killed John.

Who sent it? A note from Sawyer read, 'Unable to trace.'

Antonia scrolled down and read a message from the same source, dated the day before John died. Subject 2 needs to be transferred.

The thread ended. John must be 'Subject 2'. Antonia's blood chilled.

She opened the next sheet. Again, it started with confirmation from Lika that he'd 'received some details', this time related to someone called BB.

The next message, dated Sunday 7 November, read, BB is causing problems. Have a word. Usual fee.

Again, this was a message to Lika from a source Sawyer hadn't identified. She checked her diary. The day before the van hit Tomasz.

The reply sent two days later just said, Unable to speak to BB, spoke to assistant. She should get the message.

The bastards. She *had* been the target. She'd make sure Lika paid for what he'd done, but she needed to find out who paid him. Antonia stood, full of energy and needing to do something. She grabbed her jacket and charged out of her office.

'Ms Conti, where are you going?' Sawyer's concerned cry made her hesitate.

'I just need some fresh air, Jean.'

'You're not supposed to go out without the police—'

'I'm not a prisoner.'

Sawyer blinked, her mouth an 'o'.

'Sorry, Jean. I'm wound up.'

'Have you read the messages?'

'It's the main reason I'm wound up.'

'Are the messages useless?'

'Far from it, Jean. They're a goldmine, and I've only read three threads.'

Antonia returned to her office and resumed her examination of the messages. The thread showed nothing for two weeks, then two days ago, Lika received another message: BB needs collecting.

They *had* come to grab her. She felt sick, but she didn't have time to dwell on it and read on.

Usual fee.

Half, you messed up last time.

Whoever this client was, he had the balls to haggle with a killer.

Lika didn't object and replied the next day, BB not alone. The job will require more staff.

She scrolled down, but the thread finished. *Blast!* She needed to know Lika's next move.

She opened each tab and checked the earliest date of each thread. None older than seven months. On several, Sawyer had put the real email addresses of Lika's clients. Antonia would check them later and cross reference the 'jobs' with assaults and murders.

Antonia sat back and clasped her hands behind her head. Whoever directed these attacks wasn't the head of the Albanian mafia, so his death changed nothing. Lika was taking an enormous risk, freelancing. In the meantime, she had to find whoever paid him to attack her.

CHAPTER 18

The sight of a police car parked outside Antonia's office alarmed Chapman until he discovered why they were there. Pleased Antonia had finally seen sense, he made his way to the entrance and rang the bell. The last rays of the sun disappeared behind the skeletons of the bare trees lining the canal path opposite.

'Can I help you?' a tinny voice asked.

'Inspector Chapman. I'm here to speak to Antonia.'

'Do you have ID?'

'I came here two days ago.'

'ID please.'

Bloody hell! He held his ID card up to the camera.

'Thank you.'

Instead of the buzzer, he heard bolts draw back, then the lock buzzed and he pushed it open. Antonia's new assistant stepped back, her brown eyes, magnified by her thick-lensed glasses, wide in alarm.

'Do you have an appointment to see Ms Conti?'

'No, but I'm sure she'll see me.'

'Do you have a warrant?' She'd regained her composure and was ready to block his progress.

'What?' She must be pissed off because he'd ignored her and barged in last time. 'ANTONIA!' he shouted through the open door, earning a disapproving glare. An electric wheelchair whirred. 'Afternoon, Mrs Curtis,' he called past the woman. 'Your Rottweiler's preventing me coming in.'

'Inspector, Jean is doing her job. Jean, this is Inspector Chapman, has nobody introduced you?'

'He barged in on Wednesday, ignoring me.'

'He's like that. In my experience it's a trait common to all police. I've no idea why Antonia has decided to befriend him.' An amused glint in her eye checked his retort. 'I presume you're here to see her?'

'Thanks. Nice to meet you, Jean. Sorry about barging in the other day.' He strode through the office greeting those he recognised. Most had their heads down, seeming focused on their screens. He knocked on Antonia's door and her irritated 'Yes!' told him what to expect.

'Russell, am I expecting you?' She sounded harassed.

'I'm here to collect Nadimah,' he said. 'I'm taking the girls ice skating. But I thought you and I could have a quick chat. And by the way, your escort's outside.' He closed the door and took a seat.

'Blast. I told them six; they're early.' She charged out and returned two minutes later. 'I've told them to grab a coffee.'

'What made you change your mind about having a police escort?'

'Someone tried to kidnap me two nights ago.'

'You serious? Why didn't you tell me?' Was she paying him back for ignoring her calls when he was suspended?

'Your friend at Islington said he would. I've not stopped since.'

Chapman remembered a missed call while he spoke to his prison contact. He checked his phone. 'Yeah, he tried. So, what happened?'

'Adam and I came out of the pub—'

'You went for a drink with him?' The guy was twice her age. He'd ask around about him.

'He wrote a story for me, and if you recall, someone barged in, and he left before we finished—'

'And you could only see him in the evening?'

'Yes. God, you sound like you're my dad.'

Was she mocking him? 'Did *he* tell you about the missile?'

'You've read the story?'

'It's ruffled a few feathers.'

'Tell me about it. I've had no end of calls.'

'I'm assuming there wasn't an "unnamed witness" who saw the "firework".'

'No comment.'

'Right. And what happened when you left the pub?'

He listened with alarm as she told him. Much as he wasn't happy about this Adam, it sounded like he'd come good. 'What makes you think they wanted to kidnap you?'

'Apart from them turning up mob-handed?' She looked uneasy. 'I got given this.' She angled the screen towards him.

He wheeled his seat round the end of the desk. 'What is it?'

'This is a list of messages from someone, I don't know who, to Agron Lika—'

'Bloody hell! How have you got his emails?'

'Read them.'

He read with growing concern. Added to the evidence of the phone call, this proved beyond doubt the Albanians were behind the attacks on Antonia. 'You couldn't just piss off normal gangsters, could you?'

'I always aim high. But I don't think it's them I've upset. Lika's doing it for money.'

'And you've no idea who's paying him?'

'Nothing I can prove, but if it's not Reed-Mayhew I'll give up exercise and take up crochet.' She clicked on a tab and the screen changed.

As he read, he pondered the implications and sat for a good two minutes once he'd finished reading. 'How did you get this information?'

'You know I can't tell you—'

'It may help take Lika off the scene.'

'I doubt it. We can't prove it's his email. I know it is, but proving it? Anyway, it's the person paying him we need to find. If we get rid of Lika, they'll just hire someone else. At least this way, I can monitor his messages, see when he's coming for me again.'

Chapman didn't like it. He'd heard the same argument from senior officers justifying leaving high-level drug dealers in situ. He always wondered if any were just protecting their paymasters.

'We identified the other party in some of the message threads. I've checked some of them.' She clicked on another tab. 'These dates match up with some nasty assaults.'

'Can I have a copy?'

'Can you use it?'

'Not officially, but if we give the investigating officers the information, they can revisit those cases.' He wouldn't let someone paying to get people assaulted off the hook. And whatever Antonia said, he wouldn't let Lika walk free. He'd wait, though, until she was safe.

'I hoped you'd say that.' She slid a memory stick towards him.

A tap on the door and Jean stuck her head in. 'I'm off, Ms Conti. I'll ring you on the number you gave me if I discover *anything* of interest to tell you.' She might as well have winked.

'Thank you, Jean, have a good weekend.'

She left without looking at Chapman and closed the door.

'Bloody hell! She's your hacker, isn't she?' He could have sworn Antonia blushed, but the door opened again, saving her.

'Russell, are we going skating?'

'Hi, Nadimah, he's just finishing.' With a look of relief, Antonia turned the screen away. 'You'd better go, I've got a mountain of work before the officers come back.'

'Actually, I wanted to talk to you about the prison story you were working on. I visited Bradwell yesterday.'

'Do you want to ring me at home, over the weekend?'

'Yeah, sure.' He picked up the memory stick, said his goodbyes and left with Nadimah. Her mum was deep in conversation with Jean, who still avoided his gaze when he greeted Sabirah.

Outside, full darkness had fallen and so had the temperature. Who the hell wanted to stand in a freezing skating rink in this weather?

'Have you upset Aunty Jean?' Nadimah's question caught him by surprise.

Aunty Jean? They *were* close. 'Not really. We didn't get off on the right foot.'

'Right foot?'

He reminded himself English wasn't her first language. 'We had a misunderstanding.'

'Yes, she can be a bit funny. Mama says she's blessed by God.'

'Your mum's getting on well with her.'

'She's very kind. We're going to her house next weekend. Mama says she's got a lovely big house, even nicer than Auntie Eleanor's.'

How does an office worker afford one of those in London? What if she used her hacking skills to supplement her income? *Come on, Russell, she might have inherited it.* 'The car's over here. Let's pick Abby up. She's not shut up about this since you suggested it.'

Nadimah rewarded him with a big smile. The realisation her father would never see her grow up hit him like a gut punch, and he led the way to where he'd parked. The squad car hadn't come back and he hoped Antonia hadn't sent them home. He'd see about getting some leave so he could keep an eye on her. She took too many risks.

◆　◆　◆

Antonia's new pay-as-you-go mobile chirruped, telling her an encrypted message had arrived from Fiona. Working at new location this weekend. Should have some good stuff for you Monday. Usual time and place?

How would she manage her police escort next time she met Fiona? Too tired to think about it now, she replied OK, switched the phone off and focused on finishing her work. She'd told the police officers to come back at eight, hoping to get most of her work done by then. The message from Fiona reminded her she'd downloaded a podcast on cognitive neuroscience. If she planned to write an article, she needed to at least know the basics. She put in her earbuds and listened while she got a coffee.

While it brewed, she glanced at Sawyer's desk. The china figurines she'd decorated it with sat in a straight line, the gaps between each precise to the nearest millimetre. Antonia couldn't resist nudging one aside.

'What are you doing, Antonia?'

She jumped with a guilty start and removed her ear buds. 'Eleanor, I didn't hear you.'

'Clearly not. A bit childish, moving Jean's effects. She can't help her OCD.'

'No, I suppose not.' She moved the figure back, hoping she'd got its position right. 'What are you doing here?'

'I still work here, in case you'd forgotten.'

'You'd gone upstairs.'

'Now I'm back down. I wanted to ask you what's wrong.' Eleanor peered at her, making Antonia fear she'd done something she shouldn't have.

'What do you mean?'

'I appreciate you've had some awful experiences in the last few weeks, but you seemed to take them in your stride. Now, I think I'm mistaken.'

She couldn't tell Eleanor about the nightmares of being trapped in a burning car with John, his brain exposed through the top of his head. 'I'm fine, a bit tired. It's been a long week.'

'Are you sure? You seem more than tired. I'd say you were' – she searched for a word –'preoccupied, like when you first came to me.'

She'd been a mess when she first arrived here. A teenager who'd endured more than she should and didn't know if she could trust anyone. 'I'm over it, really.'

'What's bothering you, then?'

Do you want a list? But she didn't want to load any of her worries on to Eleanor. 'I'm worried about Sabirah.'

Eleanor's face fell. 'We all are.'

'What's happening to her? I know it's not good, but not the details.'

Eleanor glanced round the empty room. 'Shall we go to your office?'

Eleanor refused a drink, and taking her coffee, Antonia followed her and closed the door.

After a long pause, Eleanor began. 'You know I promised Sabirah your old flat? You don't need it now, as you've got Alan's house, and having property here would make citizenship more attainable for her and the children.'

'I thought you'd already sorted it.'

'Until the lovely Kate stuck her oar in.'

'What's she done?' The mention of Kate put Antonia on edge. Eleanor's estranged daughter had done her best to make Antonia's life difficult. Although in her forties and owner of a house far grander than her mother's, she had fought against Eleanor leaving her house to Antonia, and marshalled her legal forces to fight for her 'birthright'.

'Apart from blocking the transfer, she's . . .' Eleanor struggled to speak. 'She informed the immigration authorities Sabirah was taking advantage of me because of my "enfeebled state".'

The absolute cow. Despite her anger, Antonia couldn't help laughing. 'Sorry, it's not funny. But have they met you?'

'They have now, and according to Sabirah, although she wouldn't say much, they see me as some sort of fifth columnist raising traitors who wish to harm the country.'

'I presume you don't mean Kate.' Did people see *her* as a traitor? She'd lived here ten years and believed in the country. She just couldn't stand by and watch crooks abuse it.

'No, she's a perfect citizen for this kleptocracy. So now, Sabirah, instead of having UK citizenship and somewhere of her own to bring up her children, is fighting to stay in this country. All because of that greedy madam.' She hit the edge of her chair. 'I'm so angry. If I could get my legs to work, I'd walk to her bloody house in Kensington and strangle her.'

'What's Sabirah's new solicitor got to say about it?'

'Al Rahman? He didn't seem as concerned about her latest setback as I expected. Although full of himself beforehand, telling me not to worry as he'd never lost, afterwards he didn't even act annoyed he'd lost his first appeal.'

'What did he say?'

'Not a lot. He shrugged it off and rushed off to see another client.'

'What does Sabirah think?'

'She's obviously devastated, and worried sick about what might happen, but she won't hear anything against him. I suspect she blames me.'

'That's ridiculous, after what you've done for her.'

'Partly fuelled by guilt, I'm afraid, after what we put her through.'

'After what *I* put her through.' Antonia still squirmed every time she thought about what had happened to Sabirah after Antonia got her mixed up in their last investigation into GRM.

'Let's not fight over the blame, I put you in that position.' Eleanor looked suddenly old and frail. 'You looked into Al Rahman, didn't you?'

'I spoke to Geoff Stokes, who thinks he's slimy, but straight. He's represented some very dodgy people, several of whom we've investigated, but he appears honest.'

'Hmmm, that's what I found. But a woman came with us to the appeal, and I didn't like her at all.'

'Any reason?' Eleanor had good instincts, although she'd not taken to Chapman at first.

'Very charming, beautiful manners, but cold and calculating.'

'Sabirah's not easily taken in.'

'No, not usually, but this woman is from Idlib, claims to know mutual friends back home, and was at pains to impress on me how much she hates the regime in Syria.'

'You think Sabirah's got a blind spot?'

'A strong possibility.'

'What's her name? I'll get one of the guys to look into her.'

'Rosemary Juma, but you've got a lot on your plate, so I'll do it. I'm not senile yet.'

The front doorbell buzzed, and an expression of alarm crossed Eleanor's face.

Antonia checked the time. Eight. 'That's my escort.'

'Okay, you get off, I'll lock up.'

Antonia shut down her computer and packed up her backpack. She hugged Eleanor. The old woman felt insubstantial, like she might blow away in a strong breeze. The buzzer sounded again, and someone banged on the door. Antonia checked the camera. A policewoman waited at the bottom of the stairs. Antonia pulled the door open.

The woman said, 'We haven't got all night. Didn't anyone tell you? Friday night's rather busy.'

'We'd better go then, hadn't we?'

The male officer driving gave Antonia a sympathetic smile as she got in the back. She shut off her irritation at the policewoman's behaviour. She only had to tolerate them for the five minutes it took to drive her home. The car pulled out and Antonia lost herself in her thoughts.

'Where do you come from?' the woman surprised her by asking.

'Here. London. Why?'

'I mean originally.'

'I grew up in the house where you picked me up.'

'So, you were born here?'

The other officer gave his colleague a warning look.

'No. Do you have a problem with that?'

'She's just curious,' the driver said. 'Don't worry about her.'

They drove on in silence, Antonia's anger growing. The car pulled into the mews where she lived, its tyres thrumming on cobblestones. Antonia seethed as she waited for the woman to let her out. When she didn't move, the driver sighed and got out. Antonia thanked him and let herself into the house. The urge to punch something passed after she took a few deep breaths, and she went through to the small galley kitchen.

Her stomach rumbled, but she couldn't face the idea of cooking and she checked the freezer for something to defrost. Still simmering from her encounter with the policewoman, she returned to the lounge.

Although she'd painted the walls, she'd inherited the leather sofa, club chair and glass-topped coffee table from Alan Turner. She'd moved his collection of malt whiskies out of the kitchen cupboard on to the bottom of the bookshelves flanking the fireplace. Antonia rarely had a drink, but after the week she'd had, she needed one. She poured a finger of twenty-one-year-old Springbank, lit the gas fire and sat in the armchair.

A wave of sadness washed over her as she sipped the whisky and recalled pouring her heart out to Alan in this room. Now he'd gone, she had few friends she could talk to.

Antonia considered her friendship with Chapman. His unreasonable objection to Adam threatened to drive a wedge between them. Was it concern for her welfare, or something else? She wanted nothing to complicate their friendship. *And* she'd neglected Sabirah. She'd make up for it tomorrow. She wanted to take her and the children somewhere nice but didn't fancy having a police escort. If they met at a place full of people in the daytime, she should be safe without one.

The microwave pinged. As she dished the steaming food out, the landline rang. Who'd be ringing her at this time? Doubtless another 'market research' call. She carried the food through and picked up the phone.

An electronic voice said, 'Check your messages,' and cut off.

It took her a few seconds to realise who it had been. Sawyer must have intercepted another message. She retrieved her phone. She'd forgotten to turn it off and remove the SIM card, something she usually did whenever she left the office. No messages. She checked the signal. Four bars.

Of course: she'd given Sawyer the number for a phone she'd bought to communicate with Fiona. She took it out of the inside pocket of the backpack, powered it up and read the message. A screenshot of an email.

Transfer BB.

CHAPTER 19

Antonia put her head round the door of her living room. A musky masculine smell filled the room and, in the gloom, the shape on the sofa moved.

'Morning.' Adam sat up in his cocoon sleeping bag.

'Sorry, I didn't mean to wake you.'

'Don't worry about it.'

'Do you want to use the shower? I'll make coffee.'

She left him and disappeared into the kitchen. Once her panic at getting the message from Sawyer had subsided, she'd gone through her options. The police couldn't organise a safe house at such short notice, and she hated the idea of having people like the two officers who'd dropped her off to stay with her all night, even if their bosses agreed. After the way he'd handled the attack the other night, and knowing he had a military background, she'd contacted Adam to tell him she suspected another attempt on her. He'd agreed to stay the night until she arranged something more permanent.

The kettle boiled, and she made the coffee. The pump on the power-shower finished its growl as she filled two mugs and placed them on the tiny breakfast bar. As she scrolled through the news feeds on her phone he came in, drying his short hair with a towel she'd never seen before.

'I put towels out.'

'No need. I brought everything I need.'

'How did you sleep? You could have had the bed.' At times she wished she had a bigger house.

'I needed to stay downstairs. Not much use if I'm up there and someone sneaked in during the night.' He smiled at her. 'Your sofa was remarkably comfortable.'

'Coffee's here, but I've not much in for breakfast. There's a loaf in the freezer and a few eggs.'

'Eggs on toast, perfect.'

She edged round him to get to the cooker. He took his coffee and stood in the doorway. 'What are your plans long term?'

She'd not thought of anything else all night. 'The police mentioned a safe house.'

'Okay, so they stick you in a house somewhere in the suburbs. How long do you stay hidden? Can someone run your site without you?'

Eleanor, but it would be a big imposition. Was Miles ready? Although competent, he lacked experience. 'The police will drop me and pick me up.'

'Each time you go, you increase your chances of exposing your location.'

'Oh.' She'd worried about ending up in a depressing nondescript suburb like the one she and Chapman had tracked Alan Turner to, but hadn't considered the problem of getting to and from work.

'And what happens while you're at work?'

'I presume the police will have someone.'

'Who have they sent so far? A couple of uniforms in a patrol car?' She nodded.

'Are they going to deter a determined assassin?'

She imagined the officers who'd given her a lift last night facing a gunman. 'No.'

'And how long will the police spare a team to guard you? What happens long term?'

His negativity exasperated her. 'Okay. What do *you* suggest?'

He sipped his coffee. 'Short term, disappearing is an excellent tactic. But you need to get rid of the threat. You said you intercepted a message. Can I see it?'

'There are a series of them on my laptop and the latest one is on my phone.'

'Get them, and I'll sort breakfast.'

He let her past, then returned to the kitchen as she retrieved her phone and laptop. She set it up in the living room. Adam's case and neatly rolled-up sleeping bag sat in a corner and the sofa looked like it had before he arrived last night. He backed into the room accompanied by the aroma of coffee, toast and something savoury. He held a tray with two coffees and two plates. On each lay two slices of toast with rich yellow scrambled eggs piled on them. The delicious aroma came from them, making her mouth water.

'Eat up and we'll finish this later.'

Balancing the plate on her knees, she tucked into the velvety eggs. 'Hmmm, what did you put in them?'

He finished chewing and swallowed. 'A bit of cream and my secret blend of herbs and spices.'

She wolfed them down and finished her coffee, then took the dishes away and got top-ups of their drinks while Adam studied the messages. He read the one on the phone while she settled back into the chair.

'No doubt in my mind they're supposed to kill you. Who sent the messages?'

'No idea who's giving the instructions, but the guy told to "transfer" me is Agron Lika—'

'That's why you jumped when I mentioned the Albanians in the pub the other night.'

She hadn't realised she'd been so obvious. 'You know him?'

'*Of* him. How well can you link this address to him?'

How come he knew *of* this gangster and recognised the driver of the car when the men attacked them after their meal?

'One of the men who attacked me the first time rang him at the time of the attack, and then again when I saw him in Leicester Square.'

'Not enough to convict, but I'd be amazed if it wasn't him.' He looked thoughtful. 'Can I suggest a plan?'

'Yes please.'

'Go into hiding. Nothing you can do if you're dead. Then, persuade Lika to tell you who's paying him.'

'How do I do that?'

'I'm not an expert on the Albanian mafia, but I doubt they encourage freelancing, so threaten to tell his boss.'

'That's going to be a problem.'

Adam's eyes widened. 'The guy in the helicopter.' He drank the rest of his coffee. 'You could just guess who's paying him. You've upset someone enough for them to want you dead. It's because of something you're still working on. He didn't want you dead before, just scared off. They tried to kidnap you, and because the threat you present has escalated, they now want you dead. Who might it be?'

Antonia was certain it was Reed-Mayhew. 'I'm working on a story exposing GRM.'

'That can't be it. Aren't you working on anything involving career criminals? What happened just before we got attacked?'

'I met an informer on the same story. John, the dead man you cut out of the car, worked for GRM.'

'You said he was a whistle-blower. Bloody hell. You're saying someone there arranged his death and has now ordered yours?'

'I considered other possibilities, but *The Investigator* has history with GRM, and I can't see any alternatives.'

'Do you think this goes to the top, or is someone lower down behind it?'

'Does it matter?'

'GRM is a big opponent to take on. An out-of-control underling is a much easier proposition.'

'I'm pretty sure it's Reed-Mayhew, the big boss.'

Adam whistled. 'You can certainly pick them. That makes it much harder.'

'I know.' Helplessness washed over her. She couldn't see a way out.

'You have another option. You can stop investigating the story, make sure they find out you've stopped, and hope they decide you're no longer worth killing.'

She imagined Eleanor's reaction. She would back off if she knew of a threat to Antonia's life. Antonia wouldn't ask her. 'It won't happen. What if it gets out threats will scare us off?'

'I thought you'd say that.' He studied her with a steady gaze. 'Shall I tell you how I'd deal with it?'

She wanted to solve the problem herself, but part of her welcomed a ready solution. 'Go on.'

'Do you have twenty to fifty grand?'

'Do you want to buy Lika off?'

'You'd need another zero.'

She had the money from Alan's life policy, plus some of his savings, so it wasn't a problem. 'Say I can get the money.'

'First, go underground, keep yourself safe. Get a proper team to protect you, not a couple of uniformed coppers in a marked car. Then get the story out there. After that, there's no point killing you. How long do you reckon you'll need to get the story ready?'

She doubted Fiona would give her enough on Monday to break it. 'It might take a couple of weeks.'

'Okay, it could get expensive, and obviously the longer it goes on, the more chance of the bad guys getting lucky.'

'There's another problem. Reed-Mayhew is a vindictive bastard. He might get them to kill me anyway.'

'Not if you're too much trouble.'

'What do you mean?'

'Hit Lika so hard he and his dogs back off.'

'They'll just hire someone else.'

'Yes, but if it gets out you're trouble, people won't take on the job. Once the story's broken, how much effort will this Reed-Mayhew put into getting revenge?'

She didn't know, but feared his vindictiveness would know no bounds. 'How do we hit Lika and his "dogs"?'

He held her gaze. 'We both know the language they understand.'

Antonia swallowed. 'Do we know anyone who speaks their language?'

'We certainly do.'

'Are you offering?'

Adam laughed. 'Maybe twenty years ago.'

'Who, then?'

'I know people I used to work with. They've set up companies offering close protection and dynamic defence. They're my age and older, so don't do the legwork. But they've got teams of serious operators. Ex-Special Forces, guys in their twenties and thirties you wouldn't mess with.'

'What would they do?'

'We tell them what needs doing. They tell us how much, we pay them and then they do it.'

The prospect seemed so attractive. But would she be paying for someone to be killed?

◆ ◆ ◆

Sabirah sat in the kitchen and studied her children. Nadimah hadn't stopped talking of the ice skating from the night before. Her brother watched her with admiration as she regaled him with stories of her exploits on the rink. This should be a good time for her family. Losing Rashid would always hurt, but they lived in a beautiful home and the children were happy. Nadimah hadn't seen the bullies for a while and her visits to the gym with Antonia were giving her visible confidence, even after such a short time.

But instead of being happy, Sabirah worried every waking moment. And because she wasn't sleeping, her supervisor had caught her dozing at work. He'd overlooked it because of her history, but she couldn't risk it again. And although the letter they'd given her allowed her to continue working until they expelled her, she wasn't allowed to find another job. Mr Al Rahman hadn't returned her calls since the appeal had failed. The court people hadn't come to write reports on her yet, but she expected police to come round and take them any day.

How could it be that Mrs Curtis, who had been like a guardian angel, caused these problems? Her daughter had started it with her complaint, but the latest setback implicated Mrs Curtis herself.

'Are you okay, Mama?' Hakim asked, a slice of toast in his hand.

'Sorry, I'm lost in my memories. Don't let the honey drip on to the table.' She moved his hand over his plate.

'When are we seeing Antonia?' He bit the corner off the slice and chewed. Although Antonia's favourite, he'd become jealous of Nadimah going to the gym with her.

'Today she has to work, but she said she'll ring me.'

'Can we go to the zoo?'

'We do that every time,' Nadimah complained. 'Why don't we go ice skating?'

Hakim made a face. 'I'm going to be a vet, so I need to study animals.'

'I'll teach you some tricks.'

He took another bite of his toast as he considered this. At least the children didn't fight now. But what would happen to them if they ended up in a detention centre, and then where? Somewhere worse. A black dread washed over her. Tears pricked at her eyes, and she stood, turning her back as she went to the cooker. She mustn't let them see how upset she was.

She fussed around the kitchen while they finished, then cleared the table while they did their homework. Whenever she and Rashid discussed the children, they'd agreed their education came first, whatever happened. She doubted they'd get much of one in a refugee camp.

Come on Sabirah, don't give up now.

Her phone rang as she finished preparing the meat for tonight's meal. 'Antonia. Good morning.'

'Hi, Sabirah. I'm so sorry, I can't come over. I . . . something's come up and I have to work.'

'Oh. The children will be disappointed.'

Antonia sounded strange. Then she heard a man's voice in the background. 'Tell them I'm truly sorry. I'll make it up to them.'

After an awkward minute of small talk, Antonia ended the call. She was obviously lying. A surge of annoyance washed over Sabirah. But that wasn't fair. Antonia had her own life and her own problems. She didn't have any obligations to her or the children. The sense of abandonment grew stronger. Tears coursed down her cheeks, and she wiped at them. The children mustn't see her like this.

She hurried through to the hall and collected the vacuum cleaner. They knew to stay out of the way while she cleaned. Sunlight flooded into the living room through tall sash windows as she cleaned it. After half an hour of vigorous activity, she felt better.

She checked her reflection in the ornate gold mirror above the fireplace. She looked tired, but not like she'd been crying. *Don't wallow in self-pity.* She would take the children out herself. The zoo cost too much, but she could afford a family ticket to Madame Tussauds.

As she vacuumed the rug a final time, Hakim appeared in the doorway. 'There's a man at the door, Mama.'

The police? But they would come with many. It must be the person coming to write the report to decide their future. Panic made her freeze, but she must make a good impression. She glanced round the room, pleased at how she'd got it.

'Put this away.' She gave Hakim the vacuum cleaner and descended the stairs, checking her appearance in the mirror by the front door and wishing she'd had time to put on something better. After preparing herself, she opened the door. 'Mr Al Rahman?'

'Good morning, Mrs Fadil, Sabirah. Sorry to disturb you on a Saturday morning. I'm aware I've neglected to respond to your calls. Can we speak?'

Although she'd been waiting for his call, his arrival at her door threw her. She didn't want him in her home, but she needed his help. 'I'm just taking the children out for the day.'

'May I give you a lift?' He gestured to his limousine parked at the pavement.

A gasp from behind, from Hakim, as he stared at the car, his mouth open. She'd never forgive herself if she denied him the opportunity to ride in such a car.

'Thank you. We need a few minutes to get ready. Do you want to come in?'

'That's very kind, but I have calls to make. I'll wait in the car.'

She closed the door, relieved, and puzzled by Al Rahman's demeanour. What did he want? 'Get changed and tell your sister.' The boy charged up the stairs. At least Nadimah hadn't yet reached the age where she took half a day to get ready.

Five minutes later, they made their way to the car. Even Nadimah looked excited, despite her usual dismissive response to her brother's enthusiasm for cars. The chauffer got out and opened the back door. Poor man, he never seemed to have time off.

Mr Al Rahman ended a call and beckoned them in. 'Welcome, these must be your beautiful children.'

Her maternal pride kicked in and she forgot her suspicions for a moment as she introduced them. The twenty-minute journey passed with her worrying about why he'd come on a Saturday morning. He must have bad news, but he seemed relaxed and spent the journey answering the children's questions about the car and showing them the gleaming drinks cabinet. They arrived on Marylebone Road and the car pulled over into the layby outside their destination.

Al Rahman produced two twenty-pound notes and gave one each to her children. 'Get some sweets and ice creams.'

'Please, Mr Al Rahman, there's no need,' she said.

'I insist.'

The children waited for her permission. She had barely enough for the entrance fee and worried about paying for the extras they always wanted. She nodded.

'Now, wait for your mother. I need to speak to her for a few minutes. Charming children, Sabirah.'

She waited for the door to shut. 'What's happening about social services? I am still waiting for them to come.'

'Yes, that's what I wanted to talk to you about.' Al Rahman looked uncomfortable. 'You can avoid it if you do HMG a favour.'

'Who is HMG?'

He laughed. 'Her Majesty's Government. You scratch their back . . .'

She wasn't sure what he meant, but feared the worst. 'What do I have to do?'

'As they explained at the tribunal, your, er . . . hostess presents a problem. She's working to undermine trust in our government, and by extension the country.'

'I will not hurt Mrs Curtis.'

'Nobody wants you to hurt her, but you want to help the country, don't you?'

She'd heard these treacherous questions back home and knew the answers you had to give. But Al Rahman should have been on her side, protecting her from these. 'Of course.'

'Anyway, it's not Mrs Curtis we're concerned about, but her adopted daughter.'

'Antonia is my friend.'

'Would a friend take your daughter to consort with criminals?'

'What criminals?'

'The people at the gym where she took your daughter.'

How does he know about this? 'They are not criminals.'

'They are known to the police.'

'Antonia would not do that. Her friend is a policeman.'

Al Rahman sneered. 'You must know, you can't trust all policemen.'

Sabirah didn't believe Mr Chapman was a criminal, and Antonia wouldn't mix with crooks.

'Mrs Fadil, Sabirah. All we'd want you to do is find out what she's doing, and tell us. If she's not breaking the law, nothing will happen.'

Her Rashid had done nothing wrong, and they'd still killed him. But the UK wasn't Syria. These things didn't happen here.

'We don't talk about her work. If I ask now, she will be suspicious.'

'Of course.' He produced a small packet from his jacket and took out its contents. 'Place this somewhere near her desk. Somewhere she won't find it.'

She felt trapped. 'Nothing will happen to her?'

'Of course not. This is a civilised country, governed by the rule of law.'

'And if I do this, I can stay?'

'Yes, of course.'

She needed a better guarantee. 'You promise, we get Leave to Remain?'

He held her gaze. 'I promise, I will make sure you get Leave to Remain.'

Sabirah swallowed. 'I need a guarantee.'

Al Rahman's features darkened. 'I have given you my word. Do you want me to swear on my children's lives?'

Did he even have children? She'd seen no photos in his office. 'In this country, I need a written contract.'

'No, nothing in writing.' He glared, and much as she wanted to look away, she didn't.

'Okay, swear, on your mother and father's lives, that if I hide this microphone in Antonia's office you will make sure I get Leave to Remain.'

'Okay, I swear.'

'Say it properly.' Her heart raced.

With an angry sigh, he repeated her words.

She reached for the package.

'Excellent decision, Sabirah.'

Fearing she'd betrayed everything she believed she was, Sabirah put it in her bag and got out of the car. Despite the cold, her body was bathed in sweat. Hakim looked at her with concern on his young features.

Come on, smile. 'Okay children, let's go inside.' She must do this for them.

CHAPTER 20

Chapman half-listened to the lunchtime news as he worked at his computer. The spare room of his top-floor flat, where he kept his desk and laptop, would need a makeover before Christmas. He used it as a bit of a dumping ground *and* his office, but if Abby came to stay, he wanted it to be somewhere she'd want to return to.

He'd given up on the investigation into Neil Griffin's death for the moment. He hated being thwarted, but he didn't see any way he could continue without additional information.

The newsreader announced the arrest of Sami Milham, a prominent businessman accused of abusing children. Chapman had seen the name recently and turned the volume up. The man vehemently denied any wrongdoing, but they always did. Sami Milham. Where had he heard the name before? They mentioned his school, which sparked a link in his brain.

He opened a file on his laptop and found the images he'd taken while he'd waited for the CrimTech team at Aaron Futcher's twenty-second-floor office. He'd found Snowden mentioned in the diary and knew he'd seen this latest name there. And there it was. Sami Milham, Ellaby Snowden and Aaron Futcher had met for lunch three weeks earlier, just before Snowden's suicide. His mind whirred. What had linked these three, apart from the school they'd attended? Had all of them abused kids and, when they were discovered, two took the easy way out?

But there had been no suggestion of child abuse with the other two, although he'd not considered it. He found the story of Milham's arrest on the internet and checked out the investigating officer. He didn't know her, but he'd contact her on Monday. He was still dealing with the Futcher suicide, so he'd use it as a pretext for speaking to her. As he read the details, his mobile buzzed. He muted the radio and took the call.

'George, I didn't realise Islington stayed open on Saturdays. How can I help you?' Was the chief inspector ringing about the drink they'd each promised to have?

'Ha, ha. Don't like to ring on a Saturday, but just spoke to a contact who says Agron Lika's getting a crew together. He's missing two lads, and he's got a wet job.'

Chapman's thoughts raced. They had solid links between the dead guy who'd fled from Antonia in Leicester Square and Lika, and he'd bet the one the fireman had put in hospital was the other missing thug. Were they planning to kill Antonia? 'Have you got details of the target?'

'No, just pub talk. Could be nothing but didn't want to ignore it. I've rung the contact number for Ms Conti, but it's switched off.'

'She's got a phone phobia. I'll get hold of her. Thanks, George, we'll have to have that drink soon.'

He rang Antonia's mobile, not expecting to get through, then the number for her house. It rang out, so he tried the office, which went to a message. He contacted control, but she'd not requested an escort. *What the hell is she playing at?* The fear something *had* happened tempered his irritation. He closed the laptop and, getting his coat and phone, he left.

As he drove to Antonia's, he considered the options. He suspected it would take the Force a couple of days to sort something out, that's assuming they agreed this threat warranted round-the-clock protection, and there was no guarantee of that. He'd have to persuade them.

He arrived in the mews and stopped, his tyres squealing on the wet cobbles. He rang the doorbell, and not getting an answer, he peered in through the window. The neighbour came out, and he recognised her from the time the security service snatched Alan Turner from outside the house.

'Have you seen Antonia?'

'Sure, she went out with her friend, they both had a suitcase. I think he stayed the night.' She described Antonia's companion.

The bloody fireman!

Thanking her, he charged back to his car. Luckily, he'd done some checking up on Adam and had found out his address. He kept slowing to stay under the speed limit as he drove to Clerkenwell. A van pulled out of a space three doors up from the fireman's house and he swerved into it.

The house stood at the end of a crescent of four-storey Georgian houses. He rang the bell for a minute before someone answered. The fireman stood in the opening, a crowbar in his hand.

'You weren't thinking of using that?'

The fireman scanned the pavement on each side of the front door. 'Only if someone had a gun to your head.'

'Is Antonia here?'

'Come in.' He stepped aside and closed the door behind Chapman, deadlocking and bolting it.

They stood in a wide corridor with a mosaic tiled floor. Chapman recognised Antonia's blue coat on the row of hooks on the wall behind the door. A staircase ahead led down, and a door on his left led through to a kitchen.

'Through there.' The fireman pointed to the open door with his crowbar before putting it on the floor underneath the coat hooks.

'What are you doing here, Russell?' Antonia didn't look happy.

The room ran the length of the house, with the back half set up as a kitchen diner and the front, a lounge. Antonia sat in an armchair in the front of the shuttered bay window. Two sofas faced each other across a coffee table.

'Can I get you a drink?' Adam asked.

'He's not staying.'

'He's obviously gone to some trouble to find you, so at least hear him out.' Adam gestured at the nearest sofa and Chapman sat.

'How did you find me? How did you know where Adam lives?' Antonia folded her arms and glared.

'Your neighbour, Judy, told me.' He glanced at Adam, who'd put the kettle on.

'What, she told you where he lives?'

'I'm sure someone of Inspector Chapman's calibre would have no trouble finding out where I live. Coffee okay?'

'Yeah, cheers.' He appreciated the unexpected support.

'What's so urgent you needed to use police resources to track me down?'

'I came to warn you. Lika might be after you.'

She unfolded her arms. 'I know, we intercepted a message.'

'You and your hacker?'

She sank down into her seat. 'Was I supposed to just ignore it?'

Adam brought two coffees and set one each in front of Chapman and Antonia. 'That's why we came here. I'm hoping nobody followed you.'

Chapman's cheeks grew warm. He'd been so annoyed, he'd not paid attention, but he doubted Lika would have had a team ready yet. 'No, I wasn't.'

'Are you sure?' Antonia glared.

'Positive.'

Adam broke the ensuing silence. 'I'll leave you two to it.' He left the room, closing the door behind him.

'Judy said he spent the night at your place.'

'On the bloody sofa. I got the message last night and didn't fancy being killed in my bed.'

'You could have rung me.'

'Adam's ex-military, he's trained for this sort of thing.'

'So have I, and I'm not ex anything. I'll arrange a safe house for you.'

'I'm safe here.'

'What about protection? What happens if he's on duty? I'll get a police team for you.'

'How long will that take?'

That was the flaw in his plan. He couldn't even guarantee they'd get one. 'A couple of days, but it will take Lika time to sort out a team.'

'And what happens then? You stick me in a safe house in the middle of nowhere, for how long?'

'It's not ideal, but what's the alternative?'

'Adam's sorting something out.'

'What, him and his geriatric mates?'

'You're pathetic.'

He took a deep breath. This wasn't getting them far. 'Have you got the latest email your hacker intercepted?'

'Why?'

'We can't use them as evidence, but if I claim I got the material from an informer, and we get a warrant on the strength of it, we might get them legally.'

'I'll get my phone.'

She left the door ajar and thirty seconds later, footsteps sounded on the stairs. Adam came in and closed the door. He poured himself a coffee and sat opposite Chapman.

'There's nothing going on between me and Antonia.'

'I don't want to see her hurt. She's not as tough as she makes out.'

'I'd worked that out. She's a great kid, but I'm not interested in her in that way.'

'Oh yeah.'

'My relationships don't last too long, and Antonia's looking for someone special.'

'She told you?' She barely knew him.

Adam became thoughtful. 'I wanted that at her age, so I recognised it.'

The door opened and Antonia came in with a phone. She placed it on the coffee table in front of Chapman. 'Here's the message.'

Chapman read it, his anger at whoever sent it and fear for Antonia growing. 'Antonia said you're arranging some guards for her.'

'I'm waiting to hear back from guys I used to work with.'

'What's the plan?'

Antonia replied. 'I'll work from here as much as possible. When I need to go anywhere, I'll have an escort.'

'Is that what you're arranging?'

Adam nodded. 'A team of three guys will take her to and from work. They'll pick her up and drop her off in different multistorey car parks, where I'll take and collect her. And I'll tail *them* as a backup. When she gets to her destination, they stay outside until she's ready. They'll use different vehicles and drive different routes.'

'And these are all ex-forces guys like you?'

Adam laughed. 'A lot younger, they're still in the game.'

'It won't be cheap.'

'I'm getting a special deal. Mates' rates.'

'What happens if they track you here? A crowbar isn't going to do much if they're armed.'

'Adam's getting some security cameras put in,' Antonia said. 'And if by some chance they track me, he has a panic room downstairs.'

Why did a firefighter need a panic room? Chapman had been about to suggest his place, but he couldn't compete with that. 'What happens if Adam's at work?'

'I've got a friend who'll take my place,' Adam said. 'He runs a security firm.'

Chapman had to admit, they offered a far better level of protection than she'd get with the police. 'I've not been able to get leave, but I'll help out when I'm off. Ring me whenever you need me.'

Antonia mouthed, 'Thank you.'

'How long do you intend to live like this?'

'Until your IT guys can trace the messages to Lika.'

'But he's just a middleman. We need to find who's paying him.'

Antonia exchanged a look with Adam. 'We'd worked that out. It's Reed-Mayhew, or someone working for him. I'm hoping your computer experts will prove it.'

'I was afraid you'd say that.' Much as he wished Antonia was wrong, he had to agree.

Adam's phone rang and with a gesture of apology, he went through to the back of the room.

'I was going to tell you about Bradwell,' Chapman said. 'They've definitely been carrying out experiments on the prisoners.'

'What did you find out?'

'They're claiming to carry out psychotherapy, but the medic treating him was really shifty, so I suspect they were bullshitting.'

Antonia thought for a few seconds. 'I'm seeing my informant on Monday. Can I interview you after I've spoken to them?'

'Yeah, sure. And I found out—'

'Yeah, okay.' Adam's raised voice told him something wasn't right.

The firefighter ended his call and returned, wearing a troubled frown. 'Bad news, I'm afraid. We can't get anyone until later in the week. Can you rearrange your meeting with your informant?'

'I'd rather not, she might change her mind.'

A couple of colleagues Chapman worked with in diplomatic protection had gone freelance and they owed him favours. He didn't know how much it would cost, and he wouldn't ask for 'mates' rates'. He'd been saving to buy a flat, but this was more important.

'Give me a second.' He stood and stepped into the back of the room, past gleaming kitchen units, and stood overlooking a sunken garden. He found the number he wanted and pressed call.

'Russell, you old goat, how can I help you?'

'I need some guys to guard a friend. She's upset the Albanian mafia.'

'When?'

'As soon as.' Chapman heard keystrokes.

'Okay, I can let you have two Monday first thing, both ex-special forces.'

'Can you manage three?'

After another delay and more tapping, he got a negative reply.

'Okay, we'll manage. Let me know what you want up front.'

'Don't worry, Russell, I know you're good for it.'

Only just. He ended the call and returned to the others.

'Success?' Antonia said.

'Yep, only two guys, but starting Monday. Let me have your number, Adam, and they'll liaise with you.' Antonia's smile of gratitude lifted his mood.

He finished his coffee. 'Can you forward that latest message, Antonia? We'll get the warrant first thing Monday, and we can get our IT guys on it. Don't worry, they'll have slipped up somewhere.' He hoped he was right. They'd need all the help they could get to take Reed-Mayhew on.

◆ ◆ ◆

The distant voice grabbed Antonia's attention, growing louder. A vigorous knocking followed, and she opened her eyes. Confusion and alarm fought for dominance.

'Antonia, are you okay?'

Adam.

Antonia's senses returned. Were they under attack? 'What's wrong?'

'Nothing. It's ten, you asked me to wake you.'

Blast! 'Okay, thanks.'

She put on the bedside lamp. Her sheets lay in a tangled mess and perspiration coated her bare limbs. She lay there for a few moments and then swung her legs out of the bed, sitting on the edge for even longer. The images populating the nightmares that kept waking her hovered. She could almost feel the heat from the metal of the water cylinder, and its burnt metallic smell, as she hid in the cupboard. The sound of the poor girl as the monster raped her, then silence when he strangled her. Watching through a crack in the door, Antonia had wet herself and the memory was so real, she checked the rumpled sheets. Twenty-three and still worried about wetting the bed. *Come on, pull yourself together.*

Limbs heavy with exhaustion, she trudged to the shower room off her bedroom. Careful not to catch her reflection in the mirror, she stripped off and got in the shower. As the stream of water washed over her, she sobbed. The progress she thought she'd made with Haller had vanished overnight. This was the worst night she could remember as an adult.

Her fingers had crinkled, so she got out and dried herself. A cursory examination in the mirror told her she'd not escaped unscathed from the troubled night. She'd put on some make-up, not something she wanted to get into the habit of doing. She glanced at the time as she got dressed. Ten forty. Adam must be wondering what had happened to her.

She found him in the kitchen, reading the Sunday paper at the table. The aroma of coffee filled the room.

'You're clearly ready for one of these.' He poured a mugful from an insulated jug.

'That bad?' She slid into a seat opposite him.

He reddened. 'I didn't mean . . .' He folded the paper. 'You want breakfast?'

'Hmm, yes, please. What's on offer?'

'Sunday special. Bacon, eggs, beans, sausages, mushrooms and potato cakes. A northern delicacy I'm trying to introduce to you southerners.'

'Sounds good.' She sipped her coffee.

'Do you want to sit in the other room and read the paper while I cook? This is noisy.' He gestured at the extractor.

She didn't have the energy to move. 'I'm fine here if you don't mind.'

'Russell rang while you were in the shower.'

'What did he want?'

'He wanted to update you. He said he'd ring back.'

Checking up on me. 'Thanks.'

She read the headlines, hoping they'd distract her from the thoughts crowding her mind. The lead stories focused on the accusation against Sami Milham and the suggestion that dozens of other victims had come out of the woodwork. His solicitor threatened to sue the police for releasing his name, but they denied they'd done it. Although Antonia didn't want to involve *The Investigator* in such a story, the unusual name stirred a memory, and she was sure it was on the documents Sawyer had hacked. To her frustration, she

267

realised she'd left the notes she'd made in her office. She'd do an internet search after breakfast and see what came up.

Despite her efforts, Antonia's mind strayed to the nightmares that had disrupted her sleep. Although she knew she should try to forget them, her brain kept going over the details.

'You okay?' Adam set down two plates laden with breakfast.

'Sorry, just distracted.'

He sensed her reticence and didn't try to force the conversation. Instead, he read the paper. She attempted the same, but couldn't concentrate. She wolfed down the food. At least she hadn't lost her appetite.

'You need to speak to someone,' Adam said.

'What?'

'I've seen colleagues affected by PTSD. Did the crash and what happened after bring it on?'

The scene had featured amongst them, but it wasn't the most vivid of the memories haunting her.

'It's nothing to be ashamed of.'

'It's not that. I'm seeing a therapist, but it doesn't seem to help.'

'In my experience, there's not a linear progression. You don't get better every time you go. Some sessions set you back, but you need to power on through.'

'Sounds like the voice of experience.'

He gestured at her plate with his fork. 'What do you think of the potato cakes?'

'Excellent. You'll have to give me the recipe.' Haller had reluctantly given her an emergency number. Should she ring him? By the time she'd finished, she'd decided. 'I'm going to find out if my therapist can see me today.'

Adam considered this for a few moments. 'I'll give Russell a bell, see if he's available to tail us.'

'No need. As he said, they probably won't have anyone on me for a day or two.' Despite saying she wasn't ashamed of her therapy, she didn't want Chapman to know.

'I'll get my mate Byron.'

'I'm pretty sure nobody knows I'm here and nobody knows about my therapist. I've only gone twice, and I've been careful.' Had she? Especially the first time she went. She'd been such a mess.

'He can shadow us. You see if your therapist can see you. Here.' He slid his phone across the table. 'I'll clear up. Signal downstairs isn't great, but use the Wi-Fi and an encrypted service.'

Deciding not to argue, she took the phone down to her room and punched in the number. After some cajoling, Haller agreed to see her in his consulting rooms in an hour. Adam made a quick call and they waited until a text arrived. As they left, Antonia checked but didn't see any cars that could have been shadowing them. Adam drove with a studied intensity, taking a few detours and, arriving at the clinic, parked outside.

Haller opened the door dressed in chinos and a lumberjack shirt under a V-neck jumper. He led her into his consulting room. 'Keep your jacket on. The room's still chilly.'

The fire, which she'd never seen on, flickered. She declined a hot drink, and they started the session.

She told him about last night. 'I'm terrified the progress I thought I'd made seems to have disappeared overnight.'

He studied her intently. 'Have you made any changes to your life recently?'

Without explaining why, Antonia told him of her move to Adam's place.

'The change in scenery could have adversely affected you, but the reaction is extreme. Is this a friend from when you experienced your . . . difficulties as a child?'

'Are you suggesting the circumstances in which I met Adam will have an effect?'

'Association triggers memories.'

She explained how she'd met Adam.

He checked his notes. 'And did the incident feature in your nightmares?'

'Amongst others.'

His pinkie finger lifted. 'I'm assuming you're staying with this friend for a while?'

She nodded.

'We'll address the incident where you met him in today's session and hope it helps. Memories are complex and we can't guarantee it will address the problem.'

She came out ninety minutes later, drained and wanting to sleep for a week. Adam didn't ask questions and focused on driving. His phone emitted a beep, and he glanced at the screen.

'Chapman for you. Do you want me to pull over and give you some privacy?'

'I'll take it here.' She reached for the handset and examined the screen. The call came via an encrypted app. At least Chapman was learning. 'Afternoon, Russell.'

'Antonia. You had a good sleep. Late night?'

Oh, for God's sake. He'd seemed okay after his chat with Adam yesterday. 'How can I help you?'

'I've passed on the tip about Lika using encrypted emails to the team from Islington investigating the attacks on you. They'll apply for a warrant first thing Monday, and the IT guys will start a search. Hopefully, we'll get him off the streets and find out who's paying him.'

It would be an enormous relief. 'Thanks.'

'Are you okay?'

'Hmm, not great, but you know, a hit squad is hunting me.'

'Yeah, sorry.'

She was being unfair. Chapman didn't deserve it. 'No, I'm sorry.'

'Did you see the papers?'

'Yes.'

'Sami Milham went to school with Futcher and Snowden—'

'You're joking. The paper didn't mention it.'

'The first reports did, but I'm guessing the school took out an injunction.'

'What's your take?'

'Futcher met up with both Milham and Snowden in the last few weeks. I reckon they were up to something together and two of them decided to end it all.'

'I'm pretty sure Milham was involved in the business venture to bid for prison contracts with them, but I'll need to check when I get into the office tomorrow.'

'Oh, right. I hadn't realised. But how does that tie in with the suicides?'

Antonia wasn't sure. Chapman's theory explained it, but she was sure it must involve Reed-Mayhew somewhere.

A car pulled out in front of them and slammed the brakes on. Antonia gripped the phone. Adam swore and blasted the horn. The other car did a U-turn, its young occupants giving them the finger as they shot past. Antonia relaxed.

'Where are you?' Chapman demanded.

'I'm . . . We just nipped out.'

'Just the two of you? Why didn't you ring me?'

'Adam's friend is shadowing us.'

'Another geriatric has-been—'

'I'm too tired for this, Russell.' She ended the call.

She returned it to the cradle, and it beeped again, but they both ignored it. A profound sadness almost made her cry. She couldn't stand the thought of losing another friend.

CHAPTER 21

The man alongside Antonia in the back of the people-carrier focused on the exterior, checking for potential threats. Virgil and Raphael, the driver, exuded quiet competence. Although she wanted to lie back in the seat and close her eyes, she scanned the traffic and streets on her side. Anyone who looked suspicious snagged her attention and the strain of concentrating added to the exhaustion that had plagued her for the last few weeks. Haller's session yesterday hadn't helped.

The exchange from Adam's car to this one had gone smoothly, exactly as he'd outlined, making Antonia glad she'd trusted him. They arrived at work and pulled up outside the entrance. The driver spoke to someone over the mic on his collar and then gave her the okay to leave. Virgil escorted her to the front door and waited until she'd got inside before leaving.

The alarm didn't sound when she opened the main door, and she panicked for a moment until she heard the hoover and followed the noise.

'Good morning, Sabirah.'

Sabirah jumped, holding her hand to her chest. She killed the vacuum cleaner. 'Antonia, you frightened me.'

'Sorry, and sorry about the change of plans Saturday. It's a work thing . . .' Should she warn her to be aware of strangers? But she didn't want to add to her worries. 'Is everything okay?'

'Yes, thank you.'

'Have you heard any more about the appeal?'

'I have to go. I'll be late for work at the shop.' She unplugged the vacuum cleaner and wheeled it out of Antonia's office.

'You know you don't have to do this . . .' But she'd gone, and the lift doors swished open. Her cancelling on Saturday morning must have really upset her. She'd have to make it up to her, and the children, when this was all over.

She powered up her computer. A duster and can of polish sat at the back of her desk. Sabirah didn't usually leave stuff around.

She took them back to the cleaner's cupboard. A mop, bucket and dustpan cluttered up the area outside it. Antonia put them away and made herself a coffee. The lift hummed. Had Sabirah come back to clear up? The doors slid open, and an electric motor whirred.

'Morning, Eleanor. Tea?'

Eleanor paused at the doorway to the kitchen. 'What have you said to Sabirah?'

'Nothing. I apologised for cancelling on Saturday. I'd agreed to take them all out.'

'I think she's been crying. The poor woman's distraught.'

'She left some cleaning equipment out.'

'I've told her she shouldn't be cleaning our offices, especially with all she's got on her mind.'

'So have I. I wasn't criticising. I meant it's uncharacteristic.'

Eleanor's expression softened. 'Yes, she's going through hell. I wish we could help her. I'll speak to Geoff, see what he advises.'

'Good idea.' Although her investigation into Al Rahman had thrown up no issues, Eleanor's report on his reaction had convinced Antonia he wasn't the right solicitor for her friend.

'Did your cancellation have anything to do with the heavy who escorted you this morning? Although he didn't appear so heavy to me.'

How much should she tell Eleanor? 'My police escort Friday weren't very good, so I've arranged my own.'

'Can you trust them? Remember what happened . . .'

She'd never forget what had happened to Alan Turner, and every day she regretted she hadn't warned him about the security company he'd hired. 'They're friends of Russell.'

'Hmmm. Yes, please, to the tea.' Eleanor spun her chair and headed for her desk.

After dropping Eleanor's drink off, Antonia closed herself in her office and retrieved her notes. There, she'd written Sami Milham's name as one of the founders of the new company. If the suicides of two founders, as well as a fraud investigation, didn't eliminate the new company from government contracts, this latest scandal would definitely sink their chances. Even without Chapman's revelation that the three men had gone to school with Reed-Mayhew, she had no doubt he was behind it all. But how, and could she prove it?

She needed to speak to Milham, but he was on remand. Something she'd found during her internet trawl yesterday gave her hope. The reports said his wife originally met him when she came to give him Reiki treatment. Antonia entered her maiden name and, after hitting on many dead ends, found an old interview with her on an obscure alternative health website. It listed her contact details and, hoping she'd not changed her number, Antonia dialled it.

'Hello?'

'Mrs Milham?'

'Yes, who are you?' Her voice radiated wariness.

'My name is Antonia. I work for *The Electric Investigator*—'

'Why don't you people leave—'

'Don't put the phone down. I don't think your husband is guilty.'

After a long pause, Mrs Milham replied. 'Go on.'

'I think he's been set up and I want to put his side of the story. Can I speak to you?' Antonia held her breath while she waited.

'Okay. I'm not in town, but come and see me on Wednesday when I get back.' She gave her address and ended the call.

Relief and exhilaration gave Antonia a boost of energy. She'd confirmed she'd see Fiona to catch up with her about the abuse of prisoners and worked through until ninety minutes before the agreed meeting time. As she finished, the front doorbell rang. Her escorts had arrived.

As with this morning, they set off at speed and took a circuitous route to their destination. Virgil focused on the nearside and Antonia sat behind Rafael, supplementing his watchful scrutiny. She'd need to have a good reason for their presence, one which wouldn't alarm Fiona. At Kew Gardens, Rafael dropped Antonia and Virgil off at the Victoria Gate. Virgil became uncomfortable at their exposed position. In the short queue to pay, people stared at Antonia, wondering who she was as she sheltered under an umbrella while Virgil scanned their surroundings, too obviously a bodyguard.

'Virgil, can we just behave like a couple on an outing?'

He fell into step beside her, but kept an alert watch on their surroundings. Although taller than him, she held the umbrella even higher to not obstruct his field of vision. They reached the bistro and, reluctantly leaving Antonia in the entrance, Virgil checked out the restaurant. Although they'd seen nobody suspicious, anxiety gripped Antonia until he returned and beckoned her. A warm fug enveloped her, accompanied by the smell of coffee and baking. Eight elderly people occupied three tables on the right side of the restaurant. Fiona sat at their usual table at the back and looked alarmed.

Antonia smiled. 'Can you give us some privacy?'

'Sure, I'll wait here.' Virgil pointed to a table near the entrance and Antonia continued to Fiona's table.

'What the hell's going on, Antonia?' Fiona held her handbag, ready to leave. A wet raincoat hung from the hook behind her, and an umbrella leant against the wall.

'Sorry, I should have warned you. I'm doing a story on Albanian drug dealers and one of them has made threats.' Close enough to the truth.

Fiona still exuded unease but placed her bag on the seat next to her. They ordered drinks and exchanged small talk. Antonia wanted to ask if Fiona had managed to get her on one of the trials, but not wanting to seem too desperate, decided to wait until she'd briefed Antonia on the story.

Once their orders had arrived, Fiona leant forward. 'I've spent all weekend at a prison on the Kent coast. It's a right mess.'

Antonia turned her voice-to-text recorder on. 'What's happened?'

'What hasn't happened. They've got enough material to keep a decent-sized psychiatric clinic busy for months. The worst is, one of their prisoners killed himself. He hung himself using a rope he made from bedsheets.'

'Grief. Why?'

'They removed the memory of his daughter's birth. His wife had had a rough pregnancy, but they both survived. Once the memory disappeared, he convinced himself they'd both died, and he killed himself before the authorities could get them to him.'

'How awful.' Anger infused Antonia's sympathy for the poor woman and child.

'Yes, isn't it,' Fiona continued, giving the prisoner's name and details of the prison.

The other incidents, although not as tragic as this account, demonstrated a complete disregard for the rights of the prisoners involved. Antonia wrote the article in her head as she listened and made notes for follow-up questions. The material would complement what she'd already learned from John. Fiona finished, and drained her cup.

'This is great information, Fiona. I should be able to do something with it.'

'Oh, fantastic.' Fiona didn't hide her relief.

How would her guards react if she offered Fiona a lift? 'Can we drop you off? There's a spare seat.'

'No, thanks. The tube's quicker.'

'We can drop you at the station.'

'Kew's only five minutes' walk.'

Why would she refuse a lift in this weather? Antonia asked the question that had occupied her thoughts since her visit to Haller. 'The clinics you mentioned, they're not involved in the dodgy treatment?'

'Oh no. They're properly regulated and staffed by professionals. We, the company I work for, wouldn't use them as partners otherwise.'

'So, they've had no problems with their patients?'

'Absolutely none. I know I said I'd ask about including you in their trials, but I've been too busy.'

'That's okay.' Antonia tried to hide her disappointment, but now she'd got their addresses from Haller she could approach them herself.

'You won't mention them in your report, will you?'

'Of course not. I just like to get a complete picture. Are they on Montpellier Street?'

'How the hell did you know?' Fiona raised her voice.

'I'm a reporter. That's what I do, find out things.'

Fiona stood up and grabbed her coat. 'I thought I could trust you.'

'You can. I won't mention them.'

Fiona struggled into her coat and grabbed both handbag and umbrella. 'Goodbye, Antonia.'

'Fiona!'

Virgil had already got to his feet and halved the distance between them. Fiona brushed past him and charged out into the rain.

Antonia stared at the door as it swung shut, puzzled. She was sure Fiona hadn't been as annoyed as she acted.

◆ ◆ ◆

Sanchez breezed into Chapman's office. 'Afternoon, Russell. What time do you call this?'

'When you reach the dizzy heights of inspector, you can spend your Monday mornings in pointless "strategy" meetings.' He'd almost fallen asleep. Fortunately, they didn't have one every week.

'Not for me, thanks.' Sanchez looked disgustingly healthy. She'd had her hair cut to its normal razored finish and her cheeks had gained more colour.

'Someone's had a good weekend.'

'We went windsurfing in Dorset. You should try it.'

'The thought of balancing on a piece of wood while avoiding getting blown into a freezing cold sea isn't my idea of fun.' Plus, he didn't have anyone to go with. Since Brigitte had left him six months earlier, he'd had two one-night stands and an entire week with a high-powered solicitor who clearly just wanted a 'bit of rough' to show off to her friends. He couldn't imagine any of them windsurfing.

'Don't knock it till you try it.' She gestured at his computer. 'What are we on?'

Chapman glanced at the screen. 'Aaron Futcher.'

'I thought he committed suicide.'

'Probably, but I think it's linked to the Sami Milham case in the papers.'

'I heard something about it on the radio.' She moved a file from his visitor's chair and sat.

'The three of them – Futcher, Milham and Snowden – all attended the same school and in the same year. Futcher met both in the last few weeks. Two take their own lives just before we arrest the third.' He'd decided not to mention the information Antonia had given him during their ill-judged conversation yesterday. He should have rung her to see how the first day with her guards had gone, and get confirmation of the link between the three men, but he'd decided against it.

'Did you find anything suggesting Futcher abused kids?' Sanchez asked.

'Nothing, but I wasn't looking for it, and I only searched his office.'

'Did you get his office computer?'

'Yep, the forensic team took it, and his phone.' He needed to check if Islington had sorted out the warrant for Lika.

'Are you going to mention it to Superintendent Harding?'

He snorted. 'No way. The arsehole will sit on it. I'll contact the officer working on Milham and see if there's any link.'

'Who is it?'

'DI Gillich.' He'd already tried contacting her without success.

'Stevie. She's good. She gave a talk on uncovering historical abuse during my sergeant's induction course.'

'The instructors let you use their first names now?'

'Hark at you, grandad. I suppose you didn't speak unless spoken to in your day.' Sanchez produced her phone. 'I'll text her.'

Gillich responded, offering to meet them at five.

Chapman checked the time. 'I'll meet you at the car in twenty. Can you organise a warrant for Futcher's house, including all devices? I'll speak to IT first.'

To his relief, the forensic IT team had got the warrant to examine the electronic communications of Agron Lika first thing this morning. It sounded like they'd made good progress, helped by the information he'd passed on from the woman who worked for Antonia. The report on Futcher gave him less help. They'd found nothing suggesting involvement in child abuse, but they hadn't looked for it, either. They'd do a more in-depth check of the hard drive.

He met Sanchez in the underground car park. The stench of oil and fuel hung in the air, although the eye-watering fumes had reduced since they started using electric patrol cars. He should get one himself, but even with a subsidised car loan, he couldn't afford it, and trying to charge one where he lived would be a right royal pain.

They arrived at Lewisham police station just before five and found a parking space. A young constable led them to Gillich's office on the third floor.

'Alice, good to see you again.' Gillich stood to greet them. Tall, with shoulder-length black hair and the build of a cyclist, she gave them a friendly smile.

After the introductions, Chapman gave her an outline of his theory.

'So far, we've found no evidence of anyone else being involved in the abuse, and the witnesses we've got haven't mentioned any others. What were those names again?' Gillich adjusted her screen.

Chapman slid over a sheet of paper he'd printed the details on.

She typed into her keyboard. 'We've not come across either of these as possible accomplices, but it doesn't mean they're not involved. Ah, here we are. They're listed as friends. We've got emails between them, nothing suspicious.'

'When did they last meet?'

'Let's see.' She clicked on her mouse. 'The three of them last met up two weeks ago. He saw Futcher regularly, Snowden less frequently. They also exchanged emails. Hang on . . . Here, they discussed Snowden's death. He asked Futcher about Snowden's state of mind at their last meeting. Normal . . . usual self. And here's Milham, expressing shock, blah, blah, neither saw it coming, yup. As you'd expect, really.'

'Could they have used a code?'

'They could. But we've found no evidence. I'll get our guys to run their conversations through the software. If they met and discussed their activities in person, we've no chance of finding out unless he comes clean. But all indications are, he worked alone.'

Chapman tried to hide his disappointment. 'What put you on to him?'

'A psychologist. She discovered four men at her clinic who'd each suppressed the memories and persuaded them to come forward.'

'All four were *her* patients?'

'Two were hers and her colleagues treated the other two.'

'What are the chances of that?'

'They're a specialist clinic dealing with traumatic memory suppression, and there aren't many in the country. And if Milham abused large numbers . . . I've come across people who've abused dozens.'

Chapman could believe it. How many lives had the monster who'd abused Antonia blighted? 'I'm assuming you've found something apart from these men's testimonies.'

'They're compelling, and I've listened to hundreds. We've also had more come forward since the news reports. I went through them this morning, appraising the new witnesses to decide who to see first. It will take us at least a week to interview them all.'

'First impressions?'

'Some are time-wasters, but I'm expecting many to be genuine. We also found images and evidence he'd visited sites sharing abuse material and information on his laptop.'

'What's he saying?'

'Denies it all. Says the laptop isn't his, even though we found it in a safe in his property. The abuse took place in a cottage he inherited from his parents twenty-odd years ago and uses as a hideaway. And each of the victims described the layout perfectly.'

'Forensic evidence?'

'We're searching it, but he abused the men fifteen years ago. I don't expect there's any left.'

'So, he suddenly stopped.'

'Don't tell me my job, Inspector.' Her expression hardened.

'Wouldn't dream of it. Just thinking aloud.' He smiled.

'Once we interview the new witnesses, we can determine if he *did* stop.'

Chapman hesitated before asking his next question, expecting a rebuff. 'The woman treating the victims, do you have her name?'

'What do you plan to do?'

He wasn't sure, but the case felt wrong. 'I wanted to discuss the possibility that the witnesses are still suppressing memories of the involvement of others, including the two I'm investigating.'

'Hmmm. Okay, but don't contaminate my case.' She fixed him with an intense stare.

He ignored her. 'Do you have the names of the victims?'

'Now you're taking the piss.'

'I want to check if they're linked to my two in any way.'

After several long seconds, she nodded. 'Don't speak to them or their families and don't give these names to anyone else. Otherwise, being bounced down to sergeant will be the least of your worries.' She glanced at Sanchez, then printed off a sheet listing the names of the victims and the details of the person treating them.

Chapman read the name at the top. 'Edda Bartholf. German?' The address below her name stirred a memory he couldn't grasp.

'Dutch, but speaks perfect English, like most of them. She's a tall glamorous blonde, if you like the type. Half my team fell over their tongues when we interviewed her.'

'Sounds interesting. Thanks for your help, Stevie. I won't forget this.' He stood, and they said their goodbyes.

They took the stairs and as they descended, Sanchez said, 'What do you think? She didn't buy your theory, did she?'

'It's strange that all four went to the same clinic—'

'As Stevie said, there aren't many dealing with those cases, and lots more have come forward. It takes a lot of courage to admit you've endured abuse.'

Antonia never mentioned her abuse to him, even though she knew he'd read the report of her failed attempt to get her abuser charged. 'I'm still uncomfortable about it. Call it copper's instinct. They instilled it in us old-timers.'

'Right, grandad.'

His phone vibrated and he checked the number. Gunnerson. 'Hi, boss, how can I help you?'

'Where are you?' Her tone told him this wasn't a social call.

He paused on the half-landing. 'Lewisham nick. What's up?'

'Why do you want a warrant to search a suicide victim's home?'

'I'm investigating potential links to another case—'

'You're dropping it and focusing on what we discussed this morning. Superintendent Harding will take over—'

'What the hell's it got to do with him?'

'If you don't like the way we run this organisation, you know what your options are, Inspector.' She ended the call.

He'd never heard Gunnerson so rattled. What the hell was going on?

CHAPTER 22

Even sitting in the back of the people-carrier, Antonia's shoes were uncomfortable, and she tried to focus on their surroundings, knowing her inattention could risk all of them. She wished she'd brought her backpack rather than this inadequate handbag, and her dress confined her. Going back to her house to collect her outfit had been nerve-wracking, but uneventful. She'd booked an appointment at one of the clinics on Montpellier Street that Haller had told her about, posing as a wealthy heiress.

The people-carrier turned into Montpellier Street, and Antonia experienced a moment of panic. Should she go through with it? Another broken night told her she couldn't afford *not* to. She'd told Adam and her guards she'd come here working on a story. The car slowed and pulled into a parking space opposite the clinic. Antonia studied the four-storey Georgian building. An estate agent occupied ground level, with the clinic on the upper floors.

She took a deep breath. Haller had reassured her the clinic would have been vetted, something Fiona confirmed. She could always cancel if she wasn't comfortable. 'I'll go in on my own. Thanks, guys.'

Virgil looked unhappy. 'I recommend we check it out first, Ms Conti.'

'I've had a hell of a job persuading them to talk to me. How do you think they'll react if you barge in?'

Virgil remained unconvinced. 'You're paying us, so you're the boss. But I still recommend we check it out.' He saw she wouldn't change her mind and gave a resigned nod. 'Are you happy for me to walk you to the door?'

'Sure. And I may be a couple of hours.'

He got out and scanned the street, then gestured for her to join him on the pavement and escorted her to the door. A discreet metal plate beside it bore the name Syrus Clinic. A camera above it followed them and would show her guard, but it would play into her 'heiress' persona.

A disembodied voice told her to come up to the second floor. She left Virgil and closed the door. Ignoring the small lift in front of her, she climbed the stairs, tiredness making her legs heavy. The door at the top of stairs opened before she arrived and a young man in a tailored suit greeted her. He showed her into a smart salon overlooking the back of the building, furnished in Regency style, with ochre walls and oak parquet floors. A scented candle flickered on a credenza against the side wall, filling the room with the aroma of vanilla.

'I'll just need a few details, Ms Okoye,' he said in a deep voice.

Antonia had used an old alias to book the session. She'd also brought one of the burner phones they kept in the office and gave its number. When he'd taken her details, he produced a card reader from under the desk.

'Will cash do?' Antonia opened her handbag.

'Of course.'

'Daddy says always pay cash if you can, and ask for a discount.' She smiled and counted out ten fifties. She kept two thousand in the safe at work, just in case.

He checked it and placed it in a drawer in the desk, then produced a sheet of paper, which he slid across to her. 'Just a formality. The first part is a non-disclosure agreement. Our treatment is revolutionary, and we ask you don't discuss it. The second part, which you sign after the therapist has explained the treatment to you, is an indemnity to say you understand the risks.'

'Risks?'

'I didn't express myself well. Any medical procedure has the possibility of side effects, even Botox injections, not that you need any.' He showed flawless teeth. 'Your therapist will explain all the potential issues, and you're perfectly at liberty to decline once you've thought it through.'

Would I get a refund? 'Okaaay.'

'I'll show you through.' He led her out into the corridor and to the next door.

A slim woman in her fifties with short chestnut hair, blue eyes and wearing a grey suit rose from a wingback chair, one of two arranged round a low circular table. A door on the side wall led to a darkened room. A window overlooked the back of the property. The man left them and closed the door. The woman took the indemnity form off Antonia and invited her to sit in the other chair.

'Ms Okoye, my name is Lina Schiffer.' She spoke with a faint accent. 'I'll ask you some questions to determine if our treatment is suitable for you, then we can discuss the treatment. If you're uncertain about anything, please ask.'

Antonia had anticipated the questions they might ask and had memorised her fictional personal details, including previous treatments she'd had.

After half an hour, the woman smiled. 'I'm pleased to say we can help you. I'll explain the treatment. Here at the Syrus, we recognise some memories are impossible to reconcile with who you are. We use a revolutionary process, which targets the memories you want to forget, and enables us to remove them.'

'And the risks? Your colleague mentioned something.' Antonia gestured at the form that now lay on the table.

'Of course. We occasionally find the memory removal leads to unintended changes.'

'Like what?'

'Although removing memories will alter your personality, this is usually minor and will be acceptable to you. Most patients welcome these changes. But occasionally we remove a memory which causes unwelcome and major changes to your character. It may take a while to manifest, but once it happens, we can reverse the process. We record every memory we remove and can replace it.'

That sounded like what had happened to the prisoner Fiona told her about. 'When it happens, do you have to replace every memory you've removed?'

'We can usually work out which one is the likely cause of the issue. We replace one at a time until the unwelcome trait is reversed.'

'Do you then return to normal?'

'I shouldn't have used "reversed". It's more of a correction, so although you might not be *exactly* the same, the unwelcome changes will go.'

Antonia wasn't sure she wanted any changes to her personality. What would she say if the people close to her noticed?

'Ms Okoye?'

'Sorry, I was just thinking. It must be quite time-consuming.'

'It's rare, but when it happens, we often pinpoint the correct one first time. We know what we're doing, Ms Okoye. We normally have at least six sessions where we map your brain and identify where you keep your memories, in particular the ones you want to remove.'

'Six sessions?' Fiona had mentioned multiple sessions, but had given the impression it would be two or three.

'We need to make sure we've got everything we need before we start. If you're unsure you want to go through with it, say now. This isn't a quick fix.'

'No, I appreciate that.' Although disappointed she'd have so many sessions of mapping, Antonia welcomed the delay before any treatment.

'Once the treatment starts, we will expect you to keep a diary, which I will go through at the start of each session. In it, you must log any changes you notice. We will also check for changes, but as we only see you for a short time, your observations, and those of the people you live with, are vital.' She slid the sheet across to Antonia, stood and walked to a cabinet Antonia hadn't noticed behind the door.

Antonia read the standard indemnity clauses and signed, again remembering to use her pseudonym.

Schiffer returned with a large, beige faux leather-covered diary, which she passed to Antonia. 'Ready to start?'

Antonia swallowed. Although they were only mapping her brain, her mouth was suddenly dry. Would they discover her real identity when they did it? 'Yes.'

Sabirah let herself into the house, her guilt tempered by her decision to defy Al Rahman. But by doing so, had she jeopardised the children's and her future?

The lift motor whirred. She closed the front door and rushed to the stairs, not wanting to speak to anyone, but the doors opened before she'd reached the half-landing.

'Sabirah?' Mrs Curtis called.

Tempted to pretend she hadn't heard her, Sabirah stopped and turned. 'Hello, Mrs Curtis, are you well?'

'I'm more worried about you. Do you have a few minutes?'

'I have to collect the children.'

Mrs Curtis checked the time. 'I won't keep you.' She gestured to her kitchen door.

Short of being rude, Sabirah didn't have a choice and trudged down the stairs and held the kitchen door open for the wheelchair. As usual, the large stove in the centre of the run of kitchen units kept the room warm. Max, the old lady's cat, lay in his bed in front of it and lazily opened an eye before twitching an ear and going back to sleep.

'Take a seat.' Mrs Curtis gestured at a chair at the long refectory table, next to the gap where she usually positioned herself.

Sabirah walked round the table, keeping its width between them, and refused the offer of a drink. She doubted she *could* swallow. Had her treachery been discovered?

Mrs Curtis made herself a tea as Sabirah's nerves threatened to explode. After what felt like an eternity, she placed the mug on the table and wheeled herself into position.

She looked troubled and kept her gaze on the table. 'We've discussed Mr Al Rahman, and both Antonia and I have investigated him.'

This was it. She knew what he'd asked Sabirah to do. 'I'm sorry—'

'No.' Mrs Curtis held up a hand. 'You have nothing to be sorry for. I was going to say, although we don't think he's the right solicitor for you, we haven't found anything problematical with him, so far.'

'So, what did you want to tell me?'

'Mrs Juma. How well do you know her?'

'She is from Idlib. I didn't meet her there, but her husband works at the hospital where I had my children.'

'Her husband is a diplomat.'

'No!' That meant . . . no, she couldn't believe it.

'Yes, I'm afraid.'

'But Mrs Juma was almost deported for working against Assad.'

'No, she was spying for him. She infiltrated an opposition cell here in London, and several of their relatives were arrested and killed back home. She's only here because she claimed diplomatic immunity.'

Sabirah wanted to be sick. The memory of Rashid's arrest rushed at her. What had she told the woman about her family and friends back home? 'And Al Rahman?'

'I'm still investigating, but he seems clean, for a lawyer representing crooks.'

'I will sack him. You say you haven't found anything, but Mrs Juma was the one who sent me to him.'

'I'm still investigating. Please don't do anything yet, I don't want to tip him off.'

'Okay.'

Sabirah stood. She had to leave before she was sick. How could she see him again? She staggered from the room and made her way to the stairs. She realised they'd sucked her in from the start. How had she been so stupid? Had the people in the immigration centre been part of it? She could trust nobody. Except this kind woman and Antonia, and she had betrayed both.

◆ ◆ ◆

Chapman rang the bell at the main entrance to *The Electric Investigator*, his ID card ready. He needed to mend bridges with

Antonia. He'd behaved like an arse Saturday *and* yesterday. Adam seemed a decent bloke and he should take him at his word. Chapman realised he'd come close to buggering up his friendship with Antonia and he'd been an idiot to think they'd ever be more than friends. At least the news he'd come to deliver would cheer her up.

'Can I help you?' The voice dragged him out of his reverie.

'Russell Chapman. I'm here to see Antonia.'

To his surprise, the door opened without him undergoing an interrogation. Jean Sawyer stepped back to let him in.

'Good afternoon, Inspector Chapman. I'm afraid Ms Conti isn't back yet. Do you want to come in and wait?'

Sabirah was in the main office and looked startled when she saw him. 'Sabirah, how are Nadimah and Hakim?'

'Very well, thank you, Mr Chapman. Thank you for taking Nadimah out.'

'We enjoyed it. Maybe bring Hakim next—'

'They have a lot of schoolwork.' She turned to Sawyer. 'Thank you, Jean, I'll tell the children.' She said her goodbyes and scurried off.

Had Antonia told her what a plonker he'd been? No, she wouldn't. So why was Sabirah avoiding him?

Sawyer led him through to Antonia's office, took his drink order and left him in peace. Chapman set to checking his emails, but didn't have to wait long.

'Russell, Jean said you were waiting.' Antonia looked tired, but didn't seem too pissed off at him.

'You look nice. What's the occasion?'

'I had a meeting.' She sat and slipped off her shoes.

'What's up with Sabirah? She got funny about me offering to take the kids skating and couldn't wait to get away.'

Antonia's expression clouded. 'She's having problems with the immigration authorities. And you're in the police . . . You know her history.'

'But she knows I'm not like the bastards she's dealt with. Let me know if I can help.'

'You've not come here to discuss Sabirah.'

'I come bearing good news. We served a warrant to investigate Lika's emails yesterday morning and our IT guys have taken his electronic communications apart. They've found his dodgy email address – luckily, someone told them where to search. They're working on the codes.'

'Did they say when . . . ?'

'They wouldn't commit themselves, but I'm expecting a break-through imminently.'

'Great, thanks for telling me.' She focused on her screen.

Was she still pissed off? 'I wanted to go through a couple of things with you.'

'I've got to get my main article completed and published . . .'

'It's about Milham and his connection to Futcher and Snowden.'

Her attention returned to him. 'They're definitely involved in the company bidding for the new prisons,' she said. 'I think the charges against him are fabricated.'

'On the pretext of investigating Futcher's death, I saw the officer investigating Milham. She is convinced the accusers are genuine and they've found evidence on his laptop.'

She hesitated a few moments; he could almost see her thoughts in motion. 'Have they found if Futcher and Snowden are involved in the abuse?'

'Nothing so far. But I've got misgivings about her case. How much do you know about it?'

'I'm hoping it's my next lead story. What concerns you about the case?'

'It's not your usual material.'

'I guarantee it's not what you think it is, and Reed-Mayhew is mixed up in it.'

He hoped she was wrong, but suspected she wasn't. 'The four men who came forward did so after going to a specialist clinic dealing with memory recovery.'

'And?'

'The *same* clinic. Doesn't it seem strange to you?'

'Which one?' She studied him intently.

How much should he tell her? He considered Gillich's warning. 'It's in London . . .'

'But you won't tell me?'

'It's part of an ongoing investigation. I can't. Sorry, Antonia.'

'Okay. What do you want me to do?'

'As soon as I found this out, they took the Futcher case off me.'

'You think there's a high-level cover-up?'

'Of course.'

'I agree, and I think they're covering up who is behind what's happened to these three men.'

He wasn't sure who was behind the cover-up, but her theory made as much sense as any. 'Be careful, Antonia.'

'Good advice, since someone's already trying to kill me.'

'How's the security I arranged to cover you till Adam's detail is available?'

'Excellent so far, thank you. The guys seem top-notch. Different routes each day and they change cars, so they don't become familiar. Adam says his crew will be ready to take over Thursday. Let me know how much I owe your friend.'

'Don't worry, I'll sort it.'

'I can't accept. Alan left me some money, I'll use that.'

'It doesn't seem right using it for bodyguards after what happened to him.'

She frowned. 'You could be right. I'll get *The Investigator* to pay it. We're doing all right at the moment. But thank you for the lovely offer.'

His face grew warm. 'Adam seems a good guy.'

She sat back in her chair, mouth open.

'For a water squirter.'

She laughed. 'So, what *do* you want me to do about the Milham case, seeing as you won't tell me anything?'

'I can't investigate Futcher, and the officer investigating Milham isn't taking my calls any more, so I need you to do it.'

'Luckily, I'm already on it. I'm seeing Milham's wife—'

'Seriously? How?'

She tapped the side of her nose. 'I can't tell you. It's part of an ongoing story.'

'Funny.'

'Do you know anything about his victims? Anything connecting the men?'

'Just the clinic so far.' He'd not even determined how and where Milham had met them.

'Okay. I'll tell you if I get anything from his wife. Now I really must get on and finish my lead story. It's already late.'

'I intended to buy you a late lunch, as a sorry for being an arse?'

'I'd be the size of a house if you did it every time.'

He laughed. 'Fair comment. Another day?'

'The story's written, I'm just tweaking it.' She checked the time. 'Give me twenty.'

'Great, I'll get another coffee.' He stood. 'Could I read it?'

'I don't see why not. Jean's got it on her machine. Why don't you ask her to put it on one of the spare screens and read it?' She started tapping on her keyboard before he'd left the room.

After checking with Antonia, Sawyer set him up on a spare PC. He scrolled down the screen and sipped the coffee Sawyer had given him. He examined the chunky mug. He didn't remember seeing it before. He read the section on the experiments on the prisoners and choked.

'Are you okay, Inspector?' Eleanor studied him from her wheelchair.

Bloody hell, I didn't hear her come in. He waited until he could breathe. 'Yeah, it went down the wrong way. This article, it's not up yet?'

'It should have gone up twenty minutes ago, but Antonia got back late. I think she's doing it now.'

'She can't.' He jumped up and rushed to her office, barging in without knocking.

'What's wrong?' Antonia stood up in alarm.

'Have you published the article?'

'I'm just about to, if you—'

'Don't.'

'What do you mean?' Eleanor had followed him in. 'Why shouldn't we publish it?'

'Some of it isn't true.' Chapman moved the visitor's chair aside to give Eleanor room, closed the door and sat down.

'I've worked on it for months,' Antonia said. 'I've spoken to two inside sources, including one they killed, and have checked all the facts. So no, I'm not pulling the plug.' She sat with her arms crossed.

'Which parts were wrong?' Eleanor said. 'We can't risk any mistakes, Antonia.'

Chapman was still processing the information he'd read. 'The prison you mention is in Essex. It's Bradwell—'

'The one you visited?' Antonia frowned.

'Yup. I told you they experimented on prisoners at Bradwell, and one died, but it wasn't the guy you named. You were going to interview me about it.'

'Sorry, I've got enough to run the story. I was going to do a follow-up with your testimony. It will keep it in the public eye.'

'But your story's wrong.'

'Maybe two died? They no longer publish the figures for deaths in prison so I couldn't check.'

'But I can, through official channels, and after I visited Bradwell I checked if something similar had happened in other prisons. The prison in Kent you mentioned has had no unusual deaths this year. I remember because it's the only one in the southeast with a clean bill of health.'

'Did your source get the wrong prison, Antonia?' Eleanor said.

Antonia sat for a minute. 'She visited, so I'd imagine she *would* remember.' She hunched forward and attacked the keyboard.

'What are you doing?'

'I'm pulling it. We can't trust any of it.' Antonia's eyes shone with unshed tears.

'They're obviously experimenting on prisoners,' Eleanor said, 'or don't you think you can trust John's evidence?'

'I trust John's data.'

'Well, now the inspector's offered us more evidence. Can't you use that instead?'

'Possibly. It would—'

Loud voices from the main office silenced her. Antonia jumped up and reached the door as it burst open. A bulky giant with no neck and wearing a dark suit filled the opening.

'Ministry of Patriotism. We're closing you down for posting inaccurate stories.'

'Which stories?' Antonia stood her ground, although he towered several inches above her and must have been at least twice her weight.

No-neck edged into the room and a second man, shorter and slimmer, wearing black-framed glasses, followed him in. He leered at Antonia, and Chapman bristled.

'Are one of you going to answer?' Eleanor addressed the two men, pink spots on her cheeks.

'You've published an untrue story about one of our prisons which will adversely affect public confidence—'

'No, they haven't,' Chapman said.

'Who the hell are you?' The man with the glasses stepped towards him, clearly expecting to intimidate Chapman. His hoarse voice sounded like he had broken glass in his throat.

'Inspector Chapman.' He stood and produced his warrant card. 'Have either of you got any ID?'

'I recognise these two,' Antonia said. 'They were at the Ministry the day I got called in. The big guy's Grist and he's Palmer.' She waved a hand at the smaller man.

'ID. The pair of you.' Chapman moved towards them and held out a hand.

Grist waved a huge paw at Antonia. 'The lady said—'

'If you work for the Ministry, you should know how the law works in this country.'

Grist produced his ID. The look from Palmer should have melted the lenses in his glasses, but eventually he produced an ID card, thrusting it at Chapman's face.

He checked that their names matched Antonia's recollection and returned the cards. 'I suggest you check before making accusations.'

'We have,' Grist said without conviction.

'Check again.'

Grist produced a smartphone and opened a browser. Palmer stared at Chapman. As the logo for *The Electric Investigator*'s website appeared on the giant's screen, his phone rang.

'Yup?'

A panicky voice on the other end said, 'Abort, they're not—'

'I'm here now.' Grist turned away and brushed past his companion, muttering into the phone.

Palmer glared, and Chapman grinned at him.

Seconds later, Grist ducked his head into the doorway. 'We're going.'

Chapman mouthed, 'Run along now,' and waved.

After the men had left, Chapman turned to the two women. Had they heard the caller? One look at Antonia told him *she* had.

'Well, that was fun,' Eleanor said, and he believed she meant it. 'What's up, dear?'

'They knew we'd pulled it. They're listening to us.'

CHAPTER 23

The check of Antonia's office for bugs and scan of their computer system had taken until nine last night. The fact they'd not found anything hadn't improved her paranoia.

Fiona's deceit really hurt. So far, she'd resisted searching for her real identity, but it was her priority today. The laptop her IT security company lent her while they took her old one apart didn't have her passwords saved on the browser and she entered each one as she searched specialist databases.

Sawyer tapped at the door and came in. 'Morning, Ms Conti. Ooh, is this a change of image?'

'I'm interviewing someone later.' She'd thought hard about what to wear for the interview with Milham's wife and decided on her dress, again.

'You should wear a dress more often, Ms Conti. Coffee?'

The one she'd made when she arrived had cooled. 'Thanks, Jean.'

Sawyer took it and studied the mug. 'Why don't you use the insulated mug in the cupboard?'

It had belonged to Alan Turner, and Antonia didn't feel right using it. 'One of the new ones you got will do.'

Eleanor arrived just after Antonia's coffee and, closing the door, settled opposite her.

'What should we do about Jean?' She spoke in a low voice. 'She came in here alone and was the only person who could have removed a bug before they scanned the room.'

'Shall we wait until we hear about the laptop?'

'But if it's not something on it, it must be her.'

'I know.' Antonia had grown to like the woman. 'Though she was the one who identified the threat to me.'

'Unless it's an elaborate charade and there's actually no threat?'

'I didn't imagine John's death, or the two attacks on me.'

'I'm not saying you did, dear. But . . .' Eleanor exhaled. 'I don't know what to think any more.'

'Let's wait.'

'You're probably right. What are you working on now?' Eleanor looked old and Antonia wanted to hold her.

'I'm trying to find Fiona.'

'Any joy?'

'There's an article here about KS Clinical Services. A Professor Karel Swan runs it and claims to have developed a unique process to manage people's memories. I'm just investigating his company.' Antonia checked the time. 'I'm going out in half an hour. I'm meeting . . . someone about another story.' She didn't feel comfortable discussing anything sensitive in her office, even though their security company had checked and cleared it.

'Oh, very mysterious. I'll leave it with you then.'

Antonia entered the name KS Clinical Services and found their website. The 'Our People' page didn't include pictures of the staff. Antonia read the biographies of the female members and entered their names in the search box.

She quickly found images of all but one: Edda Bartholf. No photos of her on the internet anywhere, which seemed unusual. Antonia opened the website for the University of Utrecht, where

Bartholf had graduated. Her bio didn't give a year, but Antonia guessed she'd be about thirty, six or seven years older than her.

Working her way through the yearbooks took an age. She'd have to come back to it. The front doorbell rang, and she checked the time. Her lift. She'd just check the Interdisciplinary Social Science course for 2013. The class photo came up, and there she was. With growing excitement, Antonia zoomed in on the image. The name wasn't Fiona, but she couldn't mistake her. This was the woman she'd met at Kew, her whistle-blower.

A knock and Sawyer stood in the doorway.

'Thanks, Jean. I'll be two minutes.' Antonia grabbed her handbag and coat and breezed out of the door. Now she knew who Fiona was, she could decide how to deal with her.

Virgil waited outside. 'You look happy. Good news?'

'I've found out the real identity of someone who's been stringing me along.'

'Ouch, I'm glad I'm not in his shoes.'

'Her.'

Virgil paused his scan of their surroundings to give her a sidelong glance.

'It's *work*,' she told him. *God! Why did she care what he thought?*

She'd become used to checking the traffic and her surroundings as they drove and did it without thinking. Both Virgil and Raphael seemed tense.

She glanced to her left. 'Everything okay, Virgil?'

'Sure.' He kept his attention on the outside.

'You're both stressed by something.'

Virgil finally looked at her. 'We're on our own. Neither Adam or Byron can make it, so there's no backup car.'

Antonia's stomach muscles clenched. 'What about Russell?'

Virgil shook his head. 'Sorry, but I'm sure we'll be fine.' He gave her a smile. 'Would've just been belt and braces.'

She hoped so, and reassured herself she was far safer than she'd been in the back of a police car.

She tried to focus on her questions for Milham's wife, but kept checking the cars they passed. Her thoughts also kept straying to how she should deal with Fiona. *At least you didn't give her money. Just admit the woman fooled you and move on.* But her pride wouldn't let her.

A crowd waited outside the gates of Milham's mansion in Wimbledon.

'Shit!' Virgil sounded disconcerted for the first time. 'We're going to have to get them cleared out of the way. Can you speak to someone inside?'

'I've got a phone number.' Antonia retrieved the mobile she'd used to contact Mrs Milham.

They'd almost reached the house. The crowd comprised around thirty camera crew and reporters. They continued past them. A solid sliding gate blocked the opening in the high brick wall surrounding the property.

'Contact them and find out who's in there. We need to get the gates opened, but keep those monkeys out—'

'Why don't you drive up to the gate and I'll slip in? They only need to open it a fraction.'

'Anyone could be in the crowd. You stay in the car.'

Antonia bristled, but realised it made sense and called. A panicked-sounding Mrs Milham answered and passed the phone to their security guys.

Virgil gave them instructions as Rafael drove round the edge of the common and turned left, then described a square, arriving back at the house as the gates slid back.

'Okay, I'm unlocking my door.' Virgil slid out of his door, slamming it behind him. The locks clicked, and the car rolled forward. Working with the men inside, they got through the gates without anyone joining them. Once the gate closed, Antonia released her pent-up breath. The doors unlocked and Virgil opened the side nearest the house.

'Thanks, lads.' He addressed the two uniformed security guards, who inspected them from beside an SUV.

The older of the two approached. 'We'll have to search you if you want to go in.'

'You can search us, but you only check the lady's coat and bag.'

The man opened his mouth to argue, but changed his mind when he saw Virgil's expression. Antonia handed him her bag and removed her coat. Once the searches were finished, Virgil and Rafael escorted her to the front door. The house, a two-storey red-brick villa with a white column on each side of the entrance, was new, but modelled on a much older residence. A woman in a black maid's uniform opened the door.

'Madam said to show you to the den. Follow me.'

Virgil stepped up to the door. 'Okay if we check first?'

She gave a 'what do I care' gesture and clicked away on low heels. They followed, Virgil in the lead. Gaudy artwork lined the wide corridor. The floor, laid in pale marble shot through with pink veins, had a black border flecked with gold. The maid led them to a cream door with a gold handle and knocked.

'Madam, the visitors are here.'

A woman of South Asian descent studied Antonia with big brown eyes. 'Who are these men?'

Antonia used this to her advantage. 'I've received death threats because I've defended your husband.'

'I need to check the room.' Virgil pointed behind Mrs Milham.

She stepped back and gestured for him to enter. Virgil took a step in and stopped. A man of forty sat on a low cream sofa, one of two facing each other across an onyx coffee table. He wore a supercilious expression and a gaudy padded dressing gown.

'My husband,' Mrs Milham said.

That explained the reporters. Antonia suppressed her excitement and reformulated her questions. Virgil completed his survey and backed out of the room. Antonia took his place.

Milham stood, and his silk dressing gown gaped open to reveal black satin pyjamas. 'Ms Conti, charmed to meet you. Excuse my attire, I've not been home long and after my ordeal, I needed my wife to give me a thorough wash.'

God! What a creep. Antonia took the offered hand, and he lifted hers to his lips, giving her an appraising leer. She suppressed a shudder.

'Please take a seat.' He patted the cushion next to him.

Antonia chose the sofa opposite. Statues of sensuous dancers, modelled on those she'd seen in Hindu temples, sat on several of the flat surfaces. A large painting of a woman in the same style hung over the fireplace. The voluptuous figure left nothing to the imagination, and, with a shock, Antonia recognised his wife's face. He smirked when he spotted she'd made the connection.

'Do you think it does her justice?' Milham stared at Antonia's knees.

She pulled at the hem of her dress, resisting the urge to put him in his place. 'Thank you for agreeing to see me.'

He grinned and gestured to his wife to leave them. 'My wife tells me you don't believe I'm guilty. I need all the friends I can get.'

He agreed to let Antonia record him. 'You attended school with Ellaby Snowden and Aaron Futcher.'

He put on a sad expression. 'Both gone far too soon. Two tragedies.' He wagged a finger. 'I will *not* discuss them.'

'What's your relationship with Gustav Reed-Mayhew?'

'Grief. I've not had any *relationship* with that oik since we left school. I saw him at some charity gala a few months ago, but we barely spoke.'

'Were Mr Snowden and Mr Futcher there?'

'No, why?'

'Do you recall what you and Reed-Mayhew spoke about?'

'He mentioned an incident from school which must have been quite humiliating for him, but I'd completely forgotten.'

'What happened?'

'Erm, well.' He glanced to his left. 'Someone sent him a note inviting him to a drinks party at the sports pavilion, dress for swimming. He turned up in his trunks but everyone else wore white tie.'

'How did he take it?'

'Not well.'

He didn't elaborate further. Antonia said, 'How did you get on with him at school?'

He shrugged. 'We didn't *not* get on, but we weren't friends. In fact, he didn't have many friends. Too needy and pushy.'

'What about Mr Snowden and Mr Futcher?'

'I've said I'm not talking about them. It would be disrespectful to their families.'

'I meant how did they get on with Reed-Mayhew?'

'His name's Mayhew, he adopted the double-barrel in the sixth form, much to everyone's amusement.' He considered her question. 'They were both in the rowing club with Mayhew, but they got him thrown out.'

'Why?'

'Something to do with missing funds. Mayhew misappropriated the money donated for some new kit. If I recall, he denied it and they couldn't prove it, but they got the others to vote him out.'

'Did he resent it?'

'And how. He made threats, and someone forced Snowden's car off the road while they were both in it. Rumours Mayhew instigated it, but again, no evidence.'

'Do you know if either saw him recently?'

'No idea. I told you, he wasn't someone we discussed. Barely knew him. Why all the interest? You're supposed to be interviewing me.' He glanced at her knees again, and then her chest.

Ugh, you lech. 'Could he be behind the accusations levelled against you?'

'What?'

'You've denied the charges, but you have four accusers, more coming forward. Why would they make up the accusations?'

'I thought you said you believed me.'

'I do. It's a genuine question.'

He considered it for a long time. 'Mayhew said something at the charity do about making sure you paid your debts.'

'What did you think he meant?'

'They had an auction and a couple of people bid for items but didn't collect. I thought he meant that, but maybe he meant older debts.'

'Did anyone else hear it?'

'My wife and the young lady with Mayhew.'

'I believe these charges against you, and your friends' suicides, lead back to Reed-Mayhew. I don't know who your accusers are, but I suggest you tell your defence team to search for links between them and him.'

'Thank you, Ms Conti. I believe I will.'

Antonia came to the question she worried most about. 'Oh, by the way, I heard a rumour you were setting up a company with Mr Snowden and Mr Futcher, to bid for the new prisons. Have their deaths meant you're no longer going to bid for those contracts?'

His mask slipped for an instant, and surprise mingled with anger before he regained control. 'I'm sure you know by now not to pay attention to rumours.' He stood. 'Thank you again, Ms Conti.' His gaze strayed once again to her chest. 'My wife and I host interesting parties. We'd love you to attend.' He took her hand and kissed it.

She wanted to snatch it away and punch him. She'd need a long shower as soon as she got out of here, but at least now she *knew* Reed-Mayhew was involved in the deaths of Snowden and Futcher. The chance to hit back at the childhood humiliation, plus the opportunity to remove business rivals, was more motive than he usually needed. But how to prove it, and how had he managed to do it?

◆ ◆ ◆

Chapman spent the morning investigating the four men who'd accused Milham of abusing them. So far, he'd found nothing to link them to Reed-Mayhew. In fact, nothing linked them to each other, apart from the clinic they attended. He'd begun investigating it when his phone rang. George from Islington. Did he have an update on Antonia's attacker?

'Russell. We've had a breakthrough. We've linked Lika to the emails, and at least three serious assaults.'

'Fantastic. What about the people who're paying him to attack Antonia?'

George hesitated. 'We've not cracked their emails yet, but we're working on it. We're picking Lika up later. With any luck, we'll find evidence of who he's working with at his place. If not, we can pressure him to give them up.'

Good luck with that. 'When's the raid?'

'As he's a credible threat to Ms Conti, we're going straight in. Thirteen hundred at his office. If you want to come along, rendezvous at twelve-thirty. I know it's short notice.' George gave him an address in Barking.

Chapman thanked him and ended the call. He checked the time. He'd have to leave now, and even then it would be tight. He stuck his head out into the main office. Sanderson and Walker were the only two at their desks. Sanchez had already gone out with Baxter, the person he'd most want alongside him during a raid on someone like Lika.

'Louisa, get a vest. We're going out.' At the car, he gave Walker the keys. 'You drive, Louisa. We need to get there smartish.'

'Blue lights?'

'Until we get on to River Road.'

Her face lit up. Steady rain fell, and they hit traffic as they joined the Edgware Road. There was no way they'd make it. But Walker hit the sirens and bullied cars out of their way. Chapman braced himself against the dashboard. *What have I let myself in for?*

The fifteen miles took them just over half an hour. A cluster of police cars waited at the rendezvous point, the car park of a lorry depot on Thames Road. The officers had gathered under a covered area at the back of the warehouse. Chapman and Walker caught the tail end of the briefing.

'All right, Russell, didn't realise you were on this case.' The chief inspector leading the armed response team greeted him. 'Okay.' The CI checked the time. 'We go in exactly eleven minutes. Make sure you change your radios to channel seven. The rest of you follow us in convoy, stay at the entrance to the industrial estate and wait until we've cleared it. Our intelligence is that Lika and four of his heavies are on site and could be armed, so don't take any chances.'

The minibuses of the armed response team set off first and the rest followed, with Chapman's car in the rear. They didn't need to hurry, so he took over driving, much to Walker's disappointment. They arrived at the entrance to the Buzzard Creek Industrial Estate and parked up next to George's car.

The rain eased and Chapman got out, thinking he should exchange a few words with George while they waited. As he reached the car, a black column of smoke bloomed above the rooftops where the minibuses had gone. Then a loud bang and grey clouds billowed into the sky. They both stared. Was this supposed to happen? Then the radio burst into life.

'All units, abort. The target has exploded. Two casualties have exited. Fire brigade and ambulance required.'

The waiting cars started up and the front one raced down the drive toward the scene, spraying the filthy water from the puddles. Chapman ran back to his car and, jumping in, pressed the ignition button.

The instruction over the radio stopped him. 'Inspector Chapman, wait at the entrance to direct the fire guys.'

'What the fuck. If they can't see it, they want shooting.' Walker waved a hand at the cloud of smoke gathering above their target.

Chapman agreed but doubted they could do much if they attended the incident. What the hell had happened?

Up ahead, a large pickup with a double cab pulled out of a side road, spraying water and skidding as it fishtailed.

'Boss, that leads to the back of the estate.'

Chapman studied the occupants as they approached, moving much too fast. The two in the front wore scarves up round their mouths and caps pulled low. Another bulky pair sat in the rear. A surge of adrenaline energised Chapman. He put the car into gear and swung it round as they passed. He could do with Walker driving, but they didn't have time to change over.

'Call it in.' He pointed at the handset. 'Make sure you change channels.'

His wheels spun on the greasy concrete before gripping. The pickup rounded the bend and disappeared. Next to him, Walker informed control, her voice high with excitement. They followed their quarry round the bend and the pickup came into view. He put his foot down, the steering bucking in his hand as he negotiated potholes.

Flashing amber lights appeared in front of the pickup. A large trailer edged out on to the road. The pickup's brake lights flared.

'Got you, you bastards.' Walker leant forward.

The trailer continued edging out until it blocked most of the road. The pickup slewed to a stop. One of the back doors flew open and a passenger dressed in black, leapt out. He gestured at the lorry driver, who opened his door and returned an angry salute. Then the driver changed his mind and slammed his door. The trailer jerked forwards.

Walker slapped the dashboard. 'What's he moving it for?'

They'd closed the gap, and the man in black noticed them. Chapman, already slowing, braked. The man raised his arm. Flame flashed.

The windscreen shattered, then the sound of the first shot reached him followed by a second. He braked, unable to see ahead. He steered left, hoping to miss the trailer, but the wheels locked. He pumped the brakes. Then, as he waited for the impact, they stopped.

'Thank fuck! You okay, Louisa?'

She slumped in her seat, a red stain spreading across her top. He glanced out of the side window. The gunman stood less than ten paces away, his arm raised towards Chapman.

CHAPTER 24

Antonia considered how to use Milham's information as she waited for someone to unbolt their front entrance, buoyed by further vindication of her theory about Reed-Mayhew's involvement. Miles opened the door, his usually cheerful demeanour replaced by a troubled frown.

'What's happened?'

He glanced over his shoulder. 'Your laptop's back. They found nothing.'

'Oh, right.' Disappointment replaced her positivity. 'Okay, thanks for telling me.'

'Sorry.' Miles stepped back and let her in before bolting the door behind her.

Sabirah was in the office again, talking to Sawyer. They fell silent as Antonia entered and she didn't miss the haze of panic hanging over them.

Sawyer said, 'Oh, Ms Conti, the phone in your desk drawer kept ringing—'

'Did you answer it?' *Blast!* She meant to turn it off. She didn't want the clinic discovering her identity. And the fear of Sawyer or anyone here finding out her secret wasn't far behind.

Sawyer blinked rapidly, taken aback by Antonia's reaction. 'You told me not to answer your mobiles. Any of them.'

'Yes, sorry.'

Sabirah, looking as shocked, said goodbye to Sawyer and left, avoiding Antonia's gaze. Antonia watched her leave with growing sadness.

She slunk into her office and closed the door. The phone she used to contact the clinic showed three missed calls. What did they want? She punched the button to return their call, and they put her through to Schiffer.

'Ms Okoye, good news. We've got a cancellation at six this evening. Can you make it?'

Although initially frustrated that she'd need so many sessions of 'mapping' before they began any treatment, she didn't want to go too quickly. The fact she'd slept better last night than for a long time added to her reluctance. Maybe her work with Haller was kicking in. On the verge of saying she had too much on, she had an idea.

'Do you carry out memory recovery therapy?'

'I thought you wanted to forget things?'

Although she'd love more memories of her mother *and* her father, a shadowy figure partially glimpsed through a small child's vision, she had no intention of undergoing more treatment. 'Do you?'

'We don't, but I can recommend a couple of clinics.'

'Great. I'll get the details when I see you tonight.'

She ended the call and stared at her laptop. A printed report from the security consultants sat on the casing. She thumbed through it. No software or hardware on her laptop could have picked up her words. She'd disabled the built-in mic and camera when she got the device, and they remained inoperative.

As they hadn't found a bug when they swept the office, Sawyer must have removed it before the security team arrived. Nobody else could have done it. Sawyer must go, but Antonia felt a sense of loyalty to her. And she'd given her the warning about Lika.

Antonia didn't have the energy to think about it now. She returned to her research into Fiona, or Edda Bartholf; it would take her mind off having to deal with Sawyer. Antonia found the number for the lab Bartholf worked at. She hesitated for a few moments, then dialled.

After a bit of to and fro, she got to speak to Professor Swan, the director. 'Ms Conti, you say you work for *The Electric Investigator*. How do I know it's true?'

'The details are public knowledge. Do you want to look it up and ring me?'

They ended the call, and she waited, hoping she hadn't lost him. Then the light on her phone flashed and Sawyer put him through.

'Sorry, Ms Conti, I've learned to be very careful,' the director said. 'How may I help you?' His voice, wary at first, had a warm quality, like drinking chocolate.

'I wanted to speak to you about Edda Bartholf.'

He didn't reply at once and when he did, the warmth had gone. 'What about her?'

'She spoke to me about your research. She used a pseudonym, but it was definitely her.' Antonia outlined what Fiona had told her.

'Interesting. Ms Bartholf sold our secrets to GRM. I found out ten days ago. She's now an ex-employee.'

Antonia considered his revelation. Had Bartholf fed her the false information about the experiments on prisoners at the instigation of GRM? The fact those goons from the Ministry of Patriotism were also involved suggested a very high-level attack on *The Investigator*. It had Reed-Mayhew's fingerprints all over it. What about the Syrus Clinic? But she'd got the name from Haller, and she had to believe she could trust him. What he knew about her could be used to destroy her.

'Ms Conti?'

'Sorry, I was thinking about what you'd said. Would you speak to me about it?'

His breathing carried over the phone. 'Okay. I need to think about what I'm happy to share with you. I'll see you on Friday evening, at your offices. Five o'clock?'

She wanted to talk to him sooner. 'I can meet you before then, anywhere.'

'Forgive my paranoia, but I want to make sure I'm talking to the right person.'

'Okay, Friday at five it is. I'll give you the address.'

'I'll find it, thank you.'

She ended the call, looking forward to hitting back at Bartholf, and hopefully GRM. But now she needed to deal with Sawyer.

◆ ◆ ◆

The gunman steadied his aim, the barrel huge as it pointed at Chapman's head. Chapman swallowed. Then came a shout from the pickup and the gunman lowered his automatic, made a throat-slitting gesture at Chapman and grinned before jogging away to the vehicle. In another moment, it was gone.

Chapman drew in a ragged breath. Sirens sounded from up ahead. He grabbed the radio. 'DI Chapman, officer down. A gunman in a pickup has shot one of my people.' He gave their location and the details of the vehicle.

He examined Walker. A faint breath stirred the hairs on the back of his hand. The sirens came closer, and he got out. Blue lights flickered and a fire engine appeared, and behind it more lights. He flagged the ambulance down, not caring how badly Lika's people needed it.

He helped the ambulance crew get Walker out of the car and on to a stretcher, watching helplessly as they worked on her. Once they'd removed her jacket and vest, he saw the wound, high on her trapezius. It looked like the bullet had missed any major vessels. Blood soaked her top, but didn't pump out. Focused on her, he didn't see the car pull up alongside until the occupant approached.

'How is she?' the uniformed superintendent said.

Chapman didn't recognise her. 'Still alive.'

The paramedics controlled the bleeding and slipped an oxygen mask over Walker's head. The two medics wheeled the stretcher to their vehicle and told Chapman where they'd be taking her. He watched the ambulance pull away with an empty sensation in the pit of his stomach.

'Do you want to talk me through what happened?' the superintendent said. 'Get in my car. I'll need your keys. Yours is a crime scene.'

'I admit it's a bit untidy, but nobody's been quite that critical of it before.'

She smiled at his weak joke and, taking his keys, locked his car. He stared at the bloodstain on Walker's seat. If she'd driven, the gunman would have shot him, and because he was taller, the bullet would have probably hit his vest.

The superintendent's car smelt of tobacco smoke overlaid with pine air freshener. Chapman took the passenger seat as she started up the engine and put on the heater. 'Do you want to talk me through it?'

Chapman gave a detailed account of what had happened from when they saw the pickup until the gunman shot Walker.

'You were told to wait there for the fire brigade?' the superintendent said.

'I decided to pursue the four men. I surmised they participated in what had happened at the raid site and didn't want them to get away.'

'Well, they got away, and one of your team has taken a bullet.'

'If I'd known how it would pan out, I wouldn't have fucking made the decision.'

She studied him. 'Let's see what's going on.'

She dialled a stored number on her phone, engaged gear and drove towards the industrial estate as the ringtone came through the speakers. A male voice answered, 'ma'aming' her, and she gave instructions about sending someone to the hospital and getting Chapman's car collected.

The superintendent drove carefully, clearly wary of damaging her new Lexus on the rutted road. The roadway opened out into a concreted yard full of emergency vehicles. Three fire engines clustered round a single-storey industrial unit. The explosion had destroyed the roof lights and the metal cladding on the walls bulged, like a giant trapped in there had punched them. Piles of debris lay beside the two openings at the front.

The thick dark smoke of earlier had gone and a thin haze drifted out from the gaps in the walls. Hoses snaked into the building through a large gateway with the remains of a roller-shutter hanging from the top like a torn curtain. Firefighters in breathing apparatus moved in the depths of the building, ghosts in the smoke.

The superintendent's car rolled past to pull up alongside one of the armed response team minibuses. The CI saw the car and got out of the minibus, hunched in the rain, then got in the back seat.

'Didn't realise you were coming, ma'am.' He wiped moisture off his face with a large hand.

'I'm here to investigate the shooting of the inspector's companion.'

The CI stared at Chapman. 'What the hell happened?'

Chapman updated him, realising they must still be on the other radio frequency.

'What happened here?' The superintendent pointed at the smouldering building.

'Our bus arrived first and as it reached the end of the roadway, the building exploded. Two men ran out, their clothes smouldering and covered in blood.'

'Either of them Lika?' Chapman said.

'No, but I aborted the mission. We gave them first aid and asked them if there was anyone else in—'

'Was there?' What did it mean for Antonia if Lika died? Would whoever had hired him find someone else, or give up?

'Inspector, let him tell the story and save your questions for the end.' The super signalled for the CI to continue.

'There wasn't anyone else inside, but we found two bodies, neither of them Lika, behind the building. Someone had shot them.'

'Shit!' Chapman said. 'They must have put him in the back of the pickup.'

'Probably. There's a roadway leading to more units behind there, and we found a big hole in the fence. It's where the raiders came in, to avoid the cameras.' The CI pointed at the eaves of the unit on fire, where cameras covered the access road and entrance. 'They'd blown a hole in the wall at the back using a smaller device and must have come in through there.'

'Why blow the place up if they came to snatch Lika?' the superintendent said.

'Destroy his computers and paperwork.' Chapman hit the dashboard. 'It's why I'm here. He's hiring thugs out to people to settle scores. They've killed at least one person and are trying to kill another. The people who carried out this raid are also working for whoever hired him. They must be concerned we're getting close to him.' *Shit, we won't find out who instigated the threat to kill Antonia, and whoever it is knows about my investigation.*

◆ ◆ ◆

Sabirah peered through rain-streaked windows as the bus negotiated heavy traffic. Shop windows full of festive goods mocked her. Nadimah and Hakim were so excited by the prospect, but the fear they could return to a detention centre by Christmas dominated her thoughts. The bugging device Al Rahman had given her sat in her bag like an accusation. Any trust she'd had in him had evaporated, and despite her promise to Mrs Curtis, she wanted to sack him. How dare he make her choose between her friend and her children?

The information she'd learned about Mrs Juma kept intruding on her thoughts. She didn't think they'd discussed anything that could be used against friends and family in Syria, but the likes of this woman could use the slightest thing to denounce you. The thought of being deported was bad enough, but if she'd inadvertently harmed anyone back home, she wouldn't be able to live with herself. It was bad enough she'd betrayed Antonia, who'd helped her so much. She'd done it for her children, but still felt the shame and pain.

And now Al Rahman had summoned her, telling her to bring the bug. Did he know what she'd done? After hiding it in Antonia's office for one day, she'd been so tormented by guilt she'd removed it. Once again, she'd betrayed her friend for nothing.

The bus drew up near Al Rahman's office and Sabirah got off. Her umbrella kept the worst of the rain off her. She needed a better coat, but she must save her money in case they ended up in detention. People with money could get better food and extra blankets.

She hadn't bothered wearing her best clothes, and the receptionist regarded her like a beggar. The lawyer made her wait forty minutes, but at least it gave her a chance to warm up, and even the unwelcoming receptionist made her a drink. She'd known they'd make her wait and had asked Jean to mind the children. Jean was a good woman – a bit unusual, but good-hearted, and the children liked her.

A door opened and Sabirah roused herself, expecting to see Al Rahman, but an Englishman carrying a case came in through the main entrance. He glanced at her with cold, expressionless eyes, then, after a quick exchange with the receptionist, went into Al Rahman's office.

How much longer must she wait? She'd text her children. They'd be home now. She'd finished messaging them when a light flashed on the receptionist's desk.

'Mrs Fadil, you can go through now.'

The other man hadn't left. Had he gone out through another entrance? She got up and knocked on Al Rahman's door until he summoned her in. He sat at his desk, a pile of papers in front of him. The other man studied her from a chair at the corner of the desk. Sabirah wanted to run.

Al Rahman looked her up and down. 'Sit.'

She perched on the edge of the chair, conscious of the other man, but not daring to acknowledge him. Was he the man sent to write a report on her?

'What happened?' Al Rahman asked.

'You asked me to come here.'

'Yes, because the device I gave you stopped transmitting after one day. Where is it?' He held out a hand and gestured impatiently.

Sabirah opened her handbag, hand trembling, and retrieved it. Al Rahman clicked his fingers, and she wanted to throw it at him, but placed it in his palm. He glanced at it, then passed it to the cold-eyed man. The man examined it before opening his case and holding the bug against something in it.

'It's dead.'

Sabirah held her hands out in a helpless gesture and closed her eyes, hoping her guilt didn't show. One of the young men she worked with at the shop had told her about these devices and how to disable them. She'd put it in the microwave, as he'd instructed.

Al Rahman frowned. 'What might have caused it?'

The other man expelled air through loose lips. 'Several things. Possibly a blast of radiation—'

'Radiation?' Al Rahman glared at her accusingly.

'Yeah, from a microwave, or infra-red sensors. One failed because the target used an insect repelling device which, ironically, interfered with the bug.'

'Hmmm.' Al Rahman didn't sound convinced.

'They have cockroaches in the cellar and use a plug-in repellent,' Sabirah said.

'That would do it.' Cold-eye put the bug in his case and retrieved another device. 'This should work in that environment.' He held it out to her, but Sabirah couldn't move.

'Here.' Al Rahman took it off him and waved it at her impatiently.

She couldn't hide it again, but took it anyway.

The lawyer studied her from under hooded eyes. 'You can go.'

'What's happening with my citizenship?'

'They're sending someone to assess your situation. Has someone come to see you?'

'But you said if I helped you . . .'

'The device is faulty, so—'

'It's not my fault. I did what you ask, and you promised.'

'You don't expect me to help you without you giving me anything of value. Now leave, before I lose my temper, and I'll contact you when you need to come back.'

Her legs trembling, Sabirah stood. She couldn't do it again, and if she broke another one, they would know.

As she went out, she heard Cold-eye say, 'We might not need her, we've got another—'

The door closed, cutting him off.

CHAPTER 25

The calm and reassuring presence of Eleanor next to her gave Antonia courage. Sawyer knocked on her office door and came in.

'You wanted me?'

Eleanor took charge. 'Take a seat, please, Jean.'

Antonia could detect puzzlement but little nervousness as her PA settled into the visitor's chair.

Antonia needed to take a sip of water, and let Eleanor continue. 'You're aware a government department raided us yesterday?'

'Of course, I let them in.' Sawyer's confusion grew.

'They'd listened in to our conversations and knew exactly what we planned.'

'Oh my. Is that why they took your laptop away, Ms Conti? But you're very aware of electronic security. Unlike many people I've—'

'It wasn't on any of Antonia's devices. Someone planted a bug.'

'A bug. Where?'

'We didn't find one.'

'But how . . . ?'

Antonia still couldn't detect guilt or fear, and signalled she'd take over. 'Someone removed it before we searched my office.'

'Who could have done it?'

'By a process of elimination, we've determined—' Antonia needed another sip of water.

'Oh, for God's sake!' Eleanor said. 'It could only be you, Jean.'

'No!'

Antonia said, 'Nobody else came in here.'

'What about the policeman?'

'I trust Russell. And anyway, I never left him in here on his own, unlike you.'

Sawyer radiated hurt and confusion. 'I just took the empty cups away.'

'I'm sorry, Jean—'

'But it wasn't me.' Sawyer looked from Antonia to Eleanor. 'What are you going to do?'

Antonia swallowed. Sawyer still wasn't behaving like a guilty person. 'We're going to terminate your employment.'

Tears welled up in Sawyer's eyes. 'I've done nothing wrong.'

'I'm sorry, Jean.' Antonia crossed her arms.

'I helped you. I found out about those people trying to hurt you.'

Antonia didn't have an answer.

'We're all sorry, Jean, but we have to trust everyone working here. Clear your desk and leave by five. We'll pay you until the end of December.' Eleanor used a brisk voice Antonia had rarely heard.

Sawyer's mouth opened and the tears threatened to fall, but holding them back, she stood and walked out of the room.

The silence she left behind lasted until Eleanor broke it. 'I always hate these things, but she betrayed us, Antonia.'

'But we can't prove it.'

'Who else could it have been?'

Antonia still wasn't convinced. Either Sawyer was a brilliant actress, or she hadn't done it. 'Everybody who works here has access to my office. I never lock it.'

'We've gone through this.' Eleanor wheeled herself out, leaving Antonia to her thoughts.

She stayed in her office until Sawyer knocked on her door. 'Ms Conti, I've handed everything over. Thank you for giving me the job, I've enjoyed it.'

Antonia couldn't think of a reply except, 'Thank you for telling me about Lika.'

'Goodbye.' Sawyer turned away, her eyes shining, then she left.

A few moments later, Eleanor wheeled herself in. 'I know it's tough, but it's a part of leadership. You'll have to get used to it.'

'Yeah, I suppose so.' But she didn't think she ever would.

She was still brooding when Virgil appeared at the door to collect her. As she walked through the office, Sawyer's bare desk reproached her, and a mournful air hung over the place.

'Everything okay?' Virgil studied her thoughtfully.

'Yeah, thanks. The burdens of leadership.'

'Do you want to talk about it?'

She nearly said, 'I'm going to see my therapist,' but stopped herself. 'Thanks, but it's no biggie.'

The journey to the clinic for her six o'clock appointment passed uneventfully, and telling Virgil she wouldn't be more than an hour, she made her way up. A young woman had replaced the man at the reception desk. Schiffer collected her from reception and led her to the treatment room. Unlike last time, Schiffer had already laid out the mind-mapping equipment.

'Nothing wrong, Ms Okoye?'

'I'm fine, thank you.'

'You seem a bit out of sorts. Is anything troubling you?'

'Just work stuff. Nothing major.'

Schiffer looked unconvinced. 'The mapping will be ineffective if you're too disturbed.'

'I'm fine.' Antonia took a seat on the recliner.

She lay back as Schiffer placed the helmet lined with sensors and contacts on her head. Her hair now formed a dense curly mass, but Schiffer assured her the equipment would still work. Her muscles tensed as she forced herself to recall the memories she wanted to remove. Her scalp tingled and, imagining spikes piercing her brain, she had to resist the urge to wrench the helmet off. As she listened to Schiffer encouraging her to cast her mind back in a low soothing voice, and focused on the memories, her surroundings faded to nothing.

◆ ◆ ◆

A loud banging and raised voices penetrated her consciousness. Antonia opened her eyes. She dragged shattered thoughts through thick treacle, but they refused to coalesce. Where was she? She moved, and pain lanced through her head.

'What's happening?' She lay on a recliner with a contraption on her head. Was it causing the pain? The raised voices came again. She had to get up, and tried to sit, but something on her head tugged her back.

Schiffer stood at the open door talking to someone in reception, then turned to Antonia. 'Be careful, it's very delicate.' She rushed across and lifted a helmet off Antonia's head.

Recollection flowed back. She'd been getting her memories mapped. But why did she feel so groggy? More banging, and a distorted man's voice demanded they open the door. Had Lika's men found her? Antonia got to her feet but almost fell. What the hell had happened to her? Slowly, her balance returned. 'Is there another way out?'

'Yes, but why? They're your escort.'

Antonia's heart rate slowed. But why would they come into the building? Had something happened? She reached the reception as Virgil opened the entrance door.

'Antonia, you okay?'

'Of course I'm okay. What the hell are you doing?'

'You've been two hours.'

Antonia checked the time. Eight. Confusion and disbelief vied for supremacy 'I'll come right down. Can you wait for me?' She returned to the treatment room and waited until Schiffer closed the door. 'How come I was unconscious?'

'You fell asleep, so I let you. We didn't do any mapping, so I won't charge you for the session. I was able to use another treatment room for my next appointment.'

She recalled Schiffer's soothing voice, and then nothing. 'I've not been sleeping well.'

'We see that all the time with our patients, but once we finish mapping your memories, we can remove those causing you problems.' She hesitated a few moments before adding, 'Whatever happened at work today caused you real distress. If you want to discuss it . . .'

'No, it's fine.' She picked up her coat. 'Is the Friday session still on?'

'Try to relax before you get here.'

'Okay, thanks, bye.' She collected her backpack.

'See you Friday, Antonia.'

Virgil stood by the entrance to reception, his body tense. Antonia followed him downstairs, then what Schiffer had said sank in.

Nobody here knew her as Antonia.

In the lobby, Virgil texted Rafael to get the car ready to pick them up. As they waited, he said, 'What's up?'

'You used my real name. I've told them I'm . . . I'm someone else.'

'Sorry. I . . . I was worried.'

Her anger evaporated. 'No, it's okay. You did the right thing. I'm sorry I put you in that position.'

A reply from Rafael beeped, and they went outside. Icy rain lashed down, and they hurried to the double-parked car outside the entrance. It pulled away at speed, and Antonia fumbled for her seatbelt. Still groggy, she peered into the dark through rain-streaked windows. How was she supposed to see anything?

Next to her, Virgil tensed. 'The dark Ford Galaxy has now made the same turn as us three times.'

'Roger,' Rafael confirmed. 'I've got him.'

Antonia twisted in her seat to check, but Virgil said, 'We don't want him to know we've made him, and I need you to keep an eye out for any accomplices.'

Antonia's adrenaline had spiked. Feeling exposed, but very much awake, she peered into the darkness.

'Take the next left,' Virgil said, 'and see if he follows.'

The car braked sharply and turned left, then accelerated.

'He's still with us,' Rafael announced.

The tension in the vehicle increased and Antonia's insides knotted. She wanted to ask what they intended doing, but guessed she'd find out soon enough.

'See if we can lose him, Raf. Hang on, Antonia.'

The engine note increased as Rafael changed down. They'd come off the main roads and were driving down a deserted side road. Ahead on the pavement she saw movement.

'Stinger, hold on!' Rafael shouted.

The seatbelt bit into her shoulder and then, accompanied by a series of pops, the car slewed sideways. They mounted the pavement and a brick wall loomed ahead. Everything slowed, and she watched, horrified, as they seemed to skate towards it, the bricks growing bigger. Then everything disappeared as her head jerked back as from a punch. Metal screamed and glass shattered. Her neck and head jerked, and she slammed into the doorpost. Then the scene jumped like a missed frame in a movie.

Intense pain sliced through her skull as she opened her eyes. Virgil lolled against her, heavier than he should have been. Rafael lay motionless, slumped over in the driver's seat. Were they dead?

Outside, a door slammed. She needed to get out. A figure appeared at the side window on Virgil's side. By some miracle, the glass hadn't smashed. Then it shattered, and an arm reached in, searching for the lock.

Dragged out of her stupor, Antonia tried to grab at the hand. But the combination of Virgil's weight and her seatbelt held her back. She reached for the seatbelt release button, but it lay under Virgil's torso. With a heave, she freed the belt and eased herself out from under the security guard.

The hand continued fiddling with the lock. The impact must have damaged it. She again tried to grab the hand, but a forearm of knotted steel swatted her away. She tried yet again, and the hand slapped her, hard. She tried to retaliate, but the arm withdrew. Then metal creaked, and the door opened. The overhead light came on, but the door stuck. The hand grabbed the doorframe and pulled. With more groaning, it gave.

A bearded face appeared in the opening and she threw a punch at it, catching him on the cheek. He reeled away with a curse. She hadn't hurt him. She pulled her legs free, leaving her shoes behind, and leaning back on to the door, straightened them along Virgil's body so her feet were just below the broken window. The beard returned, a vicious expression above it. She waited until his head and shoulders filled the opening. Then, bracing herself against the door behind her, she twisted her hips and kicked him in the face.

Her heel slammed into his nose. He didn't even cry out, just slumped forward. Something heavy fell out of his hand and clunked on to the ground outside. A surge of anger seized her, and she kicked again and again at his motionless head.

'Antonia.' A groggy Virgil stirred. 'Get out.'

She tried her door, but nothing happened.

'This side,' Virgil hissed.

Antonia hesitated a moment but a sharp voice from outside roused her and she scrambled over the prone bodyguard and fell out on to the pavement. The bearded man lay centimetres away and Antonia struggled to her feet. She reached for Virgil.

'Leave me. Go!' Blood dripped from a cut on his head.

At least one car had pulled up behind theirs. She saw movement and ran in the opposite direction. Rain soaked through her tights and within a few paces she realised she'd injured her foot. Agony shot up her leg each time she placed it on the ground.

She checked where she was. She'd taken a side road from where the attack happened. One feeble streetlight illuminated the stretch she could see. Behind her, shots rang out. Her guards weren't armed. Had someone shot Virgil and Rafael? She hesitated, but what could she do? She ran on, ignoring the pain. Then she stumbled to a stop. In the gloom and through the pouring rain, the wall blocking the end of the short lane loomed over her.

With a curse, she ran back. A figure appeared in the darkness, and she stopped. He did the same. He was far bigger than her guards, and the faint light from the streetlamp glinted off his black skin. Her lower leg felt on fire and barely supported her weight, but she'd make sure he didn't have an easy victory.

◆ ◆ ◆

A police car dropped Chapman at Newham hospital and he arrived exhausted after two hours of questions by Internal Investigations. They'd put Walker in a private room, and he spent half an hour chatting to her mum in a low voice, while his constable dozed between them in a drug-induced sleep. The doctor treating her reassured him she'd make a full recovery. The bullet had passed through muscle without doing too much damage. He left at eight, barely able to keep awake.

At the main entrance, he tried Antonia's mobile again but got the unobtainable message he expected. When he'd rung *The Electric Investigator* to give her the news about Lika, her odd assistant hadn't answered, and his enquiry about her elicited an awkward silence. Antonia had already left, and his attempts to contact her had been predictably unsuccessful. Why the hell couldn't she carry a mobile like a normal person?

He punched in the number for the fireman's landline, but it rang out, and his irritation turned to concern. Where the hell was she? Had something happened to her? Although her security detail should have finished long ago, he tried their number, which also just rang out. Now even more alarmed, he took a cab to Clerkenwell. Despite the rain, he got it to drop him at the opposite end of the crescent from Adam's flat.

He strolled towards the house, trying to appear casual, but gripped by tension. A light glowed in the ground floor bay window of Adam's living room. He reached the front door and checked the frame. No marks signifying a break-in. He pressed the call button. A bell rang in the distance and Chapman resisted the temptation to bang on the door. Footsteps, and then locks clicked. His stomach tensed as he waited. The door swung inwards to reveal Adam in jeans and a T-shirt.

'No crowbar?' Chapman said.

'Camera.' Adam pointed to a discreet device above the front door. 'I watched you from getting out of the car. You ashamed to be seen coming to my door?'

'I need to speak to Antonia.'

Adam's expression clouded. 'She's not back yet.'

The reaction increased Chapman's anxiety. 'She's late? Why weren't you backup?'

'My mate was. Do you want to come in?' Adam stepped aside and pointed at the hallstand. Chapman removed his coat and hung it up, letting it drip on to the tiled floor. The crowbar leant against the wall behind the door. As locks clicked behind him, Chapman walked into the kitchen. Warmth enveloped him and the aroma of chilli, garlic and unidentified spices made his mouth water. Apart from a dry cheese sandwich at the hospital, he'd not eaten since breakfast. Steam rose gently from two pots on the cooker. Although desperate to ask about Antonia, he didn't want to appear too eager.

'Your turn to cook?'

'You tasted any of her cooking?'

'I have to admit, never.'

'Once was enough for me. Grab a seat.' He pointed to the lounge area. 'Drink?'

'Beer would be good. You got an IPA?' Chapman sank into the armchair in the window. Jazz, so quiet he first thought it came from upstairs, played in the background.

Adam returned with two gaudy cans covered in condensation and two glasses. He placed one of each in front of Chapman, turned the music off and sat opposite him. 'Okay, what's up?'

'*You* said she's late.'

'Yeah, but she's got three guys guarding her, including my best mate, who I trust against most people. I'm sure there's a good reason. She called in to a source on the way home.'

He doubted she'd have told Adam who her source was. 'I missed her at work and when I rang your phone, nobody picked up.'

'I've been on days, hence my mate standing in for me. So why did you need to see her?'

None of your bloody business. 'I wanted to tell her about Lika. Someone shot two of his blokes and bombed his place.'

'I heard.' Adam took a sip of his beer.

'What do you mean?' They hadn't released the details.

'How many fires do you think LFB attended today where a bomb had gone off and two men were shot?'

'You didn't go?'

'No, but one of my mates did.'

'How did you know it was Lika's place?'

'Your mate's company aren't amateurs. Once you told them who was behind the threat to Antonia, they did a thorough profile. Because I'm backup, they shared it with me.'

'Your mate who couldn't supply the security on Monday must have a few spare blokes now. Ex-military, aren't they?' Something about the way the gunman held himself had seemed familiar to Chapman.

'Mostly. Why?'

He waved the question away. Would Adam and his mates have taken Lika out? He doubted the police would have got much information from the gangster, but a group of ex-special forces guys trained in enhanced interrogation techniques might have more success. 'When did you find out where he had his base?'

Adam studied him, a smile playing about his lips. 'You think I had something to do with it?'

'Did you?'

'I wouldn't have started a fire. I won't put colleagues at risk.'

'But you'd have killed Lika's assistants and kidnapped him?'

Adam scowled. 'Why don't you look closer to home? His boss died in the helicopter crash, and I'd imagine there'll be quite a struggle to replace him.'

Adam's phone buzzed, and he checked the caller before taking it into the kitchen. Chapman couldn't make out his words, but the fireman's body language told him it was important. He ended it after five minutes and came back into the room.

'Antonia?'

'She'll be late. Do you want to eat?'

'What's happened?'

'They were on the way back from seeing her source and ran into an ambush—'

'Is she okay?'

'Sprained ankle and the driver's in hospital with whiplash and concussion. Someone used a stinger and took out all four tyres.'

'So, why is she okay? I mean, what happened to Lika's men?'

Adam returned to the kitchen and checked the pans. 'As the ambush started, another group of men arrived and took them out.'

'You serious?'

'Probably linked to the fire at Lika's office.'

Chapman digested this news. 'And your mate, he just watched?'

'She's at Kensington Police Station giving a statement. We'll get a call when she's ready to collect. Rice okay?'

'What? Yeah, fine, thanks.' Chapman didn't believe him, but what had really happened?

But the idea of another Albanian faction targeting Lika made sense. He retrieved his phone and rang the station. A contact told him they'd received a call to an incident in Holland Park. They'd found the car imbedded in a brick wall, the remains of a stinger and three dead men, all armed, but none shot. What the hell had happened?

They ate at the table in the kitchen, his seat overlooking the sunken garden, now illuminated with solar-powered lamps. He ate seconds of a spicy Sichuan chicken that made his tongue tingle, its flavour more intense than the one he normally ordered when he visited the restaurants in Soho. They loaded the dishwasher and waited, Chapman having another beer.

Adam's phone buzzed again. 'Let's go.' He slipped a polo neck over his head and headed out into the hallway, where he picked up a quilted waterproof.

Chapman drained his glass and joined him, slipping into his still-damp coat. Adam secured his flat and led them to a brand-new Prius.

'You changed your car?'

'Hired. I've used a different one each day.'

They drove in silence to a twenty-four-hour multistorey. 'Why are we here?'

Adam ignored him and drove up to the third floor. Few cars remained, but a black Range Rover sat in the centre block. The doors opened and five people got out, Antonia in their midst. A wave of relief made him light-headed. Adam drove into a space opposite and Chapman leapt out.

'Antonia, you're okay?'

A tired smile greeted him. 'Just this.' She pointed to a cast brace round her left calf.

Adam introduced the driver, a black man who towered over him, as his friend Byron Mason. Chapman recognised him from his security company profile. The other three stayed in the background. Chapman spotted Virgil, but didn't know the other two.

'Who are those?'

'They work for me.' Byron's deep voice resonated. 'After what happened, I thought we could use extra muscle.'

'So, what *did* happen?'

'Can we go home? I'm exhausted.' Antonia looked shattered.

'Sure, I'll help you into the car.' Adam offered a shoulder.

Chapman waited until she was out of earshot. 'I don't believe this shit about another gang.'

Byron fixed him with a level gaze. 'I took two of them down. They had guns and I didn't—'

'Self-defence then.'

He snorted. 'Right. How do you rate my chances?'

'I'm not a judge.' He glanced at Byron, trying to read him. 'Did you have anything to do with Lika being taken out?'

The big man frowned. 'That's not good. Wasn't Antonia monitoring his comms to find out when the next attack was coming?'

'Yeah. But whoever did it took him with them. Handy if they want to make him tell you who's behind the contract on her?'

'Risky. Someone like Lika might die before you got anything. It makes more sense to keep tabs on him and see who he reports back to. I hoped he'd meet his paymaster following tonight's failed attack. Lika will have wanted more money to continue or he'd want to back out, and he'd have told them in person. Guys like him always believe the "look them in the eye" bullshit they get from watching gangster movies.'

It made sense. Maybe Adam's friends had nothing to do with Lika's disappearance.

'What do you plan to do?' Byron said.

'I'm a serving police officer, I can't ignore information about three killings—'

'Oh yeah. Do you want to know what happened to the third?' Chapman waited.

'Antonia kicked him in the face. Knocked him straight out.'

'What should she have done? He tried to kill her.'

'No argument from me, but she didn't stop. She kicked him a few times after he passed out. What's the term for that, Mr Serving-police-officer?'

Chapman checked Adam's car. Antonia sat slumped in the passenger seat. He'd seen her kill before – each time, saving both their lives.

Byron folded his arms. 'Let me know what you want to do.'

His crew had come forward and flanked him. Antonia had her eyes shut and Adam looked into a distance only he could see. Chapman swallowed, feeling very lonely and exposed.

CHAPTER 26

The headache filling Antonia's skull had become almost unbearable as she watched Chapman talking to Byron Mason through the windscreen of Adam's car. She'd avoided taking the painkillers the nurse who'd treated her leg prescribed, but she couldn't hold out much longer. She relived the relief when Byron introduced himself. It had taken little persuasion for her to agree to give his version of the attack, especially when she considered her part in the deaths of their attackers. Yet more ammunition for her nightmares.

A wave of depression washed over her. Chapman's body language changed, and he nodded at Byron. What was keeping him? She just wanted to go home and go to bed.

She reached across and pressed the horn. 'Can we get going?'

Chapman waved and finished his conversation before getting into the seat behind Adam. The car pulled away with a squeal of tyres, leaving the four people and their Range Rover behind. They left the car park and she closed her eyes, but the stabbing pain behind them didn't abate.

'I'll drop you home,' Adam said to Chapman.

'No need, I'll get a cab from your place.' Chapman sounded despondent.

She sensed disappointment, but also concern. The idea he worried so much about her surprised her once more. She suspected he'd given Byron a hard time about what happened, but what could they have done? At least they'd dealt with the attack and Lika would need to get another team, or realise he'd bitten off too much. A piercing pain as the car went over a pothole made her grit her teeth. Nobody talked and Adam put on some music, stuff she heard on old programmes from the eighties.

She jerked awake. The car had stopped. She scanned her surroundings in a panic, but recognised the crescent Adam lived on. Chapman got out and opened her door, offering a hand, and she joined him. The cold, wet cobbles sucked heat out of her bare foot as she leant on his shoulder and hobbled to the house.

Her best dress now resembled a rag, and she'd lost her only decent shoes. Back to jeans and leather jacket tomorrow. The warmth of Adam's flat enveloped her, and the aroma of food reminded her she'd not eaten.

'Do you want a hot drink while you wait for the cab?' Adam asked Chapman.

'We need to talk.'

She guessed this included her, although she just wanted a shower and her bed. They sat in the kitchen and waited in silence. Adam put the kettle on and placed a bowl from the fridge into the microwave.

Antonia closed her eyes. 'Can you get me the painkillers from the side pocket?'

Chapman found them and Adam passed her a glass of water. The nurse told her to take two, but she'd try one and see if it made enough difference. Adam placed a bowl of steaming food in front of her and she fell on it, shovelling it into her mouth. He brought the hot drinks and sat facing her and Chapman.

The tense silence built until Chapman broke it. 'You and your mate denied it,' he said to Adam, 'but I know you were behind the attack on Lika's office.'

'When?' she said through a mouthful of rice and chicken.

Chapman told her about the aborted raid.

'Why do you think Adam's behind it?'

'Not necessarily him, but his gang of has-beens playing soldiers—'

'Where would *I* be without those "has-beens"?'

'His games have prevented us tracking down the person paying Lika.'

Adam studied him with calm indifference. 'Why would I do that?'

'You obviously think you can beat it out of Lika, which is why you've grabbed him.'

'Yeah, but you can't guarantee he'd talk before he died—'

'Your mate said the same. Are you both some sort of experts on torture?'

'Can you two stop it?' She wanted to smash their heads together.

'Sorry.' Adam took her empty bowl away and returned with two beers and two glasses and placed them in the middle of the table. 'If I'd done it, I'd have taken Lika, but left his office intact. Giving you a chance to follow the trail from there.'

Chapman picked up a can, opened it and poured. 'So, who did it then?'

'It's obvious, isn't it?' The jagged edge of her headache had blunted, but so had her brain, reminding her why she hated taking these painkillers. What was she going to say? The two men studied her, their irritation with each other turning to concern.

Adam spoke first. 'It makes sense to investigate any rivals for Lika's boss's job. Or have you considered it might be the person paying him?'

'Why would they do it?' Chapman emptied the last drops from the can.

'If they're worried you're getting close.'

'How would they know?'

'You're going to tell me none of your colleagues sell information?'

Chapman's irritation returned but then he gestured at her with the can. 'We discussed it in your office. If the same people who bugged it—'

'Whoa.' Antonia held up her hands. 'You're saying someone bugged my office?'

Chapman exchanged a puzzled look with Adam, then turned back to Antonia. 'Right. You know this, or knew it. They were listening to us when those two bozos raided.'

A faint memory, like a barely remembered dream, swam away from Antonia. She reached for it, but her headache gave her a jolt. 'I'm going to have to get some sleep.'

'Seriously, Antonia, don't you remember?'

'Russell, leave her alone. If she has a concussion, she might not. She's had a hell of a day.'

She stood, desperate to get out of her dress and get cleaned up. The stabbing pain in her head grew more intense. Taking the pack of painkillers, she shuffled out of the room. The two men's reactions told her something, but she couldn't deal with it now.

◆ ◆ ◆

Despite feeling like death the next morning, Antonia insisted on going to work at the normal time. The constant headache plus flashbacks to the attack on their car kept her awake, and she'd only managed a couple of hours. Adam, who treated her as if she was broken, drove her to the rendezvous with the security team. Her unease increased as they got closer until, by the time they entered the car park, her insides were like knotted ropes.

They made their way up to the second floor, where a VW people-carrier waited. Virgil got out and waved. Rafael, looking no worse for wear apart from a cut above his left eye, saluted her. She forced herself to get in, unable to rid herself of the sensation of getting into a coffin, and secured the seatbelt.

The ordeal of the journey lasted far too long, although her guards acted like nothing had happened yesterday. Those men had almost killed them.

They finally deposited her at Vincent Terrace and, exhausted but relieved, she let herself in. The absence of an alarm and sound of the hoover warned her of Sabirah's presence before she saw her in the main office. Sabirah stopped, looking haunted.

Guilt at having let her friend down stabbed at Antonia. 'Sabirah, do you want to arrange something with the children on Saturday? I promise I won't let you down this time.'

Sabirah reacted like she wanted to bolt. 'Saturday? Sorry, Jean has offered to take the children out. Sorry.'

Antonia hid her relief. She doubted she'd be feeling up to taking the children out by then, but at least she'd offered. 'That's a shame, maybe the following weekend?'

'Okay, I'll see.' Sabirah checked the time. 'I have to go.'

'Is everything all right? You've avoided me for a few days.'

Sabirah stood with her mouth open. 'Lots of worry about the immigration.'

'Eleanor told me. I am sorry they're giving you such a hard time. Is there anything I can do?' The way they used refugees as punchbags to distract from their failings had always angered her, but it was getting worse.

'I have to go.' Sabirah seemed so uncomfortable it made Antonia want to weep.

Had what she'd done been so awful? 'When I let you down last weekend, it was because some men wanted to kill me. I couldn't see you and put you at risk.'

Sabirah spun away and Antonia reached for her shoulder, but her friend almost ran to get away, dragging the machine and hose behind her. Antonia wanted to follow her to offer help, but a hollowness drained her of energy. She trudged to her office and tried to face the day. She stared at the screen, her brain unable to function.

'You look dreadful.' Eleanor's greeting jerked her out of her stupor. 'I bet you've stayed awake all night riddled with guilt.'

'Guilt?' Did she know what had happened with Sabirah?

'I never enjoyed it, but you can't shirk the responsibility when you're in charge.'

Eleanor sounded confused. Antonia wondered what she meant. 'I'm not complaining, but I'm pretty sure we never discussed attempts on my life during my job interview.'

'What are you talking about?'

Antonia told her about the attack, omitting her and Byron's parts in the men's deaths.

Eleanor sat for a minute. 'I'm so sorry, Antonia. That's it, we're dropping the story—'

'We're not. It's the one thing I'm certain of.'

'Don't be ludicrous. No story's worth risking your—'

'I back off now and I might as well change our strapline from "Investigating without fear or favour" to "We'll investigate if people don't get too annoyed".'

'You're being childish. Nobody expects you to risk your life.'

'What about the sixty-five journalists killed last year?'

'But none of them worked in a . . . a democracy like ours.'

Heat filled Antonia's head. 'I don't need this. I've got a head-ache, and I hardly slept. We're continuing with this story. It's my decision. That's also a responsibility of being in charge.'

Eleanor recognised she wasn't going to win and gave a rueful smile. 'Where's your coffee?'

Antonia checked the time. 'Jean normally brings one. She must be late.'

'Are you joking? Because if you are, it's not funny.'

'I know she's got a thing about being punctual, but anyone can get caught in traffic.'

Eleanor grew concerned. 'How serious was your head injury? Did you lose consciousness?'

'For a second, or even less.'

'That's it. You're not working today. I want you to have a scan, and you're not coming back until you get the all-clear.'

'Please Eleanor, I don't have the energy for this. Anyway, they gave me a scan last night. There's nothing wrong.'

Eleanor's bemusement reminded her of Chapman last night.

'You sacked Jean yesterday,' Eleanor said.

'What? Why? How could I have?'

'The why is, she'd bugged your office.'

'Chapman said the same last night. I thought he was winding me up.'

'You seriously don't remember?'

'I don't play games, Eleanor.'

'In that case, get another check-up and don't come to work until you get to the root of the problem.'

The sense of helplessness paralysed Antonia. She could always trust her memory, even cursing it because it wouldn't let go of the things she wanted to forget.

A combination of a long phone call at his desk and traffic made Chapman late getting to Vincent Terrace. Despite his desire to check up on Antonia, he'd avoided contacting her yesterday and only came now because Eleanor had invited him to the meeting with Professor Swan, the head of the lab where Edda Bartholf had once worked, and the man who had apparently devised the treatment given to Neil Griffin and the other prisoners. Eleanor had told Chapman of her concerns about Antonia's memory loss and he'd spoken to the officer who'd investigated the crash. The doctor who'd treated her had said she might not get her memory back for a few weeks.

He'd also spoken to his ex-diplomatic protection contact to increase the security she was getting, and Chapman would pay for it, despite what she said. He still wasn't sure if he bought Adam's protestations of innocence about the disappearance of Lika. Adam's suggestion it could have been Reed-Mayhew did chime with his thoughts at the incident, but that was before Byron told him he'd killed two of Lika's men. Nobody had seen the gangster since the explosion and fire at his place and Chapman suspected he'd soon be propping up the foundations of a large building, if he wasn't already doing so. Few people would shed tears over the prospect, but the ending of a line of enquiry that might have led them to the people ultimately trying to kill Antonia frustrated him.

Miles let him in, his smile strained. An air of gloom hung over the place, one he'd not seen since the murder of Antonia's predecessor, Alan Turner. He knocked on Antonia's door and walked in.

'What are you doing here?' Antonia looked exhausted. No wonder Eleanor was worried about her.

'You've forgotten our appointment?'

Confusion made her frown.

'I invited him,' Eleanor said from behind him.

Antonia glared at him. 'You think it's okay to make fun of me?'

'Sorry, poor joke.'

Antonia dismissed him with a wave and turned on Eleanor. 'Why did you invite him?'

'I thought it would be useful to have his input. He's investigated the death of one of the prisoners being experimented on.'

Antonia considered this for a few moments. 'Okay, but I've got work to do.' She returned her attention to her screen.

He followed Eleanor out of the room and closed the door behind him.

'Sorry about that, Inspector,' Eleanor said, 'and thanks for coming.'

'My fault. I shouldn't have made that stupid crack about her forgetting I was coming.'

'Not your wisest decision. Mr Swan is obviously going to be late. Cup of tea while you're waiting?'

Chapman didn't want tea; he wanted to tell Antonia how sorry he was and how worried he was about her. She'd looked lower than he'd seen her since Turner's death. He followed Eleanor through the almost deserted office into the kitchen.

After making him tea, Eleanor gave him a tablet with the notes they'd used for the article Antonia had pulled at the last instant on his advice, then excused herself, saying she needed to finalise some details with her solicitor. Chapman read them, then checked his emails and sent a text to Abby. He'd caught up with all his correspondence and had half a cup of cold tea left when Antonia appeared in the doorway wearing her coat and carrying her backpack.

'I'm going to have to go. I've got an appointment.'

He stood. 'I thought you were eager to see Swan?'

'I am, but he's over an hour late now and I've tried ringing him, but no answer. He's obviously changed his mind.'

Behind her, Eleanor finished making a call and joined them. 'I thought you said he was keen.'

'I thought he was,' Antonia said. 'He's either reconsidered or been got at.' She looked beaten.

However low she'd got, Chapman hadn't seen her like this. 'Why don't you cancel your appointment and have a break? You look shattered.'

'I think I can manage a meeting with an informant.'

'I've arranged for extra security starting Monday. Why don't you take the weekend off and you'll be able to—'

'When I want you to run my life, I'll let you know.' Antonia spun away.

Eleanor blocked her path. 'He's right, Antonia. You need—'

'Not you as well.' The doorbell rang. 'That will be Virgil.' Antonia dodged past the wheelchair and strode to the entrance.

'Antonia! Stop being ridiculous.' Eleanor clenched her fists.

Chapman followed Antonia as she opened the outer door. Virgil waited in the opening.

'Antonia!' Chapman resisted reaching out to impede her.

She held up a hand to forestall him and continued.

The slamming of the front door sounded like a full stop. His insides churned. *Why the hell do I always do this?* He trudged back and stood facing Eleanor. 'I might as well get off.'

'Sorry, Inspector, it appears we're both in her bad books—'

The doorbell rang. Had Antonia come back? He made his way to the door and checked the security camera screen, disappointed when he saw the image. The man who stood outside looked a few years younger than Chapman's forty-three. After identifying him, Chapman opened the door.

The man bustled in. He resembled a power lifter rather than an academic. 'Apologies for my lateness, I have an adequate reason. My assistant was involved in a smash outside our clinic.'

'Is he okay?' Eleanor said.

'She. I hope so. Shall we crack on?' He studied Chapman and Eleanor. 'Unless I'm badly mistaken, neither of you is Antonia Conti.'

'Sorry, she had to leave. I'll ring her.' Chapman tried her number while Eleanor led Swan into Antonia's office. As he'd feared, she didn't have her phone on.

'I can't get hold of her,' Chapman said as he joined them and took Antonia's seat, which still held the warmth from her body.

Swan refused refreshments, and they sat studying each other.

'I recognise Mrs Curtis from your website, but you say you're a policeman. Do you have your ID?' Swan's hazel eyes scanned the ID card, and he returned it. 'Before I start, what do either of you know about cognitive neuroscience?'

'Why don't you assume we're both ignorant but interested,' Eleanor said with a smile.

'All right.' He took a breath and began. 'I'm a trained psychologist, but memory and how it works fascinated me, so I specialised in cognitive neuroscience. As a reporter, and you a policeman, you'll know memory isn't fixed and is unreliable. The advantage of this is, we can manipulate memories to reduce the emotional impact of traumatic incidents or overcome phobias. We can even make people forget specific incidents.'

'Isn't it a bit hit-and-miss?' Chapman had seen too many colleagues failed by therapy.

'Up to now. Most techniques rely on a combination of drugs and therapy, but it doesn't always work, and the memory may return. And if the trauma results from several incidents or a prolonged exposure to whatever caused it, the existing techniques are

345

less effective. This is where my method is revolutionary.' A note of pride entered his voice. 'What I've done is create a device which identifies all memories associated with a particular trauma and completely erases them.'

'Oh yeah, and all we have to do is give you the contents of our bank account?'

Swan snorted. 'My research does cost money, and I don't have a huge budget like some organisations, Inspector.'

'How does your technique work?' Eleanor asked. Although Swan had agreed to let them record him, she'd already covered her notepad in hieroglyphics.

'I'd rather not give too much away, but it involves analysing brain activity during the recollection of particular memories. We detect structural changes in neurons during the process and thus identify where that particular memory is stored. It's not an exact representation of what happens, but it helps people to picture the process. We simultaneously use functional imaging techniques which I developed from researching quantum brain dynamics—'

'Not using lasers?' Chapman's head was threatening to explode. 'What gave you that idea?'

'Antonia mentioned it in the article she wrote. She must have got it from her informant.'

'Someone was having fun at her expense. Putting it simply, my device measures electrical activity in different parts of the brain.'

'Like an EEG scan?' Chapman said.

Swan looked disdainful. 'We use a much more sensitive device which not only identifies your brain activity, but allows us to focus on a specific memory. Each memory has what I call a "signature" and we can isolate it, and then remove it. And even store it.'

'If this technique is so effective, how come every clinic isn't using it?' Eleanor said.

'I'm a conscientious scientist, so I made sure I carried out thorough clinical trials and these highlighted some problems.' He hesitated, as though unwilling to admit flaws in his invention. 'What we discovered is, the brain, like nature, abhors a vacuum, and creates memories to fill the space formerly occupied by those we remove.'

'And that's a problem because . . .?'

'Anything can trigger new pseudo-memories. An actual event the subject witnesses, in which they insert themselves. A TV programme or film. Something they've heard, read or even a dream.'

'An incident you've heard about could then become a "memory"?' Chapman's mind raced. What Neil Griffin had said now made sense.

'Possibly.'

'How soon after you've removed the original memories?'

'That's another problem. There isn't a pattern. Some people replace them almost straight away, others, weeks or even months later. There's also an added complication. Some people will replace parts of the removed memories at different times, replacing them with unconnected pseudo-memories from many sources.'

'Someone subject to your treatment could end up creating these pseudo-memories forever?' The idea appalled Chapman.

'No!' Swan looked uncomfortable and pulled at one of his large earlobes. 'We think it only continues until they've replaced a similar amount of memory.'

'You think?' Eleanor looked horrified. 'And you've experimented on people?'

'Of course, we tried it out on lab animals first.'

'Traumatised rats?' Eleanor couldn't hide her scorn.

Swan reddened. 'I'm working on a solution. Anyway, these people were desperate; nothing else had worked for them.'

'It doesn't make what you did sound any better.'

'They're all volunteers. I explain the risks.' He swallowed. 'Can I have some water?'

Chapman found a jug and glasses in the kitchen and brought them in on a tray.

Swan filled a glass and took a gulp. 'Once I discovered the problem, I paused the experiments until we found a solution.'

Chapman said, 'These pseudo-memories. Can't you just remove them?'

'So far, no. And it causes other issues . . .'

'In the article Antonia wrote, your assistant said she'd removed them from prisoners affected.'

'Of course, you already know about the problems in the prisons. Another lie, I'm afraid.'

'Jesus!' Eleanor said. 'One of their staff came forward to expose the abuses, but someone killed him.'

'You're joking.'

'I don't joke about death, Professor Swan. They drove a lorry into his car.'

Swan paled. 'The accident, the reason I'm late, involved my car and a lorry. My assistant took it because I'd forgotten to charge it, and she lives close by. I'm here in her car.'

Eleanor broke the long silence. 'After the whistle-blower died, a woman calling herself Fiona contacted Antonia offering information. But she only told us some of it. She never mentioned the pseudo-memories, and she mixed her account up with enough lies to cause us problems. Luckily, the inspector here spotted the errors, and we avoided making a catastrophic mistake.'

'My former assistant, Edda Bartholf?'

'As we've since discovered. Can you explain how you prevent the rogue memories taking root?'

'I mentioned we can identify individual memories. We can record them, and we can also create new ones. We're getting better and can almost recreate exact recollections of a specific event in someone who wasn't there. You must implant the same "volume" of memories. I use the term "volume" but what we discovered is, the intensity of a memory is as important as its extent. So, an intense memory of a minor event can occupy as much space as the memory of huge, sprawling events.'

An idea occurred to Chapman. 'Could you implant a false memory in someone without their knowledge?'

'It doesn't work on everyone, but yes. If someone's susceptible, you can remove the memory of them attending a session, so they don't even know they've had any treatment.'

'So, you can make someone believe they've committed a crime, or been the victims.'

Swan nodded, now even more uncomfortable. 'You don't have to implant such memories. I discovered the problem when one of my patients decided he was a monster who'd committed unspeakable crimes.'

Excitement surged through Chapman. 'What happened?'

'He barricaded himself in the kitchen at the clinic, opened all the gas valves and then lit a match.' Swan ran a hand through his cropped hair. 'I'd just broken the door down and the place went up, taking my hair with it.'

'He killed himself?'

'I'm afraid so. Three other patients at clinics which trialled the technique tried self-harming.'

It would explain why Neil Griffin had climbed on the roof, punishing himself for imagined crimes that his cellmate had committed. But had someone deliberately implanted pseudo-memories of crimes in the minds of the two wealthy suicides, Snowden and Futcher? 'You said other clinics were involved—'

'Not any more. Once we discovered the problems, we pulled the plug.'

'None of them are implanting memories?'

'They shouldn't be. We haven't shared the technique with them yet.'

Chapman hadn't missed the obfuscation. 'But you suspect at least one is.'

Swan's discomfort increased. 'I'm not prepared to go on record about it, but, yes, I suspect one is. There's a clinic in Knightsbridge . . .'

The four 'abuse victims' and both Snowden and Futcher had gone to clinics in Knightsbridge. Antonia was right. This led back to Reed-Mayhew.

'And how did they discover your new technique?' Eleanor said.

'My former assistant knows it intimately. Her mother, Lina Schiffer, runs the Syrus Clinic—'

'That's where Antonia's gone,' Eleanor shouted.

'Isn't she undercover?' Unease made Chapman fidgety.

The colour drained from Swan's features. 'She's met my former assistant, Edda Bartholf.'

'Yes,' Eleanor said. 'She posed as "Fiona", Antonia's source for the story we pulled.'

'But Bartholf's now working with her mother at that clinic!'

'Shit!' Chapman stood. 'It's where she was coming back from when those men attacked her the other night. Bartholf must have tipped off the gunmen.' He pulled out his phone and ran for the exit.

CHAPTER 27

The thought she should confess everything to Antonia had preyed on Sabirah's mind since she'd seen her yesterday morning. At least she hadn't lied to her about spending tomorrow with Jean. Jean had rung the night before, inviting the children for a sleepover, and the children had jumped at the chance. She suspected Jean having the latest computer games swung it, especially in Hakim's case.

A gust of wind cut through her coat, and she shivered. The one she'd seen in the charity shop near her work had gone. They rarely got such good designer clothes in there. She could spend tomorrow searching for another, knowing Jean would be taking care of the children.

The bell from Hakim's school carried through the frigid air and she hurried. The enormous cars most of the other mothers came in littered the street, many half on the pavement. She reached the school gates as the children streamed out of the building. A few of the other parents acknowledged her. She'd hoped to make friends with some, but the memory of being treated as some sort of trophy to show off to her friends by one mother when she'd first arrived still stung. At least Hakim made friends easily.

She spotted him in a group of boys and waved. His smile lifted her heart. He parted from his friends at the gate and ran towards her, beaming.

He held up a badge. 'I won this for getting a hundred per cent in my maths test.'

'Well done, I'm so proud of you.' She wanted to hold him but didn't want to embarrass him in front of his friends. She contented herself with ruffling his hair. How long would this last before she could hug him in public again?

They walked to Nadimah's school together, him full of his day. She loved hearing about what he'd done and his joy in learning, just like his father. But then he said something that catapulted her into the issue dominating her waking hours.

'A man came to see me when I was in class. Everyone was looking at me.'

'Did this man say who he was?' She realised she'd been too sharp, but Hakim didn't seem to notice.

'No, he spoke to my teacher for ten minutes and then he took me to an empty classroom and asked me about Antonia and Auntie Eleanor.'

'What did you tell him?'

'I said how kind they were and how Antonia is good at fighting and took Nadimah to teach her to fight.'

She remembered the accusation that criminals ran the gym Antonia took her daughter to.

'Did I do something wrong?' A tremor entered her son's voice.

'Of course not. Why?'

'You have the expression you have when you don't think we can see you.'

Shame and sadness overwhelmed her. 'I'm just thinking. Don't worry.' She ruffled his hair again. 'Do you want to go to the pantomime next Sunday?'

'Can we?'

'Of course.' Colleagues from work had arranged an outing, and she'd book the seats tomorrow when she did the extra shift she'd arranged after Jean had offered to take the children.

They arrived at Nadimah's school, and she wanted to ask her daughter if someone had questioned her. But Hakim's excited greeting, 'Mama's taking us to the panto next week,' set the tone, and she didn't want to spoil the children's mood.

She hid her concern until they got home. Although Jean had promised them takeaways later, Sabirah insisted on giving them *manakish* spread with cheese. They wolfed it down. She should feed them English food, but didn't want them to forget their roots. And having 'foreign' food was such a British thing to do, wasn't it? She cleared up while they packed their overnight bags, making sure she didn't have any negative thoughts in case they came in and caught her out.

Sabirah maintained the facade of happiness all the way to Jean's house, although it wasn't difficult with the children's excitement at the treats they anticipated. She checked the address when they arrived. The vast house only had one bell by the front door. Certain they'd come to the wrong place, she pressed the button and waited for the inevitable disappointment.

'Oh hello, you must be Jean's latest project. Come in.' A grey-haired woman wearing a tweed skirt and hand knitted cardigan opened the door and stepped back.

'Is Jean here?'

'Any minute, she's been held up. The interview overran.'

'Interview?' Sabirah ushered the children into the warmth.

'She might have her faults, but idleness isn't one of them. She's not one to stay out of work long.'

'But Jean has a job.' The odour of lavender and mothballs pervaded the expansive hallway she'd entered. Despite its size, the dark wallpaper and heavy furniture filling it made it oppressive.

'She wasn't going to stay there with those harridans. The way they treated her was disgraceful. I'd normally advise her to get another job first, but she had to resign in this case.'

'Jean has resigned?' She wasn't sure what a harridan was, but suspected it wasn't a compliment.

'Yes, you're the cleaner, aren't you? I'm surprised you can stand it. The Conti woman is just an awful bully, like a lot of those people when they get a bit of power over us, and the old bat in the wheelchair probably thinks she can get away with treating people like muck because of her misfortune.'

'They're kind people, not bullies.' What had happened? Jean loved working there.

'Hmm.' The woman studied her through thick-lensed tortoise-shell glasses. 'I suppose where you come from, women get used to being mistreated, but my daughter isn't.'

In my country, they respected me as an architect, and didn't treat me as a second-class citizen. 'I'm sure it's misunderstanding.' Jean didn't always grasp why people did things, and Antonia was under strain, but she wouldn't bully anyone.

The woman sniffed and addressed the children. 'Take your coats off if you're staying.'

Sabirah nodded to let them know they could. Their unease made them timid, but she wouldn't leave them until Jean got home. Her introduction to Jean's mother explained why her friend behaved unusually. The dark furniture and décor continued in the gloomy living room their hostess led them into. The odour of decay and dust added to the sense of neglect. She directed the children to a large sofa with pieces of crocheted fabric laid on the arms and back. They perched on the edge of the seat.

'Are you staying then?' Jean's mother's attention made Sabirah uneasy.

'Until Jean gets back. I want to say hello.'

354

'You might as well sit down, then. Can I get you refreshments?'

'No, thank you.' And both children shook their heads, their expressions saying, 'Don't leave us.' Sabirah joined them on the sofa.

'I'm having an Earl Grey.' The woman left.

'Mama, I don't—'

'Shh.' She laid a finger against Hakim's lips, then whispered, 'We'll see Jean, then eat with her and we can decide, okay?'

He smiled, and a surge of tenderness overwhelmed her. She would do anything to keep these children safe, even betray her friends.

The large clock in a tall dark case chimed. The arm moved with a click, which echoed. Once she heard it, it dominated, counting off the seconds. She studied the room. A tiny, ancient TV sat in a corner, almost forgotten. A stuffed owl perched on a twig on top of it. Nadimah also noticed it and screwed her face up in disgust.

The front door opened, and Jean called out, 'I'm home, Mum. Sorry I'm late.'

The old woman's voice came from deeper in the house. 'We're in the parlour.'

The door swung open and Sabirah leapt to her feet.

'Oh, hello.' Jean's smile made the room almost welcoming. She withdrew and shouted, 'Why have you stuck them in here, Mum?'

'It's where we greet our guests. Should I have placed them in the kitchen?'

Jean looked at the children and rolled her eyes. 'Parents. They have no idea, have they? Come on, let's put you somewhere more comfortable.'

The children, much cheered by this exchange, followed her to a doorway at the end of the corridor. Behind it lay a modern, light and bright room. Instead of the clutter and dark furniture of the parlour, a few items of modern furniture in pale wood and upholstered in pastel fabric were arranged round a huge screen that dominated one wall.

Jean operated a remote and the screen burst into life. The scene looked like something from a film.

'You've got *Game of Thrones?*' Hakim's eyes shone.

'Of course.' She picked up a game controller from the side table and handed it to him, then gave Nadimah another.

Within seconds, Sabirah had turned from their saviour to an unwelcome distraction. 'I'll go,' she mouthed to Jean, who accompanied her out of the door. Although eager to discover what had happened between Jean and Antonia, she didn't want to sour the mood. But why hadn't Jean said anything when she rang yesterday? She'd speak to her about it tomorrow when she collected the children.

The need to focus on her surroundings had stopped Antonia thinking too much about her run-in with Chapman. Did he set out to wind her up, or couldn't he help himself? She tried to forget about him, or at least to not let him upset her. Although her headache had faded over the course of the previous day, Antonia's memory of the incidents leading up to Sawyer's sacking remained opaque. Ironic that she was going through so much trouble to forget some memories when others had disappeared so easily, accompanied by a slight headache. Although when she'd told the doctor at casualty – and the police – she'd forgotten what happened *after* the accident, he'd reassured her she'd regain her memory.

As they approached the clinic, she couldn't rid herself of the sense of dread, and even her normally imperturbable companions seemed tense. She thought of cancelling and going home for an early night, but now Swan had let her down, she needed to get more information out of Schiffer. She had five more sessions of preparation before she had to commit herself to the treatment.

At the clinic, the young woman receptionist greeted her with a professional smile and Antonia took a seat. Yet again she was the only one here and she realised she'd not seen any other patients. The sessions weren't cheap, but she wasn't paying enough to keep a place like this going. She must ask Virgil if they'd seen anyone else arrive or leave.

Schiffer arrived within minutes. 'You're a lot more relaxed today, Ms Okoye. Please come through.'

The woman, however, seemed tense, and Antonia tried to read her. She followed Schiffer to the treatment room. Again, the equipment waited in the centre of the room, and Antonia suddenly wanted to be elsewhere. She fought the urge.

'Could you give me a bit more information about exactly how the treatment will work, Dr Schiffer?'

She checked the time. 'I'm in a hurry today, I've got a theatre engagement. But next session, and certainly before we start the treatment.' Schiffer's smile lacked conviction, but Antonia couldn't get a handle on why.

She climbed on the recliner and Schiffer connected the helmet and cables. The machine emitted a low hum, making Antonia's scalp crawl. Schiffer typed some instructions into her laptop. 'Relax, Ms Okoye. You need to be thinking of the memories you want to get rid of, so we can map them.' The lights dimmed and Schiffer's soporific voice murmured more instructions. Antonia had a strong sense she should get out of there, but the thought receded as her head swam. The sensation of falling down a long tube wasn't unpleasant. Had she recently experienced the same process? Before she could focus on the thought, her descent accelerated, and the room faded to nothing.

Antonia crawled up a long dark tube lined with rubble. Was she dreaming, or had she been drugged? A figure loomed over her, and she cringed from it. Her body refused her orders and frustration made her jaw ache.

'How do you feel, Antonia? You fell asleep again.'

She knew the voice. Schiffer. Her brain churned and her thoughts fired off in all directions. 'Like I've woken from a deep sleep.'

'Would you like a drink?'

'Hmm, yes please. Water.'

Schiffer left the room. Antonia sat up, her body heavy, and tried to recall what had happened. She'd arrived and Schiffer had greeted her, but then nothing.

Schiffer returned followed by a tall blonde woman. 'You've met my daughter, Edda. But you know her as Fiona.'

'What are you doing here?' Antonia asked her.

'Here's your water.' Schiffer handed Antonia a glass.

Antonia looked past her at Fiona. 'You said you'd get back to me after you'd visited the prison last weekend.'

Fiona seemed unduly relieved by Antonia's comment. 'Sorry, things got on top of me.'

'I'll leave you and Edda to catch up.' Schiffer left, closing the door behind her.

Antonia sipped the chilled water. 'Do I call you Fiona or Edda?'

'Whichever makes you comfortable.'

Something about Fiona made her uneasy, but she couldn't quite bring it into focus. A slight headache grew more intense as she attempted to dredge up the memory.

The door burst open and Schiffer appeared, alarm etched on her features. 'Those men have come back.'

'Which men?' Antonia put the glass down.

'They've been watching the place. We saw them last time you came, but thought nothing of it.'

'Let me see.' Fiona rushed out.

Antonia couldn't remember much about what she'd done last time she came, but the attack on her way home remained vivid. Hadn't Adam's friend killed two, and she'd done the same to another? Maybe a different crew were watching the clinic, and they'd come to finish her.

Fiona barrelled into the room. 'They're the ones who followed me from our last meeting. We need to go, Antonia.'

Their alarm infected Antonia. Where were Virgil and Rafael? Something must have happened to them. They wouldn't have allowed anyone suspect to approach the clinic. Filled with concern for them, she followed Fiona out into the reception area. The receptionist wasn't there, but a screen behind her desk showed an indistinct figure at the door.

'This way.' Fiona opened a door on to a corridor leading past the treatment room to the back of the building.

Antonia hesitated, then the man outside banged on the door.

'Hurry, Antonia.' Fiona beckoned her and they ran to a narrow steel staircase going down to a door with a panic bar across it. Someone had gone through and not closed it. Outside, a small courtyard lay in darkness. The outline of a car filled most of the space. Fiona opened a back door.

'Get inside and lie on the floor.'

Antonia hesitated. This all felt wrong.

'Come on, they'll be here soon.'

The urgency in Fiona's voice propelled Antonia forward, and she jumped in. The receptionist sat in the driver's seat and started the engine. Fiona got in, slammed the door and crouched down, gesturing for Antonia to do the same. Then she pulled a rug over them as the car rolled forward. The smell of wool and rubber mingled with the scent of Fiona's perfume. The notion of going into danger paralysed Antonia as she crouched in the cramped space.

◆ ◆ ◆

The lights changed to red on the road ahead and Chapman cursed, resisting the temptation to use the blue lights. He reached for his phone in the bracket, punched redial and listened to it ring out. Then, just before he killed it, Adam answered.

Chapman didn't let him finish his greeting. 'Are you backup for Antonia?'

'No, Byron—'

'Can you contact the people guarding her? I haven't got their new phone numbers after the crash.'

'What's happened?'

'She's gone to the Syrus Clinic, but the woman who duped Antonia works for them. It's also where Antonia came from when Lika's men attacked her, and I think someone at the clinic tipped them off.'

'Shit! I'll warn them now. Give me the address and I'll see you there.'

Making Adam promise to ring back, he killed the call. The lights changed, and he overtook a bus, forcing a van coming the other way to take evasive action. He didn't celebrate his good fortune for long. Piccadilly teemed with traffic in both directions, either going home for the weekend or coming into town for the night. The rain didn't help. He passed Buckingham Palace and entered the tunnel under the Wellington Arch, hoping he didn't get stuck in there with no signal.

He passed the junction with Sloane Street and turned into the Brompton Road as his phone rang. 'Adam.'

'The guys tried to get in, but they can't get hold of Antonia and the occupiers won't let them in.'

Chapman's stomach clenched. 'Just tell them to get in there. They must have done something to her.'

'They can't just barge in. It's not the wild west.'

'Okay, I'm almost there.'

Despite the traffic, he'd covered the last mile quickly, but then everything came to a halt. A siren sounded and blue lights flickered in his mirror. He pulled over, then when the police car passed, he eased into its slipstream. At the approach to Montpelier Street, the police car slowed and indicated. Chapman followed it across the lines of traffic streaming the other way.

More blue lights strobed ahead, and Chapman found a place to stop. He jumped out, almost slipping on the slick pavement, slammed his door and jogged to where the police clustered. Virgil and Rafael were holding a heated discussion with three officers while a fourth spoke into an intercom.

'Virgil, where's Antonia?'

One of the officers approached him aggressively. 'Can you please keep out of it, sir?'

'DI Chapman.' He produced his ID. 'This man's a personal protection operative guarding a woman who was attacked two days ago.'

The officers' demeanour changed. 'We were told they were trying to break into a private clinic.'

'Our client is in there, but they won't let us see her,' Virgil said.

Chapman strode to the intercom and held his ID up to the camera. 'Police. Open this door.'

The lock buzzed, and he pushed the door, running up the stairs and through another door into a smart reception area. He recognised the room from their website and a woman he identified as Schiffer stood in front of a desk, arms folded.

'Do you have a warrant?'

'I don't need one, Mrs Schiffer. I know Antonia Conti came in here two hours ago, and I suspect she's in danger. Where is she?'

Schiffer covered up her surprise that he knew her name. 'We haven't got a patient called Antonia Conti.'

'She's not a patient.' He pointed at the discreet camera in the corner. 'Unless you've wiped it, your CCTV will show you're lying.'

Schiffer raised her eyebrows. 'I'm not in the habit of lying, Inspector.' She sat behind the desk and turned the screen of the PC so Chapman could see it.

Virgil, Rafael and one of the uniforms crowded into the room behind Chapman.

'Two hours, you say.' Schiffer punched keys, and the screen showed the entrance to the room.

The time stamp read sixteen fifty-seven. The door opened and Antonia walked in. 'That's her.'

Schiffer glanced at the screen. 'This is Patience Okoye. She had an appointment to see me at five.' She changed the screen to show an appointment calendar with Okoye P showing in the relevant time slot.

The first time Chapman met Antonia, she'd used the same pseudonym. She'd also knocked him on to his arse. 'Whatever name you knew her under, she's the woman we're here for. Where is she?'

Virgil and Rafael approached the two doors leading out of the reception area.

'Where are you going? That's private property.'

Virgil ignored Schiffer and opened the left-hand door. Rafael surged through the opening in a practised manoeuvre and Virgil followed.

'We've got private medical records in there and if you touch them, you will answer to me.' Schiffer's blue eyes blazed.

'Where does the other door lead?' Chapman said.

'It leads to the back yard.'

He gestured to the uniform, who'd been joined by a second, to check it.

Virgil returned. 'There's a locked door in the first room. Have you got the key?'

Schiffer glared at him. 'It contains very delicate equipment.'

'You can either open it or I will.'

'Inspector, will you allow this thug to threaten to vandalise my office?'

'Only because I think he'd do a better job than I would. Now, the key.' Chapman held out a hand.

Schiffer collected a key from a drawer and led the way into the treatment room. Chapman and the two bodyguards crowded round the door as she inserted the key. The lock clicked, and she put a hand through the opening, flicked a switch and stepped back. Chapman stepped into a room four feet by six, more of a large cupboard. A laptop connected to a chrome helmet covered in wires sat on a shelf.

Chapman exhaled. 'What's this for?'

'I doubt you'd understand, Inspector.'

'Try me.'

'We use it in our therapy. For patients who suffer from phobias, PTSD, etc.'

'Is it one of Professor Swan's machines?'

She reacted like he'd slapped her, then recovered. 'It's similar.'

'Did you use it on Antonia?'

'I told you, I've never met—'

'Don't mess me about.'

Schiffer swallowed. 'What passed between us is covered by patient confidentiality.'

'What did you do to her?'

A constable spoke from the doorway. 'Boss, there's nobody else here, and the chief inspector's just arrived. She wants a word.'

Schiffer gave him a look of triumph. What the hell had she done to Antonia?

CHAPTER 28

'I'd say it's pretty conclusive, Inspector.' The uniformed chief inspector indicated the screen where a bewildered-looking Antonia followed a tall blonde woman along the corridor and down the stairs, which led to the rear exit of the clinic. 'Your Ms Okoye, or whatever her name is, doesn't look like she's being coerced.'

'There's more than one way of controlling people . . .' Aware claiming Schiffer might have manipulated Antonia's memories would make him sound deranged, he contented himself with a glare at the psychologist. 'Where was your daughter taking her?'

Schiffer didn't hide her surprise he knew who accompanied Antonia. 'I've no idea, Inspector. She's an adult, as is Ms Okoye, and fully entitled to go anywhere she wants without asking my permission.'

A commotion at the door announced Adam's appearance. He still wore his uniform under his coat and a faint smell of smoke accompanied him.

'Who are you and how did you get past my people?' the CI demanded.

'He's with me,' Chapman said. 'Ms Conti is staying with him.'

'Seeing as she left of her own volition, neither of you, or you two' – she indicated Virgil and his colleague – 'have any business here.'

Chapman wanted to wipe the smirk off Schiffer's face, but he needed to find Antonia. He saw Adam had questions, but he followed Chapman out on to the pavement in silence. Two more police cars had arrived, and five uniforms hung around the entrance. A small crowd watched from a short distance.

Chapman couldn't contain his frustration and turned on Virgil. 'Why the hell did you let her—'

'Shall we move away from prying ears?' Adam said.

They left the officers and the crowd behind, and Chapman stopped.

'How did you let her get away? You're supposed to protect her.'

Virgil leant away from him. 'She wouldn't even let us check the place out before she went in—'

'But why didn't you go in and find her when she didn't come out?'

Adam cut in. 'Shall we focus on finding her, rather than apportioning blame?'

Chapman agreed, but he hadn't finished. 'How the hell did she get out? Weren't you watching the back?'

'Of course, Mr Mason was watching it.' Virgil produced a mobile and punched a button. He walked away and muttered into the handset, then ended the call and returned. 'There's two ways out the back, one through the mews and another on Trevor Place. He covered both and has photos of the cars, including number plates.'

'Where is he? Can you tell him to get round here?'

Virgil studied Chapman. 'Byron Mason's not a guy you tell. He knows we're here.'

Chapman let it go. 'At least we'll be able to trace the cars.'

'Will you be able to use your resources?' Adam said.

'Not officially, unless I can link it to an open crime.'

'Getting that data shouldn't be a problem,' Virgil said.

'Can you access the traffic cameras?' Chapman knew Antonia had done it through a hacker she knew.

'It won't be a problem,' he repeated.

Adam frowned. 'How come they overpowered her? I've seen her fight. She doesn't take prisoners.'

Virgil said, 'It looked like they'd drugged her, the docile way she went along with the woman.'

'It wasn't drugs.'

They all looked at Chapman.

'They've manipulated her memories. I'm pretty sure the blonde woman is the person Antonia got a story from. She fed her a pack of lies and I'd have sworn Antonia would kill her the next time they met.'

'I didn't see her clearly on the CCTV, but the woman Antonia left with is the one she met in Kew,' Virgil said. 'The woman stormed off after their last meeting.'

Chapman didn't know what this meant, but suspected it wasn't good.

'What do you think's happened?' Adam said.

'They've wiped some of Antonia's memories, including the ones of the woman's betrayal, and either added a new one, or not . . .' He hoped to God it wasn't the latter. She could have absorbed all sorts of experiences by now.

'They can do that?' Adam looked doubtful.

'Frightening, isn't it.'

Virgil's phone emitted a series of pings. 'Mr Mason's photos.' He held the screen up. It showed a middle-aged man wearing an anorak, hurrying in the rain. He swiped past similar images until the picture of a car appeared.

'Can you send them to me?'

'Give me your number.' Virgil punched it in and a few seconds later, Chapman's phone started its own symphony of chimes.

He scrolled through the images, ignoring the pedestrians. He'd captured the number plates of every car but hadn't got many of the drivers. The last two images were blurred, but clear enough to read the numbers. What the hell was Antonia playing at? Had she been getting treated at the clinic? What he'd learnt from Swan about the risks filled Chapman with panic.

A commotion from the entrance to the clinic broke this silence as Byron argued with the uniforms.

'Byron!' Adam shouted and waved.

He left the uniforms and strolled towards them. The bulky tweed coat he wore made him seem even bigger than the last time Chapman had seen him. He greeted Adam and the two guards.

'Inspector Chapman, we meet again.'

'What happened to you?'

He smiled. 'I heard them stalling Virgil at the front door, so I guessed Antonia was still in there, or had only just left. I followed the next car which came out of the rear alleyway, just in case.'

'You didn't get any cars that left after you drove off?'

Byron looked amused and retrieved a device from his pocket. 'It's a motion-activated video camera. I left it hidden at the back. It picked up two more cars. They're the last two I sent you.'

'Oh, right. What about the car you followed?'

Byron retrieved his phone and showed Chapman the image of a small Tesla pulling on to Trevor Place. A young woman, smartly dressed but looking worried, drove.

'Was anyone in the rear?' Chapman said.

'Not that I saw, but I didn't get very close.'

'Can I see please, Mr Mason?' Virgil reached for the phone and studied the image. 'That's the receptionist.'

A surge of adrenaline energised Chapman. 'How far did you follow them?'

'Not far. She drove into the car park under a tower block.'

'Which one?'

Mason gave a name Chapman recognised. The office block Futcher had fallen from.

Adam also knew of it. 'A subsidiary of GRM owns the offices on the upper floors.'

'How do you know?'

'Antonia told me about her problems with Reed-Mayhew. We keep records of all big commercial buildings at work. I collated them.'

'Is she still there?' It might be a coincidence, but he doubted it.

Mason shrugged. 'For a start, we don't know she ever arrived. I never saw her in the Tesla. It didn't stay long, and she wasn't in it when it left.'

'So, she's probably still in there, unless she's left in the back of a van.'

'That's what I thought.' Mason grinned. 'Which is why I left two of those cameras covering the car park. We'll have every vehicle leaving or going in.'

'Could be hundreds.'

'Over the weekend? Do you have a better idea, Inspector?'

Chapman had to admit, he didn't.

Rafael held out his hand. 'I got into the laptop we found while you argued with the owner. Some idiot had stuck the password on a post-it in the cupboard.' He passed a memory stick to Chapman.

'What's on it?'

'I'm not sure. I copied most of the files I found. One's a list of names. People they treated?'

'Was there a Snowden or Futcher on it?'

'Sorry, I didn't read it.'

Chapman studied it. Could this give him the breakthrough he needed *and* help him find Antonia?

◆ ◆ ◆

The headache that had started before she fell sleep took hold of Antonia and seized her skull in its grip. She opened her eyes, and hazy light filtering through insubstantial curtains illuminated the room. She sat up, grimacing as the vice gripped tighter, and inspected her surroundings. It resembled a soulless, high-end hotel room. Mirrored wardrobes lined the wall on her right and a desk sat under the windows that ran the length of the wall to her left, a leather-covered chair tucked under it. On the wall in front of her, at the foot of the bed, hung a huge television.

She pulled the heavy duvet off her legs and swung them off the bed. After they'd escaped from the men at the clinic, they'd changed vehicles in an underground car park. Instead of crouching under a blanket in the cramped rear of the first car, she and Edda, or Fiona as she still thought of her, had travelled in the rear of a comfortable people-carrier with blacked-out windows. She had no clue where they'd gone, but they'd driven for at least an hour, stopping once halfway through the journey.

Standing made her head spin, and she waited until it stopped, then made her way to the window. She worked out how to operate the pull-cord and opened the curtains. An opaque film covered the glass, letting in light but obscuring the view. Antonia examined the frame for a lock but couldn't find one. Frustrated, she pressed her forehead against the glass but could only make out vague shapes in the distance. She remembered riding up in a lift, so guessed they must be a long way up.

'What are you doing, Antonia?' Fiona stood in the doorway.

'How did you get in without a key?'

'We don't have locks on the doors.'

'Just the windows?' She straightened and tapped the glass. 'And what's this?'

'It's a sealed building and we're thirty floors up. It's for your own safety. And the film on the glass is to make sure nobody can take a shot at you.'

'From thirty floors up?'

'There are several buildings of similar height within a mile, and it only takes a marksman . . .'

The skin on Antonia's neck crinkled, and she backed away from the window. 'Why would marksmen shoot at me?'

'Those guys we ran from last night are ex-military. They work for dangerous people. Don't underestimate them.'

How do you know so much about the people chasing me? What had happened to Virgil and Rafael at the clinic yesterday? Surely, they'd come searching for her. Something must have happened to them. The thought added to her despondency. But Eleanor and Chapman would make sure they found her unless they too . . . no! She couldn't think that.

Fiona smiled. 'Shall we get a coffee?'

'Good idea.' For all Fiona's friendliness, Antonia had a niggling sensation she shouldn't trust her. She tried to remember why, but her headache grew more intense, filling her skull with pain.

'You coming? You seem in a trance.' Fiona waited in the corridor wearing an expression of concern that didn't seem genuine.

'I'm fine, just unsettled.' Antonia followed her past a shower room into a short corridor. There *was* no lock, and five more doors led off the corridor, one at each end and two on each side. They went through the one opposite into a large open-plan living-dining room. The same film covered the windows, making the room feel claustrophobic.

Two men sat at the dining table and Antonia stopped. 'Who are they?'

The men turned to study her. The nearest filled the chair he perched on, making it appear too small to contain his bulk. He rose to greet her and despite having no neck, he stood several centimetres taller than her. 'Morning, Antonia. I trust you slept well.'

The memory of him driving the people-carrier last night returned, along with a less distinct recollection. His companion, who'd also been in the van, waved a knife smeared with butter and continued chewing. Light glinted off his shiny black glasses.

'You guys saved us any coffee?' Fiona's cheerful greeting sounded forced.

'Why are you here?' They were obviously guarding her, but as a prisoner, or to protect her?

'We're here for your protection. Some dangerous men are looking for you.' No-neck didn't talk like a thug.

Again, why did *he* know about who was after her? Did he work for the same people who employed Virgil? She didn't think so. He wasn't like any of the others, and his companion made her uneasy, not confident and safe. She sensed a threat, but in a nebulous fashion, like an abstract danger in a nightmare that never gets defined. Coffee and something to eat would help.

No-neck poured two coffees and slid them across the table. Antonia nodded her thanks and took one. The aroma comforted her, and she sipped the rich liquid. In the centre of the table sat two laden platters. One contained a selection of pastries and bread rolls, the other several cheeses and sliced meats. Her stomach reminded her she hadn't eaten last night, having been unable to face food. Antonia took a plate from a small pile and helped herself. She devoured four of the fresh bread rolls.

'Ready for that, weren't you?' The man with the glasses spoke in a hoarse, rasping voice that seemed familiar, although she didn't recall him talking last night.

'Where do I know you from?'

'He came with us last night, Antonia.' Fiona gave a dismissive wave, but an air of alarm passed between her and the two men.

Trying to recall where she'd seen him made Antonia's headache spike, and she gasped.

'What's wrong?' Fiona asked. 'You still got the headache?'

'A bit.' It took on a life of its own, pushing all thought away.

'Hmm, you sometimes get one following a stressful incident. I've got some painkillers—'

'No drugs.' *God, I can't bear this.*

'Shall we try some therapy? No drugs, and it will soothe you.'

Anything to stop it. 'What do I do?'

She led Antonia back into the hall and through the door next to the bedroom. Instead of a bed, it contained a chair and a low recliner facing the windows opposite the door. These too had an opaque coating on the glass. Behind the recliner, on a table, sat a laptop and a chrome helmet.

'What's that?' Antonia pointed at the device.

'Don't worry, it will help you. Take a seat, we'll soon have you sorted.' Fiona directed her to the recliner.

Another shaft of pain seared Antonia's skull, and she staggered. Fiona grabbed her arm and supported her. A distant voice told her to get out of there. But first, she must stop the pain.

◆　◆　◆

After finishing her extra Saturday morning shift Sabirah arrived back at Vincent Terrace and let herself into the house. How many more times would she be able to do this? To take her mind off her worries, she'd spend the next couple of hours cleaning the offices, then collect the children. As she mounted the stairs, the lift started, coming up from the basement. Sabirah waited until the doors opened, and Mrs Curtis wheeled herself out. She looked exhausted.

'Hello, Mrs Curtis, are you working today? I want to clean the offices.'

'I've told you before, you don't need to. You can't today, in any event. We've got to find— We're working on a big story.'

'Oh, okay.'

'Where are the children? You normally take them out on Saturday.'

'They stayed with Jean. They had a sleepover.'

'Jean?' Mrs Curtis looked concerned. 'You know we had to sack her?'

Sabirah felt she'd been slapped. 'She said she resigned. She and her mother was very rude about you and Antonia.'

'I imagine she was trying to save face.'

'Why do you sack her?'

Mrs Curtis hesitated. 'I suppose you're bound to find out. She's been spying on us. We think she planted a listening device in Antonia's office.'

Sabirah's cheeks grew hot as shame hit her. She couldn't let Jean take the blame. 'Mrs Curtis, I have confession.' She held the banister and slumped on to the second step. 'I did it.'

Mrs Curtis studied her with concern. 'What did you do?'

'I . . .' The words stuck in Sabirah's throat, but she forced them out. 'I placed bug in Antonia's office.'

The old woman blinked. 'But why? What possessed you?'

Hot tears coursed down Sabirah's cheeks. 'My lawyer, Mr Al Rahman, told me I must, so we can stay here.'

'What do you mean?'

'When they refuse my appeal because of you. I saw him afterwards. He gave me a—'

'They refused your appeal because I appeared for you? Are you sure?'

'They said you are a bad influence and have corrupted Antonia.'

'Oh my.' Mrs Curtis placed a hand on her chest. 'Did Al Rahman say that?'

'The woman on the panel, the one like a shrew, she said.'

Mrs Curtis scowled. 'Oh, her. We have a history. I'm so sorry, Sabirah.'

'*I* am sorry. I betrayed you. And Antonia. Now Jean is in trouble because of me.'

'Yes, we have got into a right pickle. What did Al Rahman say?'

'He gave me bug and said I must hide it in Antonia's office. Then they would let me stay.'

'He promised you Leave to Remain if you bugged her office?'
'Yes.'

Mrs Curtis slapped the arm of her chair. 'My God. I can't believe they'd stoop so low. They engineered this to get you to spy on Antonia.'

'I'm sorry?'

'Can't you see? All this they've put you through was to make you place that bug. Have you got your Leave to Remain?'

Anger and shame made Sabirah hot. 'He says I have to do it again because the bug is broken.'

'After all that, they've left you facing the threat of deportation.' She hit her chair again. 'I'll make sure that scum pays for this.' The anger drained from her face. 'Are you saying the bug you placed didn't work?'

'No. Yes, it works, but I broke it. Then he called me to his office.'

'It was a brave thing to do.'

Sabirah snorted. Brave would have been to refuse. 'A boy I worked with said I should put in the microwave to damage circuits. So they think it's accident.'

'Clever you. When did you do this?'
'I broke it Monday night.'

'Are you sure?'

'Yes.'

'Oh.' Mrs Curtis frowned. 'The bug was there on Tuesday, working—'

'No, I took it Monday night.'

'I understand, dear, but the people listening overheard us on Tuesday afternoon. So, not your bug. It must have been Jean, because someone removed it later that afternoon, and only she had the opportunity.'

Sabirah couldn't take this in. Had she sabotaged her children's chances of staying for no reason? She fumbled for a tissue.

'Don't be upset, dear. I understand why you did it. You're very brave confessing, but it's Jean's fault.' Mrs Curtis wheeled herself closer and gripped Sabirah's hand. 'And after all that, you didn't get what you wanted.'

The tissue disintegrated and tears cascaded into her lap as Sabirah shook her head.

'Here, take these.' Mrs Curtis thrust a small pack of tissues into her hand. 'And don't worry, you don't have to see Al Rahman again. Have you got the device he gave you?'

'I took back, but he gave me another.' She opened her bag and took out the envelope she'd kept it in since he'd given it to her. 'It has his fingerprints.'

'Well done.'

'I also record him telling me to do it. On my phone.'

Mrs Curtis almost clapped her hands. 'Good girl. Send it to me.'

Sabirah's shame diminished. But she realised what she'd done. Jean was the spy, and she'd trusted her children to a traitor. She rose. 'I have to go. Jean has the children.'

'Wait.' Mrs Curtis produced some notes. 'Get a cab. Get yourself presentable and I'll order one.'

'Thank you.' Sabirah took the money and hurried up to her flat, returning as the taxi arrived. She thanked Mrs Curtis again and rushed off. She sat in the taxi, too anxious to enjoy the unfamiliar luxury. The more she considered what Jean had done, the angrier she got. What excuse had she for betraying Mrs Curtis and Antonia? And to accuse them of cruelty made it even worse.

As they got closer to Jean's house, her anger turned to apprehension. What if she'd done something to the children? They'd sounded happy when she'd spoken to them this morning, but that was four hours ago. Tempted to ring them, she got her phone out. But what to say? Best to just turn up and bring them home. Jean wouldn't harm them. But what about her mother? Sabirah stared at the display, paralysed by fear and indecision.

'Is this okay, madam?' The taxi sat outside the house on the semi-circular drive.

She paid the driver and stared at the house as the taxi pulled away. It was still afternoon, but a light showed in the hall. Taking a deep breath, she strode to the door and rang the bell. She waited a long minute and rang it again. Then she seized the lion-head knocker and banged it three times. The sound echoed but nobody came. Sabirah grew frantic and peered through the front windows but couldn't see anyone. A locked gate blocked the path to the rear of the house. She pushed the letterbox open and peered into the empty hallway.

'NADIMAH! HAKIM! ANSWER ME PLEASE?'

'Are you okay, young lady?'

The question made her jump. A bald man in his sixties studied her from the pavement.

'I can't find my children.'

He walked to her, his rubber boots crunching on the gravel. He held a pair of hedge clippers in his gloved hand. 'A young girl, so high, and a boy?'

'Yes, did you see them?'

'About an hour ago. A car picked them up.'

'What car?'

'A limousine. A very smart vintage jobbie.' He described Al Rahman's car.

Her legs almost gave way, and she held on to the wall. He must be working with Jean. What had she done? She'd let a monster take her children.

CHAPTER 29

This Saturday, the office of *The Electric Investigator* was as busy as on a normal weekday. Chapman's eyes smarted as he worked at Antonia's desk, where he'd also dozed intermittently, having been there since the previous night. The panicked sense that he needed to find Antonia urgently kept him from resting. The smell of stale fish and chips assaulted his nostrils and he reminded himself to empty the bin. Even working through the night and morning, he'd not finished checking the information on the memory stick. Realising the size of the task, he'd rung Sanchez and persuaded her to come in to help him.

Apart from the data on the memory stick, they worked to identify all the cars they'd photographed. Without the resources of the Met, they struggled to process the information quickly enough. The traffic footage wasn't a problem. Virgil and his team, in another office, along with people from Mason's company working off-site, had tracked down the vehicles they'd seen leaving the rear of the clinic. The issue was accessing the traffic cameras in real time.

They'd identified the Tesla belonging to the receptionist as the vehicle most likely to have removed Antonia. Consequently, the tower block she'd driven to became the focus of their attention. Adam got hold of plans of the building and sat in a corner of the main office, determining the best way to gain entry. Mason had replaced the remote cameras with bodies and they kept the site under surveillance, gathering details of cars leaving and entering. These all needed checking. So far, only one vehicle warranted further investigation, a people-carrier with blacked-out windows, which had left soon after the Tesla arrived. Mason's people were working to identify where it had gone and Chapman waited impatiently for their findings.

Miles and Eleanor, the only people who belonged here by right, helped where they could. Chapman rubbed his eyes. The data he'd found on the memory stick didn't relate to anyone he could identify, and he began to fear none of it did. The dread that they'd been allowed to copy it to throw them off track grew with every fruitless search. If Sanchez didn't find something in the folders she was checking, he didn't know what they'd do.

He opened yet another folder, not expecting anything different. He spotted a name that made him sit up. The folder contained a series of sub-folders, including one bearing Antonia's pseudonym, Patience Okoye. Had it only been in March he'd turned up to arrest her, imagining he and Sanchez could 'manage' a woman? How wrong he'd been, but he wouldn't make the same mistake again.

Chapman opened the sub-folder, but his excitement turned to frustration when he couldn't open the files inside with anything on Antonia's computer. The computer's offer to search the internet for anything suitable ended in failure.

'Alice?' he called into the outer office.

She arrived wearing an expression he recognised.

'You've found something?' he asked her.

'They treated both Snowden and Futcher, just before they killed themselves.'

A surge of excitement made him forget his frustration. 'Yesss! Was Futcher their patient before Snowden?'

'Yeah, how did you know?'

Chapman tapped the side of his nose. 'His wife said a school-friend recommended the clinic. I bet they planted the idea he recruit Snowden.' He produced a sheet of paper and slid it across the desk. 'What about these four?'

She picked it up and read the names. 'You going to tell me who they are?'

If they were victims of abuse, the guys deserved anonymity, but he suspected they were victims of a con. 'They're the four who accused Milham of sexual abuse.'

Sanchez glanced at the door and pushed it shut. 'You should be more careful about sharing their names.'

'You're the only person I've discussed this with.'

This seemed to satisfy her, and she left, returning twenty minutes later wearing a puzzled expression. She placed the piece of paper he'd given her on the desk, her notes now added to his writing. 'You'd better explain everything.'

'Grab a seat. I'll tell you what I think's happened.' He waited for Sanchez to sit. 'I found links between Snowden and Futcher. They'd gone to school together and stayed close, but I wasn't sure what linked their deaths until we arrested Milham. He'd also gone to the same school.'

Sanchez frowned. 'A sex abuse ring?'

'That's what I thought, but Antonia disagreed. She had information they were involved in setting up a business to bid for prison contracts—'

'Stepping on GRM's toes?'

'Exactly. And they'd also gone to school with Reed-Mayhew—'

'Two birds, for Reed-Mayhew?'

'You know, Alice, you can really take the wind out of someone's sails.'

'Sorry, I'm just guessing.'

'Right.' He explained Antonia's theory: 'These guys went to school with the bastard and treated him like an outcast. Antonia thought he'd somehow got them to kill themselves—'

'How?'

'I'll explain later. Anyway, Antonia interviewed Milham and decided he was innocent, and that Reed-Mayhew had engineered his problems as well.'

'How? Pay the four guys to claim he'd abused them?'

'No, too easily disproved, especially by someone like Milham with plenty of money. The four guys needed to believe the abuse happened. Reed-Mayhew also planted a laptop with incriminating images in Milham's house.'

'How did he persuade them they'd been abused? And what about the suicides?'

'Griffin had convinced himself he'd committed his cellmate's crimes and killed himself because of it. With him it happened by accident, but what if they implanted memories convincing Snowden and Futcher they'd done something terrible—'

'I still don't buy the stuff you told me about implanting false memories.'

'You mean you don't want to believe it. It makes our job impossible. But it all fits, Alice.'

'Okay, they implant false memories in the two guys, but you're saying they also convinced four random men that Milham abused them?'

'Yep. They just had to be the right age and from London. You found the clinic had treated all six.' He examined the sheet she'd brought back. Sanchez had written two dates alongside each name. He pointed to the second column. 'Those the last dates they attended the clinic?'

'Yes.'

'They all went there the week before they accused Milham. They must have primed them then.'

Sanchez stayed silent for a long time. 'It makes a sort of sense, if you accept what this guy Swan told you, but it's all circumstantial.'

But did he have enough to get a search warrant? They needed to see the treatment notes and so far, they'd not found any.

'What did you want me for, boss? You called me in before you gave me the names to check, if you remember.'

'Oh yeah, I found these files, but I'm struggling to open them. Do you want to have a go?' He turned the screen so they could both see it.

'Yeah, I found the same for the guys I looked into. I couldn't open them. Some were plus and others minus—'

'Are they?' He'd not noticed.

'Yeah, all these are minus.' She pointed at the three file names. A set of figures under each corresponded to dates that week, including yesterday.

'Shit!' Something Swan had mentioned returned. With a growing sense of dread, he reached for his phone and punched the dial button.

'Professor Swan, can I help you?'

'Sorry to bother you, Professor, but I need your help.' He explained what had happened to Antonia. 'We've found some files labelled .sklp.'

'Those would be the files used to store memories—'

'And a minus sign means it's one you've removed?'

'And a plus, for those you've added. You were listening.'

Chapman ignored the supercilious tone. 'Antonia's files show just a minus sign.'

'Where are you? Is she with you?' Swan's tone increased Chapman's apprehension.

'I'm at *The Investigator*, but we don't know where Antonia is.'

'Well, you must find her. I'll come straight over.'

◆ ◆ ◆

'Antonia, wake up.' Fiona's insistent voice dragged Antonia back to consciousness.

The thick, woolly sensation of waking too early in a sleep cycle made her think she'd only just lost consciousness. Hands tugged at her head. *What's going on?* She wanted to resist, but her arms were too heavy. She opened her eyes and tried to turn.

'Don't worry, I'm just taking this off.' Fiona's soothing voice came from behind her. Then the tugging stopped.

She recalled where she was, remembering Fiona's calming tones as she got Antonia to relax on the recliner and placed the helmet on her head, with the promise it would ease her headache. Had it? It wasn't all-pervading, but a sharp jab in her skull as she moved reminded her it hadn't gone.

'Have you finished? I'm absolutely drained.'

Fiona didn't respond, but the sense of someone watching her made Antonia's skin tingle. Was someone else in the room? With great effort, she rotated her shoulders. A figure lurked just inside the door.

'Who are you and why are you watching me?' Sleep made Antonia's voice hoarse.

The man came into the room where she could see him better. Of average height, with short brown hair and bland features, he resembled a mid-level accountant. She sensed something familiar about him, but couldn't bring it to mind.

'Has she completed her treatment?' He spoke over Antonia's head to Fiona.

'We were just starting when you arrived.'

He frowned at the implied rebuke.

Antonia had thought him ordinary-looking, but the cold intensity of his hazel eyes made her shiver. 'Are you going to answer me?'

'You haven't changed, have you? Still full of your own importance, imagining you're on some sort of crusade to save the world, but all you're doing is selling a fantasy of holding the powerful to account.'

She had met him, but had no memory of when or where. A sense of dread told her she hadn't enjoyed it.

'You're certain she won't recall any of this?' He spoke over her head again.

'When we've finished her treatment, she won't remember her own mother.' Fiona had dropped the soothing tone.

The words made Antonia's blood chill.

'Really?' the man said.

'We can't do it all at once, not if you want her to remain viable afterwards.'

Remain viable? The woman talked about her as if she was something to be used. Sweat poured into Antonia's eyes as she strained to get up, but although she made her legs twitch, she couldn't lift them off the recliner.

'You sure she can't move?'

'Don't worry, I gave her a muscle relaxant in her coffee. She'll be like this for a few hours.'

I will make you pay for this. If she 'remained viable'. What if she didn't?

The visitor returned his attention to Antonia. 'You're going to become Gustav Reed-Mayhew's greatest cheerleader.' He gauged her reaction.

So that's who you are? She'd read about him, but why couldn't she recall his appearance? Chunks of her memory were missing. *Oh*

God. Fiona was erasing parts of her memory, and not those Antonia wanted her to. What if she forgot about the people she loved?

Reed-Mayhew gave her a chilling grin. 'You remember me now, don't you?' Then he addressed Fiona. 'Make sure she doesn't recall anything about me except her new memories of how much she admires me.'

'Of course, sir.'

'I'd love to see the bitch in the wheelchair's reaction when it happens, but at least I'll hear it as you bicker in your office.'

Antonia still couldn't move, but she could talk. 'Forget it. We got rid of your spy.'

'Oh, you have, have you?' He laughed, a surprisingly loud sound. 'Well, Ms Conti, I'm sure it will please you to know you were right about my old school pals. I wouldn't have bothered with them if they hadn't tried to attack my business. Well, maybe a lesser punishment, when I had time to enjoy it. Unfortunately, I didn't witness Snowden's demise, but I have remarkably good footage of Futcher's swan-dive from the twenty-second floor of this building. And I can't tell you how much I'm enjoying Milham's discomfort. Wait until they find the evidence I've hidden in his mother's former home.'

The confirmation of his identity and that she'd been right gave her little satisfaction. 'What about the young men who believe Milham abused them, because of your perverse desire for petty revenge?'

'What about them?' Reed-Mayhew made a gesture of dismissal.

A surge of anger energised Antonia, and she thrust her arms forward, lifting her torso off the recliner. 'You arrogant monster.'

His look of fear as he leapt back a step gave her a small measure of satisfaction.

'You'll pay for that, Ms Conti. Not directly, but through some-one you care about. You can enjoy trying to guess which one of the social cripples you surround yourself with I will choose.' He lifted his gaze to Fiona. 'Can you make sure she remembers this promise, without recollecting the rest of our meeting?'

'I'm afraid it's too fraught with risk. It's best to wipe everything from your arrival.'

'A pity.' He turned back to Antonia. 'But at least you can suffer for the next few minutes, and you obviously will once it's happened. I'm sure we'll find a way to ensure you know of your complicity in your friend's fate. Whichever one I choose.' He checked the watch on the inside of his left wrist and addressed Fiona. 'Let me know when you've finished with her. How long will you need?'

'Ideally a week—'

'You have until Monday.'

'We need time between implanted memories to ensure they've—'

'If I wanted to know how you do it, I'd have asked you. Your mother will help, and you can take it in turns.'

'I'm concerned about the patient.'

'You hypocritical liar!' Antonia shouted.

Reed-Mayhew laughed again. 'She clearly doesn't reciprocate your concern for her wellbeing. And if she becomes incapable because of your ministrations, so be it. I'm sure it will break the old woman, and if not, I'll find another way.' He fixed his icy gaze somewhere above Antonia's head. 'So, by Monday then?'

'Yes, of course, sir,' Fiona said.

'Well, goodbye, Ms Conti. Don't get up, I'll let myself out.' He chuckled at his joke.

The door slammed and a needle jabbed Antonia's arm. 'Just in case, Ms Conti.' Fiona removed it with a rough jerk. Antonia fought to stay awake, but a black tide overwhelmed her.

◆　◆　◆

Swan arrived by cab and rushed into Antonia's office still removing his coat. 'Can I see those files?'

Chapman gave up Antonia's seat and hovered as the Professor operated the mouse. Sanchez occupied the visitor's chair and Eleanor rolled into the open doorway, Adam behind her.

Swan ignored his audience and studied the screen. 'Yes, those relate to my treatment. These' – the cursor hovered next to the file dated with Antonia's first visit – 'are memories removed from the subject.' He right-clicked and checked the file properties. 'Thankfully, they didn't do much in this session.' He checked the other two and stayed silent.

Chapman couldn't stand it. 'What is it, Prof?'

'During the second session, they removed close to the maximum threshold. But yesterday they went much further.'

'What does maximum threshold mean? Have they caused her permanent damage?'

Swan backed away from Chapman's outburst. 'Sorry, I didn't mention it yesterday, but we discovered you can remove a few memories without triggering the replacement process. Once you exceed that, then the brain will create replacement memories, unless you create artificial ones and "upload" them.'

'How long does she have?' Sanchez said.

'Impossible to say. It may have already happened.'

Chapman remembered his poor joke about Antonia forgetting their meeting and wanted to throw up.

'Can you reverse it?' Eleanor gestured towards the screen. 'Can you replace those memories?'

Swan blew out his cheeks. 'In theory, but they're sometimes unusable.'

'You said "sometimes". How frequently?'

'One out of three. Maybe forty per cent.'

'You mean nearly half?' Chapman wanted to smash his fist on to the desk.

Swan looked uncomfortable. 'We also don't know if these are all they've removed. We need to get the laptop.'

How the hell were they going to do that?

A phone rang in the doorway and Adam answered. 'Great, you got the address?' He listened some more. 'Yup, I'll let you know.' He ended the call. 'They've tracked the people-carrier with the blacked-out windows. It stopped at a block of flats for a few minutes, then returned to the office block.' His phone pinged, and he studied the screen. 'Here's the address.' He held it for Chapman to read.

Shit! It didn't help.

'Can I see, boss?' Sanchez took the phone. 'They'll all be private, so finding out who owns them will be horrendous.'

'Yes, thanks, Alice.'

Adam took his phone back. 'Byron's searching for the owners of the freehold, but he's going to struggle to discover who owns each flat on a Saturday.'

'Can I see?' Mrs Curtis reached for the handset and studied it. 'MILES?' she called out. He appeared behind her, and she handed him the phone. 'Is it one Antonia investigated?'

Miles's brow furrowed. 'Yes, I should have a copy on my desktop. I can print it off.' He hurried away.

'What's happening?' Chapman said.

'Antonia investigated the ownership of property in London, including all blocks of luxury flats over six floors.'

It was about time they caught a lucky break. Miles returned with five printed sheets and placed them on the desk. Each sheet had twenty addresses with a name next to each one. Many had BR or CY in one of the columns.

'What's this?'

Miles placed a finger on the column. 'Those are owned through "tax-efficient vehicles" in either Bermuda or the Cayman Islands.'

Chapman's optimism evaporated as he checked each sheet. 'So, we don't know who owns more than half of them?'

'It was rather the point of the report, Inspector,' Mrs Curtis said.

'This list is bloody useless.' He shoved it away.

'As a condition of getting government contracts, GRM agreed to no longer use tax havens, so we can ignore those and focus on the others.'

'Assuming Reed-Mayhew stuck to the agreement.'

Adam picked the sheets up. 'We'll go through these and cross-reference them with GRM subsidiaries or senior employees.' He led Miles out of the room.

'I'll help them.' Mrs Curtis looked to have aged since Chapman arrived last night. Then again, he doubted *he* looked his best, either.

He swallowed his disappointment and his thoughts returned to how to recover the laptop Rafael had copied the data from while Chapman kept Schiffer busy. Could he persuade DI Gillich to arrange a search of the clinic? He'd need Swan's help. He explained what he needed, and Swan agreed.

Gillich answered within a few seconds. 'Inspector Chapman, how can I help you?'

'I've found something linked to the Milham case. The four victims—'

'I told you to stay away from them. What have you done? Have you contacted them?' Her anger made Chapman hold the handset further away.

'Nothing of the sort. I received information about the clinic the two suicides I investigated had attended. While checking the data, I saw the names of your witnesses. You've got a serious problem.'

'Oh yeah, what?'

'Can I get Professor Karel Swan, an expert in cognitive neuro-science, to explain it?' He passed the handset, and a weight fell off his shoulders. 'Coffee?' he mouthed to Sanchez, and she nodded.

By the time he returned with two mugs, Swan was winding up his conversation. 'Thank you, Inspector. Shall I hand you over to Inspector Chapman?'

Chapman placed the mugs on the edge of the desk and took the handset. 'Are you convinced?'

'Your Professor Swan is very persuasive. I'll get the principal officer to sign an emergency warrant and meet you there. What's the full address of this clinic?'

Chapman recited it and, after agreeing to meet her there in an hour, ended the call. As the handset passed over the two mugs, it emitted a shrill screech. He did it again, with the same effect.

Sanchez opened her mouth to speak, but he shushed her and, scooping the mugs up, rushed through to the kitchen. He smashed the first mug in the sink. There, amidst the brown liquid, lay a tangle of wires. He broke the second and found the same. He checked the cupboards and found four others, identical. Resisting the urge to smash them, he placed them all in the sink before filling it with water. When he'd submerged them all, he turned the tap off, closed the door and walked back to Antonia's office, feeling sick.

'How much do you think they heard before you broke it, boss?'

'They will at least know where we're going.'

CHAPTER 30

Blue lights reflected off the windows of the shops on the corner of Brompton Road and Montpellier Street. Chapman gave thanks and snuggled further into his jacket as he waited for the vehicles to appear. Two came in a short procession: an unmarked car and a liveried minibus. He left the inadequate shelter of the estate agent's doorway and jogged across the road through the freezing drizzle.

Gillich got out of the car dressed in slick waterproofs, and examined him. 'Why didn't you wait in your car?'

'Alice has got it, round the back.' He shivered. 'You got the warrant?'

'Yep, anyone in?'

'There's a light on.'

'Okay. I'll brief the guys. You say Alice Sanchez is out the back? I'll get someone to accompany her in case anyone tries to sneak out.'

She strode to the minibus, briefing her team while Chapman checked on the clinic. Nobody appeared at the front windows.

Gillich returned, her team following. 'Let's see what they've got to say for themselves.'

Chapman let them go ahead and tacked on to the rear of the procession. Gillich spoke into the intercom, the door opened and she led them in. Chapman followed, grateful for the warmth that enveloped him. He made it to the top of the stairs and edged into the crowded reception area. The young receptionist who'd driven the Tesla sat behind her desk, her face a mask.

Schiffer appeared. 'What's the meaning of this? I have a severely traumatised patient who you mustn't disturb.'

'We have a warrant to search the premises.' Gillich thrust a paper at the psychologist.

'I must object to this invasion of our clinic. I'll be speaking to our solicitor—'

'Be my guest. In the meantime, my people will search your premises and we need the clinical records of these people.' Gillich pointed at the warrant.

Schiffer read it, colour draining from her face. 'These are confidential documents—'

'Which is why we've got a warrant. Now get these for me and move out of our way.'

Schiffer made eye contact with the receptionist, who reached for her mouse.

'Move away from the computer. Now!' Chapman reached her desk in two strides.

The woman dropped the mouse and stepped back.

Chapman addressed the nearest constable. 'Seize the computer. Can you power it down and get it bagged?'

Gillich gave instructions to the rest of the team, who dispersed.

Schiffer returned to her room.

'Ms Schiffer,' Gillich called after her.

Schiffer stepped back into view. 'Dr Schiffer.'

'Whatever. Inspector Chapman will search your treatment rooms.'

'I have a patient in there.'

'Get them out.' Gillich turned her attention to the receptionist, who sat with arms crossed.

Schiffer glared at Chapman. 'I need to warn my patient before she sees you. She's in a fragile state and having a man barge into the treatment room could traumatise her.'

Chapman suspected this was bullshit, but gestured to the nearest woman constable. 'Go with her. Don't let her touch anything.'

He stayed in the corridor and watched them go in. After a couple of minutes, a tall woman of about thirty came out of the room. She gave Chapman a confident smile as she passed him.

He entered the room. 'We need any devices which contain information of the patients listed on the warrant. Where's the laptop you attach to your memory machine?'

Schiffer recovered her surprise. 'Memory machine. What's one of those?'

Chapman strode over to the cupboard where they'd seen it yesterday and tried the handle. 'Can you open this?'

Schiffer didn't object, making him uneasy. When he opened the door, he realised why. 'Where's the stuff you had in here yesterday?'

'We often share equipment with our other clinics. It's possible we've lent it to someone.' She gave him a supercilious smirk he wanted to wipe off her face.

'It's got recordings of the memories you removed from your patients. Now where is it?'

'What a fanciful idea, Inspector.'

He stepped up to Schiffer and spoke in a low voice. 'I know what you've been doing, and you *will* pay for it. Where's Antonia?'

'I'm afraid we don't have any—'

He jabbed a finger at her. 'Stow it.' He addressed the constable who'd positioned herself at the desk. 'Seize everything in the desk and don't let her delete anything.'

He left before he did something he might regret. A check of the other rooms confirmed his fears. The laptop wasn't there. He returned to the reception where Gillich supervised the removal of bagged items of evidence.

'What's up, Russell?'

'They had a laptop and device they used to alter those people's memories, but they're not here now.'

'Could they be using them somewhere else?'

'Shit!' Were they still using them on Antonia?

The biting cold and freezing rain chilled Sabirah to her core. Desperate for some respite, she slipped into the café with the steamed-up windows. Warm, humid air infused with the odour of bacon and fried food enveloped her.

She ordered tea and sat on a stool at a bench facing out of the window. The steamed-up glass made the people rushing through the rain appear as shadows. The tea arrived and she wrapped her frozen hands round the warm pottery. She'd spent two hours touring the shopping centres closest to Jean's house, hoping she'd taken the children there and her neighbour had made a mistake.

How would Al Rahman know Jean? She realised she knew very little of the woman she'd trusted with her precious children. Had he placed her in Antonia's office so she could spy on her? Sabirah recalled Jean got the job after the young man who'd started got hit by a car. Had it been to get Jean in the office? Sabirah didn't doubt Al Rahman could do something so terrible.

But why did he want Sabirah's children? To pressurise her? But he, or the people he worked for, could get her deported. More than enough leverage to get her to betray her friend. What more did they need? Had he taken the children for another reason? Or was Jean getting revenge for being sacked? Her head spun with horrifying thoughts.

Unsure where to go next, she retrieved her phone and checked the local map. It rang.

'Mrs Curtis. Everything okay?'

'No, Sabirah, I need to speak to Jean. I've been trying to call her, but her phone keeps ringing out. Are you at her place?'

'She's not home. I don't know where she has taken Nadimah and Hakim. I try to call her, but she doesn't answer.'

Mrs Curtis let out an exasperated sigh. 'That explains it. She's as bad as Antonia about being tracked. She won't have taken it if she's gone out. What about Nadimah's phone? Has she got it with her?'

Mrs Curtis paid for a phone for Nadimah after she learned about the bullying. 'She has turned it off.' Or had someone else?

'And you don't know where they might have gone?'

'I think Al Rahman take them in his car.'

'Really? Does Jean know him?'

Sabirah related her theory about how Jean had got the job.

'But she didn't place the bug. We've discovered a bugging device hidden in those new mugs. I've made a dreadful mistake. Jean had nothing to do with it.'

Sabirah wasn't sure how to react: there was relief that Jean wasn't a spy, but confusion about what she'd done with the children, and why. Whose car were they in? 'That's why she is so angry.'

'Oh, my,' Mrs Curtis said. 'Okay, I'll contact the police. Where are you?'

'In a café. I'm searching for the children, and I got cold.'

'Go back to Jean's. I'll send the police there.' Mrs Curtis ended the call.

'You all right, love? You seem upset.' The woman who'd served her stood at her shoulder, a tray in one hand and a cloth in the other.

'Sorry. My children . . . Can you tell me where is taxi rank?'

'You won't get one in this weather. I'll get you one, just wait here.' Three minutes later, she returned. 'Go out the back, he'll be here any minute.' She waved a hand at the fire exit door at the rear of the shop and picked up the dirty mug.

'Thank you.' Sabirah picked up her bag, fastened her coat and rushed out through the exit as a cab drew up.

The driver sensed her impatience and made good progress through the heavy traffic, but Sabirah willed him to go even faster. When they arrived, a police car sat outside Jean's house. Sabirah paid the driver and rushed to the front door, where two officers waited.

'Mrs Fadil?'

'Yes, my children, have you found?'

He shook his head.

Sabirah pointed at the house. 'I think she take them in car.' She described Al Rahman's limousine as best she could.

'This one, you mean?' the shorter policeman said, pointing behind them.

A chauffeur-driven limousine drew up outside the house. The driver got out and opened the rear door. It wasn't the man who drove Al Rahman and now she'd seen it, the car was much newer than his and sported a discreet sticker for a limousine hire company.

Jean got out and stared at the police. 'What's happened?'

Before Sabirah could speak, Nadimah and Hakim bounced out of the car.

'Mamma, we saw a film in a big cinema in Leicester Square,' Nadimah started.

'Then we had cream cakes,' Hakim cut in.

Sabirah rushed to embrace them, relief and happiness competing with shame she'd doubted her friend.

'Why are you here?' Jean asked the police.

Sabirah's shame increased as they explained. The officers left and as they drove away, she turned to face Jean.

'Sorry, Jean, I was so worried. But I have good news.'

◆ ◆ ◆

Sanchez drove and Chapman spoke to his boss, DCI Gunnerson.

'This all seems far-fetched, Russell. Removing and replacing memories.'

'It did to me as well, boss, but I've spoken to the guy behind it, and so has DI Gillich, and she persuaded the principal officer to authorise a raid on the clinic.'

'What are these addresses you want me to search?'

'We think they took Antonia Conti there. We traced a vehicle we believe they took her in to that address. All the flats on the top two floors are ultimately owned by the same company—'

'Yeah, GRM. Are you trying to make my ulcer worse?'

'Sorry, boss.'

'And you're not even sure she's there?'

'I'm really worried about Antonia. I don't think we have much time.'

'Okay, Russell.' Gunnerson sighed. 'I'll take some crews over to investigate. If the occupants are in, we'll ask them to let us search their flats. If any refuse, or they're empty, I'll revisit the decision.'

He realised Gunnerson wouldn't do much more without concrete evidence.

'And, Russell, how did you discover this vehicle's movements?'

'Sorry, boss, you're breaking up.' He ended the call.

'Is she doing it?' Sanchez asked as she manoeuvred his car past a bus disgorging passengers.

'She's meeting us there—' An incoming call from Adam interrupted and he took it. 'Good news, Adam, I've—'

'Change of plan,' Adam said. 'We think she's still at the office block.'

'What?'

'A Humvee visited earlier. We think it belongs to Reed-Mayhew—'

'Did anyone see him?'

'No, but Rafael just saw Schiffer go in, driving like a lunatic.' Adam swore and the sound of horns blared from the handset.

'Where are you?'

'Me and Virgil are on our way. Byron's coming with some more people.'

Chapman made a quick decision; they were five minutes away. 'I'll meet you there.'

'Okay, but turn your phones off.'

'Why?'

'Just a precaution. We don't know what we're going to come across or what we need to do.'

Chapman's misgivings about Adam returned, but he could always switch them back on if he needed to. 'Okay, see you in five.' He ended the call and gave Sanchez an update. He'd leave Gunnerson to search the flats, just in case they'd made a mistake.

Adam's car sat in the entrance to the car park, preventing the barrier closing. Sanchez parked behind it, and they got out. Inside the car park, three bulky figures waited by two lift doors. Virgil carried a battering-ram, but the others were empty-handed. Both lifts waited with doors open.

'Adam!' Chapman and Sanchez jogged toward him.

'Schiffer went up to the thirtieth floor, Rafael followed her car into the building.'

Chapman's mind raced as he considered their tactics. 'How far away are the reinforcements?'

'Byron's at least fifteen minutes—'

'Too long. We need to go up now.' He stepped into the lift car and waited for the others to join him.

Adam checked him as he reached for the control panel. 'Get off at a lower floor and take the stairs. The sound of the lift will warn them, and we don't know what they're carrying.'

He realised Adam and the other two wore tactical vests under their coats. Too late to worry about it now. He punched the button for the twenty-eighth floor. As the lift rose, he briefed the others. 'When we reach the thirtieth floor, we must find Schiffer. We can assume she's gone to Antonia. We spread out and search. Once we find the right room, we'll meet up outside it. Virgil, you take the door and I'll go through first—'

'Nope,' Adam said. 'I'll do the door and Virgil and Rafael take the first room. We've rehearsed it. And you haven't got a vest.'

'I'm the police officer—'

'Yup, and we're all ex-forces. These two do it all the time, but I'm rusty, which is why I'm on the door.' Adam reached into his jacket and produced an extendible cosh. 'You got one of these?'

'I've got these.' Sanchez produced one and a can of Mace.

Chapman had nothing. 'Take this.' Adam thrust the cosh at him and took the battering ram off Virgil. 'Once they've gone through, I'll follow, then you two, in whatever order you want.'

Chapman slipped the cosh into a pocket. 'Alice, you'll have to stay on the landing to guard the lifts. In case they get round us and try and use them.'

'Why don't we just block the doors so they can't summon them?' Sanchez didn't look happy.

'Reinforcements will need them. We send them to the ground floor—'

'No need. I've operated the fireman's switch.' Adam winked at Chapman. 'The call buttons on the other floors won't work until it's reset. This one will stay on our floor until we need it and the other one is waiting for Byron and his team at ground floor.'

Smartarse. But at least he knew what he was doing.

'We split up on arrival at twenty-eight. You two take the service stairs' – Adam addressed Virgil and Rafael – 'then check the north corridor. Make sure you search the toilets, we don't want any surprises.'

Chapman didn't like being usurped, but this wasn't the time for a power struggle.

Adam continued. 'The thirtieth has five office suites. Two corridors lead north and south. The entrances to the suites are off those. I reckon she'll be in one of the three smaller ones. They're across the south side of the building. The two on the north side are bigger—'

'Why focus on the small ones?'

'A smaller area is easier to control. They'll keep the numbers involved to a minimum. They're still a few hundred square metres each and comprise several rooms.'

Chapman couldn't fault the logic. They rose past the twentieth floor, and a tense silence filled the lift car. Butterflies took off inside him, then the lift stopped on twenty-eight. After a long pause, the doors opened. Everyone looked relieved when they stepped on to an empty landing.

'You two through there.' Adam directed the two bodyguards to their right. They hurried away on silent shoes.

'And you follow me.' Adam headed to a door with the silhouette of stairs on it, the battering-ram cradled like a baby. Chapman still had to hurry to keep up with him as he ran up the stairs with an easy stride. Sanchez extended her cosh with a snap and Chapman followed suit. At the top, Adam paused and signalled to the two police that he'd go through the door and head right and they should go left.

He held the ram on his shoulder, like an oversized baseball bat. After a silent three, he pushed the door open and sprang out. Chapman went left. Straight ahead of them sat an empty reception desk.

A door burst open on their right and a figure barrelled out, moving too fast to see clearly, followed by a second going the oppo site way. Chapman's heart raced, then he recognised Virgil and Rafael.

They signalled OK, then disappeared down the north corridor. Adam signed they should each investigate one office suite and sent them on their way. Chapman gripped the cosh, his hand hot and damp. He headed to the south-west corner. A solid door led off the corridor, but he didn't need to check it. Schiffer's distinctive perfume led to the door like a trail. He placed his ear against the hinge and heard raised voices.

Taking care to make no noise, he rushed back to the lift.

He'd found Antonia. Now all they needed to do was get her out, and quickly.

CHAPTER 31

Raised voices woke Antonia. She opened her eyes and stared at a pale-yellow ceiling. Who was talking and where was she? She moved her head and a shard of pain spiked behind her forehead. She stopped moving and took stock. Something rested on her head. A helmet? She raised her left hand, the arm impossibly heavy, and patted a metal contraption.

What's going on? She used both hands to ease it loose and the tingling sensation she'd barely noticed stopped.

The sounds of disagreement ended and a door behind her opened. She snatched her hands away, but the device stayed on her head. She pretended to sleep.

'If we do that, we might as well wipe her mind and leave a blank slate.'

A visceral hatred set Antonia's limbs tingling.

'So be it. We can't risk it.'

This second, accented voice provoked a less intense reaction. Who were these women?

'We'll effectively destroy her personality,' the first woman said. 'Nobody's ever done it before, and we can't be sure she'll survive as a viable person.'

Antonia swallowed. What did she mean? The urge to flee seized her, but she should wait. The way her arms responded told her they'd drugged her. The longer she took to recover, the more chance of her strength returning.

'So what, Edda?' the accented voice pressed. 'She means nothing to us. If we leave any memory, we could end up in prison.'

'But she won't remember anything, I've already wiped everything between us in the last three weeks, from when she first met me. Including the sessions she had with you.'

She must know these women, but how, and what 'sessions' did she mean?

'You always were an idealist. They've spoken to Swan. Now, even the stuff she knew before you met her could put us at risk. And if any of this blows back to Reed-Mayhew, prison will be the least of our worries.'

The mention of Reed-Mayhew made Antonia's skin clammy. What did this have to do with him?

The accented voice continued. 'You saw what he made us do to Snowden and Futcher, and what he's doing to Milham is just sadistic.'

'You didn't object to doing it, though. Enough money buys off your conscience, doesn't it?'

'Grow up. If you won't do it, I will.'

The sound of keystrokes came from behind her. Antonia tensed her muscles. Whatever they intended to do to her, she wasn't going without a fight.

The keystrokes ended, and the accented voice spoke. 'You haven't connected it. What the hell have you done, Edda? You idiot.'

'I did.'

A hand pressed on the device on her head. Antonia twisted away from the pressure. She heard a sound like a saucepan lid hitting the floor. The shocked, pale face of a young blonde woman loomed over her. Ignoring the pain in her head, Antonia thrust her right hand at her, two fingers aimed at the blue eyes.

With a screech, the woman reeled away.

'Edda, what is it?' the woman with the accent said.

Antonia forced reluctant legs to work and scrambled to her feet. She staggered and her vision wavered, but she held on to the back of the recliner and stayed upright. An older woman watched her, her mouth open in alarm. Feeling her balance returning, Antonia released her support and took a step towards the woman.

The woman retreated. 'I won't hurt you,' she said – this was the accented woman – but her body language betrayed the lie.

Radiating panic, the woman searched for a weapon. She scooped up the laptop next to her and threw it. Antonia batted it away. The one called Edda slammed into her back, thrusting her forward. Instead of resisting, Antonia continued the forward momentum, accelerating towards the older woman, who didn't move, seeming paralysed.

Antonia dropped her forehead and caught the shorter woman across her nose. Blood spattered on Antonia's skin. The pain made the earlier headache seem like a twinge. She staggered, but kept her feet. The woman's body slumped to the floor, coming to rest against Antonia's shins.

With a shrill scream, Edda launched another attack from behind her, punching Antonia in the kidney and grabbing her waist.

Gasping in pain, Antonia swung her elbow, making contact with a torso. A second blow made Edda release her. Antonia's relief didn't last. Her left foot slid away on a slick of blood that had spread from the fallen woman's head. When she grabbed the edge of the desk to stop her falling, her right knee hit the tiled floor with a sickening crunch.

She didn't have time to react as Edda leapt on to her back, grabbed a handful of her hair and slammed her head toward the desk. Antonia twisted her shoulders and caught her neck on the edge. A whooshing in her head and she collapsed. She landed on the floor, Edda on top of her, her hands scrabbling for Antonia's throat.

Antonia twisted and bucked, almost unconscious, but aware enough to know she must fight. She thrust her left palm into Edda. Her attacker swung a desperate punch, but it lacked power and bounced off the top of Antonia's head. Antonia swung her right fist, smashing Edda on the cheek and dislodging her.

Antonia scrambled to her knees. A strike to the woman's neck knocked her to the floor. Antonia rose to her feet and, as the woman pushed herself into a kneeling position, kicked her in the jaw. With a sickening click, her head snapped back. An arc of blood sprayed the wall behind her, and she lay still.

Antonia stood, breath rasping, light-headed with relief. Then a sound made her freeze. She glanced at the doorway. A huge man with no neck filled the opening. An automatic in his right hand.

Adam stood to the left of the door, battering ram held by his side, holding it by the grips. Virgil and Rafael waited on the other side, extendible batons and cannisters of pepper spray in their hands. Chapman held his baton, his mouth dry. Next to him, Sanchez stared ahead, pale with her lips a compressed line.

'After three,' Adam mouthed.

Then a screech came from behind the door. Chapman's racing pulse spiked. Was it Antonia? He wanted to rush in now, but Adam counted, then swung the lump of metal at the lock. The door splintered and flew in. Virgil disappeared into the opening, followed by Rafael.

Adam slung the battering ram over his shoulder and charged in after them. Chapman raced behind him into a reception office with a desk to one side and a sofa opposite. Five doors led off the room, as Adam had stated in the quick briefing he'd given them: two on each side and the other straight ahead.

The first door on the left swung open, and Virgil rushed out. Adam approached the door on the right and pulled it open before barging through. Chapman followed. Grey light through the windows illuminated an empty office with four desks arranged in two rows. A second scream came from behind him. Chapman reversed out, almost knocking Sanchez over. She pointed to the middle door.

Chapman charged to it and pushed it open. A door on the right of the short corridor gaped open, revealing a bedroom. The next contained a bulky figure filling the doorway. He held an automatic in his hand. The top of the doorframe protected him from a downward strike. Chapman accelerated at the man and hit him with all his strength. He wished he hadn't. It was like running into a block of concrete. The man grunted and staggered a step forward. Chapman bounced off him and hit the doorframe. The impact ripped the cosh out of his grip.

He took in the scene at a glance. Antonia stood over a fallen woman. Another lay on the floor behind her, a halo of blood smeared round her head. The man he'd barged into, huge and with no neck, spun with deceptive speed and uncoiled a punch. Chapman recognised Grist as he ducked. What the hell was a Ministry of Patriotism goon doing here? Chapman gasped as pain exploded across his skull. He fell and landed in a heap. Hot liquid flowed from a cut on his scalp.

A boot smashed into his ribs, emptying his lungs.

He fought for air, agony spreading from the impact. Acting on instinct, he rolled. Pain from his ribs spread like fire. He hit something soft and warm. The woman's body? He looked up. Grist loomed over him and grinned as he lifted a boot. Chapman pushed against the body, but it didn't move. He lifted a forearm across his head and closed his eyes as the boot slashed towards him.

Grist grunted, but the expected blow never landed. Chapman looked, saw blood pour from Grist's nose as Antonia landed a second punch. The giant swung at Antonia, but she moved out of range. Grist raised his other arm. The automatic. Chapman forced himself upright, his ribs screaming in pain. The cosh lay by his foot, and he reached for it, but realised he'd be too slow.

'GRIST! Can't you take on a man?' The metal scraped across the tiled floor as he picked up the cosh.

Grist sneered and altered his aim. Chapman swallowed. Then a blur of movement and a shot exploded. It flew high. Antonia grappled with Grist, attacking his gun arm while he slapped her with the other. The force of his blow snapped her head back, but she held on. Chapman struggled to his feet, his legs like jelly. Grist hit Antonia again, sending her sprawling across the room.

Chapman staggered two steps and swung the cosh at Grist with his remaining strength. The blow landed on the giant's shoulder. Grist bellowed and swung his automatic at Chapman. It smashed into his temple. He fell to his knees, his vision blurring and stars exploding in his head. A huge hand seized his neck and squeezed. He told his arms to resist, but they didn't obey. The pressure increased and his hands lost feeling. The cosh clattered to the floor. He gagged, and blackness descended.

◆ ◆ ◆

Antonia opened her eyes. She lay in the corner. Her cheek hurt, and so did the back of her head. Had she passed out again? Chapman knelt at Grist's feet. The giant gripped his throat. Chapman's struggles weakened as she watched and his puce complexion and protruding tongue told the story. Antonia pushed herself off the floor, struggling to control her limbs. Grist turned on her as she cried out in frustration.

He lifted the automatic and aimed at her, steadying his aim. She wouldn't beg or show fear. Then, Grist hurtled forward, releasing Chapman. His thighs hit the table and sent it crashing across the room.

Adam, still latched on to the giant, drove him into the wall. He released Grist and staggered back. What was he doing here? Of course, he must have come with Chapman.

Grist lashed out with the gun. Adam blocked the blow and grabbed his wrist. The two men struggled but the bigger man pulled Adam's arm. Instead of resisting, Adam leapt forward and headbutted Grist. The giant dropped the gun and fell to his knees. Adam sprang back from him, a streak of blood on his forehead.

Antonia straightened, swaying as blood rushed from her head.

Adam leapt at the gun, but Grist grabbed his arm. Adam pulled himself free. Instead of throwing a punch, his right foot shot out, catching Grist on the nose. The already bloodied head snapped back. Moving quicker than she'd have believed, Grist grabbed his foot. Adam punched him, but he held on and twisted. Adam grimaced in pain and panic. Antonia, her balance returning, pushed herself from the wall and, taking careful aim, launched a kick. It hit Grist's head as a second punch came in from Adam. With a sickening crack, Grist fell. He lay still, blood oozing from his head wounds.

Antonia and Adam stared at each other for a moment, breathing hard. Chapman still lay where he'd fallen. She needed to help him. Then, a cry of pain came from outside, followed by two shots. Adam moved first. Scooped up Grist's gun and ran for the door. Antonia, her head full of shards of broken glass, followed. As she passed Grist, a foot swung out, catching her ankle. She crashed to the floor face first.

◆ ◆ ◆

A gunshot dragged Chapman into consciousness, then another, convincing him he'd not dreamt it. Antonia lay on the floor, face down and still. Grist crouched near her feet, attempting to rise. A surge of fear and anger lifted Chapman to his feet against the screaming of his ribs. The pain transferred to his head.

Grist continued uncoiling himself, blood dripping from what remained of his nose.

Although wanting to run, Chapman stepped toward him. A metallic clunk told him he'd kicked something. The cosh. He picked it up. Grist used one arm to support his torso. Chapman raised the cosh and swung it at the man's elbow. It struck with a nauseating snap. With a scream, Grist fell forward.

Chapman swallowed the acid in his throat and followed up his attack.

When certain Grist no longer posed a danger, he dropped the bloody weapon and rushed to Antonia. She wasn't moving, but a strong pulse reassured him.

A scream issued from the outer rooms. He knew the voice. A second shriek confirmed it. Sanchez. He rushed into the reception area.

Sanchez stood on tiptoe in front of a man wearing black-framed glasses, shielding him from Adam, who stood with his back to Chapman, levelling Grist's pistol at them. The man held

Sanchez's left arm up behind her back. His other arm held an automatic under her chin.

'Don't come closer, plod,' the gunman said to Chapman, his voice rasping.

Chapman recognised Palmer, the other thug from the Ministry, as his momentum took him one step further into the room. Sanchez cried out.

'You deaf?' Palmer sneered. 'You don't look so tough now.'

Chapman didn't reply.

Deciding Chapman posed no threat, Palmer returned his attention to Adam. 'I won't tell you again, put the gun down.'

Adam, his arm steady, said, 'That won't happen.'

Behind Sanchez and the gunman, Chapman could make out someone on the floor. He recognised Rafael. *Where's Virgil?* Then he saw him, further in, but as still. *Shit!* The two shots.

Sanchez cried out again, a shrill screech of agony. 'I reckon her shoulder will go next time.' Palmer enjoyed causing her pain.

Chapman swore to make the man pay.

'In which case, she'll fall,' Adam said, sounding unfazed. 'Leaving you exposed.'

Palmer swung the automatic at Adam. Sanchez screamed. The door behind Chapman slammed open and Palmer turned towards it, exposing his head. An explosion in Chapman's right ear deafened him as Palmer's head jerked backwards and a red mist painted the wall behind him. He and Sanchez fell. *Who the hell shot him?*

Antonia stood behind Chapman, arm outstretched, holding a small automatic in her fist.

'Where did you get that?' Chapman's voice sounded small and far away.

She stared at him in a daze and mouthed, 'Grist had it.'

He held out a hand and she passed it to him, her hand trembling. 'You okay?' Blood covered her battered face and dripped down her chin. *Of course she isn't, you idiot.* 'Here, sit down.' He gestured at a chair but she resisted. 'Come on, it's all over.' She let him lead her and slumped into the seat.

Across the room Adam crouched beside Sanchez, dragging her clear of the dead gunman. Antonia's bullet had shattered one lens of his glasses. Sanchez cradled her left arm as Adam helped her sit. Sprayed blood covered her hair, left ear and her neck below it.

They needed an ambulance. He scanned the room. They needed a fleet of them. Chapman retrieved his phone and his finger hovered over the power button. How the hell would he explain this? Especially Grist's blood all over him, and what about Antonia? Shit! He couldn't call an ambulance. Then he remembered the last time he'd come here. Whoever manned the security desk would have seen them arrive and break into the office. Why weren't the police here?

Then the main door crashed open and dark-clad figures swarmed in.

CHAPTER 32

Antonia struggled to her feet and took a few steps towards the door to the apartment. She should run. But where to? Then she recognised the tall figure at the front of the phalanx of invaders and relaxed.

Chapman recognised him at the same moment. 'Am I glad to see you, Byron.'

Byron took in the situation, then his rumbling voice delivered calm orders. 'Two of you check the people in that room. You help Adam. The rest of you clear the place and don't take any chances.'

Two people carrying backpacks rushed into the next room and a third approached Sanchez, taking over from Adam. Others swarmed through doorways and dispersed. Antonia's attention returned to the man she'd shot, his glasses askew and a pool of blood surrounding his head. She'd never shot someone before. Would it count as self-defence? He hadn't been aiming at her.

'Who you calling?' Byron's question to Chapman broke her thread.

Chapman stared at the phone in his hand. 'I was going to call an ambulance—'

'Not a good idea.'

'I know, but it's too late, there's a security guy monitoring the front desk.'

Did they have cameras in the offices? Antonia realised she'd face serious charges for what she'd done to those women, and having seen Grist, so would Chapman.

But Byron said, 'Not today. He left before the Humvee arrived and nobody's replaced him. One of my guys went straight there and checked. Someone's turned the cameras off.'

Chapman's shoulders slumped and a weight fell off Antonia.

Byron pointed at the door behind her. 'Who's through there?'

'I think they're beyond help.' She'd bitten her tongue when she'd fallen and sounded drunk.

Chapman studied her with a look of concern. 'Can one of your guys check her out?'

Exhaustion and pain suffused her body, and she allowed Chapman to lead her to the chair before she collapsed. Another of Byron's crew approached, unzipped his backpack and put on some disposable gloves. Chapman released her forearm, leaving her feeling abandoned. The medic cleaned up Antonia's injuries, the disinfectant stinging as it seeped into her wounds. As he worked, she closed her eyes and let her mind drift. In the background, Byron's voice rumbled, issuing orders over a phone.

With a jerk, she straightened. She must have dozed. A figure on a stretcher was being carried out of a side office. The attendant at the head carried a drip. a good sign. Adam followed, his manner grim.

He came over, favouring his right knee. 'How you doing?'

'Been better, but also worse.'

'Yeah, you and me both.' Blood had dried on his forehead, but she didn't see a wound.

'Who's on the stretcher?' She gestured at the medical team disappearing through the exit. 'I heard shots.'

'Rafael.' He stared into the distance. 'They shot Rafael *and* Virgil.'

'How's Virgil?'

He gestured at the black body bag on a second stretcher.

The sight made Antonia blink. 'Can I see him?'

'Hold fire, guys.' Adam spoke to the stretcher-bearers.

One of them unzipped the body bag, the sound of it bringing back unpleasant memories. Virgil didn't look at peace. A jagged hole in his throat told her how he'd died. Dried blood stiffened what she could see of his top. 'Who shot them?'

Adam pointed to the man she'd shot. 'He guessed they wore vests and aimed high.'

Chapman and Byron walked out of the door leading to the apartment, deep in conversation, Chapman walking like he felt every one of his years and leaning over to his right to protect his ribs. He held a wallet in his gloved left hand. 'Did you recognise the big guy, Antonia?'

'Should I have?'

'He works at the Ministry of Patriotism. He raided the office on Tuesday along with him.' He pointed to the man she'd shot.

She tried to remember, but nothing came. Frustration made her want to throw something. 'I've got huge gaps in my memory. I heard the two women talking about wiping it—'

'Shit! Did you find a laptop in there?' Chapman grew animated.

Someone had recently thrown one at her. 'There's one in the room you found me in.'

He rushed back through the door, leaving a bemused Byron, and returning with a battered laptop in his other hand. 'You deal with this as we discussed.' He handed the wallet to Byron. 'We need to go, young lady.'

'Where?'

'Swan's clinic. He's on standby.'

'Who's Swan and what's the rush?'

'I'll explain on the way.' He almost dragged her to the exit. Relief she didn't have to worry about clearing up this mess vied with irritation at the way Chapman was behaving.

Adam exchanged a few words with Byron, then caught up with them. 'I'll drive, you tell me where.'

One lift car waited at the floor, and they hurried into it, Adam punching the basement button.

The doors shut, and she untangled her arm from Chapman's grip. 'Russell, please, what's going on?'

'If they've tampered with your memories, it might have caused permanent damage.'

'What do you mean?' A phrase from the conversation she'd overheard came back. Was she now not a viable person? How could she tell? The way she felt, she didn't think she was.

Antonia fell asleep soon after they left the tower block. She lay on the back seat of Adam's latest hire car. The thought she might still be a target made the skin on Chapman's neck itch and he kept glancing back to check for a tail.

'You know you're grunting each time you do that?' Adam said. 'Is it your ribs?'

'They're a bit sore. The big bastard gave me a good kicking.' His throat felt like he had a sand-covered ball bearing stuck in it.

Adam gave him a long look.

'What?'

'Did you see how you left him?'

How could he forget? He'd discussed it with Byron, who'd reassured him he'd take care of it before he left. He stared ahead, but didn't recognise their route.

'Where are we going?'

'We're swinging by my place.'

'Antonia needs attention straight away. We can't risk—'

'We're talking about an extra half an hour. We're covered in dead people's blood.' Adam rubbed at the dried smear on his forehead. 'We don't know who will be at this clinic and imagine if we got stopped . . .'

It made sense. Why the hell hadn't he thought of it? 'What about our clothes and the car?'

'Byron's swinging by later with a team.'

Chapman pictured what they'd left behind, imagining he was investigating. 'Forensic teams are really thorough. They can't afford to miss anything.'

'He's got some good guys. They've done it before.'

Chapman didn't ask. Adam had some strange friends for a firefighter. 'Will they keep their mouths shut?'

'They either worked with or knew Virgil, and he was very popular.' Adam hesitated. 'What about your sergeant? Will she say anything?'

Chapman hadn't considered Sanchez's reaction. He'd been so eager to get Antonia out, he'd not spoken to her. She'd have a serious problem explaining her presence there, but she could be a stickler for the rules, a real girl scout.

'You're hesitating, which suggests you don't know.'

'I'll give her a bell.'

'And say what? I assume both your phones are traceable.'

Shit! He was right. If they conspired to cover it, they'd both be in serious trouble. Trying not to worry, he checked on Antonia, who hadn't moved. Was it already too late for her?

They arrived at Adam's and he got out and opened the back door. 'Antonia, you need to get out.' He gently lifted her head and shoulders off the seat.

She woke with a start. 'What? Oh, it's you.'

'Come on, let's get you out of here.' Adam helped her out on to the pavement, and she let him lead her to his front door.

Her passivity and helplessness distressed Chapman; he could hardly reconcile her with the woman he knew. How seriously had the treatment damaged her, and could Swan piece her memories back together? As she hobbled across the pavement, he got out and collected the laptop, wincing as his ribs compressed. He didn't intend letting it out of his sight. It could be their only chance of restoring Antonia. He scanned the crescent and followed, exhaling in relief when they got inside. Warmth enveloped him, and with it, the desire to sleep.

'You use the main bathroom and Antonia can use the en suite in her room.' Adam took them downstairs to the sleeping quarters. 'I'll take that and clean it up.'

Chapman examined the laptop, noticing the stains for the first time. He also saw the big dent in the casing. 'Bloody hell! What if it doesn't work?'

'Don't worry, I've used much worse. You can imagine what firefighters do to delicate equipment.'

Chapman gave it up and staggered into an immaculate bathroom with a bath and free-standing shower in opposite corners. It smelt of cleaning fluid and soap and a stack of towels sat on a corner unit. He sat on the toilet lid. Dark spots covered his trousers. Bugger, he didn't have any clean clothes. He'd have to borrow some.

Adam knocked on the door. 'I've put some stuff out here. The clothes belong to my younger brother, they should fit you. Put everything you remove in these bags. There's a coffee.'

Chapman forced himself to get up and opened the door. Neatly folded clothes and a pair of shoes sat next to a stack of bin bags and a steaming coffee. He took them into the bathroom and sipped the coffee, wishing he hadn't when it hit his throat. He left it to cool and completed undressing, standing in one bag while he placed his clothes in another.

Under the shower, he scrubbed his skin until he'd removed every trace of Grist. Conscious they needed to get Antonia treated, he got dressed and made his way upstairs. The stench of bleach filled the hall.

Adam stopped mopping and inspected Chapman. 'Very smart. I'll get showered if you want to wait in the kitchen.'

The laptop sat on the table, now devoid of the dark marks but not the dent. He sat and finished his now-cold coffee, helping himself to bread, cheese and tomatoes, which Adam had left in the centre of the table. By chewing it well, he swallowed enough to take the edge off his hunger. What would happen if his part in today's events came out? A few years in prison at least, *if* they accepted he'd acted in self-defence. Otherwise, life. And the same for Antonia.

Adam returned with her, breaking into Chapman's reverie. Although more alert, she still looked dreadful.

'That bad, eh?' She gave a lopsided grin, her jaw and lips swollen.

Chapman's cheeks grew warm, and any regrets at what he'd done to Grist disappeared. Adam rescued him by suggesting they get a move on. Darkness had fallen and the temperature had dropped. Adam's ski jacket engulfed Chapman, but he appreciated its warmth. Adam led them to a different car, leaving the one they'd arrived in behind.

He drove at just above the speed limit and as they neared King's College Hospital, Antonia, dozing in the back, grew agitated until they drove past and pulled into a business park next to it. Swan's clinic stuck out, the only one with the lights still on.

They parked by the front door and two figures rushed out, one pushing a wheelchair. Swan and his assistant arrived as Adam got Antonia out. They ignored her protests and made her sit, the assistant wheeling her inside.

Chapman handed the laptop to Swan. 'We rescued this from where they kept her prisoner. It had wires attached to it and a sort of metal helmet.'

'Well, you've got the right machine. You don't know how much they erased?'

'Sorry, no. But she's very confused.'

They arrived inside the clinic and Swan locked the doors behind them. 'Don't worry, I'll get everything off this. I've already uploaded the information on the memory stick your friend gave me. Make yourselves at home, gentlemen' – he swept an arm around a reception area with comfortable seating, drinks and a selection of food – 'and leave the rest to me.'

He followed his assistant and Antonia through the doors. Chapman and Adam looked at each other. They could do nothing but wait.

◆ ◆ ◆

Sabirah was relieved Jean had spoken to Mrs Curtis and accepted her apology, agreeing to return to work on Monday. To Sabirah's embarrassment, Jean insisted on paying for the cab to take them home. It slowed at the mini roundabout at the end of Graham Street and drove into Vincent Terrace. The thought of getting home and having a hot bath, then sitting with the children in front of the fire in their living room, presented a heavenly prospect. But a car sat outside their house and a knot started in her stomach.

'Nice motor,' the cab driver said, as he pulled up behind it.

Sabirah, sitting in the back between her children, peered through the windscreen. There was no mistaking Al Rahman's car this time. The knot grew tighter. She thanked the driver and, giving him a generous tip, ushered the children towards the house as they stared at the car.

'Is that the nice man who took us to Madame Tussauds?' Hakim said.

'Come on, let's go inside.'

'What do you think he wants, Mama?'

Sabirah didn't dare think, but it wouldn't be anything good. 'We don't even know he's here to see us. Other people live in this street. Now, come on.' She regretted her tone straight away.

The rear door of the car opened, and Al Rahman got out. Sabirah's knot got bigger. *Please go away and leave us alone, just for one day.*

'Why are you here?' she demanded.

Then the other back door of the car opened and Rosemary Juma got out.

Sabirah's heart contracted. Had she come here to gloat? Then a surge of anger made her want to beat the woman senseless.

Nadimah squeezed her hand. 'Are you okay, Mama?'

She returned the pressure and addressed Al Rahman. 'Are you going to tell me?'

The door to the house opened and Mrs Curtis called, 'You can come in now.'

She understood now. Mrs Curtis must have summoned them. 'Go inside, children.' Sabirah ushered them to the house and the two visitors followed her, Al Rahman at the rear. The thought of the coming confrontation drained Sabirah's strength with every step she took, and by the time she reached the door, she didn't think she could go any further.

Mrs Curtis greeted them. 'Welcome home, Hakim, Nadimah, Sabirah.' Her welcome smile disappeared when she spoke to the two visitors. 'Go through here.' She gestured towards her living room. 'Children, go upstairs and get washed and changed. I'm treating us to a takeaway later, whatever you want, even chicken wings and pizza.'

The children's disappointment at being excluded evaporated, and they raced each other up the stairs. Sabirah looked at the old lady for an explanation. She winked and wheeled herself into the living room. The fire gave the room a cheery air at odds with Sabirah's mood. Al Rahman and Mrs Juma stopped in the middle of the room.

'Sit.' Mrs Curtis directed them to the blue leather sofa opposite.

They sat. Mrs Curtis directed Sabirah to a chair facing them and pulled up in a space next to her. They studied the unwelcome visitors in a thick silence broken only by the hiss of the fire. Sabirah, who would have once gabbled to cover her nerves, stayed silent.

Al Rahman ran his tongue over his lips and Mrs Juma kept brushing at her skirt.

Sabirah jumped as Mrs Curtis broke the silence. 'I've asked you to come here to explain what you're going to do to ensure Mrs Fadil and her family stay in this country.'

'I don't take orders from you.' Al Rahman's defiance lacked conviction.

'That's as may be, but you forgot one thing when you decided to blackmail my friend, Mr Al Rahman. The Nationality and Borders Bill applies to both of you, as much as to Sabirah.'

'I didn't blackmail anyone. How could you suggest such a thing?' Al Rahman gestured at Sabirah. 'Tell her.'

Mrs Curtis signalled Sabirah to stay quiet. 'I'm sure the Law Society would take a very dim view of you conspiring with the chair of an Immigration tribunal.'

'What are you talking about? I've not come here to be insulted. Come on, Rosemary.'

'I've spoken to the gentleman, and he confirms you persuaded him to strip Sabirah of her Permit to Reside—'

Sabirah let out a cry. 'It was *you*?'

Al Rahman wouldn't look at her. 'She is a danger to this country. Like *you*.' He jabbed a finger at Mrs Curtis. 'People like you don't appreciate when they're well off, complaining about a democratic government. Try living under a dictator.'

'So, you don't deny it?'

Al Rahman laughed. 'It wasn't a surprise to him, or the other two on the panel. You don't think it was my idea?'

'Whose idea was it?'

'You don't expect me to tell you. And I was happy to do it, because I care about this country. I did nothing wrong. Your daughter started it.' He jabbed a finger at Mrs Curtis, who grimaced.

'But placing a listening device in a private property, without a warrant, is a criminal offence.'

'I didn't.' He pointed at Sabirah. 'She might have; in which case, she is the one who will face the weight of the law.'

Was this true? Sabirah didn't know, but Mrs Curtis didn't look worried.

'The fact she feared for her own and her children's safety is adequate defence. Sabirah, can you confirm that Mr Al Rahman, while acting as your solicitor, coerced you into placing a listening device in the basement office here?'

Sabirah pointed at Al Rahman. 'You told me to place a bug if I wanted to stay.'

'Rubbish. It's my word against yours, and who is going to believe a cleaner, who's been sent to prison, over a respected lawyer?'

'You may be right,' Mrs Curtis said, 'but the forensic evidence will show you're lying.'

'Forensic evidence? You don't have any.'

'Your fingerprints are on the device you gave Sabirah.'

'She gave it—' Al Rahman looked worried, but then he gave a sly smile. 'She asked me for it. I explained the legal position to her. You can ask Rosemary.'

Mrs Curtis produced her phone and clicked a button. Al Rahman's voice came out of the speaker, promising Sabirah Leave to Remain if she hid the bug.

The colour drained from his features, and he coughed. Sabirah couldn't help smiling at his dumfounded expression.

Rosemary Juma spoke for the first time. 'You people are snakes. You criticise Mr Al Rahman for spying on a criminal, but you do it to him, an honest man, and think it's okay.' She got up and bent towards the fireplace. Standing up with the ornamental poker from a set beside it, she approached Mrs Curtis and gestured at the old lady's phone. 'Give me that.'

Mrs Curtis shook her head and Juma stepped closer, lifting the poker.

'Rosemary, don't!' Al Rahman held up his hands.

'Why not? I have diplomatic immunity.'

Sabirah roused herself and stood. As the poker descended, she grabbed Juma's arm. The woman was stronger than she looked and snatched it free. Then she swung at Sabirah. She lifted her arm and the bar struck, just below her elbow. Sabirah screamed and fell back.

Juma lifted the poker again and advanced on her.

Clutching her arm, Sabirah retreated. Her foot caught on the rug, and she tumbled backwards with a cry.

Juma came at her with a sneer. 'You are the worst type, coming here and telling lies about our great leader. Snivelling that they killed your husband. He died because he was a traitor, like you.' Juma raised the weapon.

'Mamma!' The cry came from the doorway and Nadimah flew at Juma.

'Nadimah! Don't—'

Juma took a swing at the girl, but Nadimah ducked, then did something Sabirah couldn't believe. She lifted her hands and punched Juma in the mouth, then, almost too quick to see, in the stomach, and then twice more to her head. Juma dropped the poker, then fell to the floor, wheezing.

Sabirah scrambled to her knees and picked up the poker. Nadimah helped her up and held her, sobbing. 'Mamma, are you okay?'

Her arm hurt but she'd live. 'Yes, my dear. Thank you, thank you.' She held on to the poker and kept Juma in sight as the woman lifted her bloodied head off the rug.

'I think it's time you left,' Mrs Curtis said, in a calm voice, like she was ordering tea in a café.

'What do you want me to do?' Al Rahman, pale, his voice shaky, couldn't take his gaze off the injured woman as blood dripped off her nose.

'You must speak to the members of the tribunal and convince them to reverse their decision.'

'How do I do that?'

'I really don't care, Mr Al Rahman. Tell them you have recordings of your conversations—'

'That's not true.'

'I do not care. I'm sure you can be convincing.'

Al Rahman stood for several moments. 'I'll do it next week.'

'You'll do it Monday.' Mrs Curtis looked fierce.

Al Rahman nodded, and he helped Juma to her feet, her immaculate make-up and hair askew. Sabirah untangled herself from her daughter and followed them to the front door, poker gripped tightly in her good hand. She closed and locked the door and leant against the wall, in pain, exhausted, but relieved. She returned to the living room and the sound of laughter.

Mrs Curtis said, 'There's a bottle of champagne in my fridge. Do you want to fetch it and some glasses, Nadimah?'

Nadimah looked at her mother, and she nodded. Sabirah had only drunk champagne once, with Rashid at a Christian wedding they attended in Lebanon when they first married. She realised this would be a good time to have it again.

CHAPTER 33

The hours dragged by, and Chapman tried to make himself comfortable. Not that the chair was uncomfortable, but his ribs hurt like hell. He'd also convinced himself the authorities had found the bodies and would soon identify him as a killer. He'd avoided checking the news because he didn't want to know yet, but was telling himself it was because he didn't want to disturb Adam, emitting gentle snores on the next sofa. How the hell could he sleep, knowing Antonia was undergoing a procedure which, if it failed, would irreparably harm her?

'Okay, I give up.' A sleepy Adam sat up and gave him an annoyed stare.

'What?'

'You're doing it again, the huffing and grunting. Why don't you ask them for painkillers? I'm sure they'll have them.'

'I don't want to interrupt the procedure.' Antonia hated taking drugs, and doing so while her future hung in the balance didn't feel right.

Adam sighed and, getting up, limped to the reception desk. A first aid kit hung off the wall behind it and he placed it on the counter and opened it. 'Ibuprofen four hundred. You're not allergic?'

'No.'

Adam removed a blister pack and swung by the refreshment table, where he retrieved a bottle of water from a small fridge. He set up the coffee-maker before returning with tablets and water.

'I'd rather not take them.'

'Why not?'

'Are you taking some for your knee?' Chapman swept a hand at the leg.

'No.'

'Well, then.'

'What? Did I keep you awake with my groaning?'

Chapman didn't have an answer. 'Can we just leave it?'

'Sure.' Adam returned the tablets. 'Do you want a coffee?'

'Yeah, okay.'

'What are they doing in there?'

'I'm no expert,' Chapman said, 'but as Swan explained it, those women removed some of Antonia's memories and they're on the laptop I gave him. He's going to try to restore them.' He attempted to explain how leaving her with gaps in her memory could result in her creating pseudo-memories.

'Anything she's experienced or heard? So, a film, or what about a book she's read?'

'Yes, according to Swan. Neil Griffin, a lad I put in prison, believed he'd abused and killed children, crimes his cellmate had committed. The guy must have told Neil about it, and he absorbed it into *his* memory.'

Adam whistled. 'But Swan can replace her old memories? He mentioned something about them being unusable. What would happen then?'

'I asked him what he could do if we didn't find the laptop. He said he'd implant something benign.'

'And Antonia would just lose the original memories?'

426

'He said he can approximate them. For example, if she forgot about staying at your place, you could tell Swan about her stay, and he could create some and implant those.'

Adam was quiet for a long moment, looking off across the room. Then he turned to Chapman. 'As a copper, doesn't it bother you? You can't rely on any eyewitness testimony.'

Chapman had given the idea a lot of thought. 'Yup. Even if it's corroborated by several witnesses, they might all be false.'

Adam whistled again and sipped his coffee.

Chapman checked the time. Gone midnight. They'd sat there seven hours. Although tired, he doubted he'd sleep until Antonia came out.

'Do you mind if I put the news on?' Adam said.

Chapman wanted to wait until he'd found out what had happened to Antonia before worrying about his fate, but he couldn't avoid it forever. 'Be my guest.'

The picture came on without sound. Adam changed the channel several times before Chapman recognised the scene above a 'breaking news' banner. The building they'd driven away from with Antonia eight hours earlier. Anxiety squeezed his insides. Adam's rapt attitude told of *his* reaction.

Chapman took the remote from him and punched the volume button.

'*. . . police and fire service have been on site for almost an hour and firefighting continues. The cause of the fire on the thirtieth floor hasn't been established, but according to eyewitnesses, it spread rapidly to engulf the corner of the building. Several explosions have been heard. The office suite involved was undergoing refurbishment, so one early theory is that the workmen caused the fire.*'

Chapman lowered the volume. 'Did you know Byron was going to set fire to it?'

'He didn't.'

'How can you be sure?'

'He wouldn't put my colleagues at risk.'

Chapman wasn't convinced. What better than a severe fire to get rid of the forensic evidence? He increased the volume.

'We've been told the fire brigade have recovered several bodies, but as the premises were unoccupied, their identities are a mystery. Sources have confirmed the building has the latest hidden surveillance system—'

'Shit!' Adam swore.

Chapman agreed. 'Did you know about the surveillance system?'

'Of course not.'

'You did the reconnaissance—'

'Believe it or not, hidden surveillance systems aren't something we note on our fire plans.'

Chapman realised he was being an arse. It didn't matter. They were buggered. Would the cameras show him killing Grist? If they did, he'd do a long stretch. A phone rang and Adam retrieved one from inside his jacket.

'I thought we agreed to turn them off?'

'It's a burner I got off Byron.' Adam took the call. 'Byron, I'm with Russell at the clinic.' He scanned the otherwise deserted reception area. 'I'll put you on speaker.'

'Someone's set fire to the office we cleaned up.' Byron's voice rumbled out of the speaker.

'I'm watching it now. You knew about the hidden surveillance?'

Byron chuckled. 'Oh yeah. One of the installers works for me now. I told my guys to hack it after I followed the car there.'

'You knew they'd taken Antonia there?' Chapman said.

'I didn't know, but it was a possibility, and if we controlled the surveillance I hoped we'd be able to check. But they don't cover the offices, just the car park, lifts and circulation areas. By the time we took control, the people carrier was in the car park, and they'd gone.'

'And you had nothing to do with the fire?'

'Behave! We finished cleaning up around four hours ago and left. We'd set up a loop on the surveillance system before you turned up, so it showed an empty building for six hours. When it ended and showed images in real time, they'd have seen the damaged door. Anyway, a car arrived soon after the six hours finished – my guys were still watching the place. Then two more cars came. An hour later, they all left and so did my guys.'

The fact he hadn't been compromised sank in and relief made Chapman's hands tremble.

'Did your guys recognise the people who arrived?' Adam said.

'They've got photos. I'll send them over. How's Antonia?'

'We're still waiting.'

'Tell me how she gets on.' Byron ended the call.

Chapman drained his coffee, thanking his lucky stars. Adam's phone emitted a series of beeps and he examined it before handing it over. A series of photos showed vehicles in the car park under the building, and people getting out.

'Bloody hell,' Chapman said. 'Superintendent Harding. Well, well.'

'Friend of yours?'

'He's riding interference on a couple of cases linked to the clinic.'

'Dirty, then.'

'I've always suspected so, but not had the evidence.' He swiped through the photos and stopped. 'Shit!'

'What?'

Chapman held the phone so Adam could see it. 'The woman in the overalls is his wife, Jolanta Dobrowski, a senior crime scene technician. She'll have gone to process the scene.'

'I wouldn't worry. If Byron says they've removed all evidence, they have. Don't forget, we expected a full police investigation.'

'It's not what I'm worried about. I don't mind dropping Harding in it, in fact I look forward to it, but Dobrowski was once a good friend.'

'You don't need to forward her picture. In fact, I'd keep Harding's back as insurance, unless you want him dealt with now.'

Chapman considered it. *Could be a good idea.* He handed the phone back. 'Can you let me have copies?'

'Sure, I'll forward them.'

Voices came from behind the doors Swan had taken Antonia through. They opened and Antonia strode through, tired and battered, but unmistakably herself. A surge of relief and affection propelled him out of the seat, and forgetting his sore ribs, he rushed to meet her.

◆ ◆ ◆

Antonia put the finishing touches to her article on the Syrus Clinic and its links to two suicides and the false accusations levelled against Sami Milham. Unable to trust any of the information Bartholf/Fiona had given her, she'd only hinted at the experiments on prisoners. But the information she'd got from John, and more recently, Chapman, enabled her to give it enough meat to prompt the authorities to act. She pressed send and relaxed.

Chapman came through the door first, having been banished to the main office while she finished.

'You're quick,' she said. 'I've only just sent it to you.'

'Have you seen this?' He brandished a tablet, open at the site of one of the major news outlets, placed it on the desk and sat.

Antonia read it. The headline screamed, 'FIRE VICTIMS IDENTIFIED'. The report described Schiffer and Bartholf as 'respected psychologists working at the cutting edge of the science'. *Wait until my article hits.* According to the account, they were visiting the offices to expand their 'thriving practice'.

An escape of propane from workmen's equipment had collected in the offices and caused them to pass out. A phone call to one of their mobiles had ignited the mixture and led to an explosion and fast-developing fire.

She showed Chapman the paragraph. 'I'll ask Adam if it's even possible when I see him this evening.'

She read on.

Two passing security consultants had tried to rescue them but had succumbed to the effects of smoke.

'The first time smoke has made a hole in someone's skull. Who the hell did the autopsy?' She put the tablet down.

'Someone in Reed-Mayhew's pay. But it stinks, it's a whitewash. Those guys held you prisoner and tried to destroy you. One of them killed Virgil.' Chapman picked up the tablet, barely able to control his anger.

'My article puts people straight about what happened at the clinic.'

'But making those Ministry thugs out to be heroes . . .'

'They're dead.' Although Swan had restored the memories, she had only vague, disjointed recollections of Grist and Palmer, remembering only her fight with the first and shooting of the second.

Chapman gave her an odd look.

'What?'

'The old Antonia wouldn't have given them any quarter.'

She frowned in irritation. Eleanor had said something similar, but she didn't agree, although how would she know if she couldn't remember?

The door burst open, and Eleanor wheeled herself in. 'You mention nothing about what they did to you.'

'I . . . I didn't think it was wise. Where do I say they took me? And what happened then? If I'd mentioned anything about the tower—'

'Say they took you somewhere else, or you don't recall.'

'And what if the receptionist who drove us there comes forward?' Antonia realised it was irrational, but those two women fooling her embarrassed her, and she had no intention of sharing it with her readers. 'I've not pulled any punches on their complicity in what happened to Snowden and Futcher, or what they did to the men they convinced were victims of abuse.' She found the latter unforgivable, and had few regrets about killing them.

'I wonder what motivated them. It couldn't have just been money.'

'We tracked links to several accounts that contained nearly seven million. That's quite a lot of motivation for many people.'

Eleanor didn't look convinced. 'Russell, did you contact the young men?'

Chapman put his tablet down and leant forward in the visitor's chair. 'DI Gillich informed them. I understand they're getting psychiatric help and Swan has offered to try and remove the false memories. He said he's found a way of removing them since he worked on Antonia. I informed Milham and the families of the two suicides.'

'Murder victims.'

'I agree, Eleanor, but technically they killed themselves.'

'What about your friend, the young prisoner?'

'Neil Griffin? His mum's got a lawyer and they're talking a lot of noughts.'

'Good, the more they take from Reed-Mayhew the happier I'll be. Shame you don't remember him visiting you, Antonia.'

'Unfortunately, we don't know he visited Antonia.'

'We're pretty sure he was there for at least half an hour, Russell,' Antonia said. 'And I'm pretty sure he would have wanted to gloat over what they'd done to me. He can't resist crowing whenever he thinks he's won.' Antonia wondered how much this reversal would wound Reed-Mayhew's ego. He'd definitely want revenge, but she couldn't worry about that.

Despite Swan's best efforts, he hadn't been able to restore some of Antonia's recent memories. She could recall events up to a point, then a blank filled the hours in between. The only memories she had of Bartholf/Fiona, apart from killing her, came from the memory stick. They'd deleted them from the laptop, not realising Rafael had copied some of it. Antonia had discovered who the real Fiona was, a colleague of John's who'd died in an 'accident' a few days after he had.

Chapman finished reading. 'Good article, Antonia. Nice balance between emotion and logic, without overdoing it.'

The compliment made her warm. 'Thank you, sir.'

'One minor quibble—'

'Of course, there would be.' She folded her arms. 'I presume it relates to Virgil.' Unwilling to make his body disappear, Virgil's employer, working with Byron, had set up an 'ambush' in which 'unknown assailants' had shot him and Rafael. The narrative that he'd died a heroic death defending his colleague was close enough to the truth. Rafael was now recovering in a private clinic.

'I spoke to the SIO investigating the "ambush" and he's not happy. There's evidence someone moved the body after death, and he thinks Rafael's claim to remember nothing about the incident, or how he arrived at the clinic, is bullshit.'

'What's he doing about it?' Antonia hadn't been happy when she'd learned of the plan through Adam, but agreed, Virgil's death needed acknowledging. She didn't want Adam's friends to suffer any blowback.

'Not much he can do. The local cameras were down and no witnesses. He's pretty pissed off it will go down as an unsolved unless something breaks.'

Sawyer came to the door. 'Drinks, everyone? DI Chapman, Sergeant Sanchez says she's going to be a bit late.'

'Thanks, Jean.'

They gave their orders and waited until she'd left.

Chapman lowered his voice. 'How did the mugs end up in the office?'

Eleanor said, 'Jean ordered them from our office products catalogue, but the courier delivered them to the wrong address where they supposedly sat for six days.'

'And who were they delivered to?'

'A small start-up which has since folded. Owner's a brass plate in a tax haven.'

Chapman raised his eyebrows. 'Reed-Mayhew, or someone at the Ministry of Patriotism?'

'Both, I suspect,' Antonia said. 'Millie Forman's boss took sudden "early retirement" and is moving to somewhere without an extradition treaty. I believe she's been cleared of involvement, denied knowing Grist and Palmer were dodgy, and she's even been promoted. Has Sanchez told you what she intends doing? I presume she's said nothing so far.'

'I called round hers last night. She's off sick with her shoulder, torn muscle and stretched ligaments. She told them she injured herself coming off her bike. She won't say anything about you shooting Palmer, the man who *actually* injured her.'

A weight Antonia hadn't been aware of carrying lifted off her shoulders. 'Eleanor, apart from not mentioning my visits to the clinic, you're happy with the article?'

'It's excellent, Antonia, your best. As Russell put it, well written. I assume Geoff Stokes and his team have vetted for legal issues? You don't hold back on the insinuations of Reed-Mayhew's involvement.'

'I had to take out a few bits which Geoff thought would have attracted legal action. I'd mentioned he'd hired Lika to kill me, but since nobody's been able to find him, and someone destroyed his records . . .'

'Unfortunately, we still haven't tracked down the guys who did it and shot my officer,' Chapman said. 'We will though, someone always talks. You should have left it in and seen him in court.'

'I stood by everything I put in, but I was concerned about losing our licence.' She hated having to censor herself in order to survive. 'You're okay with the Virgil story, Eleanor?'

'Not sure if I approve of fictionalised accounts, even though it agrees with all other news sources.' Eleanor's expression told Antonia she approved. 'What's happening to his family? He had children, didn't he?'

'Two little girls. They'll get compensation from his employer, plus a pension.' The thought of them growing up without their dad saddened Antonia the most. Another one to chalk against Reed-Mayhew when she finally settled his account.

Sawyer returned with a tray of steaming mugs. 'Who wants the one with the listening device?'

Everyone laughed, although embarrassment tempered Antonia's merriment. 'What time's the table booked, Jean?'

'Six thirty. I've booked the cabs for six.'

Antonia checked the time. 'I'd better get this published then. Everyone okay with it?'

Chapman and Eleanor both agreed, and she pressed publish. Her fear that one of her rivals would publish a spoiler hadn't materialised, so they would get all the plaudits. The consortium Reed-Mayhew had tried to destroy had won the contract they'd bid for when the police dropped the charges against Milham. Not only would this have really hurt him, but her article would raise enough questions about his existing contracts to put them at risk and Reed-Mayhew would face some tough questions. This article wouldn't bring him down, but it would weaken him.

Antonia was still determined to make sure he paid for the death of Alan Turner. And she could wait.

Acknowledgements

This is the bit where I can, in a small way, acknowledge those who've helped me on my journey to get this novel published.

The support of my family and friends is as important as ever, and I want them to know I never take it for granted. Members of my writing group, South Manchester Writers' Workshop, give me constructive advice on my writing, and have contributed greatly to improving it.

My beta-readers. Thank you, B. E. Andre – Boz, Mark Thomson and David Qualter, who read the early drafts and gave me such valuable feedback. Cliff Chen, who gave me helpful pointers on the sections relating to memory, stopping me making too much of a fool of myself. Any errors remaining are entirely down to me.

C. J. Harter, Chris, whose comprehensive report significantly enhanced the manuscript.

My agent, Clare Coombes from The Liverpool Literary Agency, who read my manuscript over the Christmas holidays whilst suffering from Covid-19. Despite this, she made sure she gave me the help I needed to knock the manuscript into shape and meet my deadline. Her professionalism and continued support is much appreciated.

Finally, the people I've dealt with at Thomas & Mercer – starting with Victoria Haslam, who continues to be very positive and supportive, championing my work.

David Downing of Maxwellian Editorial Services, Inc., who made editing this novel as pleasurable as working on the first one. His continued wisdom and positive comments, even when I make his life difficult by rewriting chunks between edits, give me confidence in my writing.

Gill Harvey, who again copyedited the manuscript, never complained, even though I keep making the same stupid errors. Her suggested changes continue to improve the work.

Frankie Bertoletti, who made sure I didn't make any unintentional crass errors.

Jill Sawyer, who did the proofread. Her thoroughness has given me confidence that very few, if any, of my many mistakes have slipped through.

Dominic Forbes, whose excellent cover design complements the brilliant one he designed for *A Long Shadow*.

Sophie Goodfellow and Emma Mitchell from FMcM, who have ensured my books get a fantastic level of exposure.

I've taken some liberties when describing how memory works and how it may be changed. Part of this is a consequence of my incomplete understanding of the subject – despite Cliff's best efforts – but I also had to make the plot work, and I hope it does.

About the Author

Photo © 2021 Steve Pattyson Photography

David Beckler writes fast-paced action thrillers populated with well-rounded characters. Born in Addis Ababa in 1960, David spent his first eight years living on an agricultural college in rural Ethiopia where his love of reading developed. After dropping out of university he became a firefighter and served nineteen years before leaving to start his own business.

David began writing in 2010 and uses his work experiences to add realism to his fiction. David lives in Manchester, his adopted home since 1984. In his spare time, he tries to keep fit – an increasingly difficult undertaking – listens to music, socialises and feeds his voracious book habit.

Follow the Author on Amazon

If you enjoyed this book, follow David Beckler on Amazon to be notified when the author releases a new book!
To do this, please follow these instructions:

Desktop:

1) Search for the author's name on Amazon or in the Amazon App.
2) Click on the author's name to arrive on their Amazon page.
3) Click the 'Follow' button.

Mobile and Tablet:

1) Search for the author's name on Amazon or in the Amazon App.
2) Click on one of the author's books.
3) Click on the author's name to arrive on their Amazon page.
4) Click the 'Follow' button.

Kindle eReader and Kindle App:

If you enjoyed this book on a Kindle eReader or in the Kindle App, you will find the author 'Follow' button after the last page.